P9-DMG-362

MRS. FLETCHER

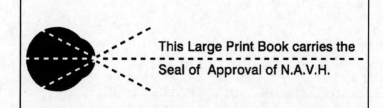

This Large Print Book carries the
Seal of Approval of N.A.V.H.

MRS. FLETCHER

TOM PERROTTA

THORNDIKE PRESS
A part of Gale, a Cengage Company

POQUOSON PUBLIC LIBRARY
500 CITY HALL AVENUE
POQUOSON, VA 23662

GALE
A Cengage Company

Farmington Hills, Mich • San Francisco • New York • Waterville, Maine
Meriden, Conn • Mason, Ohio • Chicago

Copyright © 2017 by Tom Perrotta.
Thorndike Press, a part of Gale, a Cengage Company.

ALL RIGHTS RESERVED
This book is a work of fiction. Any references to historical events, real people, or real places are used fictitiously. Other names, characters, places, and events are products of the author's imagination, and any resemblance to actual events or locales or persons, living or dead, is entirely coincidental.

Thorndike Press® Large Print Core.
The text of this Large Print edition is unabridged.
Other aspects of the book may vary from the original edition.
Set in 16 pt. Plantin.

LIBRARY OF CONGRESS CATALOGING-IN-PUBLICATION DATA

Names: Perrotta, Tom, 1961- author.
Title: Mrs. Fletcher / by Tom Perrotta.
Description: Large print edition. | Waterville, Maine : Thorndike Press, a part of Gale, a Cengage Company, 2017. | Series: Thorndike Press large print core
Identifiers: LCCN 2017028268 | ISBN 9781432842291 (hardcover) | ISBN 1432842293 (hardcover)
Subjects: LCSH: Middle-aged women—Fiction. | Mothers and sons—Fiction. | College students—Fiction. | Domestic fiction. | Large type books. | BISAC: FICTION / Literary. | FICTION / Family Life. | FICTION / Coming of Age. | GSAFD: Humorous fiction.
Classification: LCC PS3566.E6948 M77 2017b | DDC 813/.54—dc23
LC record available at https://lccn.loc.gov/2017028268

Published in 2017 by arrangement with Scribner, an imprint of Simon & Schuster, Inc.

Printed in the United States of America
1 2 3 4 5 6 7 21 20 19 18 17

"The way up and the way down is one and the same."

— Heraclitus

■ ■ ■ ■

PART ONE:
THE BEGINNING OF
A GREAT WHATEVER

■ ■ ■ ■

THE OBLIGATORY EMOTICON

It was a long drive and Eve cried most of the way home, because the big day hadn't gone the way she'd hoped, not that big days ever did. Birthdays, holidays, weddings, graduations, funerals — they were all too loaded with expectations, and the important people in her life rarely acted the way they were supposed to. Most of them didn't even seem to be working from the same script as she was, though maybe that said more about the important people in her life than it did about big days in general.

Take today: all she'd wanted, from the moment she opened her eyes in the morning, was a chance to let Brendan know what was in her heart, to express all the love that had been building up over the summer, swelling to the point where she sometimes thought her chest would explode. It just seemed really important to say it out loud before he left, to share all the gratitude and pride she felt, not just for the wonderful person he was right now, but for the sweet little boy he'd been, and the strong and decent man he would one day become. And she wanted to reassure him, too, to make it clear that she would be starting a new life just the same as he was, and that it would be a great adventure for both of them.

Don't worry about me, she wanted to tell him. *You just study hard and have fun. I'll take care of myself . . .*

But that conversation never happened. Brendan had overslept — he'd been out late, partying with his buddies — and when he finally dragged himself out of bed, he was useless, too hungover to help with the last-minute packing or the loading of the van. It was just so irresponsible — leaving her, with her bad back, to lug his boxes and suitcases down the stairs in the sticky August heat, sweating through her good shirt while he sat in his boxers at the kitchen table, struggling with the child-proof cap on a bottle of ibuprofen — but she managed to keep her irritation in check. She didn't want to spoil their last morning together with petty nagging, even if he deserved it. Going out on a sour note would have been a disservice to both of them.

When she was finished, she took a few

pictures of the van with the back hatch open, the cargo area stuffed with luggage and plastic containers, a rolled-up rug and a lacrosse stick, an Xbox console and an oscillating fan, a mini-fridge and a milk crate full of emergency food, plus a jumbo bag of Cool Ranch Doritos, because they were his favorite. She uploaded the least blurry photo to Facebook, along with a status update that read, *Off to college! So happy for my amazing son, Brendan!!!* Then she inserted the obligatory emoticon and launched her message into space, so her 221 friends would understand how she was feeling, and could let her know that they liked it.

It took a couple of tries to shut the hatch — the damn rug was in the way — but she finally got it closed and that was that. She lingered for a moment, thinking of other road trips, vacations they'd taken when Brendan was little, the three of them heading to Cape Cod to stay with Ted's parents, and that one time camping in the Berkshires when it rained and rained — the earth turning liquid beneath their tent — and they had to pack it in and find a motel in the middle of the night. She thought she might cry right then — it was going to happen sooner or later — but before she could get herself started, Becca zoomed up the driveway on her bicycle, moving so swiftly and silently it felt like a sneak attack.

"Oh!" Eve flung up her arms in self-defense, though she was in no danger of being run over. "You scared me!"

Becca shot her a withering *what-planet-are-you-from* look as she dismounted, but the contempt came and went so quickly it was almost like it hadn't been there at all.

"Good morning, Mrs. Fletcher."

Eve bristled at the greeting. She'd told Becca numerous times that she preferred to be addressed by her first name, but the girl insisted on calling her *Mrs. Fletcher,* as if she were still married.

"Good morning, Becca. Shouldn't you be wearing a helmet?"

Becca released the bike — it balanced on its own for a moment before toppling dreamily onto the grass — and patted her hair with both hands, making sure everything was where it was supposed to be, which of course it was.

"Helmets are gross, Mrs. Fletcher."

Eve hadn't seen Becca for a few weeks, and she suddenly realized how pleasant the interlude had been, and how she'd failed to appreciate it, the same way you fail to appreciate the absence of a stomachache until

12

the cramps return. Becca was so petite and adorable, so totally put together — that cute little turquoise romper, those immaculate white sneakers, all that makeup, way too much for a teenager riding her bike on a summer morning. And she wasn't even sweating!

"Well, then." Eve smiled nervously, acutely conscious of her own body, the doughy pallor of her flesh, the dampness spreading from her armpits. "Something I can do for you?"

Becca shot her that frosty look again, letting her know that she'd used up her quota of stupid questions for the day.

"Is he inside?"

"I'm sorry, honey." Eve nodded toward the van. "We're just about to leave."

"No worries." Becca was already moving toward the house. "I just need a minute."

Eve could have stopped her from going in — she totally had the right — but she didn't feel like playing the role of bitchy, disapproving mom, not today. What was the point? Her mom days were over. And as much as she disliked Becca, Eve couldn't help feeling sorry for her, at least a little. It couldn't have been easy being Brendan's girlfriend, and it must have hurt pretty badly to get dumped by him just weeks before he left for college, while she was marooned in high school for another year. He'd apparently done the dirty work by text and refused to talk to her afterward, just crumpled up the relationship and tossed it in the trash, a tactic he'd learned from his father. Eve could understand all too well Becca's need for one last conversation, that vain hope for closure.

Good luck with that.

Figuring they could use a little space, Eve drove to the Citgo station to fill the tank and check the tire pressure, then stopped at the bank to withdraw some cash she could slip to Brendan as a parting gift. *For books,* she would tell him, though she imagined most of it would go for pizza and beer.

She was gone for about fifteen minutes — ample time for a farewell chat — but Becca's bike was still resting on the lawn when she returned.

Too bad, she thought. *Visiting hours are over . . .*

The kitchen was empty, and Brendan didn't respond when she called his name. She tried again, a little louder, with no more success. Then she checked the patio, but it was pure formality; she already knew where they were and what they were doing. She could feel it in the air, a subtle, illicit, and deeply annoying vibration.

Eve wasn't a puritanical mom — when she went to the drugstore, she made a point of asking her son if he needed condoms — but she didn't have the patience for this, not today, not after she'd loaded the van by herself and they were already way behind schedule. She made her way to the foot of the stairs.

"Brendan!" Her voice was shrill and commanding, the same one she'd used when he was a child misbehaving on the playground. "I need you down here *immediately*!"

She waited for a few seconds, then stomped up the stairs, making as much noise as possible. She didn't care *what* they were doing. It was a simple matter of respect. Respect and maturity. He was leaving for college and it was time to grow up.

His bedroom door was closed and music was playing inside, the usual thuggish rap. She raised her hand to knock. The sound that stopped her was vague at first, barely audible, but it grew louder as she tuned in to its frequency, an urgent primal muttering that no mother needs to hear from her son, especially when she was feeling nostalgic for the little boy he'd been, the sweet child who'd clung so desperately to her leg when

15

she tried to say goodbye on his first day of preschool, begging her to stay with him for *just one more minute. Please, Mommy, just one little minute!*

"Oh shit," he was saying now, in a tone of tranquilized wonder. "Fuck yeah . . . Suck it, bitch."

As if repulsed by a terrible odor, Eve lurched away from the door and beat a flustered retreat to the kitchen, where she made herself a cup of soothing peppermint tea. To distract herself while it steeped, she flipped through a catalogue from Eastern Community College, because she was going to have a lot of time on her hands from now on, and needed to find some activities that would get her out of the house, maybe bring her into contact with some interesting new people. She'd made it all the way up to Sociology, circling the classes that seemed promising and fit her schedule, when she finally heard footsteps on the stairs. A few seconds later, Becca stepped into the kitchen, looking rumpled but victorious, with a big wet spot on her romper. At least she had the decency to blush.

"Bye, Mrs. Fletcher. Enjoy the empty nest!"

The previous summer, when Eve and Bren-

16

dan were visiting colleges, they'd had some lovely long drives together. Lulled by the monotony of the highway, he'd opened up to her in a way she'd forgotten was possible, talking easily and thoughtfully about a multitude of normally off-limits subjects: girls, his father's new family, some of the options he was pondering for his undergraduate major (Economics, if it wasn't too hard, or maybe Criminal Justice). He'd surprised her by showing some curiosity about her past, asking what she'd been like at his age, wondering about the guys she'd dated before she got married, and the bands she'd liked, and whether or not she'd smoked weed. They shared a motel room on the overnight trips, watching TV from their respective beds, trading the Doritos bag back and forth as they laughed at *South Park* and Jon Stewart. At the time, it had felt like they were entering a gratifying new phase of their relationship — an easygoing adult rapport — but it didn't last. As soon as they got home they reverted to their default mode, two people sharing the same address but not much else, exchanging the minimum daily requirement of information, mostly, on her son's side, in the form of grudging monosyllables and irritable grunts.

Eve had cherished the memory of those

intimate highway conversations, and she'd been looking forward to another one that afternoon, a last chance to discuss the big changes that were about to unfold in both of their lives, and maybe to reflect a little on the years that were suddenly behind them, gone more quickly than she ever could have imagined. But how could they share a nostalgic moment when all she could think about were the awful words she'd heard through the bedroom door?

Suck it, bitch.

Ugh. She wanted to press a button and erase that ugly phrase from her memory, but it just kept repeating itself, echoing through her brain on an endless loop: *Suck it, bitch . . . Suck it, bitch . . . Suck it . . .* He'd uttered the words so casually, so *automatically,* the way a boy of her own generation might have said, *Oh yeah,* or *Keep going,* which would have been embarrassing enough from a mother's perspective, but not nearly so disturbing.

She probably shouldn't have been surprised. Back when Brendan was in middle school, Eve had gone to a PTA presentation on "Web-Savvy Parenting." The guest speaker, an assistant county prosecutor, had given them a depressing overview of the internet landscape and the perils it posed for teenagers. He touched on sexting and cyberbullying and online predators, but the thing that really bothered him was the insane amount of pornography that kids were potentially exposed to every day, a tsunami of filth unprecedented in human history.

This isn't a copy of Playboy *hidden in the closet, okay? This is an unregulated cesspool of degrading images and extreme sexual perversion available to everyone in the privacy of their own bedrooms, regardless of their age or emotional maturity. In this toxic environment, it will take constant, unwavering vigilance to keep your kids safe, to protect their innocence and guard them from depravity. Are you prepared to meet this challenge?*

Eve and the other mothers she'd spoken to were shaken by the grim picture he'd painted, but they agreed afterward that it was a little overdone. The situation was bad — there was no use denying it — but it wasn't all *that* bad, was it? And even if it was, there was no practical way to monitor your kids' every mouse click. You just had to teach the right values — respect and kindness and compassion, pretty much *do unto others,* not that Eve was religious — and hope that it provided a shield against the harmful images and sexist stereotypes that they would inevitably be exposed to. And that was what Eve had done, to the best of her ability, though it obviously hadn't worked out the way she'd hoped.

Suck it, bitch.

It was a little late in the day for a big sex talk, but Eve felt like she had no choice but to let Brendan know how disappointed she was. What he'd said to Becca was not okay, and Eve needed to make that clear, even if it ruined their last day together. She didn't want him to begin college without understanding that there was a fundamental difference between sexual relationships in real life and the soulless encounters he presumably watched on the internet (he insisted that he stayed away from all that crap, but his browser history was always carefully scrubbed, which was one of the warning signs she'd learned about at the PTA meeting). At the very least, she needed to remind him that it was not okay to call your girlfriend a bitch, even if that was a word you used jokingly with your male friends, even if the girl in question claimed not to mind.

And even if she really is one, Eve thought, though she knew it wasn't helpful to her cause.

Brendan must have sensed that a lecture was imminent, because he did his best to seal himself off in the van, tugging the bill of his baseball cap low over his sunglasses, nodding emphatically to the hip-hop throbbing through his sleek white headphones. As soon as they got on the Pike, he reclined his seat and announced that he was taking a nap.

"I hope you don't mind," he said, which was the first halfway polite thing to emerge from his mouth all day. "I'm really tired."

"You must be," she said, larding her voice with fake sympathy. "You had a really busy morning. All that heavy lifting."

"Ha ha." He propped his bare feet on the dashboard. "Wake me when we get there, okay?"

He slept — or pretended to sleep — for the next two hours, not even leaving the van when she stopped at a rest area outside of Sturbridge. Eve resented it at first — she really did want to talk to him about sexual etiquette and respect for women — but she had to admit that it was a relief to postpone the conversation, which would have required her to confess that she'd been eavesdropping outside of his door and to quote the phrase that had upset her so much. She wasn't sure she'd be able to say it out loud, not without grave embarrassment, and she had a feeling that Brendan would laugh and tell her that she'd heard wrong, that he would never say, *Suck it, bitch,* not to Becca or anyone else, and they'd end up disputing the basic facts of the case rather than discussing the issues that really mattered. He could be a pretty slippery customer when he needed to be; it was another trait he'd inherited from his father, a fellow master of denial and evasion.

Just let him rest, she thought, inserting a Neil Young CD into the slot, mellow old songs that left her with a pleasant feeling of melancholy, perfect for the occasion. *We can talk some other time.*

Eve knew she was being a coward, abdicating her parental responsibility, but letting him off the hook was pretty much a reflex at this point. The divorce had left her with a permanently guilty conscience that made it almost impossible for her to stay mad at her son or hold him accountable for his actions. The poor kid had been the victim of an elaborate bait and switch perpetrated by his own parents, who, for eleven years, had built a life for him that felt solid and permanent and good, and then — just kidding! — had ripped it out of his hands and replaced it with an inferior substitute, a smaller, flimsier version in which love had an expiration date and nothing could be trusted. Was it any wonder that he didn't always treat other people with the kindness and consideration they deserved?

Not that it was Eve's fault. Ted was the guilty party, the selfish bastard who'd abandoned a perfectly good family to start over with a woman he'd met through the Casual Encounters section of Craigslist (he'd falsely claimed his marital status was "Separated," a self-fulfilling prophecy if there ever was one). Eve had been blindsided by his betrayal and devastated by his refusal to get counseling or make even a token effort to save the marriage. He just pronounced it dead and buried, unilaterally declaring the past two decades of his life to be a regrettable mistake and vowing to do better on his next try.

I have a second chance, he'd told her, his voice quivering with emotion. *Do you see how precious that is?*

What about me? she'd replied. *What about your son? Aren't we precious, too?*

I'm a jerk, he explained. *You both deserve better.*

The whole world acknowledged her status as an innocent victim — even Ted agreed! — but Eve still felt complicit in the breakup. The marriage had been floundering for a long time before Ted found his way to

23

Craigslist, and she hadn't done a thing to make it better, hadn't even admitted there was a problem. Through her own passivity, she had enabled the disaster, letting her husband drift away and her family fall apart. She'd failed as a wife, and therefore as a mother, and Brendan was the one who'd paid the price.

The damage he'd suffered was subtle and hard to pinpoint. Other people marveled at what an impressive young man he was and how well he'd weathered the divorce. Eve was delighted by the praise — it meant everything to her — and she even believed it, up to a point. Her son did possess a number of good qualities. He was handsome and popular, a gifted athlete who never lacked for female attention. He'd done well in school, good enough to be admitted to Fordham and Connecticut College, though he'd ultimately settled on Berkshire State University, partly because it was more affordable, but mainly, as he cheerfully informed anyone who asked, because BSU was a party school and he liked to party. That was how he presented himself to the world — as a big, friendly, fun-loving bro, a dude you'd totally want on your team or in your frat — and the world seemed happy to take him at his word.

To Eve, though, he was still the bewildered boy who couldn't understand why his father had left and why they couldn't just make him come home. For the first couple of months after Ted moved out, Brendan had slept with a picture of his dad under his pillow, and more than once she'd found him wide awake in the middle of the night, talking to the photo with tears streaming down his face. He'd toughened up over time — his muscles turned wiry and his eyes got hard and the picture disappeared — but something had gone out of him in the process, all the boyish softness and vulnerability that had touched her so deeply. He just wasn't as nice a person as he used to be — not nearly as sweet or as kind or as lovable — and she couldn't forgive herself for letting that happen, for not knowing how to protect him, or how to fix what was broken.

They hit a traffic jam on the edge of campus, a festive convoy of incoming freshmen and their families. Inching toward the Longfellow Residential Area, they were cheered along the way by clusters of upperclassmen in matching red T-shirts who were apparently being paid to greet the newcomers. Some of them were dancing and others were holding up handmade signs that said, *Wel-*

come Home! and *First Years Rock!* However mercenary its origins, their enthusiasm was so infectious that Eve couldn't help grinning and waving back.

"What are you doing?" Brendan muttered, still grumpy from his nap.

"Just being friendly," she said. "If that's all right with you."

"Whatever." He slumped lower in his seat. "Knock yourself out."

Brendan had been assigned to Einstein Hall, one of the infamous high-rise dorms that made Longfellow look like a public housing project. Eve had heard alarming things about the party culture in this part of campus, but the vibe seemed reassuringly wholesome as they pulled into the unloading area and were swarmed by a crew of cheerful and efficient student movers. Within minutes, the movers had emptied the van, transferring all of Brendan's possessions into a big orange bin on wheels. Eve stood by and watched, happy to be spared another round of sweaty labor. A scruffy kid whose T-shirt identified him as *Crew Leader* shut the hatch and gave her a businesslike nod.

"Okay, Mom. We'll take this fine young man up to his room now."

"Great." Eve locked the van with the

26

remote key. "Let's go."

The crew leader shook his head. Despite the ninety-degree heat, he was wearing a knitted winter cap with earflaps, the material so sweat-stiffened that the flaps curled out like Pippi Longstocking's pigtails. "Not you, Mom. You need to move your vehicle to the Visitors Lot."

This didn't seem right to Eve. She'd seen lots of other mothers heading into the dorm with their kids. An Indian lady in a lime-green sari was accompanying her daughter at that very moment. But even as Eve began to point this out, she realized that the other mothers must have had husbands who were taking care of the parking. Everyone seemed to agree that this was the proper division of labor — the men parked the cars while the women stayed with their kids. Eve softened her voice, pleading for clemency.

"I'll just be a few minutes. I need to help him unpack."

"That's great, Mom." An edge of impatience had entered the crew leader's voice. "But first you have to move the vehicle. There's a lot of people waiting."

I'm not your mom, Eve thought, smiling with excruciating politeness at the officious little shit. If she had been his mother, she would have advised him to lose the hat.

27

Sweetie, she would have told him, *you look like a moron.* But she took a deep breath and tried to appeal to his humanity.

"I'm a single parent," she explained. "He's my only child. This is a big deal for us."

By this point, Brendan had tuned in to the negotiation. He turned and glared at Eve.

"Mom." His voice was clipped and tense. "Go park the car. I'll be fine."

"Are you sure?"

The crew leader patted her on the arm.

"Don't worry," he assured her. "We'll take good care of your baby."

The Visitors Lot was only a short drive away, but the walk back to Einstein took longer than she'd expected. By the time she made it up to Brendan's room on the seventh floor, he was already in full-tilt male bonding mode with his new roommate, Zack, a broad-shouldered kid from Boxborough with a narrow, neatly trimmed beard that hugged his jawline like a chin strap, the same ill-advised facial hair that Brendan had sported for most of senior year. They were wearing identical outfits, too — flip-flops, baggy shorts, tank tops, angled baseball caps — though Zack had spiced up his ensemble with a puka shell necklace.

He seemed nice enough, but Eve had to work to conceal her disappointment. She'd hoped that Brendan would get a more exotic roommate, a black kid from inner-city Boston, or a visiting student from mainland China, or maybe a gay guy with a passion for musical theater, someone who would expand her son's horizons and challenge him to move beyond his suburban comfort zone. Instead he'd gotten paired with a young man who could have been his long-lost brother, or at least a teammate on the Haddington High lacrosse team. When she arrived, the boys were admiring their matching mini-fridges.

"We could dedicate one to beer," Zack suggested. "The other could be for non-beer shit, lunch meat and whatever."

"Totally," agreed Brendan. "Milk for cereal."

"Arizonas." Zack fingered his puka shells. "Might be cool if we stacked one on top of the other. Then it would be like one medium-sized fridge with two compartments. Give us more floor space that way."

"Sweet."

Eve went straight to work, putting sheets and blankets on Brendan's bed and organizing his closet and dresser just the way they were at home, so he wouldn't be disoriented. Neither boy paid much attention to her — they were strategizing about maybe lofting one of the beds and moving a desk underneath, freeing up enough space for a couch, which would make it easier to play video games — and she told herself that it was completely natural for a mother to be ignored in a situation like this. This was their room and their world; she was an outsider who would soon be on her way.

"Where would we get a couch?" Brendan wondered.

"People just leave 'em out on the street," Zack explained. "We can go out later and pick one up."

"Is that sanitary?" Eve asked. "They could have bedbugs."

"Mom." Brendan silenced her with a head shake. "We'll figure it out, okay?"

Zack stroked his beard like a philosopher. "We could cover it with a sheet, just to be on the safe side."

It was almost five thirty by the time Eve got everything unpacked. She saved the area rug for last, positioning it between the two beds so no one's feet would be cold on winter mornings. It was a nice homey touch.

"Not bad," she said, glancing around with satisfaction. "Pretty civilized for a dorm room."

Brendan and Zack nodded in that sub-dued male way, as if they could barely rouse themselves to express agreement, let alone gratitude.

"Who wants dinner?" she asked. "Pizza's on me."

A quick, wary glance passed between the roommates.

"You know what, Mom? A bunch of guys from the floor are going out in a little while. I'll probably grab some food with them, okay?"

Jesus, Eve thought, a sudden warmth flooding her face. *That was quick.*

"Sure," she said. "Go ahead. Enjoy your-selves."

"Yeah," Brendan added. "This way you won't have to drive home in the dark."

"All right, then." Eve scanned the room, searching fruitlessly for another task. "Looks like that's it."

No one contradicted her.

"Okay." She smoothed Brendan's bed-spread one last time. She had a slightly diz-zying sense of being overtaken by time, the future becoming the present before she was ready. "Guess I better be going."

Brendan walked her to the elevators. It wasn't an ideal place to say goodbye — too many kids milling around, including a crew

31

of student movers pushing an empty bin — but there was nothing they could do about that.

"Oh, by the way . . ." Eve fumbled in her purse and found the cash she'd withdrawn that morning. She pressed the bills into Brendan's hand, then gave him a fierce hug and a quick kiss. "Just call me if you need anything, okay?"

"I'll be fine."

She hugged him again when the elevator arrived. "I love you."

"Yeah," he muttered. "Me too."

"I'm going to miss you. A lot."

"I know."

After that, there was nothing to do but climb aboard and wave to her son until the doors slid shut. For a few seconds, the elevator didn't move. Eve smiled awkwardly at the other passengers, all of them students, none of whom responded in kind. They were chatting excitedly among themselves, making plans, bubbling over with enthusiasm, utterly oblivious to her presence. Eve felt old and excluded, as if everyone else was going to a party to which she hadn't been invited. *It's not fair,* she wanted to tell them, but they were already going down, and nobody would have believed her anyway.

MEAT BOMB

I was still a little dazed when we headed out to dinner, headachy from my daylong hangover — tequila shots will do that to you — and a little freaked out by my new surroundings, the high-rise buildings and unfamiliar faces. It was hard to believe I was finally in college, after all the endless build-up, a whole year of tours and tests and applications and interviews, the drama of choosing your future, graduating high school, saying goodbye to your friends and family and coaches, all that weepy shit.

It was exciting, I guess, to have the freedom I'd been dreaming about, the ability to do what I wanted when I wanted, no one to answer to but myself. But it was kind of a letdown, too. The truth is, I would've been just as happy to spend another year at Haddington High, where I knew everyone and everyone knew me, where I could be a varsity starter in pretty much any sport I chose, and get straight Bs without breaking a sweat. I had a slightly queasy feeling walking into town — the same feeling I got in airports and train stations — like there were way too many people in the world, and none of them gave a shit about me.

At least the fresh air did me some good. It had gotten pretty claustrophobic up in the dorm room, my mother doing that manic thing of hers, fixing everything up, offering all kinds of advice nobody had asked for, like it was rocket science to do your laundry, and she was the head of NASA. When she finally got on the elevator, I felt a deep sense of relief, which isn't the way you want to feel toward your mom at a moment like that.

Zack put his arm around me, very casually, as we walked, like we'd known each other for years. It reminded me of my friend Wade, who used to do all kinds of homoerotic shit like that in the hallways. Sometimes he would even kiss me on the cheek or the side of the head, or give my ass a little squeeze, which was only funny because we were lacrosse players and everybody knew we weren't gay.

"Bro," he told me, "we are gonna have mad fun this year. Alcohol will be consumed in massive quantities in Room 706."

"Weed will be smoked," I said. "Parties

will be had."

"Dicks will be sucked!" he added, in such a loud voice that these two Asian girls walking ahead of us turned and gave us a look, like we were a couple of assholes.

"Not by me," Zack assured the girls, quickly withdrawing his arm from my shoulder. "But you ladies should totally go for it, if that's your thing."

The girls didn't crack a smile. They just turned and kept walking.

"It's okay," I told him. "No one's judging you. Lots of people come out in college."

"Eat me, douchebag."

"That's hate speech, dickhead."

"*Douchebag* is hate speech?"

"Yeah. It's offensive to douchebags."

"Huh." He nodded, like that made a lot of sense. "Then I apologize."

"That's okay," I said. "We're here to learn and grow."

There were only supposed to be four of us at the pizzeria — me and Zack, plus Will and Rico, these chill dudes from our floor — but unbeknownst to us, Will had invited his camp counselor buddy, Dylan, and Dylan had brought along his roommate, this annoying kid named Sanjay.

I mean, it wasn't like there was anything

wrong with Sanjay, and no, I'm not preju-
diced against Indian people or anyone else.
It was just awkward. The rest of us were
jocks and hard partiers, and Sanjay was a
skinny nerd who looked like he was about
twelve years old. And that's fine, you know?
Go ahead and be a nerd if that's what makes
you happy. Go design your app or whatever.
Just don't ask me to give a shit.

"Sanjay's in the Honors College," Dylan
informed us. "Majoring in Electrical Engineering. Talk about badass."

I guess you have to give Dylan some
credit. He was trying to be a good roommate, doing his best to include Sanjay in
the conversation and make him feel comfortable. It was just a waste of time, that's
all. Sanjay wasn't going to be friends with
us, and we weren't going to be friends with
him. You could take one look at our table
and know that for a fact.

"Nice," said Rico, who was a white guy
with curly blond hair, a former high school
wrestler. His real name was Richard Timp-
kins, but the Spanish teacher called him
Rico, and his friends thought it was hilarious, so the nickname stuck. "I thought
about Engineering, but I kinda suck at
math. Plus I smoke way too much weed."

"Maybe there's a connection," said Will,

an ex–football player whose neck was wider than his head. "Just putting it out there."

"It's possible," agreed Rico. "Bong hits and calculus are not a winning combination."

"Actually," Sanjay said, "I'm thinking about switching to Architecture. That's my first love."

I glanced across the table at Zack, but he was already reaching for his phone, swiping at the screen and tapping away with both thumbs. His text arrived a few seconds later:

My first love is architecture!

I texted back: *My second is sucking cock!!!*

Zack snorted and we bumped fists across the table.

"Guess what Sanjay got on the Math SAT?" Dylan asked.

Nobody wanted to know, so the question just sort of floated away. Sanjay looked as relieved as the rest of us.

Will glared at Dylan. I don't think he was mad. He just had one of those faces that looked pissed off a lot of the time. You couldn't really blame him, I guess. He'd been one of the best high school linebackers in the state, heavily recruited by Division 3 schools, but he blew out his knee in the season opener of his senior year, and that was that. Full retirement at age seventeen.

"How come he's not living in the Honors Dorm?" he asked, as if Sanjay couldn't speak English and needed Dylan to translate.

"It's too elitist," Sanjay explained. "I don't think we should have a separate dorm from everyone else. We're all one community, right?"

My phone buzzed again. I figured it was Zack, but it turned out to be Becca.

Hows it going college boy

Out w the guys, I texted back.

Miss me?

I was tempted to tell her the truth — *nope, not at all* — but I took pity on her.

Sure

Can we skype later

going to a party

What time

Ten

How about 9:30 you owe me for this morning!!! Ha ha☺

I knew this would happen. That was why I'd dumped her in the first place, so I wouldn't have to deal with this long-distance shit in college. But then last night I'd drunk-sexted her, begging to get with her one last time before I left town. She told

38

me to fuck off, which I definitely deserved. I didn't remember any of it until she showed up at my house in the morning, and totally ambushed me, in the best possible way. *It's your going-away present,* she'd said, kneeling down in front of me and tugging on my boxers. And it was a great blowjob, too — way better than usual — but I didn't think that meant we were back together, or that I owed her for anything, though I could see how she might feel otherwise.

Fine 9:30
Luv ya!

The pizza arrived — one large pepperoni, one large sausage, and one large cheese — and of course Sanjay turned out to be a vegetarian. We started giving him shit for it, until Dylan explained that it was a religious thing, which meant, according to PC regulations, that you weren't allowed to joke about it.

"I forgot how much I love pizza," Will told us. "I didn't eat any all summer. Couldn't even look at it."

"Why not?" Rico asked.

Will shrugged. "I had a bad experience. You don't want to hear about it while you're eating."

But we did, so he told us. The day after

graduation, Will had gone to a party at this rich girl's house, in the biggest McMansion he'd ever seen, with an indoor pool, a home gym, and something like eight bathrooms. The girl had been very clear that there wasn't going to be any alcohol at the party, so Will had hit the pregame hard, multiple shots of Jack plus a THC-infused lollipop donated by someone's uncle who suffered from chronic shoulder pain and had an understanding doctor. He had the munchies pretty bad when he got to the party, and it was like he'd walked into heaven — there was this amazing spread of fried chicken, lasagna, barbecue, an honest-to-goodness ten-foot-long sub, tons of great stuff. He'd already sampled a lot of it when the doorbell rang, and a delivery guy walked in with a stack of a dozen pizzas. A crowd had gathered around the buffet table, and one of Will's buddies bet him twenty bucks he couldn't eat a large pizza by himself. And not just any pizza. The one they call the Meat Bomb. Will said, *Bring it on, bitch!*

"No way," said Rico.

"It was a throwdown," Will explained.

He inhaled the first four slices like a machine. Midway through slice number five, though, he realized there was a problem.

"You know how it is. You're feeling good, totally on top of your game. And then, out of nowhere, your stomach just clenches up and says, *That's enough, bro. Do not take another bite.* But I still had three slices to go."

"You didn't eat them?" Rico said.

"The fuck I didn't," said Will. "I just kept shoveling that shit down my throat. But I knew it wasn't gonna stay there."

The spectators broke into applause when he finished, but Will didn't stick around to enjoy it. He pushed through the crowd and made his way to the nearest bathroom, only to discover that the door was locked. He pounded on it a few times, but the occupant told him to wait his turn. He didn't panic, because there was another bathroom off the kitchen. Unfortunately, that one was really popular. There were five or six people standing in line, and Will couldn't really talk, which meant that he couldn't explain his dilemma, so he just turned and headed upstairs, holding his stomach and gritting his teeth.

It was like a bad dream. Every time he found a bathroom, the door was either locked or a bunch of kids were waiting in line. So he just kept moving, hoping to find a toilet before it was too late. It was a huge house, and he pretty much gave himself the grand tour, visiting all three floors before he finally made it to the master bedroom, which was totally spectacular — a huge round bed and a wall that was all glass, looking out on a meadow — though Will didn't have time to appreciate the view. He headed straight for the bathroom, and Praise the Lord, the door was unlocked. His stomach was already lurching when he burst in there and found himself staring at six of the prettiest girls in his school, all of them in bikinis, sitting in this giant Jacuzzi.

"Oh shit," said Dylan. "Did you barf on them?"

Will shook his head. "I just gave them this sad little wave, like I was dropping by to say hello, and then I fucking bolted. I barely made it out to the hall, and that was it, the end of the road. I ducked into this little kid's room. I thought there'd be a trash can or something, but I couldn't find one, so I just yanked open a dresser drawer, pulled out all the clothes, and puked right in there. That whole fucking Meat Bomb pizza. And then I shut the drawer, wiped my mouth, and got the fuck outta there."

"Did you tell anyone?" Dylan asked, when we were finally done groaning and laughing.

"Fuck no. What was I supposed to say? Oh, by the way, your little brother might not want to open his pajama drawer . . ."

"At least you took out the pjs," Rico said. "That was thoughtful."

"What could I do?" Will had that pissed-off look again. "Eight fucking bathrooms, and I can't find a toilet to puke in? You can't blame me for that."

He shrugged and reached for another slice. Sanjay was just sitting there with his mouth hanging open, like he'd forgotten how to speak.

"Whaddaya think?" Rico asked him. "Too late to get back into the Honors Dorm?"

Zack and I returned to the room just in time for my Skype session with Becca. I asked if he'd mind giving me a little privacy.

"No problem," he said. "I'll put on my headphones."

"Think you could maybe clear out for five or ten minutes? Won't be more than that."

"Why?" He gave me a sly look. "You gonna rub one out?"

"We just need to have the talk. We were broken up for most of the summer, but then we kinda backslid. I have to let her down easy."

"Say no more, bro. I'll go see who's in the

lounge. Text me when you're done."

"Thanks."

I got out my laptop and logged on to Skype. Zack was on his way out when I placed the call, but then he changed his mind and sat down next to me on my bed, just out of camera range, as Becca appeared on the screen.

"Hey, baby." She was wearing a little white tank top, tight enough to give her some cleavage, which wasn't easy with her little boobs. "How's it going?"

"Pretty good," I said. "How about you?"

"I'm okay." She was talking in a breathy whisper, way more seductive than her normal voice, which could be kinda loud and bossy. "Where are you?"

"In my room."

She licked her glossy lips. "Are you alone?"

I glanced at Zack, trying to let him know that the joke was officially not funny anymore, but he pretended not to understand. He mouthed the words *She's cute!* and pumped his fist up and down over his crotch.

"Brendan?" she said. "Is somebody there?"

I should have just said, *Yeah, it's my roommate and he's being a dick,* but I didn't want to embarrass him.

"No," I said. "Just me."

"I miss you, baby." She gazed soulfully into the camera. "I'm still thinking about this morning."

"Yeah," I said. "That was a really nice surprise."

"Just nice?"

"It was fucking awesome."

"Good." She looked a little bashful, but sort of proud, too. "I watched an instructional video on YouTube."

That made sense. She'd given me a few BJs in the past, but she was never really into it. She was clumsy and gagged a lot, and mostly just seemed relieved when it was over. But that morning she was a porn star.

"Yeah, you brought your A game."

"It was a mental thing," she explained. "I just decided to have a positive attitude. It really makes a difference."

It was ridiculous — and kind of embarrassing — to be having this conversation with Zack sitting right next to me, but there was nothing I could do about it now except try not to look at him. I didn't want to know what he was thinking, or how close he might be to cracking up.

"I thought I'd be able to swallow," she said, "but I just . . . I don't know. I'll have to keep working on that."

"With who?" I said.

Zack made the tiniest sound just then, a single suppressed giggle way in the back of his throat, but Becca didn't seem to hear it.

"You, you asshole. Unless you want me to find someone else."

"Practice makes perfect," I teased.

Zack was waving his hand, trying to get my attention. I could see him out of the corner of my eye, pointing at his dick and mouthing the words *I'll help.*

"Hey," she said, and her voice was normal now, like the sexy part of the conversation was officially over. "Did your mom say anything after I left?"

"No, why?"

"I don't know. She gave me this weird look when I said goodbye, like she knew what we were up to."

"Don't worry about it. She was in a bad mood all day. It had nothing to do with you."

"Good." Becca seemed relieved. "So do you like it there?"

"I think so. Just trying to get used to it, you know?"

"Well, if you ever need to talk, just give me a call." She looked down for a few seconds, so all I could see was the top of her head, that shiny brown hair that always smelled so good. When she looked up, she sniffled and wiped her eyes. "I missed you so much this summer."

Zack was leaning forward now, into my field of vision. He had this sad clown expression on his face, his bottom lip pushed way out like he was about to cry. I held out my arm where Becca couldn't see it and gave him the finger.

"I like your shirt," I told her. "It's really hot."

"Yeah?" She perked right up. "I wore it special for you. I'm wearing the red thong you like, too."

She stood up to show me, pulling down her pj pants and turning so I could appreciate her tight little gymnast butt. Zack was impressed.

"Smokin'," I told her.

"You should come home for a weekend," she said. "Or maybe I could come visit you."

Zack cast a silent vote in favor of the second option.

"We'll see," I said. "I'm probably gonna be pretty busy."

"Yeah, that's what I figured."

We were quiet for a few seconds, and I knew the time had come to say what needed to be said, to apologize for the way I'd treated her over the summer, and then to explain, as tactfully as possible, that I didn't want a long-distance relationship, and that we both should be free to hook up with other people if we wanted to. But it was hard to think straight with Zack sitting right there, flicking his tongue in the V between his index and middle fingers.

"All right," I said. "I should probably go."

She smiled sadly and nodded. But then she leaned a little closer.

"Hey, Brendan."

And then, without any warning at all, she lifted her shirt and bra and showed me her boobs, which filled the entire laptop screen. It happened and then it was over. The shirt came back down and I was looking at her face again as she blew me a kiss.

"Good night, baby."

Zack was punching the air with both hands, silently screaming the word *Yes!* over and over, like he'd just scored a goal.

"Thanks," I said. "You have a good night, too."

It was hard to stay mad at Zack. He acted totally innocent, like his eavesdropping on my private conversation was totally hilarious and not creepy at all, a great bonding experience for both of us. And he was really complimentary about Becca and very excited about her pink nipples, which he compared to *little eraser nubs.*

"Why would you want to break up with a girl like that?" he asked me.

"Because I want a clean slate."

"Just keep her on the hook. I mean, Jesus, dude. She's watching how-to blowjob videos on YouTube. That'll spice up your Christmas vacation."

"Maybe you have a point."

"Hey," he said. "If you don't want her, send her my way. I'll give her some expert instruction."

The rest of the night was kind of a bust. Zack had been invited to an off-campus house party by a friend of his older brother, and it turned out to be a lot farther away than we thought. It took us about a half hour to walk there, and the party was already breaking up when we arrived. Somebody said there was a kegger a couple of blocks away, but we couldn't find it, so we ended up trudging all the way back to the dorm.

It was on the early side, but we were both pretty exhausted. We brushed our teeth together in the bathroom, then headed back to our room, where we stripped down to our boxers and got into bed. It was like having a twin brother.

I lay there for a while in the dark, thinking that college was probably going to be okay. I knew I'd lucked out on the roommate front, and I was grateful for that. I mean, what if I'd gotten stuck with someone like Sanjay, a kid I had nothing in common with? It would've sucked, having a nerd tagging along everywhere I went, being forced to eat with him and pretend to admire his architectural drawings and superhuman test scores. It was so much easier with Zack, a bro who partied and laughed at the same stupid shit I did. I knew my mother would have preferred Sanjay, but she wasn't the one who had to live with him.

"Oh shit," I muttered.

"What?" mumbled Zack.

"I forgot to text my mom."

I got out of bed, found my phone, and wrote, *College is awesome!!!* I figured she was probably wide awake at home, wondering how I was doing. She'd been talking a lot about how sad she'd be after I left, and how hard it would be to get used to living in an empty house.

"No offense," Zack said, when I'd climbed back into my bed, "but your mom is pretty hot."

"Dude," I said. "Seriously. This is not an appropriate subject of conversation."

"I'm just saying," he said. "She's kind of a MILF, don't you think?"

This wasn't the first time one of my friends had said this about my mom. She still dressed kinda young, and had a pretty good body for a woman her age. But she was my mom, and I didn't like to think about her in those terms.

"What about your mom?" I said. "Is she a MILF?"

"My mom's dead," he said, in this really sad voice. "I miss her so much."

"Oh shit." I sat up in bed. "I'm really sorry."

"Dude," he said, laughing at my sadness. "I'm just fucking with you. My mom's alive and well. But she is definitely not a MILF."

DEPARTMENT OF AGING

When Eve took inventory of her life, her job stood out as the conspicuous bright spot, the sole arena in which she judged herself a success. She was executive director of the Haddington Senior Center, a thriving facility that provided an impressive array of services to the town's older residents. The Center was not only a source of companionship, mental stimulation, and age-appropriate exercise for the elderly; it was also a place where low-income seniors could come to eat a federally subsidized meal and then get their blood pressure checked by a nurse and their problem toenails trimmed by a kindhearted podiatrist. The Center ferried a busload of clients to Market Basket twice a week, and also acted as a clearinghouse for handymen, landscapers, home health aides, and the like, referring trusted local businesses to older residents in need of assistance. Eve was proud of the work she did and, unlike a lot of people she knew, never had to ask herself what the point was, or wonder if she should be doing something a little more important with her life.

When she thought about how much she liked her job, she tended to focus on activities like chair yoga, memoir-writing workshops, and Thursday afternoon karaoke. What she didn't think about were situations like *this,* when it fell on her to deliver bad news to people who already had enough trouble in their lives.

"Thank you for coming on such short notice," she began, smiling in spite of herself at George Rafferty, whom she'd clearly interrupted in the middle of some filthy plumbing job. There was a smear of grease on his face, and the knees of his work pants were darkened with what looked like years of shiny, caked-on grime. He'd once come to Eve's house at six a.m. on Thanksgiving morning to fix an overflowing toilet, which only made the conversation they were about to have that much more difficult. "I know it's inconvenient."

George didn't smile back. He was a stocky, squinty guy with rust-colored hair, a rusty beard flecked with gray, and an air of permanent impatience, as if there was always something more urgent he needed to be attending to. He glanced apprehensively at his eighty-two-year-old father, who was sitting beside him on the couch, making loud smacking noises with his lips.

"What'd he do this time?"

Eve heard the wariness in his voice. The last time George had been summoned to the Center in the middle of the day, his father had somehow managed, by standing on his seat, to urinate out the window of the Elderbus on the way home from the supermarket. It was an impressive feat for a man his age, even if, as eyewitnesses claimed, he'd only been partially successful.

"Mr. Rafferty?" Eve turned to the older man, who was watching her with a vague, placid expression. "Do you mind telling your son what happened after lunch?"

Roy Rafferty snapped to attention.

"Lunch?" he said. "Is it time for lunch?"

"You already had lunch," Eve reminded him. "We're talking about what happened when it was over. The reason you got in trouble."

"Oh." The old man's face tightened into a scowl of futile concentration. He was one of Eve's favorites, a longtime regular at the Center, one of those chatty, friendly guys who moved through life like a politician running for reelection, shaking everyone's hand, always asking after the grandkids. He'd been healthy and lucid up until about six months ago, when his wife died of a massive stroke. His decline since then had been rapid and alarming.

"What happened?" he asked. "Did I do something wrong?"

"You went in the ladies' room again."

"Oh, shit." George stared at his father with a mix of pity and exasperation. "Jesus Christ, Dad. We talked about this. You have to stay out of the ladies' room."

Roy hung his head like a schoolboy. Eve knew his whole life story, or at least the highlights. He'd fought in Korea, and had come home with a Purple Heart and an urge to make up for lost time. Within six months, he'd married his high school sweetheart and taken over the family plumbing business, Rafferty & Son, which he ran for the next forty-five years, before handing it off to George. He and Joan had raised four kids, the eldest of whom — Nick, a high school vice principal — had died in his early fifties of pancreatic cancer. Eve had gone to the funeral.

"Mr. Rafferty," she said. "Do you remember what happened in the ladies' room?"

"I'm not supposed to go in there," he said.

"That's right," she told him. "It's off-limits for men."

"Okay," George said briskly. "We're all agreed on that. Now could you tell me what he did? I gotta get back to work."

"I'd like you to hear it from your father," Eve told him.

"My father can't remember!" George snapped. "He probably doesn't know what he had for lunch."

Eve let that hang in the air for a few seconds. It helped to have him say it out loud.

"Your father was exposing himself." She decided to leave it at that, to not specify that he was masturbating, or that he'd invited poor Evelyn Gerardi, who wheeled an oxygen tank around everywhere she went, to *come and get it*. At least he'd called her *sweetheart*.

"Oh, God." George didn't look surprised. "That's not good."

"Some of the ladies were very upset."

"I bet."

Eve turned from the son to the father. She really hated this part of her job.

"Mr. Rafferty, I speak for the whole staff when I say that I've enjoyed your company over the years. You've been so kind and considerate to so many people, and everybody likes you. But I'm afraid you won't be able to come here anymore. We can't allow it. I'm sorry."

"What?" George looked shocked. "You're kicking him out?"

"I don't have a choice. This is a community center. Your father needs a nursing home."

"Can't you give him one more chance?"

"We already did that," she said. "George, this isn't going to get better. You know that, right?"

"But he loves it here. This place is all he has left."

"I'm not sure you understand." Eve's voice was soft but firm. "Your father was touching himself and saying some very inappropriate things. One of the witnesses wanted to call the police and file charges. It was all I could do to calm everyone down and let me handle it like this."

George closed his eyes and nodded slowly. He must've known this moment was coming.

"What am I supposed to do? I can't watch him all day. My wife's getting chemo. She's in bad shape."

"I'm sorry." Eve had heard about the recurrence of Lorraine Rafferty's cancer. That was the kind of news that spread quickly at the Senior Center. "I don't know what to say."

"She's a fighter," he said, but there wasn't a lot of conviction in his voice. "It's in her lungs and liver."

"Oh, God. It must be really hard on you."

"Our daughter's taking the semester off. To watch her mother die." He laughed at the sheer awfulness of it all. "And now I gotta deal with this shit?"

He glanced at his father, who was sitting patiently on the couch, humming to himself, as if he were waiting for his number to be called at the DMV.

"There are resources available for people like your dad," Eve explained. "We have a social worker on staff who can talk you through your options."

No one spoke for a while. George reached out and took his father's hand. The old man didn't seem to notice.

"It just sucks," George said. "I hate to see him like this."

"He's a good man." Even as she said this, Eve realized how rude it was to refer to Roy Rafferty in the third person, so she addressed him directly. "You're a good man, Roy. We're going to miss you."

Roy Rafferty looked at Eve and nodded, as if he understood what she was saying and appreciated the kindness.

"Okey dokey," he said. "How about we get some lunch?"

This happened on a sleepy Friday afternoon at the tail end of summer, no meetings or activities scheduled for the rest of the day. After the Raffertys left, Eve shut her office door and turned off the light. Then she sat down at her desk and wept.

It was hard sometimes, dealing with old people, having to cast out the unfortunate souls who could no longer control their bladders or bowels, trying to reassure the ones who couldn't locate their cars in the parking lot, or remember their home address. It was hard to hear about their scary diagnoses and chronic ailments, to attend the funerals of so many people she'd grown fond of, or at least gotten used to. And it was hard to think about her own life, rushing by so quickly, speeding down the same road.

It didn't help that she was staring into the abyss of Labor Day weekend, three blank, desolate squares on her calendar. She'd been so preoccupied by the logistics of getting Brendan off to school that she hadn't even thought about trying to make plans until yesterday. First she'd called Jane Rosen — her most reliable dinner and movie and walk-around-the-reservoir companion — only to learn that Jane and Dave had made a spur-of-the-moment decision to get out of town. They were coping with empty nest issues of their own — they'd just dropped off their twin daughters at Duke and Vanderbilt — and thought that a couple of days at an inn on Lake Champlain might rekindle the romance in their marriage.

I'm terrified, Jane had confided. *What if there's no spark? What if we have nothing to talk about? What are we supposed to do then?*

Eve did her best to be a good listener and a supportive friend — she owed Jane at least that much, having subjected her to countless heartbroken soliloquies during the darkest days of her own separation and divorce — but it hadn't been easy. Jane was having second thoughts about a nightgown she'd bought, pale pink and diaphanous, very pretty, but maybe not the most flattering shade for her skin tone, especially with the hot flashes coming so frequently. And sex made her so sweaty these days, though Dave insisted that he didn't mind. *I guess I'm not feeling very attractive,* she confessed. Eve murmured encouragement, reminding Jane that she was still beautiful and that Dave adored her, but it took all the restraint she possessed not to burst into laughter and say, *Are you kidding me? That's your problem? You sweat when your husband fucks you?*

After Jane, she tried the rest of her usual suspects — Peggy, the mother of Brendan's friend Wade; Liza, who'd been divorced and single even longer than Eve; and Jeanine Foley, her old college roommate — but no one was available on such short notice. Her only real alternative was to drive down to New Jersey and spend a couple of days with her widowed mother and never-married sister, who were living together in the house where Eve had spent her childhood. She was overdue for a visit, but it was always so exhausting to see them — they bickered constantly, like an old married couple — and she just didn't have the patience right now.

Eve didn't cry for long. She'd never liked feeling sorry for herself, and knew there were worse fates to endure than three sunny days with nothing in particular to do. She thought of George Rafferty, with his dying wife and brain-addled father, and knew that he would have traded places with her in a heartbeat.

Enough of this bullshit, she told herself. *You have nothing to cry about.*

Unfortunately, she hadn't quite pulled herself together when Amanda Olney, the

Center's newest employee, opened the door and poked her head into the office.

"Quick question," she began, and then froze, taking a moment to register the dimness of the room and her boss's forlorn posture. "Are you okay?"

"I'm fine." Eve sniffled, dabbing at her nose with a crumpled tissue. "Allergy season."

Amanda opened the door a little wider. She was short and buxom, with Cleopatra bangs and multiple lurid tattoos that she made no effort to conceal, despite the disparaging comments and disgusted head shakes they never failed to elicit from the old folks. They were particularly horrified by the cobra winding its way around her left calf and shin, its forked tongue flicking across her kneecap.

"Can I help you with something?" Eve inquired.

Amanda hesitated, overcome by a sudden shyness.

"It's not about work," she explained. "I was just wondering if you were doing anything tonight. I thought maybe, if you were free, we could get a glass of wine or something?"

Eve was touched, despite her irritation. She liked Amanda and could see that it had taken some courage for her to reach out like this, however awkwardly. She was fresh out of grad school, recently broken up with a longtime boyfriend, and probably a little lonely, looking for mentorship and reassurance. But the first lesson Eve needed to teach her was that she was an employee, not a friend. There was a boundary between them that needed to be respected.

"I have other plans," she said. "But thank you."

"No problem." Amanda shrugged, as if she'd suspected as much. "Sorry to bother you."

"Not at all," Eve told her. "Have a nice weekend."

Her evening at home passed pleasantly enough, rolling along the usual track. First stop, dinner (Greek salad, hummus, pita), followed by way too much Facebook (a problem she was going to have to deal with), a couple of glasses of wine, and three episodes of *Friends* on Netflix (another problem, though she figured it would eventually fix itself, once she made it through all ten seasons). She kept meaning to start *The Wire* or *Breaking Bad,* but the time never seemed right to plunge into something so dark and serious. It was the same with books, always easier to pick up something breezy and upbeat than to crack open the copy of *Middlemarch* that had been squatting on her nightstand for the past nine months, a Christmas gift from her English professor cousin, Donna, who'd insisted that it was *deceptively readable,* whatever that meant.

Aside from the shock of Brendan's absence — still fresh and omnipresent — the only real shadow on her mood was a faint but lingering sense of regret that she hadn't accepted Amanda's invitation. A drink and some conversation would have been nice, a little way station between work and home. It was true that she had an unwritten policy of not socializing with her staff, but that was more a preference than a hard-and-fast rule, based as much on a lack of chemistry with her colleagues (most of whom were married, and even more of whom were dull) as it was on some nebulous sense of propriety. In any case, it was a policy she probably needed to rethink, now that she was retired from parenting and had more than enough time to herself. At this point in her life, she couldn't afford to be ruling out potential new friends on a technicality.

The phone rang while she was brushing her

teeth, and the sound made her heart leap with pleasure — *It's Brendan!* But when she hurried into the bedroom, wearing only pajama bottoms — because she couldn't find the top, and what difference did it make? — she saw that it wasn't her son at all.

"Ted?"

"Hey, I hope I didn't wake you."

"I'm awake. Is everything okay?"

"Just thought I'd check in. See how you're holding up. Hard to believe our little boy's in college, huh?"

Whose little boy? she thought, a reflex from angrier days. But it was true. Their little boy was all grown up.

"He seems happy there," she said. "I think he really likes his roommate."

"Yeah, Zack." Ted chuckled like he was in on the joke. "I just talked to him. Seems like a good kid."

"You talked to Zack?"

"Just for a minute. Little while ago. I called Brendan, and he passed the phone to Zack."

That was Ted all over. Mr. Glad-to-Meet-You. Always looking for the next stranger to charm.

"How's he doing?"

"Zack?"

"No, Brendan."

"Pretty good." Ted paused, recalibrating his response. "Pretty wasted, actually. But I guess that's a given your first weekend at college."

"I hope it's not gonna be a problem."

"College kids drink a lot. I know I did." He sounded proud of himself. "I can barely remember sophomore year."

"What a great role model."

"Don't worry about Brendan. He's got a good head on his shoulders."

"I hope so." She wanted to tell him about the awful thing he'd said to Becca the other day, but she heard a child screaming on Ted's end, and a woman's soothing voice, and it didn't seem like the right time to get into it. "I really miss him."

"He misses you, too. You know that, right?"

"It's hard to tell sometimes."

"Eve," he said. "Brendan really loves you. He just doesn't always know how to communicate."

She wanted to believe this, and she was grateful to Ted for saying it out loud. His guilty conscience had made him a lot nicer than he used to be.

"What about you?" she asked. The crying

had subsided for the moment. "Everything okay?"

"Up and down. Jon-Jon likes his new school. And the gluten-free diet seems to be helping a little."

Jon-Jon was Ted's four-year-old autistic son, an adorable child with severe behavioral problems. When Eve first heard about the diagnosis, she'd reacted uncharitably, considering it a form of karmic justice for Ted and his bad-girl wife, Bethany. How ironic and gratifying it had seemed at the time to see their Casual Encounter disrupted by reality. But they hadn't cracked under pressure the way she'd expected. Instead the ordeal had brought out the best in them. They were devoted to their son, totally immersed in the minutiae of his care. Ted had become an amateur expert on cutting-edge autism therapies. Bethany had quit her job and gone back to school for a master's in Special Ed. All this rising to the occasion had made it hard for Eve to sustain the hatred and contempt she'd felt for them in the immediate aftermath of her divorce.

"That's good," she said, glancing down at her bare chest. The room was chillier than she'd realized, and her nipples were hard, which made her remember how much Ted had appreciated her breasts. *They're perfect,* he used to tell her, not that it mattered much in the end. *Absolutely perfect.* "Maybe we should all stop eating gluten. Everybody who gives it up goes around telling everybody else how great they feel."

"That's because eating it made them sick."

"I guess."

The screaming started up again, louder than before, and Eve found herself wincing in sympathetic distress. Brendan had told her that Jon-Jon's tantrums could be pretty terrifying.

"All right," he sighed. "I better go deal with this. Have a good night, okay?"

"You too." She almost said *honey,* a reflex from a different era of her past. "Thanks for calling."

Eve was exhausted, but she stayed up well past midnight, playing Words with Friends against a random opponent, though that was just an excuse to keep her eyes open. What she was really doing was waiting for a message from Brendan. Over the summer he'd promised to keep in touch by sending her at least one text every single day. He was free to send more if he felt like it, or to call her, or even to arrange a Skype session if he was especially homesick. But one text per day was the agreed-upon minimum.

He'd kept his word for the past three days, texting her exactly once every twenty-four hours, even if his messages all said pretty much the same thing: *College is awesome!!!* (Tuesday); *Another AWESOME day!!* (Wednesday); and *Still totally awesome!* (yesterday). She was happy for him — though slightly concerned by the steady decline in the number of exclamation points he used — and grateful not to have been completely forgotten in the midst of all that awesomeness.

But no text had arrived today. It was Friday, of course, and he was drunk, as Ted had just informed her, so there was her explanation. But still — was he really going to break his promise on Day Four? Was he that irresponsible? She could have contacted him, of course, just typed out a quick *miss you xxoo,* and waited for him to respond, but that wasn't the deal. The deal was that he would reach out to her, and she wanted him to do it of his own free will, without any badgering, because he loved her and wanted to include her in his life. But she already knew, long before her match with Heather0007 was over (a decisive victory for Eve), that she was kidding herself. He wasn't going to text her tonight, and probably not tomorrow night, either. He just wasn't that kind of kid, the kind who'd think about his mother while he was out having a good time with his friends, or flirting with a pretty girl from down the hall. From now on, she'd hear from him if and when he felt like it — probably when he needed something — and she'd be lucky if it was once a week.

She must have dozed off with the phone still in her hand, because the vibration of the arriving message shocked her awake. *Thank God,* she thought, lurching upright, squinting groggily at the blurred and blinding screen, blinking hard to get the words into focus.

U r my MILF! Send me a naked pic!! I want to cum on those big floppy tits!!!

For a second or two, she was deeply disturbed, unable to understand why Brendan would text her something so disgusting, no matter how drunk he was. It just didn't seem possible. *Big floppy tits?* But then she double-checked, and saw, to her immense relief, that the text had come from a cellphone number she didn't recognize. It was just some anonymous jerk, a stupid prank she wouldn't even remember in the morning.

ORIENTATION

Those first few days of school, before the grind of classes started up, were pretty awesome. They had tons of activities for the freshmen, including this Welcome-to-BSU Field Day on the main quad with tug-o'-war and ring toss, water balloons and a Slip 'N Slide, all kinds of summer camp shit like that. And the weather was beautiful, which meant that lots of hot girls were wearing cutoffs and bikini tops, and more of them than I'd expected had tattoos that were good conversation starters. Some of the less hot girls stripped down too, and everybody tried to be cool about it, because body image and all that. Zack and I took our shirts off, because we'd both been working out over the summer and why wouldn't you, if you were ripped?

Mostly those days were about me and Zack. We did everything together, from the moment we woke up to the moment we crashed. One afternoon we hit the gym and did some lifting. We could both bench one eighty, but Zack could do five reps, and I could only make it to four. The day after that we checked out the climbing wall in the Student Center, but we'd gotten good and baked beforehand, so neither of us could manage a route higher than a 5.6.

It was pretty scary once you made it halfway up the wall, clinging to those knobby bolted-on handholds like your life depended on it, stuck in place until your forearms started to quiver and you had no choice but to reach for something higher. One time I lost my grip about thirty feet up. I fell like Humpty Dumpty, my arms swimming through the air, until the auto belay kicked in, the harness crushing my ballsack as it yanked against gravity. I was suspended up there for a few painful seconds, dangling like a limp dick until I floated slowly back to earth. Zack thought it was hilarious.

"You shrieked like a little bitch! I bet the whole school heard you!"

"Fuck you," I said. My chest felt hollow and my legs were shaky, and I guess he could hear it in my voice.

"I'm only kidding, bro." He clapped me on the shoulder, more gently than I would have expected. "Let's get some lunch."

Everybody had to meet their academic advisor at some point during Orientation Week to finalize their schedule and get one last pep talk about college. My guy was Devin Torborg from the Anthropology Department. I made the mistake of calling him "Professor," which was apparently a sore subject.

"Technically I'm an instructor," he explained, running his hand through his stringy hair, which looked like it hadn't been washed in a while. He had these little round eyeglasses like John Lennon, and his eyes were baggy and tired behind the smudged lenses. "Not currently on the tenure track. But I prefer 'Devin' anyway." He gave this sad little shrug and glanced at the folder on his desk. "So. Brendan Fletcher. This must be an exciting time for you. The beginning of a great . . ."

His voice trailed off, and he scowled like he couldn't remember the next word.

"Adventure," I said, helping him out.

"Ah," he said. "You're an optimist."

He opened the folder and examined the single sheet of paper lying inside. It must have listed my high school GPA and test scores and whatnot. He slid two fingers in between his face and his glasses and gave his left eyelid a thorough massage, clockwise first, then reverse.

"So tell me, Brendan." He paused to make a run at the other eye, working pretty hard on the loose skin, tugging it up and down and sideways. "What do you want from college?"

I knew I couldn't tell him the truth, which was that I wanted to party as much as possible and do the bare minimum of studying, but I didn't have a lie handy, so I just kind of stammered for a while.

"I . . . I . . . well, that's . . . you know. Good question. Just a degree, I guess."

"A degree in what?"

"Econ. Possibly. If I can survive the math requirements."

"Why Econ?"

"You know. So I can get a job when I graduate."

"What kind of job?"

"Any kind. Long as it pays six figures. I mean, maybe not right away, but pretty soon. That's my main goal."

He looked impressed, but only in a sarcastic way. "Good luck with that."

Then we went over my schedule, which wasn't very complicated. I had to take Econ 101, and also get the required freshman

Writing and Math classes out of the way. That left room for just one elective, which I had narrowed down to either Basic Concepts in Accounting or Intro to Statistics, neither of which sounded all that exciting.

"That's one strategy," he said. "You could sign up for a practical class like that and learn something useful and so forth. But my advice would be to stretch a little, try something new and impractical, maybe even a little off-the-wall. Learn a language. Take a poetry class. Study African History or Linguistics or Drawing. There's a lecture class on Polytheism that you might want to check out. Taught by yours truly." He smiled, kind of hopelessly. "You never know. It might change your life, or at least open up some new avenues for exploration."

I didn't know what Polytheism was, and I honestly didn't give a shit. But I didn't want to hurt his feelings, so I pretended to think it over.

"Maybe next semester," I said. "I'll probably just stick to Stats this time around."

"All right. Your call." He checked the time on his phone. "What about extracurriculars? Any ideas about that? Any clubs or teams or community service organizations?"

"I'm hoping to go Greek next year," I told him. "I'm not sure which fraternity, though."

"I wouldn't know about that," he said. "Where I did my undergrad work they didn't allow frats."

I had the feeling he wanted me to ask where that was, but I didn't take the bait. Especially since he didn't seem all that impressive to me anyway, a grungy non-professor in a shithole of a basement office, wearing a Journey T-shirt under his tweed jacket, which I guess I was supposed to find amusing.

"That must've sucked," I said.

"Not at all," he replied. "I certainly didn't miss them."

Then we just sat there for a few more seconds, staring at each other. I could hear singing out on the quad, an a cappella group doing a pretty cool version of "Livin' on a Prayer." Somebody had a great falsetto. I thought it might be fun to be in a group like that, if I could sing and it wasn't so gay.

"Are we done?" I asked.

He nodded and I stood up. As I was heading for the door, he called after me.

"Brendan," he said. "You know about consent, right?"

"Excuse me?"

"It's a pretty simple concept. No means no. And an intoxicated person can't consent to sexual activity. You understand that, right?"

"Yeah," I said. "I'm not an idiot."

"All right, then. Have a great semester."

Zack was meeting with his own advisor, so I killed some time at the Activities Fair on my way back to the room. It was crowded, dozens and dozens of tables set up under a huge circus tent, a good chunk of the freshman class milling around. Apparently, anybody could start a club and get funding from the university. There were Beekeepers, Hula Hoopers, Paintballers, Vegans, Future Real Estate Professionals, Brothers and Sisters in Christ, Atheists United, Triathletes, Stroke Victims, Cancer Survivors, Bicycle Mechanics, Slavic Folk Dancers. You could ride horses, row crew, play rugby, boycott Israel, learn to juggle or knit. Some of the people behind the tables were in costume — the Quidditch Club officers carried brooms and sported fake Harry Potter glasses, and one of the volunteers for the Muslim Student Union wore a full burka, or whatever they called it — and others just looked exactly like what their names said they were: Queer People of Color, Dungeons and Dragons Enthusiasts, Cannabis Reform Coalition, League of Young Conservatives, Bearded Hipster Alliance. I guess I must have spaced out a little, because I didn't even know where I was standing when the girl behind a table spoke to me.

"Hey," she said. "What's your name?"

"Excuse me?"

She laughed in a way that made me feel like she already knew me and liked me.

"It's not a trick question." She looked like a farm girl, freckles and a blond ponytail, and big shoulders, almost like a guy. "You know your name, right?"

"I used to," I said. "But I had a bunch of concussions last year."

She liked that, too, enough that she volunteered for a high five, which I delivered very gently, basically just pressing my palm against hers, earning a few more points in the process. I was a couple of inches taller than she was, but our hands were the same size.

"I'm Amber," she said. "Nice to meet you."

"Brendan."

"Do you know someone on the spectrum, Brendan?"

That was when I looked at the sign on her table: *Autism Awareness Network.*

"No, I —"

I was about to tell her that I'd just stopped

there at random when two things occurred to me. The first was that I did know someone on the spectrum, and the second was that this girl was really pretty. I hadn't noticed at first, because I was so distracted by her shoulders.

"I mean, yeah," I said. "My half brother."

She nodded, as if she'd expected as much.

"My little brother, too." She smiled at the thought of him. "He's obsessed with Matchbox cars. It's pretty much all he cares about. Yesterday he sent me a text with a picture of two of them. Nothing else. Just two little cars."

She thought this was adorable, though it seemed kind of pathetic to me.

"Mine doesn't talk much," I said. "He just has these scary tantrums about nothing. We don't even know what he's screaming about."

"What's his name?"

"Jonathan. But we call him Jon-Jon."

"That's cute."

I agreed, mostly because she seemed so nice and had such a positive attitude. The truth was, nothing about Jon-Jon was cute. It was awful to watch him get all red-faced with rage and frustration, and not know how to help him.

"Do you have a picture of him?" she asked.

I shook my head. It had never occurred to me to take a picture of Jon-Jon.

"This is Benjy." She handed me her phone. The screensaver was a photo of Amber and her brother on the beach. I'd expected him to be a little kid, but he was a skinny teenager with an intense, almost angry expression, only a year or two younger than she was. She was wearing a navy blue one-piece bathing suit in the picture, the no-nonsense kind competitive swimmers wear. Her body was thick and strong-looking, not usually what I went for, but sexy in a way I hadn't expected.

"You can give that back now," she said, but not in a pissed-off way.

"You a swimmer?"

"In high school. But not anymore. Here I just play softball."

"Cool," I said. "What position?"

"Pitcher."

She tried to look humble about it, but I could see she was proud.

"You know what?" I said. "You look like a pitcher."

"Why?" She pretended to take offense. "Because of my massive shoulders?"

"I didn't say that."

"It's okay." She struck a bodybuilder pose, turning sideways and flexing her arm. "I worked hard for these muscles. And I do have a wicked fastball, if I say so myself. You should come watch us. We're pretty good."

"Maybe I will."

She gave me a look, like I was probably full of shit. But it was kind of flirty, too.

"We're not all dykes, you know."

"I never said —"

"I'm just kidding," she said. "A few of us are bi."

I must have looked shocked, because she laughed this big-hearted laugh and slapped me on the arm as a nervous-looking girl stepped up to the table.

"It was nice meeting you," she said, stepping toward the new arrival. "You should come to one of our meetings. Third Thursday of every month."

That night I got epically shitfaced. Zack and I pregamed with vodka, and then we visited a bunch of room parties in Einstein, wandering from one to the next like it was Halloween, taking a bong hit here and a shot of Jager there, a slice of pizza in a room that belonged to a skinny white dude named Evan who was supposedly a great rapper.

There was dancing in a room where two girls named Kayla lived — Hot Kayla and Less-Hot Kayla — and a foosball tournament in the fifth-floor lounge.

At Will and Rico's, I drank some jungle juice that really knocked me on my ass. My father called when I was there, the first time I'd heard from him since I arrived at BSU. I must not have been making much sense, because Zack grabbed the phone out of my hand and started chatting with him like they were old buddies. All I remember after that was puking in the bathroom, and bumping into that douchebag Sanjay on my way out. He was wearing pajamas and a plaid robe, and carrying a little bucket with all his toiletries in it.

"You okay?" he asked. "You don't look so —"

"I'm fine," I said, giving my mouth one last wipe. "Ready for round two."

I went back to the room to change my shirt, but I guess I must have crashed, because the next thing I knew it was three in the morning and Zack was stumbling around in the dark, totally wasted, telling me that he'd tried to hook up with Less-Hot Kayla, but she wasn't into it, which was fine, because he wasn't really into it, either.

"I mean, if it was Hot Kayla, that would

be another story, right?"

After a while he got into bed, and it was quiet again, but I couldn't get back to sleep. I was thinking about maybe getting up and seeing if anybody was still awake when Zack started jerking off. I could tell he was trying to be quiet, but our beds were pretty close together.

"Dude," I said. "Seriously?"

"Oh shit," he said. "I thought you were asleep."

"Nope. Wide awake."

"You want me to stop?"

"Nah, it's okay. Just, like, hurry it up, okay?"

I don't know how long it took after that. Maybe just a few minutes, but it felt like a long time, long enough that I said fuck it, and decided to join the party. I thought about Becca for a while, but she was already far away, almost unreal. And then I tried the two Kaylas, imagining a threeway in their room, which was kind of interesting, but only up to a point. It was Amber from the Autism Awareness Network who got me across the finish line. And the weird thing was, we weren't even doing anything. She was just standing on the beach in her one-piece bathing suit, smiling at me with her pretty face and those big shoulders, and for some reason that was enough.

"G'night," Zack said, in this soft, peaceful voice when he was finished.

"Night, bro," I said, floating on the same cloud that he was. "Catch you in the morning."

LIVE AND LEARN

Suffering from a mild, not entirely unpleasant case of back-to-school jitters, Eve wandered through the Humanities Building of Eastern Community College, searching for Room 213. She was relieved to pass a number of "nontraditional students" like herself in the corridors, some of them even older than she was.

The chairs in her classroom had been arranged in a circle, group-therapy style. Eve chose one and sat down, not noticing until it was too late that some bored artisan had carved the words *I AM SO HORNY* into the desktop, and then highlighted the incisions with a red marker. She covered the graffiti with her brand-new notebook, and opened it to the first page. It was a heartening sight, all that blank white space waiting to be filled, the fresh start she'd been hoping for.

Once she was settled, she looked up and gave a friendly nod to the handful of students who'd arrived even earlier than she had. Only one nodded back, a worried-looking black man who appeared to be in his early thirties. The other three were staring at their phones, unaware that a greeting had been extended, let alone that they'd missed a chance to respond.

Eve already had a master's in Social Work, which she'd earned by attending night classes for four long years back when Brendan was in elementary school. Ted's resentment of her absences, and the parental responsibilities they shifted onto his shoulders, had been one of the major tensions in their marriage. His subsequent lack of interest in her work — his refusal to take it seriously — had been another, though that seemed mostly ironic in retrospect, now that he was raising an autistic child and had to rely on all sorts of specialists in the caring professions.

In any case, she didn't need another advanced degree, and had no interest in polishing her résumé. Her decision to return to school was purely personal. She wanted to read and think and reconnect with her collegiate self, which had been so much more open and fluid and hopeful than the versions that had succeeded it. And it was nice to have a reason to escape the empty house twice a week without having to convince someone else to join her.

The class she'd signed up for was called "Gender and Society: A Critical Perspective," a writing-intensive seminar that met on Tuesday and Thursday evenings from seven thirty to nine. She had no special interest in the topic; it was actually her third choice, after "Vegans vs. Carnivores: The Ethics of Sustainable Eating," and "From Jane Austen to *Downton Abbey:* The English Country House in Fiction and Film," both of which were full. But the class itself wasn't the point. The important thing was that she was here, trying something different, meeting new people, making her world bigger instead of hunkering down, disappearing into her own solitude.

At seven thirty on the dot, a tall, striking woman in a black pencil skirt and stiletto heels breezed through the door, her eyes widening in faux astonishment at the sight of the assembled students, as if this were a surprise party in her honor.

"Well, hello there," she said, in a throaty, oddly seductive voice. She was slender and athletic-looking, with narrow hips and attention-grabbing breasts bulging against the fabric of her tailored blouse. "I'm Dr.

Margo Fairchild, adjunct professor." She took a moment to let that sink in. "In case you're unfamiliar with academic terminology, *adjunct* is another word for *very badly paid.*"

A handful of students, Eve included, chuckled obligingly as Dr. Fairchild entered the circle and sat down, smoothing her skirt and crossing her enviably muscled legs at the ankles.

"Let's wait a minute or two for the stragglers," she said, languidly tucking a strand of dark hair behind her ear. "There are always a few lost souls on opening day."

It was tough to guess the professor's age — anywhere between thirty and forty-five, Eve thought — though her face seemed a little older than her body. Even that was open to debate, however, because of the prodigious amount of makeup she wore, a thick, almost theatrical coat of expertly applied cosmetics that seemed more appropriate for a beauty pageant runway than a community college classroom. Eve realized that she'd been expecting someone a little more like her cousin Donna, a no-nonsense scholar who wore her graying hair in a thick braid and had a different North Face pullover for every day of the week.

Her fellow students were an impressively

diverse bunch — half college kids, half older people (including a spry lady in her eighties), two black men (one of whom turned out to be Nigerian), one black woman, a Chinese immigrant man with an indecipherable accent, a young woman in a Muslim headscarf, one really cute undergraduate boy with a skateboard, and a butch woman in biker gear, complete with a black leather vest and a motorcycle helmet resting on the floor between her scuffed engineer boots. Eve was surprised to note that twelve of the twenty students were male, including a few middle-aged white guys who didn't strike her as natural candidates for a class in which students would be required to "write autobiographically and analytically about their own problematic experiences on the gender spectrum, with special emphasis on the social construction of identity, the persistence of sexism in a 'post-feminist' culture, and the subversion of heteronormative discourse by LGBTQIA voices." But this small mystery was cleared up as soon as they got started, when Professor Fairchild asked everyone to introduce themselves and talk about their reasons for enrolling in the class.

"My name's Russ," said the first guy to speak. He was wearing a Red Sox cap and a

Bruins T-shirt that seemed to have been shrink-wrapped around his beer gut. "I was supposed to be in Briggsy's class, but that got, uh . . . canceled, and this was the only other writing class in the time slot, so . . ."

"Poor Hal," said Professor Fairchild, and several heads bobbed in melancholy assent. "He was such a nice person."

There turned out to be three other transfers from the same class, "The Modern Coliseum: Sports in Contemporary Society," which was apparently one of the most popular course offerings at ECC. It had been taught by Hal Briggs, a former sportswriter for the *Herald,* who had just died of a heart attack at a Labor Day barbecue, right in front of his wife, kids, and neighbors. Eve had seen his obituary in the newspaper.

"He was too young," said Professor Fairchild. "Only forty-nine."

"Were you there?" asked a bearded guy named Barry, who said he owned a sports bar in Waxford. "At the cookout?"

"No, thank God." The professor twirled a lock of hair around her index finger, as if she were still in junior high. "Briggsy and I were just colleagues. We used to play in a faculty basketball league on Sunday mornings." The memory made her smile. "He had the ugliest jump shot I ever saw."

"Was that a coed league?" asked Dumell, the black guy with the worried expression.

"I'm glad you asked that," said the professor. "That's exactly the sort of assumption our class is going to examine throughout the semester. The way our preconceptions about gender condition our responses to the social world. But I think we need to unpack your question."

"What's that mean?"

"It means I'd like you to articulate the question behind your question. In other words, what are you *really* asking?"

"Okay. I get it." Dumell nodded uncertainly. He looked a little more worried than before. "Uh, were there other ladies besides you on the team?"

Professor Fairchild had to give this some thought. "What if I told you that our players ranged widely across the gender spectrum? Would that be a satisfactory answer to your question?"

"I guess," Dumell said. "But it's kinda complicated, don't you think?"

"I do," said the professor. "And rightly so. Because there's nothing simple about gender. Nothing natural. It's an ideological minefield that we walk through every minute of every day. And that's what this class is about. How to walk through the minefield without hurting anyone's feelings or blowing yourself up."

When class was dismissed, Eve headed out of the building with Barry, the bearded bar owner, tagging along beside her, totally uninvited. They'd been randomly paired off for an in-class exercise, and had spent the better part of the past hour exchanging "gender histories," focusing, per the professor's instructions, on moments of gender-related confusion, doubt, and/or shame.

"That was pretty intense," he said. "I have ex-wives who don't know me as well as you do."

Eve didn't say so, but she doubted Barry's ex-wives would have complained about not knowing him well enough. He was a what-you-see-is-what-you-get sort of guy, a blustery jerk who began his conversation by insisting that he'd never in his life experienced a single moment of confusion, doubt, or shame in relation to his gender identity. The story of Barry's life, as narrated by Barry, read as follows: first he was a boy, and then he was a man. The path from Point A to Point B had been straight, self-explanatory, and fun to travel.

"I don't get the point of all this navel-gazing," he'd told her during the exercise.

"I was born with a penis. End of story."

Eve had tried to draw him out, asking if he'd ever wished he could get pregnant or breast-feed a child. Ted had once called the ability to bear children a female superpower — he was trying to cheer her up at a particularly bloated and trying moment in her third trimester — and the description had stuck with her through the years.

"It's kind of a miracle," she said. "Feeling that little person growing inside you, and then feeding it with your body when it comes out. I imagine most men would be at least a *little* jealous."

Barry chuckled appreciatively, as if congratulating Eve on a good try.

"God bless the ladies," he said. "And thank you for your service. I really don't know how you do it."

And then he'd launched into a long and needlessly graphic account of the toll that childbirth had taken on his first wife's body — especially her breasts, which were never the same afterward, he was sorry to say. He'd hoped they would bounce back, so to speak — they were her finest attribute — but no such luck. At least he'd learned his lesson. When his second wife got pregnant, he persuaded her to bottle-feed, and it was a smart decision. The baby didn't give a shit, and *mama's hooters* — those were his actual words — remained miraculously perky. She did thicken a bit around the waist, but that wasn't what caused the marriage to go south. They had bigger problems, most notably his affair with a twenty-five-year-old waitress who would soon become wife number three. With that one, he laid down the law — *no fucking kids* — and she was all right with that until she turned thirty, at which point she wasn't anymore, and that was that.

"Jesus," Eve wondered. "How many ex-wives are there?"

"Just the three. I've had a few girlfriends since then, but it's not that easy to convince someone to be Wife Number Four. Believe me, I tried."

In the classroom, Eve had listened to Barry's checkered history with scientific detachment; the point was to write a profile of the subject, not to judge him on his shortcomings. Out in the parking lot, though, a sense of retroactive revulsion came over her, exacerbated by the fact that he was crowding her as they walked, occasionally bumping shoulders with her in a way that might have seemed friendly, or even intriguing, if he hadn't just outed himself as a heartless creep.

"I'm a big girl," she told him. "You don't need to walk me to my car."

"And I'm a gentleman of the old school. Nothing wrong with a little chivalry, right? Women say they don't like it, but in my experience they're pretty grateful if you hold the door or pick up the check or bring them flowers."

Eve didn't want to admit it, but she knew he had a point. Things had changed so much over the course of her lifetime that women her age had all these different models of behavior jammed into their heads — you could be a fifties housewife and a liberated professional woman, a committed feminist and a blushing bride, a fierce athlete and a submissive, needy girlfriend. Most of the time you could switch from one role to another without too much trouble, and without even realizing that you might be contradicting yourself.

"There's some gender confusion right there," she observed. "I guess I learned something tonight."

"Well, if you're gonna study this crap, you might as well do it with a shemale, right?"

"Excuse me?"

"You didn't know?" Barry seemed pleased by her cluelessness. "Our professor used to be a he."

"Really?"

"Yup. Margo was Mark Fairchild. He was a great college basketball player. Even played pro in Europe for a couple of seasons." He tugged his beard. "Not a bad-looking woman, actually."

Eve's surprise was short-lived. The signs were there, now that she knew what she was looking for — the voice, the hips, the incongruous breasts, the riddle of the "coed" basketball league. But she never would have guessed it on her own.

Live and learn, she thought.

"I've never met a transgendered person before," she said. "At least I don't think so."

"Not that I'm attracted to her," Barry added, in case she'd misunderstood his earlier comment. "I mean, to each his own, right? But that's a bridge too far for me. I wonder if she tells the guys she dates beforehand."

"How do you know she dates guys?"

"Just the general vibe I'm getting. You think she got the surgery? I'm not really sure how that works."

Eve was relieved to arrive at her car. She'd had more than enough of Barry for one night.

"All right." She clicked her remote key, and the van flashed its lights. "Guess I'll see you next class."

"Hey," he said, as she reached for the door handle. "You want to get a nightcap? My bar's right down the street. Drinks on me."

"It's been a long day," she told him. "I need to get home."

"Suit yourself," Barry said with a shrug. "I'll take a rain check."

It was too bad she didn't like him a little better, because a drink after class would have been nice. At the very least it would have given her an excuse to stay out for another hour or two, to delay the inevitable moment when she returned home and had to once again confront the enormity of her son's absence — the fact that he'd grown up and left her, and the knowledge that this was good and proper — exactly what nature intended — and that she had no right to complain.

The fact that her life had turned into *this:* this lifeless hush, this faint but elusive whiff of decay. This absolutely-nothing-to-complain-about.

She didn't linger downstairs, just poured herself a glass of wine, grabbed her laptop, and headed up to her bedroom. She locked the door behind her, not a real lock, just a hardware store hook-and-eye that wouldn't have kept out a determined intruder, but might give her a few seconds of advanced warning, hopefully enough time to grab her phone and dial 911. She'd installed it six or seven years ago, after a couple of embarrassing incidents where Brendan had wandered in while she was getting dressed. He'd insisted that these were honest mistakes, but she wasn't so sure — he was just at that age when boys get curious — and decided that a little deterrence would go a long way.

For the past few years, ever since she'd opened her account, Facebook had been an integral part of Eve's bedtime ritual. She found it soothing to scroll through her news feed one last time before turning in, paying a visit to her various friends and acquaintances, reminding herself that she wasn't really alone. They were always right there where she'd left them, the usual suspects posting about the usual stuff: recipes, pithy sayings, scanned photos from the good old days, the inevitable pets, the banal declarations, witty memes, deep thoughts, political rants, viral videos. A group from her hometown had a new thread rhapsodizing about the Freezy Cone Ice Cream Stand on Franklin Street — gone for at least two decades — that included eighty-seven comments, most of which expressed sentiments like "Yum!" and "BEST. ICE. CREAM. EVER." and "Vanilla with Rainbow Sprinkles!!!"

She forced herself to read every last one of them. That should have been enough to put anyone to sleep, but Eve was still wide awake when she finished, still as restless and aroused as she'd been when she started. So there was nothing to do but the thing she'd promised herself she wouldn't do, though it was, admittedly, a promise she'd made with her fingers crossed, knowing it would probably have to be broken.

For a sexually liberated person in her mid-forties, Eve had had, until a few days ago, a fairly limited acquaintance with pornography. She remembered thumbing through a friend's brother's stash of magazines as a teenager, being intimidated by the airbrushed beauty of the centerfold models in *Playboy,* and genuinely shocked by the "beaver shots" in *Hustler.* Her visceral distaste turned ideological in college, where it was a feminist article of faith that porn degraded and objectified women while exploiting them for financial gain. Why would you want to have anything to do with a dirty business like that?

After she graduated, she began to notice that this opinion wasn't universally shared. Lots of supposedly enlightened men she knew seemed to like porn — or at least they liked joking about liking porn — but she was surprised to learn that a number of her women friends were fans, too. Her grad school colleague Allison reported that she and her fiancé had a standing Friday night porn date that they both looked forward to all week. (Allison also had a vibrator that she'd nicknamed Black Betty and half jokingly described as the best thing that had ever happened to her.)

Succumbing to peer pressure early in their marriage, Eve and Ted had rented a movie called *Fuck My Secretary* — this was back when every video rental store had an XXX section, usually hidden in a basement or tucked away in a separate room — but they only made it through a couple of minutes before throwing in the towel. The actors had seemed like freaks, the secretary endowed with gravity-defying breasts while the boss sported an erection the size of a prize zucchini. It did absolutely nothing for Eve or Ted, so they turned off the VCR and made love, cheerfully enough, with their own serviceable, human-sized equipment. Her XXX history had pretty much stopped there. She'd never surfed for porn on the internet, and hardly ever thought about it, except in an anxious parental capacity.

Which was why it was so disorienting to find herself returning, for the sixth day in a row, to milfateria.com ("World's Biggest Buffet of All-You-Can-Eat Amateur MILF Porn!"), scrolling through the thumbnails of recently uploaded clips. *Lovely Wife BJ, Anal MILF with Creampie, Abby Loves BBC, Sexy Samantha First Time on Camera, Saucy Soccer Mom Takes It Like a Champ.* Saucy soccer mom. Eve smiled at the description and clicked on the link. That seemed worth a look.

It was the anonymous text that had led her here, the one that had arrived last Friday night. She'd forgotten all about it until Saturday morning, when she turned on her phone and saw that idiotic message staring back at her:

U r my MILF!

She wasn't sure why it had bothered her so much. It was probably just a harmless prank, the handiwork of a drunk teenager getting his late-night kicks. Texts like this were the digital equivalent of obscene phone calls.

Send me a naked pic!!

All she had to do was delete it and get on with her day. But she kept squinting at those words, floating so innocently in their cartoon bubble, as if they had every right to inhabit her phone. Before she realized what she was doing, she'd typed a reply of her own.

I'm not a MILF, you little shit

Luckily, her good sense kicked in before she pressed Send. There was no point in engaging with an anonymous pervert, giving him the satisfaction of a response, a reward for his harassment.

MILF.

She knew what the acronym stood for, of course — she hadn't been living under a rock — or at least thought she did. In her mind, it was just an updated name for the old Mrs. Robinson stereotype, the predatory middle-aged woman with a taste for younger men, maybe even boys who were Brendan's age. That was the main thing that creeped her out, the possibility that the text had come from one of her son's friends, or maybe even his new roommate.

I want to cum on those big floppy tits!!!

What kind of person would say something like that to a friend's mother? And what if it was Wade or Tyler or Max, boys she'd known since they were in preschool, whom she'd taken to the beach, who'd slept over at her house? It made her queasy to imagine one of them thinking about her body in such prurient detail.

And they're not that floppy, she thought indignantly. *They've actually held up pretty well.*

One thing that she'd learned from her web search that morning was that she'd been conflating the terms *cougar* and *MILF,* which turned out not to be synonymous at all. MILF was a broader, more passive category, basically just "any mother that is sexually desirable." What that meant, Eve realized, was that you couldn't really say, *I'm not a MILF,* because a MILF was in the eye of the beholder. The other thing she'd learned was that you shouldn't google the term if you didn't want to find yourself swimming in an ocean of porn.

There was no doubt about it — milfateria .com was part of that "unregulated cesspool" the assistant DA had warned about so many years ago at the PTA meeting. Eve was regularly shocked and frequently disgusted by what she found there. She disapproved of the site — she would have been horrified if she'd ever found anything like it on her son's computer — and sincerely wished it didn't exist. But she couldn't stop looking at it.

A few of the allegedly "Amateur MILFs" were clearly porn stars, with huge fake boobs and full Brazilians, but the vast majority looked like ordinary people. They had stretch marks, C-section scars, pimples on their faces and butts, bruises and rashes, cellulite, underarm and pubic stubble. Some of them wore glasses while they had sex, and more than you might have expected kept their socks on. A lot of them seemed to live in drab houses or cramped apartments. While a few of the women seemed embarrassed by what they were doing, others looked straight into the camera, as if they were a lot more interested in whoever might be watching them than they were in their partners. And the men! They were (most of them, anyway) a parade of horrors — hairy and potbellied, wheezy and much too talkative for Eve's taste. They loved to narrate their orgasms in real time — *Here it comes, baby!* — as if the whole world was waiting for an update.

In the past week, Eve had spent more time watching milfateria videos than she would have liked to admit, and she'd barely scratched the surface. The site was organized by category (Oral MILF, Anal MILF, Threesome MILF, Lesbo MILF, Ebony MILF, Solo MILF, etc.), body type (Busty MILF, Shaved MILF, Big Booty MILF, Redhead MILF), but also by nationality (Turkish MILF, German MILF, Canadian MILF, Japanese MILF, Israeli MILF, Iranian MILF, and on and on), a global community of women in their thirties, forties, fifties, and even older (Granny MILF), united by their willingness to have sex in front of a camera and to share the experience with the rest of the world (unless a man was sharing it without their permission, which probably happened a lot). The sheer number of videos was overwhelming; you could never watch them all, not that you'd want to. There were so many that it seemed like only a matter of time before Eve would find herself looking at someone she knew, a high school classmate, a neighbor, maybe her old friend Allison.

Her reaction was the same every time she started a session: *Ugh!* How could they do it? How could people expose themselves like this? Just the sight of all that naked flesh was overwhelming and off-putting. She cringed at the unimaginative dirty talk and the predictability of the action. She especially hated the clips that focused solely on the genitalia, the close-ups of penises and vaginas. So many assholes. She needed to see faces, to get a sense of the person she was watching. That was the only thing that mattered.

It was like a blind date or a party. Some people you liked right away, some you didn't. Some you weren't sure about. The saucy soccer mom was horrible, a giggly woman performing a clumsy striptease with the TV blaring in the background. Eve clicked out of that, tried "Swedish MILF Pink Dildo!" then "Italian Wife Deepthroat" and "Sexy Abigail Morning Fuck." None of them did anything for her.

But there was always another one. And eventually — tonight it was "Classy Lady Loves That Cock!" — something would click. The couple on her screen would seem inspired, or even blessed — you could see how alive and happy and unself-conscious they were — and maybe you envied them a little, but you also wanted to thank them for sharing this moment with you, and then that last barrier would crumble, and maybe for a minute or two you'd feel that you were right there with them, like when you heard a good song on the radio and the next thing you knew you were singing along.

■ ■ ■ ■

PART TWO:
THE END OF
RELUCTANCE

■ ■ ■ ■

TROUBLE IN SUNSET ACRES

It was only Thursday afternoon, but Amanda Olney could already feel the weekend coming on like an illness — a mild case of the flu or some mid-level gastrointestinal distress, the kind of ailment that didn't leave you bedridden but kept you confined to the couch, unfit for human interaction. You just had to wait it out in your sweatpants, bingeing on Netflix and herbal tea, a forty-eight-hour quarantine until Monday rolled around and you could head back to work.

She understood how pathetic that sounded, exactly the opposite of how you were supposed to feel if you were a young-ish single person with an office job that paid less-than-peanuts and made a mockery of your expensive education; a job, moreover, that required you to spend a good part of your life in the company of old people, some of them physically and/or mentally infirm, and many others just plain ornery. You were supposed to love the weekend, that all-too-brief window of freedom, your only chance to wash away the stink of boredom with a blast of fun. Use it to drink and fuck yourself into a state of blissful oblivion, the memory of which would power you through the work week that followed, at the end of which you could do it all over again, ad infinitum, or at least until you met the right guy (or gal) and settled down.

Well, Amanda had tried all that, and it had depressed the shit out of her. Better to be a nun than to spend every Sunday beating herself up about the bad choices she'd made on Friday and Saturday night. In fact, at this particular juncture in her life, she wouldn't have minded if the weekend were abolished altogether. She would have been fine coming to work seven days a week, barricading herself behind her beige metal desk, making phone calls and filling out paperwork, finding budget-conscious ways to keep the geezers of Haddington occupied while they ran out the clock on their golden years.

Aside from organizing events and activities at the Senior Center, Amanda was responsible for putting out a monthly newsletter called *Haddington Happenings*. One of the regular features was a chatty roundup of notable events that had transpired since the last issue — the birth of Eleanor Testa's seventh grandchild, Lou LeGrande's excellent recovery from open heart surgery, Dick and Marilyn Hauser's golden anniversary. She was adding a few items to the list — *Three cheers for Joy Maloney, who came in fifth in the Seventy-and-Over Division at last month's 5K Fun Run at Finley Park. Way to go, Joy! You're an inspiration to us all! And congratulations to Art Weber on the ten-pound bluefish he caught on Cape Cod. It was almost as big as the one that got away, right Art?* — when Eve Fletcher poked her head into the tiny windowless office.

"Hey," she said. "Did you figure out the bus thing?"

Amanda nodded, pleased to be the bearer of good news.

"It took some doing, but I finally got through to the owner and explained the situation. He says they'll give us a motor coach for the same price."

"With a working rest room?"

"That's what he said."

Eve heaved a theatrical sigh of relief.

"Thank God. There was no way I was gonna put a bunch of old people on a school bus for a trip to Foxwoods. That's a recipe for disaster."

"We're all set on our end," Amanda assured her. "The rest is up to Frank Sinatra Jr."

"I'm sure he'll be great." Eve's voice was confident, but her face expressed an alternative viewpoint. "I wish I could join you, but I have a class that night."

"No worries," Amanda told her. "I got this."

"Excellent." Eve brought her hands together in a soundless clap. "Well, enjoy the rest of your day. I'm checking out a little early."

"Lucky you."

"Not really. I'm going to a wake. Roy Rafferty."

"Oh." Amanda grimaced in sympathy. "I heard about that. Poor man."

"You wanna come?"

Amanda glanced at her computer screen. "I kinda have to finish this article."

"No worries," Eve said, retreating from the doorway. "I'll see you tomorrow."

The final chunk of the workday felt endless, that infinitely expanding space between four thirty and five, when there was nothing left to do but surf the web and pretend to look busy in case one of her co-workers wandered by in the hallway. In a more humane and rational workplace — one of those Bay Area tech companies with ping-pong tables and espresso machines and nap rooms that she was so sick of hearing about — she could have called it a day and headed out into the fresh air, but the Senior Center was old-school government work. You got paid for keeping your ass in the chair, not for the quality of your ideas or the tasks you accomplished. It was one more example of how upside-down everything was. Wouldn't it be a lot fairer if drones like her got to have the flexible hours and the hipster amenities? The people with the six-figure salaries could buy their own damn macchiatos.

On reflection, she wished she'd accepted Eve's half-serious invitation to join her at Roy Rafferty's wake. Not that it would have been much fun, sitting in a funeral home at the tail end of a beautiful fall afternoon, but at least they would have been able to drive there together, maybe go out for a drink afterward. Just a chance to hang out a bit, get to know each other a little better outside the context of work.

Amanda wasn't sure if she wanted Eve to be a mentor or a friend, but there was room in her life for both. Or maybe she was just missing her mother — it had only been six months since her death, though most of the time it felt like yesterday — and looking for a substitute, an older, wiser woman to lean on for emotional support, not that Eve was anywhere close to her mother's age, or had shown any interest in being part of Amanda's support system. If anything, she seemed a little sad herself — Amanda had totally caught her crying in her office that one time, though Eve had denied it — which just made Amanda like her that much more, and wish they could slip past the rigid, artificial boundary that separated boss and employee, and find a way to meet each other as equals.

She was clicking through a viral list she was pretty sure she'd seen before — *29 Celebs You Totally Didn't Know Were Bi* — when the phone rang. Her laptop clock said 4:52, late enough to make the call seem like an imposition, if it wasn't some sort of emergency.

"Events," she said cautiously. "Amanda speaking."

"Hello, Amanda," said the sandpapery female voice on the other end. "This is Grace Lucas."

"Okay." The name meant nothing to Amanda. "Can I help you?"

"You don't know me," Grace Lucas continued. She sounded a little off, possibly medicated. "I'm Garth Heely's wife."

Of course you are, Amanda thought irritably. When you had a job like events coordinator, there was always someone making your life miserable. At the moment, for Amanda, this someone was Garth Heely, an obscure local author scheduled to speak at the Senior Center's monthly lecture series in November. A retired lawyer, Garth Heely had self-published three novels featuring Parker Winslow, a silver-haired sleuth who plies his trade at Sunset Acres, a senior living community with an unusually high murder rate. Amanda had read them all — it was her job! — and they were better than she'd expected, except that the killer in all three books turned out to be a person of color — a Jamaican nurse in *Trouble in Sunset Acres,* an Indian urologist in *More Trouble in Sunset Acres,* and a Guatemalan physical therapist in *Mayhem in Sunset Acres.* When she'd pointed out this unfortunate pattern — diplomatically, she thought — Garth Heely got immediately defensive, telling her he was fed up with all this PC crap you heard nowadays, everybody so focused on the color of everybody else's skin, rather than the content of their charac-

115

ter. Then he suggested that maybe *she* was the racist, lumping all non-white people into a single category, as if there were no difference between Kingston and Calcutta.

Have you ever been *to Calcutta?* he demanded.

Amanda admitted that she hadn't.

Well, I have, he said. *And believe me, honey, it ain't a bit like Jamaica!*

Amanda wasn't surprised by his attitude of aggrieved innocence. It was something she'd gotten used to, working at the Senior Center. A lot of old white people acted like it was still 1956, like they could say whatever they wanted and not have to take any responsibility for their words. Soon after she'd gotten hired, she'd called out a couple of women for using the N-word in casual conversation — they were both knitting baby sweaters — and they'd looked at her like she was making a big deal out of nothing, since there were no black people within hearing range. There rarely were; Haddington was that kind of town.

Garth Heely wasn't an out-and-out racist, just a prosperous, occasionally charming white man of a certain age, blind to his own privilege, predictably smug and condescending. The only thing that surprised her was what a diva he had turned out to be, considering that he was a writer no one had ever heard of, with an Amazon ranking somewhere in the millions.

"What can I do for you, ma'am?"

"I'm calling on behalf of my husband," Grace Lucas said. "I'm afraid you're going to have to cancel his speaking engagement."

Oh Jesus, Amanda thought.

Just yesterday, she and Garth Heely had butted heads about the flyers the Senior Center had designed to promote his lecture. He thought they looked boring — *guilty as charged* — and suggested that they be printed on several different shades of eye-catching colored paper, preferably pink, yellow, and light blue. Amanda explained that this wouldn't be possible, since the Senior Center's budget didn't allow for colored paper.

"Hello?" Grace Lucas said. "Are you still there?"

"I'm here." Amanda's skin felt clammy beneath her dress. She'd only been working at the Senior Center for a few months, and the last thing she needed was to walk into Eve's office and explain that the November speaker had canceled over a trivial dispute. "Please tell Mr. Heely that I misspoke. We'll be more than happy to supply colored paper for the flyers."

The silence on the other end of the line felt more puzzled than frosty. Amanda was about to add an apology to the offer when Grace Lucas finally spoke.

"Garth is dead, dear."

"What?" Amanda started to laugh, then caught herself. "I talked to him yesterday morning. He was fine."

"I know." There was a note of quiet wonder in Grace Lucas's voice. "He died right afterward. You were the last person to speak to him. He was still holding the phone when I found him."

Oh my God, Amanda thought. *I killed him.*

"I'm so sorry," she said.

"Thank you, dear." Grace Lucas gave a resigned sigh. "I just wish he'd been able to finish the book he was working on. He said it was going to be his best Parker Winslow yet. Now we'll never know who the murderer was."

Amanda wanted to ask if there was a nonwhite health care worker in the book — *There's your killer!* — but she was distracted by an embarrassing feeling of relief, the knowledge that Garth Heely's sudden death was going to be a lot easier to explain to Eve than a disagreement over colored paper would have been.

"I'm going to bury him in his blue suit."

Grace Lucas's voice was dreamy and private, as if she were talking to herself. "He always looked so good in blue."

Wakes and funerals were an inescapable part of Eve's professional life, and she tried to approach them with a businesslike sense of detachment. She showed up in her official capacity, she paid her respects to the family of the deceased, and she went home. No fuss, no muss, no tears.

Tonight, though, she was a bit of a wreck. The news of Roy Rafferty's death had upset her deeply, coming so soon after she'd banished him for exposing himself in the ladies' room. She didn't feel guilty about her decision — as an administrator, she'd really had no choice — but the memory of it still made her sick at heart. It seemed so cruel and pointless in retrospect, humiliating a sick old man who had only a month to live, not that she had any way of knowing that at the time. All she knew was that she'd inflicted pain on someone she cared about, and that always cost you something, even if you were just doing your job. It left you feeling dirty and mean, exposed to the laws of karma. It also made her wonder if she was doing the right thing by coming here.

A lot of the wakes she went to were woefully underpopulated affairs, a corpse and some flowers and a handful of bored spectators, no one even bothering to pretend that it was a big deal. Eve was relieved to see that this wasn't the case tonight. The parking lot was packed, and so was the viewing room, an impressive line of mourners massed along the side wall, inching their way toward the open coffin. The turnout was a tribute to Roy's lifelong ties to Haddington, his membership in a variety of civic organizations, and his long and successful career as a plumbing contractor, not to mention the fact that he'd been a genuinely nice guy before the dementia kicked in.

Instead of joining the procession, Eve slipped into a velour-cushioned chair in the second to last row of the viewing room, near a group of ladies who were regulars at the Senior Center. One of them was Evelyn Gerardi, the emphysemic woman who'd been the victim of Roy's indecent overtures.

"So sad," Eve whispered. "Such a shame."

The ladies nodded in mournful agreement, murmuring that Roy was a sweetheart and a good father and so handsome when he was young. Eve turned to face the coffin, which was obscured by a wall of dark suits and somber dresses. She sat quietly for a while, trying to summon a mental image of the dead man — not the confused trouble-maker he'd been near the end, but the gruff, garrulous man she'd gotten to know a decade earlier, a stocky guy with a silver-gray brush cut and an impish twinkle in his eyes. He always wore Hawaiian shirts on Friday — his favorite had pineapples and parrots on it — and he liked to flirt with the female employees of the Center, Eve included.

What she remembered best about him was the way he'd cared for his wife after the death of their oldest son, five or six years ago now. Joan had taken it hard — how could she not? Nick was still her baby, even if he'd been fifty-two years old at the time of his death — and it seemed like all the joy and vitality drained out of her after that. Roy began holding her hand in public, something he'd never done before, and treating her with immense politeness, pulling out her chair before she sat down, helping her on with her coat, checking on her in a soft and solicitous voice. That was the man Eve was here to honor, and she hoped the Rafferty family would accept her condolences without bitterness, and forgive her for the unfortunate role she'd played in the final chapter of his life.

The line had shrunk considerably by the

time she got up and made her way to the viewing pedestal, breathing through her mouth to avoid the sickly odor of the funeral bouquets, which always made her a little light-headed. She hated this part of the ritual, that chilling moment when you were face-to-face with an object that appeared to be a clumsy wax replica of someone you knew but was, of course, the actual person. As usual, everything about the presentation seemed slightly off, from the gray suit Roy was wearing — in Eve's opinion, a windbreaker and a Hawaiian shirt would have been the way to go — to the pack of Camels and the bag of beef jerky that had been placed in the coffin to speed him on his way. Neither item seemed appropriate: Roy had quit smoking and sworn off red meat years ago. But the real problem was the vacant look on his face. Roy was a people person, always happy to see you, and interested in what you had to say, even if you were just chatting about the weather. Apathy didn't suit him at all.

Some people kissed the dead person's forehead, but it seemed both creepy and theatrical to Eve, not to mention vaguely unsanitary. She settled for patting him twice on the hand, very quickly.

"Goodbye," she whispered. "We're gonna

miss you."

All three of Roy's surviving children were standing on the receiving line, and none of them seemed to think it odd or presumptuous for her to be there. Both of the daughters — Kim and Debbie were their names, though Eve couldn't remember which was which — hugged her and told her how much their father loved coming to the Senior Center, and how highly he'd spoken of the people who worked there. Eve assured them that the feeling was mutual, and that their father was a lovely man who'd brightened everyone's day.

George Rafferty was more reserved than his sisters, but he didn't seem like he was holding a grudge. He seemed a little dazed, or maybe just exhausted.

"Thanks for coming," he said, shaking her hand with robotic indifference. "Tough day. Good to see you. Means a lot."

Eve wasn't even sure he recognized her, which left her feeling vaguely offended as she left the funeral home. *Come on, you know who I am!* She was about to laugh at the selfishness of her reaction, but she was distracted by the cool evening air when she stepped outside, the dusky blue of the sky, and the freshly paved street in front of her, its blackness bisected by a bright yellow line, a world so inexplicably beautiful that she forgot what she was thinking about and just stood still for a moment, breathing it all in.

The Bikram instructor that night was Jojo, not Amanda's favorite. She would have preferred Kendra, the soulful, slightly overweight woman who read inspirational meditations about self-acceptance during Savasana at the beginning and end of class. Kendra roamed the studio like a benign spirit, the goddess of encouragement, always ready with a supportive comment. Sometimes that was all you needed, a trinket of praise to get you through the most brutal poses, Utkatasana or Balancing Stick, the ones that made you hate your body and wonder why you even bothered.

"Let's go, people!" Jojo clapped his hands as if summoning a dog. "Where's the energy? There's no such thing as halfway in Bikram!"

Jojo was a beautiful Asian man with the body of a gymnast and the soul of a drill sergeant. His adjustments were rare and brusque and sometimes borderline inappropriate, as if his lack of sexual interest in women gave him license to touch them wherever and however he pleased.

Even so, Amanda knew that complaining about Jojo was pure luxury, like whining about the prices at Whole Foods. The real miracle was that *anybody* taught Bikram yoga in Haddington. Ten years ago, when she'd left for Sarah Lawrence, there hadn't been a single yoga studio in her hometown. Now there were three — Bikram, Prana, and Royal Serenity, whatever that was — as well as a CrossFit gym, a decent vegan restaurant, and a tattoo parlor whose owner had a degree from RISD. Without realizing it, she'd been part of a hipster reverse migration, legions of overeducated, underpaid twenty-somethings getting squeezed out of the city, spreading beyond the pricey inner suburbs to the more affordable outposts like Haddington, transforming the places they'd once fled, making them livable again, or at least tolerable.

Another reason for gratitude: Jojo's classes were more sparsely attended than Kendra's, so she had some room to spread out, no worries about her personal space getting invaded by a rude neighbor, or slipping on a puddle of fresh-squeezed man-sweat. She hated to be sexist, but it was undeniable: men were gross at Bikram. Everybody perspired, but certain guys took it to a freakish extreme, dripping like faucets throughout the entire ninety minutes of class, the foam of their mats squishing underfoot.

Tonight there were only five males in the class, none of them familiar, thank God. A couple of weeks ago she'd found herself standing one row behind a guy she'd hooked up with on Tinder, a forty-two-year-old graphic artist named Dell, with long graying hair and a sad little belly bulging over the waistband of his Speedo. Their eyes had met in the front mirror and he'd smiled in happy surprise. She was aware of his scrutiny throughout all twenty-six postures, and it had completely ruined her concentration. And then he'd tried to chat her up in the parking lot, as if they were old pals, rather than strangers who'd fucked once, just because they both happened to be bored and lonely at the same time.

She wasn't sure why the encounter had unnerved her so much. Dell was a pretty nice guy — they'd actually done okay in bed together — and she was ninety-nine percent sure his presence at the studio was pure coincidence, not the beginning of a stalking nightmare. But it didn't matter; it was just creepy to see him there, totally out of context, as if he were an actual human being, rather than a figment of her sexual imagination. She went home that night and deleted her Tinder account, so nothing like that would ever happen again.

At the Senior Center, Amanda's tattoos were a constant source of friction with the clients, and, apparently, an open invitation to criticism, like one of those bumper stickers that read, *How's my driving?* She wished she could have supplied a toll-free number, so the irate old folks could call at their leisure and leave a message, instead of accosting her in the crafts room to inform her that she'd made a terrible mistake, that she could have been a pretty girl, and what the heck was she thinking?

At least wear some long sleeves, the sweet old ladies told her. *A turtleneck and some dark tights might not be such a bad idea, either.*

Something subtler, and far more frustrating, went on in the Bikram changing room, where a number of the younger women had tattoos of their own, though of a more decorous suburban variety — a dolphin on a shoulder blade, a constellation of three or four stars around an ankle, a cheerful little bird on the nape of the neck. The first time she undressed there, she felt a sudden chill of separation, her own more drastic aesthetic marking her as an instant outsider, the bad-ass chick with the cobra wrapped around her leg, the hand grenade on her breast, the anarchist bomb on her thigh, and the meat cleaver — the only one she truly regretted — dripping blood on her upper arm.

She tried to compensate by being extra friendly, smiling at everyone she passed, but the others rarely smiled back. Most of them avoided eye contact altogether, the same way Amanda used to avert her gaze from the anorexic woman at her old gym, the one who seemed intent on committing suicide by elliptical. You wanted to look — how could you not? — but you didn't want to be rude, so you just minded your business and pretended she wasn't there.

Five years ago, when she'd been living in Brooklyn with Blake, she would have enjoyed this outcast feeling, the knowledge that she was a little too edgy for the yoga moms and single ladies of Haddington, but she wasn't that person anymore. She was lonely and looking for new friends, and it broke her heart a little every time she showered and changed without exchanging a single pleasant word or sympathetic look with anyone.

She'd gotten so used to being ignored, she wasn't sure what to think when she emerged from the shower, a much-too-skimpy towel wrapped around her torso, and noticed a slender, pretty woman staring at her with a quizzical expression. Amanda had never seen this woman at Bikram before, but she'd been aware of her throughout the class. It was hard not to be — she was one of those front-row yoga goddesses, enviably fit and limber, observing herself in the mirror with an air of scientific detachment as she tied herself in elegant knots, barely breaking a sweat.

It was a cramped space, a single wooden bench set between two rows of lockers, with several women milling about in various states of undress, trying not to get in one another's way. Amanda had just released the towel when she sensed a presence at her side.

"Excuse me?" The woman's voice was surprisingly casual, considering that Amanda was naked, and she herself was wearing nothing but yoga pants. "I think we know each other."

The stranger was even prettier up close, with black pixie-cut hair and blue eyes that seemed pale and bright at the same time. A tiny tattoo peeked from the waistband of her pants, something dark and swirly, a tornado or maybe a comet.

"You went to Haddington?" she continued. "We were in AP English senior year?"

Her voice sounded vaguely familiar, but Amanda searched in vain for a name to connect to the face. It didn't help that she was distracted by the woman's breasts, which were small and pert, with optimistic upturned nipples. She couldn't help wondering what that would feel like, having boobs that defied gravity, and a stomach so flat it might actually be concave. She glanced with longing at her own discarded towel, lying uselessly on the floor.

"I'm sorry," Amanda said. "Your name is . . . ?"

"Beckett." After an awkward moment of silence, the woman smiled, realizing her error. "In high school I went by Trish? Trish Lozano?"

Holy shit, Amanda thought. *Trish Lozano.* She could see it now, the ghost of the girl she'd known hidden inside a whole new person.

"I didn't recognize you," she said. "You were blond back then."

"Of course I was." Trish shook her head. "I was such a cliché. The cute little cheerleader from hell."

Amanda wasn't sure how to respond. She'd never thought of Trish Lozano as a cliché. She was more like the platonic ideal of an American high school girl, pretty and bubbly and super-popular, always at the center of the action. And she'd been smart, too, which seemed even more unfair.

"Your name's Beckett now?"

"I changed it in college. I got into acting and Trish just seemed so blah. We were doing this all-female production of *Waiting for Godot,* and I don't know, Beckett seemed like a cool name." Trish rolled her eyes, amused by her younger, more pretentious self. "Turns out I'm a terrible actor, so the joke was on me. But I kept the name. It's a big improvement."

Amanda could feel herself nodding a little too emphatically, as if she were receiving news of profound importance, and it made her queasy to think of what she must look like, plump and flushed and naked, listening so intently to a beautiful, bare-breasted woman who called herself Beckett.

"You look great," Trish said, touching her gently on the arm. "Are you still living here?"

"It's just temporary." Amanda's face warmed with embarrassment. "I was living with my boyfriend in Brooklyn, but . . ." It was a long story, not one she wanted to go into just then. She turned toward the open locker, rifling through her clothes until she found her bra. "What about you?"

"Visiting my mom." Trish made a sour face, as if this were an unpleasant obligation, like jury duty. "I live in L.A. now. I went out there for film school and never looked back. My fiancé's a DP. You know, a cinematographer? So I think we're pretty much stuck there."

Involuntarily, Amanda's gaze strayed to Trish's left hand, the small diamond gleaming tastefully, not the least bit boastful or obnoxious. Just a fact.

"Wow." Amanda hooked her bra, then gave the underwires a little tug, getting everything in alignment. "That's exciting."

She grabbed her panties — they were black and high-waisted, with stretchy lace panels on the sides — and pulled them on. She felt a little better now that she was decent, glad it was a good underwear day.

"Do you work in the movie business, too?"

"I was a PA for a while, but now I teach at Soul Cycle. Probably do it for a few more years, till we're ready to start a family." Trish shrugged, not unhappily. "You?"

"Single," Amanda said, trying to sound matter-of-fact. "Just getting my life in order. I'm the events coordinator at the Senior Center. They actually have a pretty good lecture series."

Trish nodded, but there was a faraway look in her eyes, as if she wasn't really listening.

"This is so weird," she said. "I still think about you sometimes."

"Me?" Amanda gave a puzzled laugh. She and Trish had barely exchanged two words in high school. "Why?"

"To be honest?" Trish said. "You kinda freaked me out. You were always staring at me like I was this horrible, stuck-up, shallow person, and I couldn't understand why you hated me so much."

"I didn't hate you," Amanda said. "I didn't even know you."

"It's okay," Trish told her. "I had this epiphany in college. It just hit me one day, like, *Fuck, I was a mean girl! That's why she hated me!* Sometimes, even now, I wake up in the middle of the night, and I'm just so ashamed of the way I treated people, how fucking selfish I was, such a little princess. So when I saw you here, I just thought I should come over and apologize. Make things right."

"You don't need to apologize."

"I am so sorry," Trish said, and the next thing Amanda knew they were hugging, Trish's proud little cheerleader boobs mashing into her chest. "I am really and truly sorry for the person I used to be."

Eve couldn't remember the last time she'd gone to a restaurant by herself — not a coffee shop or a hole-in-the-wall pizzeria, but an actual sit-down restaurant with waiters and cloth napkins, a place where the other diners glanced at you with pity when you were first seated at your table for one, and then did their best not to look at you after that, as if you were disfigured in some way, and shouldn't be made to feel self-conscious about it. And that was actually preferable to seeing someone you knew, giving them that sheepish little wave across the dining room — *Yup, here I am, all by myself!* — and then keeping your eyes glued to your plate for the next half hour, until either you left or they did.

But Eve had decided to do it anyway, to lean into the awkwardness and try to conquer it. Her inspiration was an article a newly divorced acquaintance had posted on Facebook — *Going Solo: Fifteen Fun Things to Do by Yourself . . . for Yourself!* — that had pointed out that too many single women deprive themselves of all sorts of pleasures out of simple fear of embarrassment, of being seen as less-than because they weren't part of a couple or a friend group. Just face up to this fear, the article suggested, and do what *you* want to do, and you might come to realize that there was nothing to be afraid of in the first place.

Go ahead, the writer concluded. *I dare you!*

Some of the suggested activities seemed lame — *Take a Long Hot Bath; Cook Yourself a Gourmet Candlelight Dinner* — and also beside the point, if the point was to overcome the stigma of being a woman alone in public. Others seemed unduly ambitious — *Go Kayaking; Run a Marathon* — or financially infeasible — *Take a Caribbean Cruise; Visit a New Continent.* But there were a few that landed right in her sweet spot — simple, inexpensive ways to treat yourself that required little more than the courage to get out of the house: *Sing a Song at Karaoke Night; Go to a Bar and Order a Fancy Cocktail; Take Yourself Out to Dinner.*

The restaurant she picked was Gennaro's, a homey red sauce Italian place on Haddington Boulevard. It was Brendan's favorite, always his first choice on those nights when Eve had worked late or was too tired to cook. The hostess, a high school girl with glamorous false eyelashes, led her to an out-of-the-way table near the rest room hallway. Eve didn't mind the subpar location. She was happy just to be there, surrounded by the familiar décor — the lovingly, if inexpertly, painted mural of the Neapolitan coast that took up an entire wall, the framed photographs of a Vespa and a bunch of grapes — and the comforting hum of other people's dinnertime conversation.

She wished she'd thought to bring a book for company; next time she'd know better. For now, she was reduced to perusing the old-school paper placemat — it hadn't changed for as long as she could remember — featuring a map of Italy, illustrations of the Leaning Tower and the Colosseum, and a handful of helpful facts about the country.

Population: Sixty Million
Religion: Roman Catholic
Language: Italian

Brendan had always gotten a kick out of that last one. *What a shocker,* he'd say. *Italians speak Italian. Never woulda guessed.* Thinking he'd appreciate the reference, she texted him a picture.

Dinner at Gennaro's, she wrote.

Cool, he replied, with gratifying promptness. *Who with?*

Just me. Wish you were here.
Me too I miss that chicken parm!

It got easier once her wine arrived, a house chianti as unchanging as the placemat. She'd only taken a couple of sips when Gennaro emerged from the kitchen and made his way through the restaurant, going table to table like a politician. He was a sweetheart, a diminutive, blue-eyed Italian with a ruddy complexion and a thick head of silver hair, one of those slender continental types who managed to look elegant even in a dark green apron. When he spotted Eve, his face broke into a big, incredulous grin.

"Ay, long time no see. Where's your boy?"

"College," she told him. "Freshman year."

"Smart kid." Gennaro tapped his skull with the tip of his index finger. "How's he like it?"

"Pretty well. Maybe a little too much for his own good."

Gennaro waved his hand, as if batting away an insect.

"Ah. He's young. Let him enjoy himself." He peered at Eve, his eyes narrowing with concern. "What about you? What's new?"

"Not much," she said. "Just work. Keeping busy."

Gennaro shrugged with good-natured resignation.

"What can you do? Gotta pay the tuition." He patted her supportively on the shoulder. "Nice to see you, pretty lady. You come by anytime, we take good care of you."

He moved on, leaving Eve slightly deflated. She knew Gennaro meant well, but there was something about that question — *What's new?* — that never failed to depress her. Maybe she was being paranoid, but it always felt like an intrusion, an indirect way of inquiring about her romantic life. And when she replied, *Just work,* that was code for *I'm still alone,* as if she were apologizing for being single, as if there was something wrong with that.

On the other hand, at least he'd bothered to ask, which implied that he thought there was still a possibility that something *might* be new. That was a point in her favor. And it wasn't even true that there was nothing new in her life. For one thing, she was taking a class in Gender Studies and actually learning something. And, oh yeah, she'd also gone and gotten herself addicted to internet porn, not that that was anything to brag about.

She understood that it was a little extreme, or maybe just premature, to call her problem an addiction — it had only been going on for a month or so — but what other label could you use when you did something every night, whether you wanted to or not? Tonight she knew she would go home and visit the Milfateria — it felt like a fact, not a choice — probably checking out the Lesbo MILFs, her current go-to category. Last week it was Blowjob MILFs — lots and lots of blowjobs — and the week before that had been a more eclectic period — spanking, threesomes, butt play — just to get a sense of what was out there.

Addiction was a bleak word, though, a hundred percent negative. Maybe *habit* was a better term. People were addicted to heroin. But their morning coffee was just a habit.

I have a porn habit, Eve thought, trying on the word for size.

There were definitely some upsides to it. She was having a lot more orgasms than she used to, which was helping her sleep better, and improving her complexion. Several people had commented on how good her skin looked. She was also picking up some techniques that might come in handy down the road, if she ever did find a partner. For example, she'd learned that her blowjob skills were seriously out-of-date. When Eve was young, a can-do attitude — really, just making the effort — had been more than enough to earn a passing grade. These days the bar was a lot higher.

But there was a big downside to porn, beyond the feminist objections that still made her uneasy. The real problem was spiritual: it made you feel like you were wasting your life. This wasn't so much a matter of lost time — though that was part of it, all those hours you squandered clicking on video after video, trying to find the one that would light up your brain — as it was a matter of lost opportunities. Watching too much porn made you feel like you were out in the cold with your nose pressed against a window, watching strangers at a party, wishing you could join them. But the weird thing was, you *could* join them. All you had to do was open the door and walk inside, and everybody would be happy to see you. So why were you still outside, standing on your tiptoes, feeling sorry for yourself?

Thank God, she thought, when her lasagna finally arrived.

It only took a minute for Amanda to reactivate her Tinder account. Her old matches were gone, but she didn't care about that. She used the same profile photos as before — they'd never let her down — and stuck with her tried-and-true tagline: *If you're nice, I'll show you my other ones.* She set the match distance for fifteen miles and the age range for 35–55. That was the key, in her experience. The older guys were out there, checking their phones every two minutes, just itching to be called out of retirement. And they'd happily drive through a blizzard with a flat tire if a woman in her twenties was waiting on the other end.

Amanda understood that this was a bad idea, not to mention a blatant violation of her recently instituted no-hookup policy. Tinder was like tequila — fun today, sad tomorrow — but sometimes you didn't have a choice. That unexpected reunion with Trish Lozano had really messed with her self-esteem. The thought of going home and eating a salad in front of the TV had triggered a wave of self-pity that bordered on rage.

That's the highlight of my day? A fucking salad?

It would have been fine, or at least marginally tolerable, if Trish had still been Trish, a grown-up version of her teenaged self, cute and predictable, flaunting a tacky rock, bragging about her fratboy stockbroker boyfriend. At least that way Amanda would have preserved her sense of intellectual superiority, the illusion that she was an adventurous bohemian who'd chosen the road less traveled.

But Trish — *Beckett* — was a completely new person, living the kind of life Amanda had always imagined for herself. *My fiancé's a cinematographer!* How the fuck did that happen? It just seemed so unfair — the girl who'd been deliriously happy in high school was the one who'd reinvented herself, moving to a glamorous city and falling in love with an artist who loved her back, while Amanda, who'd dreamed of nothing but escape, had ended up right back where she started, with only a few stupid tattoos to show for all her trouble.

I work at the Senior Center. They have a pretty good lecture series.

She'd felt so stupid saying that, she'd wanted to die. And then Trish had had the gall to hug her, to fucking *apologize* for her happiness, which was way worse than bragging about it.

I am so getting laid tonight, Amanda thought, before they'd even let go of each other.

Her match arrived in less than an hour, knocking furtively on the front door. She studied him through the peephole, amazed, as always, that this was even possible, that you could swipe at a photo of a stranger, and the flesh-and-blood person would show up on your doorstep. This one was a little heavier than she'd expected — he claimed to be an avid cyclist — but he bore an otherwise reassuring resemblance to his profile pic, which had been taken in an apple orchard on a sunny day. It showed him standing beneath a fruit-laden tree, squinting into the camera, smiling in a way that made him look worried rather than happy.

His name was Bobby and he seemed charmingly ill-at-ease in the living room, like a teenager picking up his prom date. He wanted to know if it was all right to keep his shoes on, and asked permission before sitting down on the couch. He said no to her offer of a beer, then changed his mind a few seconds later, but only if it wasn't too much trouble. Middle-aged men were often like this, tentative and overly polite. The guys her own age had more of a swagger, as if they were stopping by to pick up a well-deserved award.

"How was the traffic?" she asked.

"Piece of cake," he said. "Only a problem at rush hour."

"Well, thanks for making the trip."

"Thanks for hosting." He surveyed the décor with a skeptical expression, taking in the matching gray furniture, the gas fireplace, the vases and baskets full of dried flowers. "This your place?"

"I'm house-sitting. My parents are on a cruise. They're coming home tomorrow."

This was the lie she always told, because she didn't want any Tinder dudes ringing the doorbell at two in the morning, drunk and looking for company. Besides, the real story was too complicated — her mother's unexpected death from a heart attack at the age of sixty-two; her own return from the city to make the funeral arrangements and deal with the legal and financial crap (she was the only child of divorced parents, so it was all on her); and the fact that she'd just *stayed,* because life in the city had gotten complicated — she'd broken up with her boyfriend and was living in a temporary sublet — and here was a whole house that suddenly belonged to *her,* though she couldn't bear to redecorate or even clean out her mother's closet. At some point, if the opportunity arose, she'd tell Bobby that her dad was a retired cop, also not true — her dad wasn't retired, wasn't a cop, and in any case was no longer in touch with Amanda — but certain precautions were advisable if you were going to invite strangers into your home and have sex with them.

"I went on a cruise once," he said. "It wasn't that great."

"You couldn't pay me enough," she told him.

When he finished his beer, they went out on the back deck to smoke the joint she'd asked him to bring. She wasn't a big pothead, but weed worked faster than alcohol, and had the added benefit of making everything seem a little more unreal and a lot funnier than it would have been otherwise, which was definitely helpful in a situation like this.

"Nice night," he said, nodding at the sky. "Moon's almost full."

Amanda didn't reply. She wanted to keep the small talk to a minimum. That had been her mistake with Dell — they'd talked for an hour before taking their clothes off, and it had ended up feeling a little too much like a real date, which was probably what caused all the confusion when they ran into each other at yoga class.

"I'm divorced," he said. "In case you were wondering."

"I wasn't."

At least he could take a hint. They smoked the rest of the joint in a strangely comfortable silence, as if they'd known each other a long time and had exhausted every possible topic of conversation. For a moment — it coincided with the realization that she was very high — she imagined they were a married couple, committed to spending every remaining night of their lives together, until one of them got sick and died.

Me and Bobby, she thought. *Bobby and me.*

It was a ridiculous idea, but just plausible enough to make her laugh.

"What's so funny?"

"Nothing." She shook her head, as if it wasn't worth explaining. "It's stupid."

"You have a nice laugh," he told her.

They went back inside, into her childhood bedroom. The walls were pale pink, with ghostly rectangles where posters used to hang, but it all looked the same color by candlelight. He sat on the edge of her narrow bed and watched her undress.

She made a little striptease out of it, undoing the buttons on her dress one by one, very slowly. He was a good audience.

"Oooh *yeah,*" he said, more than once. "You are fucking gorgeous."

The dress fell to the floor. She stood there for a moment in her black bra and panties, along with the knee-high boots she'd tugged on for the occasion. He nodded for quite a while, as if something he'd long suspected had turned out to be true.

"You're killing me," he said. "You are totally fucking killing me."

As far back as she could remember, Amanda had had mixed feelings about her body. She was shorter and heavier than she wanted to be, with big, full breasts that weren't great for yoga or running, but made a very positive impression in situations like this.

"Oh Jesus," he muttered, as she dropped her bra on top of the dress. "Look at those fucking tits."

Standing next to Trish Lozano in the harsh light of the changing room, Amanda had felt the way she had all through high school, chubby and dull and hopeless. But right now, shimmying out of her panties in the trembling yellow light, with Bobby studying her like a painting in a museum, she felt like something special.

"Want me to keep the boots on?"

"Whatever's easier," he told her. "I'm good either way."

Eve wasn't sure a Manhattan qualified as a "Fancy Cocktail," but it was close enough that she felt entitled to check off a second box on her *Going Solo* checklist. And besides, even a simple Manhattan seemed plenty fancy for the Lamplighter Inn, which was the hands-down favorite dining spot of Haddington's senior citizens, who'd been holding their annual banquet here since time immemorial.

Eve would have been fine with never eating another iceberg wedge or fillet of sole at the Lamplighter for as long as she lived, but she had a soft spot for the bar, a cozy hideaway with red leather stools and a half-dozen booths that would have been perfect for a romantic nightcap, if there'd been any romance in her life. At eight o'clock on a Wednesday evening, it was pleasantly uncrowded without seeming desolate, only four other people at the bar — a grimly silent older couple who looked like serious drinkers, and a pair of blue-collar guys watching a ballgame on the muted TV. One booth was occupied as well, by two women engaged in an emergency heart-to-heart discussion.

"Do I know you?" the bartender asked. He was a nice-looking guy around her own age, with close-cropped gray hair and an appealing residue of boyishness in his face. "Aren't you Brendan's mom?"

Eve admitted that she was. The bartender held out his hand.

"Jim Hobie. I was his soccer coach way back when. He must have been in kindergarten or first grade. Our team was called the Daisies."

"Oh my God," Eve laughed. "I forgot about the Daisies. They were adorable."

In the earliest phase of youth soccer, all the teams were coed and named after flowers, and nobody kept score. That lasted for two years, and then things got cutthroat and stayed that way.

"It was pure chaos," Hobie told her. "Brendan was the only kid on our team who knew what he was doing. A couple of times we had to tell him to stop scoring goals and give everyone else a chance."

Eve studied the man's face, trying to place him on the sidelines of those long-forgotten Saturday mornings.

"I thought Ellen DiPetro was the coach."

"I was her assistant," Hobie explained. "I had more hair back then, and a little goatee, if that rings a bell."

Bells were not ringing, but it was a long time since Brendan had been a Daisy.

"You had a kid on the team?"

"My daughter. Daniella."

"Daniella Hobie. That sounds familiar."

"She was salutatorian," he said proudly. "Gave one of the speeches at graduation."

"That's right." It was a very long and boring speech, if Eve remembered correctly, about all the wonderful lessons she'd learned from participating in the model U.N. "How's she doing?"

"Great. She's a freshman at Columbia. Seems to love it."

"Wow. An Ivy Leaguer. Good for you."

"She didn't get it from me," Hobie assured her. "I barely squeaked through Fitchburg State."

"Maybe she got it from her mother."

"I don't think so. Her mom — my ex — didn't even graduate. Though I guess that was mostly 'cause I got her pregnant." He shrugged, like it didn't really matter. "I just think Dani was born smart. I could see it in her eyes when she was a little baby. Like she was just taking it all in, you know? Figuring it out. Our son — her older brother — he was nothing like that. He spent about a year trying to swallow his own fist. That was his big project."

"They are who they are," Eve agreed. "All we can do is love them."

Hobie glanced down the bar, toward the older couple. The man was holding his arm in the air, like he was trying to hail a cab.

Hobie sighed. "Excuse me."

While he was attending to his duties, Eve

took out her phone and texted Brendan.

Do you remember Daniella Hobie? I just ran into her dad. Your old coach from the Daisies.

"What about Brendan?" Hobie asked. "What's he up to?"

"He's at BSU."

"Still playing lacrosse?"

"Not anymore."

Her phone dinged and she picked it up.

Ugh she gave that brutal speech the daisies were so gay

"Speak of the devil," she said, slipping the phone back into her purse.

"It's nice that he stays in touch," Hobie observed. "I don't hear much from my kids these days. Their mom and I got divorced about ten years ago."

"Same here," she said. "It's tough."

"Irreconcilable differences." Hobie laughed sadly. "She hated my guts."

"Mine was a cheater," said Eve. "Nice guy otherwise."

"Can I ask you something?" He looked a little shy, like he knew he was broaching a delicate subject. "Does Brendan have a girl-friend?"

"I don't think so. He had one in high school, but they broke up over the summer. I wasn't crazy about her, to be honest."

"Only reason I ask is because Dani never

mentions boys. *Never.* If I ask her straight up, she just says she's too busy for a relationship. But then you read these stories in the paper about the kids binge-drinking and hooking up at parties and friends with benefits and all that stuff, and it sounds like a nonstop orgy."

"They're adults," Eve said. "They get to make their own mistakes, just like we did."

"Friends with benefits." Hobie shook his head in rueful amazement. "I don't even have a *job* with benefits."

"Good one," Eve said, toasting him with her almost empty glass.

He asked if she wanted a refill. Eve said what the heck, it was still pretty early. She was enjoying the conversation, which had confirmed the value of simply getting out of the house, and elevated the status of her night from small experiment to minor accomplishment.

Hobie mixed the drink with his back turned, giving her an opportunity to admire the snugness of his jeans and the tailored fit of his tucked-in white Oxford. He was in good shape for a man his age.

A man my age, she reminded herself.

"You're a nice surprise on a Wednesday night," he said, placing the fresh cocktail in front of her as if it were a trophy. A trophy just for showing up, like the ones they gave to the Daisies.

"I went to a wake. Didn't feel like going home."

"Sorry to hear it. Somebody close?"

"Just an acquaintance. Guy I knew from work. He was eighty-two."

"Oh." Hobie seemed relieved to hear it. "What can you do?"

In the mirror, Eve watched as the therapy session in the booth came to a conclusion, the two woman friends putting on their jackets and heading for the door. A few minutes later, the baseball fans made their exit as well. Only Eve and the old lushes remained.

"Slow night?" she asked.

"About average."

"I guess you make up for it on the weekends."

"Saturdays are pretty busy," he said. "But that's not my shift."

Eve made a sympathetic noise, but Hobie shook her off.

"My choice," he assured her. "Weekends are sacred. That's me-time. Necessary for my mental health and well-being."

He told her about the pickup basketball game he played on Saturday mornings, a bunch of Haddington High alums, former varsity players of all ages. Hobie was one of the older guys, but he could still keep up.

"Can't jump as high as I used to," he conceded. "But I still have a decent outside shot."

"Sounds like a good workout."

"The best." Hobie grinned. "Sundays I do a group bike ride with a few buddies. Usually thirty or forty miles. We did a big charity ride this summer."

It was easy to imagine him on a fancy bike, decked out in spandex like it was the Tour de France, breathing hard as he crested a steep hill, his face glowing with cheerful determination.

"My ex-husband did that a couple of times," she said. "You gotta really be in shape."

"I try," Hobie said with a touch of false modesty that Eve did her best to ignore. "What about you? What do you like to do on the weekends?"

"This and that," she said, wishing she had a sweaty and exciting activity of her own to boast about — rock climbing or kickboxing, even tennis. But all she ever did was read and watch movies and go for slow walks around the lake with Jane and her arthritic bichon frise, Antoine. In the summer there was yard work, cutting grass and pulling weeds and watering her little garden, meditative tasks she would have enjoyed a lot more if she wasn't so worried about ticks. These days she was looking longingly at the trees, waiting for the leaves to change so she could go outside and rake on a chilly autumn morning, pathetic as that sounded. "I just like to relax, I guess."

"Absolutely," he said. "That's the whole point."

Hobie turned and watched as the elderly couple dismounted their stools, the old woman assisting the old man, who needed a few seconds to get his feet properly connected to the floor.

"You guys okay?" he asked.

The man waved dismissively, as if Hobie did nothing but bother him.

"We're fine, dear," the woman said, taking her unsteady partner by the arm. "See you tomorrow."

After they'd shuffled out, Hobie explained that they lived right around the corner, which was a good thing, since they'd both had their driver's licenses revoked, with good cause.

"This is their ritual," he said. "They come here every night and drink whiskey sours. Barely say a word to each other, and then they walk home. Last year was their fiftieth."

"That's a long time," Eve said. "I guess they're all talked out."

Hobie shrugged. "Least they have each other."

Eve nodded, distracted by the realization that they were alone now. There was something undeniably porny about the situation — the handsome bartender, the lonely divorcée. She could see the video in her head, shot a little shakily from the man's point of view, the MILF looking up, licking her lips in anticipation as she undid his belt. It was an image that would have been unthinkable at any other time in her life, but now seemed weirdly plausible. There was literally nothing stopping her. All she had to do was slip behind the bar and kneel down. Hobie gave her a searching look, almost as if he were reading her mind.

"One more?" he asked hopefully. "On the house."

Later that night, after she'd watched her porn and gone to bed, Eve wondered why she hadn't taken him up on his offer. It was just a drink, a half hour of her time. He was reasonably good-looking and easy to talk to, and it had been a long time since she'd had a fun flirtation, let alone a fling. If she'd been advising a friend, she would have said,

Give it a shot, see where it leads, he doesn't have to be perfect.

It wasn't so much the sexual fantasy that had thrown her off — that had come and gone in a flash — as it was the nagging sense of familiarity that had snuck up on her over the course of the night, a feeling that Jim Hobie was more of the same, another helping of a meal she'd already had enough of. He wasn't as obnoxious as Barry from class, or as charmed by himself as Ted had been, but he was in the same basic ballpark. She could go to bed with him, she could even fall in love, but where would it get her? Nowhere she hadn't been before, that was for sure. She wanted something else — something *different* — though what that something was remained to be seen. All she really knew was that it was a big world out there, and she'd only been scratching the surface.

Amanda was a wreck the next morning, not because of her sexual exertions — Bobby only lasted a couple of minutes — but because it turned out to be one of those nights when sleep wouldn't come, when there was nothing to do but lie awake in the darkness and watch the bad thoughts float by, an armada of bleak prospects and unhappy memories. It had been close to five by the time she drifted off, and then she was up at seven, nursing a headache that two ibuprofen and three cups of coffee hadn't managed to eradicate.

"Are you okay?" Eve Fletcher asked when Amanda arrived at her office for their ten o'clock meeting. "You look a little pale."

"I'm fine," Amanda insisted, suppressing the usual urge to open up to Eve, to tell her about her rough night, and ask if she had any strategies for dealing with insomnia. "Just cramps."

Eve gave a sympathetic nod. "I'm almost done with all that. I'm not gonna miss it."

Amanda would have liked to pursue the subject, to hear Eve's thoughts about menopause and growing older, but she decided that was out of bounds, too. Eve was her boss, not her friend, no matter how much Amanda wished it were otherwise.

"So you got my email about Garth Heely?"

"I did." Eve looked upset, but only for a second. "Was it a heart attack?"

"His wife said stroke."

"You know what? That's how I want to go." Eve snapped her fingers. "Quick and painless. In my own bed. That's one thing you learn, working with old people. You really don't want to die in a hospital."

Amanda murmured agreement, trying not to think about her mother. Going fast wasn't that great, either. She'd been dead for a couple of days before the neighbors even started wondering if she was okay.

"Any ideas for a replacement?" Eve asked. "We need to nail this down sooner rather than later."

"I'll email you the short list by the end of the day."

"Perfect." Eve nodded briskly. "That it?"

"I think so."

Amanda rose uncertainly. She felt like she'd forgotten something important, like there was one more thing they needed to discuss, but the only possibilities that occurred to her were Trish's perky nipples and the puppy-like whimpers Bobby made right before he came, neither of which were appropriate subjects for workplace conversation.

"By the way," Eve said, "if you still want to get a drink sometime, I'd be totally up for that."

JULIAN FUCKING SPITZER

When you walk into the dining hall with someone else, you kinda melt into the scenery. Nobody even knows you're there. Walking in by yourself is a totally different experience. It's like you're radioactive, like your skin is giving off this sick greenish glow. You can feel everybody staring.

I have friends, you want to tell them. *They're just busy right now.*

Usually I ate my meals with Zack, but he'd slipped out after receiving a booty text at three in the morning and still hadn't returned, the first time that had ever happened. He wouldn't tell me who he was hooking up with, but he usually rushed out and came back an hour or two later, tired but happy, like a volunteer fireman who'd done his duty for the town and needed to rest up for a bit. I texted him — *dude where r u* — but he didn't respond. I tried Will and Rico, too, but those guys were probably still asleep.

The Higg that morning was an ocean of strangers, so I headed past the crowded tables to the less-populated section in back. It was a reject convention back there. I guess I could have taken a book from my backpack and pretended to study — that's what the other losers were doing — but it seemed like an asshole move, like, *Hey look at me reading a textbook!* At least my breakfast was pretty good, though it was common knowledge that the Higg omelettes weren't made with real eggs — it was some kind of sludgy yellow liquid that came in a can.

One thing you realize when you're on your own is how happy the people who aren't alone look. There were a bunch of couples eating together, and most of them were pretty smiley, probably because they'd just woken up and fucked. Other people were laughing with their friends. A professor with crazy-clown hair was lecturing a bearded grad student who kept nodding like his head was on a spring.

There were two groups I couldn't stop looking at. One of them was a bunch of girls who reminded me of Becca. Super-skinny, straight hair, lots of makeup. They were all wearing short skirts and sneakers, like they were still in middle school and thought it would be fun to coordinate their outfits. They kept erupting in laughter that sounded fake and a little too loud, like they wanted everyone to look at them and wonder what the hot girls thought was so funny.

Next to them was a table of football players, seriously big guys chowing down on plates piled high with ridiculous amounts of food. Unlike the girls, they were quiet and serious, maybe discussing the upcoming game, or wondering why coach had been so pissed off at yesterday's practice. I had this weird urge to pick up my tray and join them, just so I could feel like I was part of the team again. I really missed that feeling.

There I was, people-watching and eating my omelette, and the next thing I knew my throat swelled up. And then my eyes started to water. I realized I was two seconds away from bursting into tears like a little bitch, right there in the Higg. I actually had to squeeze my eyes shut and take a few deep breaths to get a hold of myself.

Little by little I could feel the pressure letting up, the rubber ball dissolving in my throat. It was a huge relief. But when I finally opened my eyes, that douchebag Sanjay was standing right in front of me, watching me like I was a science experiment.

There was nothing on his tray but an apple and a tiny container of yogurt.

"Hey, Brendan," he said. "You okay?"

I hadn't seen him for a couple of weeks — he wasn't hanging out with Dylan anymore — but it seemed to me that he was slightly less nerdy than before. New glasses maybe, or a different haircut. Cooler clothes. Something.

"Fine," I said. "Just a little hungover."

He nodded, but it was annoying the way he did it, like it served me right for getting drunk on a Monday night. *Fuck him.* I wiped my mouth and stood up, even though there were still a few bites left of my omelette.

"Gotta run," I said. "Catch you later."

I carried my tray over to the dish line and put it on the belt. I glanced back at Sanjay as I headed for the exit. He was sitting at my table, all by himself, reading a book and munching on his apple. He seemed totally fine, like he didn't even know I'd ditched him.

Losing my shit in public like that was a wake-up call. I mean, I knew I was drinking too much and fucking up in my classes. I'd flunked a unit test in Math and gotten a D on my first writing assignment for Comp —

What Does White Privilege Mean to Me? — a grade the instructor claimed was "an act of charity" on her part. I was having trouble in Econ, too, but that was mainly because I couldn't understand the prof's heavy Chinese accent. That afternoon, he was droning on about "sooply sigh" and "deeman sigh" when I started zoning out. But instead of checking Facebook or texting Wade, I decided to be constructive for once and make a to-do list, which my dad claimed was one of the Eleven Habits of Highly Successful People or whatever. It went like this:

- Homework!
- Pay Attention in Class!!
- No Drinking on Weekdays (if poss.)
- Call Mom
- Laundry!!!
- Way Less Super Smash (vid games in gen.)
- Bday Card for Becca!
- Return Dad's Email
- Hang w ppl Besides Zack
- Break Up w Becca?
- Shave Chest & Balls
- Extra-Currics?

It had a calming effect to write it all down, to take my sense of impending doom and divide it into a dozen problems that could actually be solved, some more easily than others. I decided to start small, heading straight to the laundry room after class and washing every item of clothing I owned, plus the sheets and towels, which were pretty disgusting. It was a real morale booster, except that some of the white stuff came out pink.

That night I went to the library to do my homework, which I hardly ever did. I was trying to read this book about climate change, how it was almost too late for humanity to save itself, but maybe not quite, not if we all made a decision to change our wasteful lifestyles *immediately.* It was pretty interesting, but I had trouble keeping my focus. For one thing, I was sitting at a big table in the main reading room and the girl next to me was chewing her gum really loud. And this dude across from me kept sighing hopelessly as he erased the answers on his problem set, like he wanted the whole world to know he was struggling.

But all that was just background noise. What was really bugging me was the phone call I'd just had with my mom, which hadn't gone the way I'd expected. I figured she'd be happy to hear from me, since we hadn't spoken in a couple of weeks. But she kind of blew me off.

"I'm on my way out the door, honey. I have class tonight."

"What?"

"I told you about my class. At ECC? Gender and Society, every Tuesday and Thursday night?"

"Oh yeah," I said, though it was news to me. She'd been talking about going back to school for so long I pretty much just tuned out whenever the subject came up. "How's that going?"

"Great. It's really exciting to be back in the classroom."

For a person who was on her way out the door, she had a lot of time to rave about her class. Apparently, the teacher was a really unique person, the students were super-diverse, and the reading was challenging and thought-provoking, exactly what she needed at this particular moment in her life.

"Cool," I said, though it bugged me to hear her talking about college like it was the greatest thing in the world. I was the one who was really in college, and in my humble opinion, it was a mixed bag. Also, she was taking *one fucking class*. Try taking four, and then tell me how much fun you're having.

"Oh, by the way," she said. "One of the other students said he went to high school with you. Julian Spitzer? That ring a bell?"

I froze for a few seconds, trying to convince myself I'd misheard. But I knew I hadn't.

"I remember the name," I said, after a long pause. "But I didn't know him that well."

"He told me to say hello."

I seriously doubted that Julian Spitzer had asked her to say hello. Unless he was fucking with me, in which case I couldn't really blame him.

"Hey," I said, trying to change the subject. "I got another email from Dad about Parents Weekend —"

"You know what, honey? I really have to go. I'll call you back tomorrow, okay? Love you."

Technically speaking, I wasn't lying to my mom about Julian Spitzer. I really didn't know him that well. He'd moved to Haddington in seventh grade, too late to make much of an impression on me and my buddies. In high school he was part of the skater posse. You'd see them cruising through town sometimes, zipping down the middle of the street in a big pack, like they didn't give a fuck about oncoming traffic. I remember Julian standing up really straight on his board, hands on his hips, long hair streaming behind him like a girl's.

I didn't witness the incident at Kim Mangano's house. I was upstairs with Becca — it was the first time we hooked up — in a bedroom that belonged to Kim's little twin brothers. Meanwhile, Wade was in the kitchen, trying to talk to Fiona Rattigan, his on-and-off girlfriend who'd broken up with him a few days earlier. I guess she was ignoring him, and he got kind of upset. He grabbed her by the arm and wouldn't let go. She said he was hurting her. A couple of people tried to intervene, but Wade told them to mind their own business.

He's abusing me! Fiona said, in a really loud voice. I think she was pretty drunk herself. *Somebody call 911!*

Julian Spitzer happened to be in the kitchen, because that's where the keg was. When he finished filling his cup with beer, he walked over to Wade and tossed it in his face.

Are you deaf? She asked you to leave her alone!

It took Wade a couple of seconds to wipe the beer out of his eyes and recover from the shock, and by then a couple of our lacrosse teammates had grabbed hold of him so he couldn't do anything stupid. It was the middle of the season and our team was doing really well. The last thing we needed was for the party to get busted, and a bunch of our best players to get suspended for drinking and fighting. But Wade was furious.

For a week or two it was a big deal in school, like, *Hey, did you hear about Wade and Spitzer?* But then it just kinda died down. There were other parties, other incidents. Wade got back with Fiona, our team made it to the state quarterfinals, and then it was summer vacation. The whole beer-in-the-face thing seemed like ancient history, except that Wade couldn't stop brooding about it. We ignored him, because everybody knew that Wade could be a nasty drunk. When he's sober, he's one of the sweetest, most laidback guys you could know.

It was just bad luck that night in August. Wade and Fiona were on the outs again, Becca and I were fighting, and our buddy Troy hated his camp counselor job, which required him to spend his days with whiny five-year-olds. We tried to cheer ourselves up by drinking a bottle of Popov vodka in the woods by the golf course, but getting wasted didn't improve our mood.

Afterward, we drove around in Troy's Corolla for a while, circling past the same familiar landmarks over and over — the high school, the cemetery, the lake, the high school again — because nobody felt like going home, and at least we could be bored together, and complain about the songs on the radio.

And then, on maybe our eighth or ninth lap around the town, we just happened to see him — Julian Fucking Spitzer, all alone on a dark stretch of Green Street. He was riding his skateboard at a good clip, pushing off with one foot and then gliding for a while, not a care in the world.

"Look at that," Troy said. "It's your little buddy."

He slowed down until we were right on Julian's ass, and then gunned it, swerving around him and jackknifing the Corolla so it blocked the road. Julian had to jump off the skateboard to keep from plowing into us. He could have run, but for some reason he just stood there, paralyzed, as Wade stepped out of the passenger seat.

"Get in the fucking car," he said. "We're going for a ride."

"What if I say no?" asked Julian.

"Just get in the car, asshole."

Julian didn't argue. It was like he'd been expecting this for a long time, and figured he should just get it over with. He picked up his skateboard and climbed obediently into the backseat. Wade ducked in right behind him, so there were three of us back there, with Julian squashed in the middle. Troy started the engine and we headed off.

"How's it going, dude?" Wade asked in a fake friendly voice. "Having a good summer?"

"Not really," said Julian.

"Awesome," said Wade. "Happy to hear it."

He slipped his arm around Julian's shoulders like they were boyfriend and girlfriend. I could smell someone's sweat, sharp and sour, but I wasn't sure whose it was. It was like we were one person back there, three bodies glued together.

"I've been looking all over for you," Wade said, in this weird flirty voice. "You never answer my texts."

Julian didn't reply. He kept glancing in my direction, pleading for help, but there was nothing I could do. This was between him and Wade.

"You shouldn't have thrown that beer in my face." Wade squeezed him a little tighter.

"That was a big mistake."

"I'm sorry." Julian's voice cracked a little, like he was maybe gonna cry. "I'm really sorry."

"I bet you are," Wade agreed. "But it's way too late for an apology."

Julian nodded, like he'd figured as much. His voice was small and scared. "What are you gonna do to me?"

Wade didn't answer for a while. He took his arm off Julian's shoulders and gazed out the window at the dark houses with their neat front yards, attractive homes full of decent people.

"I'm not a bad person," he said. "I'm really not."

I could totally see his dilemma. He'd talked so much about the hardcore vengeance he was going to inflict on Julian, and now he had to deliver. You couldn't just drive around with the kid for a half hour and then let him off with a stern warning.

"You should fuck him in the ass," Troy suggested. "I bet he'd like that."

I guess it could've been worse. There was no violence, no bloodshed, no tears. Nobody got fucked in the ass. It was just the four of us standing in front of a disgusting Port-A-John near the soccer field in VFW Park. I swear, you could smell that thing from twenty yards away, a cloud of human waste and chemical perfume that had been fermenting in the sun for the whole summer. Wade held out his hand and asked Julian for his phone.

"Why?" Julian asked. "What are you gonna do with it?"

"Just give it to me, asshole."

Once again, Julian did as he was told. Wade shoved the phone into his pants pocket. Then he pointed at the Port-A-John.

"Get in there," he said.

I had my hand on Julian's shoulder. I could feel his whole body stiffen.

"No way," he said.

"Oh, you're going in," Wade told him. "I guarantee you that."

"Please," Julian said. "I already apologized."

Wade poked him in the chest. "I'm not gonna say it again."

Julian just sort of went limp. All the fight went out of him.

"That's all?" he said. "You're not gonna hurt me?"

"That's all," Wade told him.

"You promise?"

"I promise. Now get the fuck in there."

It was all very civilized. Wade opened the

door to that reeking closet and Julian stepped inside.

"Enjoy your evening," Wade told him.

Julian turned to face us. The Port-A-John was slightly elevated, so it was almost like he was on stage. I guess he felt like he had nothing to lose.

"You guys suck," he said. "I hope you know that."

"Shut the fuck up," Troy told him. "You're getting off easy. If it was up to me —"

"I'm serious," Julian continued. "Guys like you are what's wrong with the —"

Wade slammed the flimsy plastic door before Julian could finish his sentence. Then he sealed it shut using the duct tape he'd found in Troy's glove compartment. He wrapped it really well, using every last bit of tape on the roll, turning that Port-A-John into a prison cell.

"Yo, Julian," he said. "I'm leaving your phone out here."

"Fuck you." Julian's voice sounded muffled and far away, though he was right next to us. "You're a terrible person. All three of you."

Wade dropped the phone in the grass.

"Catch you later, dude."

Julian started yelling as we walked away, calling us morons and scumbags and begging us to open the door, but his pleas had dwindled away to nothing long before we reached the parking lot. We tried to laugh about it in the car, congratulating ourselves on the genius prank we'd just pulled, but our hearts weren't really in it. I was about to say we should go back and let him out, but Troy spoke first.

"He can breathe in there, right? He's not gonna suffocate or anything?"

"There are vents in the side," I said. "I checked."

"Can you imagine how bad it smells?" Troy asked. "Could you actually die from that?"

"He'll be fine," Wade said. "People will be walking their dogs at like six in the morning. They'll let him out."

"That's five hours from now," I said.

"Don't feel sorry for that fucker," Wade said. "He's lucky he's not in the hospital."

I went home and got into bed, but I couldn't fall asleep. All I could think about was Julian Spitzer, trapped in that gnarly box, far from anyone who could help him. I wondered if his parents had realized he was gone, if they were maybe calling the phone that Wade had left in the grass.

I couldn't take it. Around five that morning I got out of bed and rode my bike over to the park. It had seemed so sinister the night before, a creepy place where anything could happen. But it was beautiful in the early morning, with the sun coming up and birds chirping like crazy. I could see houses through the trees, not nearly as far away as they'd seemed in the dark.

I was relieved to find the Port-A-John empty, the tape seal broken. Maybe Julian had only been in there for a little while before someone came along, or he figured out a way to free himself. Maybe I'd stayed up all night worrying about nothing.

We had a few bad days after that, wondering if he'd told anyone what we'd done, his parents or maybe the cops or even just his friends. We weren't sure if it was a crime to tape someone inside a portable toilet, but it was the kind of prank you could get in pretty bad trouble for, a serious lapse in judgment you wouldn't want to have to explain to your parents or coaches, or to a college admissions officer.

But nothing happened. We never heard a word about it.

That was the summer before our senior year. When we got back to school in September, Julian Spitzer was mysteriously absent. Some people said he'd dropped out, others that he'd transferred to private school. I was just glad he was gone, so I didn't have to see him or think about him. By the time we graduated, I'd pretty much erased him from my memory, which was why it was such an unpleasant shock to hear my mother mention his name that afternoon, dropping it so casually into the conversation, asking if it rang a bell.

You know how sometimes, if you try not to think about something, you become that much more aware of it? That's how it was with me and that girl in the library. I kept trying to concentrate on my book — the melting glaciers and rising sea levels — and she kept chewing away, making this crackly gum-and-saliva noise that went right through me.

Jesus Christ, I thought. *Can you even hear yourself?*

It was actually a relief when the protesters arrived. There were maybe twenty of them, and they entered the library like a tour group, huddled together near the main entrance, whispering and looking around. Some of the kids at my table were already rolling their eyes and shaking their heads.

"Not again," moaned the chewing machine.

"Every friggin' night," said the kid with the eraser.

The protesters organized themselves in single file, stretching all the way down the center aisle. The girl closest to my table had blue hair and black lipstick. She glanced nervously at the Muslim girl next to her, who just had the headscarf, not the face-mask. They lifted their arms.

"Hands up! Don't shoot!"

It was kind of lame that first time, like only half the group got the memo, and not all of them read it at the same time.

"He was a thug!" somebody shouted from one of the tables.

The blue-haired girl and her Muslim friend raised their arms higher and chanted with more conviction.

"Hands up! Don't shoot!"

I'd heard about these Michael Brown protests — they were supposedly happening all over campus — but this was the first one I'd actually seen. A lot of people were complaining about them, saying that it was really disrespectful, the way the protesters barged into classrooms and harassed the fans at sporting events. But it was kind of cool to have them invade the library like this, filling that quiet space with their chant, which became louder and more confident the more they repeated it.

"Hands up! Don't shoot!"

The line was moving now, new faces filing past me in a slow parade. To my amazement, one of them was waving at me. It took me a second to recognize Amber, from the Autism Awareness Network, and by then she'd broken from the line and was heading straight for my table.

"Dude!" she said in this jubilant voice, like I'd come back from the dead. "Where have you been? We missed you last meeting."

"Too much work," I said, holding up my book so she could see I was reading about climate change.

Even though she was out of formation, she raised her hands and shouted along with the others, begging the invisible cops not to shoot. She was wearing sweats and a hoodie, and I noticed again how strong she looked, with those linebacker shoulders, and how pretty she was, blond hair and blue eyes and farm-girl freckles, her cheeks all flushed with excitement.

"It's terrible what happened in Ferguson," she told me. "This shit's gotta stop."

I didn't know what to say to that. The more I heard about Michael Brown the more confused I got. Was he minding his business or had he robbed a store? Was he surrendering or trying to grab the cop's gun? I'd heard different people say different things, and didn't know what to believe.

"It's fucked up," I said. "That's for sure."

Amber smiled, like I'd passed some kind of test. She held out her hand, like she was asking me to dance.

"Come on," she said. "We need your voice."

I was shy at first, and worried about my backpack, which I'd left at the table.

"Hands up! Don't shoot!"

"Come on!" Amber told me. "Say it like you mean it!"

Some people heckled us, but others got up from their seats and joined the conga line as we moved through the library. We marched past the circulation desk and snaked through the stacks to the Computer Commons.

"Hands up! Don't shoot!"

It got easier the more I did it, and a lot more fun. Some people were swaying and others started raising the roof. For a little while Amber and I were holding hands, our arms aloft like we'd just won a medal.

"Hands up! Don't shoot!"

We did three circuits of the main floor and

then exited through the metal detector, chanting the whole time. It felt great to step out of the library into the chilly October night, everybody high-fiving and congratulating everybody else, the moonlight shining on Amber's hair as she hugged me.

When I got back to the room, Zack was lying on his bed with these huge DJ headphones clamped over his ears. I wanted to tell him about the protest, but he yanked off the headphones and sat up before I'd even had time to shrug off my backpack.

"Dude," he said. "Can I ask you something?"

"Sure."

"Would you ever hook up with a fat girl?"

"I doubt it," I said. "That's not really my thing."

"Yeah, but what if there's a fat girl you really liked? Would you hook up with her?"

"Is this for a class?"

"No, I'm just curious."

"Depends." I sat down on my bed, directly across from him. "If she's one of those plus-sized models I might."

"Not a model. Just a regular fat girl. But she's pretty and has a great personality."

"Are you trying to set me up with someone?"

181

"Dude, I'm asking you a simple question."

He sounded annoyed, which was a little unfair, since I'd already answered him twice.

"Fine," I said. "I'll hook up with her. Why not, if she's as great as you say?"

Zack nodded approvingly, like I'd finally given the correct answer.

"Okay, so you hook up with this girl a couple of times and it's fun as hell, but totally casual. No strings. But then one night she starts crying, and you're like, *What's wrong?* And she's like, *Why don't we ever go out in public? Are you ashamed of me? Is it because I'm fat?* What do you say then?"

It was all so obvious, I almost laughed in his face.

"Dude, are you hooking up with a fat girl? Is that where you go at three in the morning?"

"No," he said, in that same put-upon tone. "This is a completely hypothetical scenario."

"All right," I said. "Speaking hypothetically, I'd probably say, *Bitch, maybe if you dropped a hundred pounds we could go to the movies. In the meantime, could we get back to the blowjob you were giving me? I'm tired and I have to meet my asshole roommate for breakfast in the morning.*"

"Dude, that's so mean. She can't help it if

she's fat."

"Not my problem, bro."

"Wow." Zack looked impressed. "You're an even bigger dick than I am."

"Thank you," I said. "You wanna get baked and watch some *Bob's Burgers*?"

"I could go for that," he told me. "But I can't stay up too late. I'm tired and I gotta meet my asshole roommate for breakfast in the morning."

"That's funny," I said. "So do I."

We bumped fists and Zack broke out his weed, and pretty soon we were lit and laughing our asses off, talking shit about my hypothetical ex-girlfriend, the fat girl who'd been fun for a while, until she turned all weepy and started getting on my nerves.

THE CONFIDENT ONE

When Eve invited Amanda out for a drink, she hadn't meant it to be a date. It was a casual social thing, two colleagues hanging out after work, getting to know each other a little better. And it wasn't even Eve's idea. All she'd done was belatedly accept an invitation that Amanda had extended more than once, and that she herself had felt guilty about declining. There was no hidden agenda; she was just being polite, making amends, and giving them both something to do on an otherwise empty Friday night.

And yet it felt like a date, which was weird, because Eve didn't date women. Of course, she wasn't dating any men either, though that was only for lack of opportunity. If a man had asked her out, she would have happily said yes, unless it was creepy Barry from Gender and Society, who, unfortunately, was the only man expressing any interest at the moment, with the possible exception of Jim Hobie, the chatty bartender, though all he'd done was offer her a free drink, which hardly qualified as a romantic overture, and which, in any case, she'd declined.

But if tonight wasn't a date — and it definitely wasn't — then what accounted for the fluttery feeling of anticipation she'd been experiencing ever since she'd marked it on her calendar? And why had she chosen to wear this silky green blouse that went so well with her eyes, and then unbuttoned it one button lower than usual? The answer to these questions, Eve knew, was as simple as it was embarrassing: she'd been watching too much porn, and it had infected her imagination, making her hyper-aware of the sexual possibilities embedded in the most innocent situations. It would have been funny if it hadn't been so pathetic.

"I meant to tell you," said Amanda, who seemed quite clear about the fact that she wasn't on a date. "The maple syrup guy can't do the November lecture, so I'm scrambling to find a replacement."

"Uh-oh." Eve stretched her mouth into an expression of mock horror. "Sounds like a sticky situation."

Amanda looked puzzled for a moment, and then made a sound that resembled a chuckle.

"Sorry." Eve frowned. "Humor's not my specialty. At least that's what my ex-husband used to tell me."

"Nice," Amanda said. "I'm sure you appreciated his honesty."

"Absolutely. He was full of constructive criticism."

"Sounds like my old boyfriend," Amanda observed. "He was very concerned about my weight. If he caught me with some Ben and Jerry's, he'd pull the container right out of my hand. He'd say, *I don't want you to regret this.*"

"Really?"

"It was all for my own good, you know?"

Eve wanted to say something supportive but not inappropriate about Amanda's curves — that was one good thing about the Milfateria, it had given her an appreciation of the sexual appeal of all sorts of body types — but they were interrupted by a couple of middle-aged frat boys who wanted to know if the stool next to Amanda's was free. The guy who asked was jolly and bloated, with thinning blond hair and an alarmingly pink complexion. He made no effort to disguise his interest in the hand grenade tattooed on Amanda's left breast, only partially obscured by the neckline of

186

her dress.

"All yours," she told the guy, scooching toward Eve to make room. Their knees bumped together, and Eve felt the subtle electric jolt you sometimes get from accidental contact. Amanda shifted again, undoing the connection.

"Ted — that's my ex — used to tell me I was a bad storyteller," Eve continued. "He said it was like a Victorian novel every time I went to the supermarket."

That didn't sound too bad to Amanda. "I like Victorian novels. At least I used to. I haven't read one since college."

"They can be kind of daunting," said Eve. "I've been meaning to start *Middlemarch* for the past year or so. Everybody always says how great it is. But it never seems like the right time to crack it open."

Amanda looked wistful. "There's so much to read, but all I do is watch Netflix and play Candy Crush. I feel like I'm wasting my life."

"It's hard to concentrate after a long day at work. Sometimes you just want to turn your brain off."

"I guess. But even on the weekends, I'll read five pages, and then I have to get up and check my phone. It's not that I want to, it's that I *have* to. It's a physical urge, like the phone is part of my body."

Eve was a little too old to have that sort of relationship with her phone, but she understood the larger point all too well. It was mortifying to be an adult and not be able to control yourself. She didn't used to be like that.

"Hey," she said. "Maybe we could find a retired English professor to talk about Dickens or Jane Austen. We haven't done anything like that for a while."

Amanda's nod was grudging at best. "We *could*. But I was hoping we could maybe try something different. Get outside the box a little."

"Like what?"

"I don't know. There are a lot of fascinating topics out there. Let's hear about global warming or immigration or the rise of feminism or the history of the birth control pill. The anti-vaccine movement. I mean, just because you're old doesn't mean you can't handle a new idea, right?"

Eve heard the implicit criticism in these suggestions. Her policy, ever since she'd taken charge at the Senior Center, had been to avoid controversy when booking the lecture series. No religion, no politics, nothing divisive or threatening. The series, as currently conceived, leaned heavily on nostalgia (FDR and the Greatest Generation, the *Titanic* and the *Hindenburg,* the Civil War and wagon train pioneers), continuing education (Backyard Wildlife, Know Your Night Sky), and uplifting human interest stories (a mountain climber with a high-tech prosthetic leg, an ex-nun turned cabaret singer), with the occasional author appearance or travelogue sprinkled in.

"I hear what you're saying. But you know who we're dealing with. A lot of the seniors are set in their ways. They don't like anything upsetting or unfamiliar. Trust me, they don't want to hear about global warming."

"I get it." Amanda nodded ruefully and tossed back the last swallow of wine in her glass. "I didn't mean to rock the boat."

"It's okay. That's why I hired you. Sometimes the boat needs to be rocked a little."

In the lesbian MILF videos that Eve liked best, there was only one basic scenario: a confident woman seduces a reluctant one. Many began with the reluctant woman grumpily washing dishes or mopping the floor when the doorbell rings. The visitor — the confident one — usually arrives with a bottle of wine, a sympathetic expression, and a bit of exposed cleavage. Cut to the two women on the couch, deep in conversation, usually sitting close together. Often their knees are touching.

It is so good to see you, the confident one says, stroking her friend's thigh or upper arm in a comforting, arguably nonsexual way. *But you look a little sad.*

The reluctant one doesn't deny it.

It's been a rough day, she sighs.

Maybe she lost her job. Maybe her husband left her. Maybe the bank turned down her loan application. But whatever the problem might be, it's nothing that can't be solved by a backrub and some cunnilingus.

Eve relaxed a little once they relocated to the restaurant section. They hadn't planned on eating, but they'd polished off the first two glasses of wine in under an hour, and neither of them wanted to drink a third on an empty stomach. It was only seven o'clock — way too early to call it a night — and a table happened to be available, so here they were.

"I love these potatoes," Amanda said.

"Should we get another order?"

Amanda dabbed at her mouth with the stiff cloth napkin, leaving a smudge of lipstick on the white fabric.

"That's very decadent of you."

"I don't get out much," Eve explained.

"Might as well take advantage."

"You should've come to Foxwoods the other night," Amanda teased. "I could've used the company."

Eve grimaced. "Was it horrible?"

"It was actually okay," Amanda said. "I just felt sorry for Frank Jr. It must be depressing, doing an impersonation of your dead father. At least Nancy got to wear go-go boots and sing some songs of her own."

"She did look good in those boots," Eve said. "But I really don't think they were made for walking."

She glanced around, trying to get a bead on their elusive waiter. Aside from the iffy service, Casa Enzo was as good as everyone said, a cozy tapas place — the first ever in Haddington — with a dozen tables packed into a room that wasn't quite big enough to accommodate them. It was even louder here than at the bar, but at least Eve wasn't experiencing the restlessness that often plagued her in restaurants, the nagging sense that she was marooned at one of the boring tables while the interesting conversations were happening elsewhere.

"We should do this more often," Amanda said. "I'm usually just sitting home on the weekends, eating too much chocolate."

Eve plucked an oily green olive from the bowl. "So you're not seeing anyone?"

Amanda shook her head, more in resignation than sadness. "It's kind of a romantic wasteland around here. There aren't a lot of single people my age. At least I haven't figured out where they're hiding."

Feeling a little self-conscious, Eve removed the olive pit from her mouth and placed it daintily on her plate. There were six of them now, lined up like bullets, with bits of stray flesh stuck to the surface.

"These things are addictive," she said.

"What about you?" Amanda asked. "Are you involved with anyone?"

"Not even close. Haven't had a date in six months. Haven't had a good one in at least two years, and even that one wasn't all that great."

"Really?" Amanda seemed genuinely surprised. "How come? I mean, you're a very attractive woman."

"Thanks. That's sweet of you."

"I'm serious," Amanda insisted. "I hope I look half as good as you when I'm your age."

Eve forced herself to smile, hoping it would hide her irritation.

"Hey," she said. "Did I tell you about the class I'm taking?"

Some of the videos Eve had stumbled upon skipped straight to the bedroom, two naked women already engaged in the usual licking and groping. She clicked out of them as soon as she realized her mistake. She needed to start at the beginning and observe the negotiation, to see how the small talk turned into flirting, to hear the magic words that got the reluctant one to accept the first kiss, or allow her blouse to be unbuttoned.

The really hot part was the epiphany, the moment when the reluctant one suddenly understands that she's been seduced. All the good stuff happened then. The quickening of the breath. The parting of the lips. The silent granting of permission. The understanding that everything that came before had been leading inevitably to *this:* one mouth discovering another, a hand cupping a breast, knees spreading apart. The end of reluctance. When it was good, you could forget you were watching porn and accept it, if not as the truth, then at least as a glimpse of a better world than the one you lived in, a world where everyone secretly wanted the same thing, and no one failed to get it.

■ ■ ■ ■

Dessert arrived and Eve did the honors, poking her spoon through the brittle crust of the crème brûlée into the golden custard below.

"Wow," she said, pushing the dish across the table. "You gotta try this."

Amanda took a little bite. Her eyes widened with theatrical wonder.

"Oh my God. If I'm still single when I'm thirty, I'm going to marry the person who made this."

"I hope you don't mind a ménage à trois," Eve told her, "because I just had the exact same thought. Except for the turning thirty part."

"I'm game if you are." Amanda glanced toward the kitchen. "But I guess we'll have to see what our husband thinks. Or wife."

"I'm sure they won't mind."

Amanda nodded, but her face had turned serious.

"So how old is your professor?"

"Around my age. But she's only been living as a woman for a few years. Before that she was a heterosexual man, a professional athlete with a wife and child. But she was an emotional wreck, self-medicating with alcohol and prescription drugs. She went on a business trip and tried to kill herself with an overdose. Apparently, she came pretty close. When she came out of the coma, the first thing she said was, *I'm a woman. I've been a woman all my life.*"

"That's so cool," Amanda said. "Studying gender theory with a trans professor. You're really lucky."

"It's pretty interesting. She's an attractive woman and there are all these middle-aged straight guys in the class. They don't know what to make of her."

"Really," Amanda said, as if Eve had been holding out on her. "Any cute ones?"

Eve shook her head. "It's a motley crew. And believe me, at this point in my life, my standards are not especially high."

"Come on." Amanda smiled encouragingly. "There's gotta be someone."

Of course there was someone. There always was, at least since junior high. It wasn't a class if you didn't have a little crush on *someone.*

"It's crazy." She lowered her voice, in case anyone nearby was listening. "The only person I'm the least bit attracted to is a kid. Eighteen years old. Just a baby."

Amanda looked delighted. This was better than she'd hoped.

"That's pretty kinky," she said, as if *kinky* were a term of high praise. "I didn't know you liked the young ones."

"It's not like that," Eve said. "I just find myself watching him a lot, thinking, *If only I were your age.*"

"What's he look like?"

"He's really thin, almost like a girl. Not too tall. Long hair. Beautiful eyes."

"Smart?"

"I'm not sure." Eve had only talked to Julian once, and he hadn't said very much. "Kinda hard to pin him down. For the first couple of classes, I thought he might be gay. But it turns out he identifies as straight."

"How'd you find that out?"

"We do these peer interviews where we're supposed to articulate all this stuff people usually just take for granted."

"What did you say?" Amanda seemed genuinely curious, as if Eve's sexuality and gender identity were shrouded in mystery.

"I said straight. Cisgender. Nothing too exciting."

Amanda nodded, as if she'd figured as much. Did she look disappointed, maybe just a little? Eve wished she could qualify her answer, explain that she was very turned on by lesbian porn at the moment, and was trying to figure out what that meant. But she'd need a few more glasses of wine before she'd dream of making a confession like that.

"So would you ever do it?" Amanda asked. "Hook up with a guy that young?"

"No way." Eve grimaced at the thought. "He went to high school with my son. I'm old enough to be his mother."

"You're a MILF," Amanda said, very matter-of-factly. "It happens."

Eve was momentarily startled by the term, and the ease with which Amanda had used it in public. In her mind, it was a dirty word, not to be spoken out loud. But also a compliment.

"I don't know about that," she said, smiling modestly.

"Look at it this way," Amanda told her. "If a guy your age went out with a college girl, people would congratulate him."

"I wouldn't. I'd think he was a creep. And I'd feel sorry for the girl."

"Even if she didn't feel sorry for herself?"

"It's not gonna happen," Eve said. "It's not even in the realm of possibility."

"I'm sure the kid would be thrilled. It's like a porn fantasy come true. *I did it with my best friend's mom.*"

"They're not best friends. They barely knew each other."

Amanda scraped the last bit of crème brûlée from the bowl. Her face turned thoughtful as she sucked on her spoon.

"I wouldn't mind dating a younger guy. I've only been hooking up with older men lately, and I could definitely use a change."

"Really? How much older?"

"Mostly forties. Some fifties."

"Wow." Eve nodded in a way that she hoped came off as nonjudgmental. "Is that a preference or just a coincidence?"

"Little of both." Amanda's tongue flicked out, expertly removing a stray dab of cream from her upper lip. "They're nicer than guys my age."

"Where do you meet them?"

"Tinder, mostly." She watched Eve closely, trying to gauge her reaction.

"So you meet strange guys and have sex with them?"

Eve wanted the question back as soon as she'd asked it. But Amanda didn't seem to mind.

"They're not *that* strange," she said, smiling at her own joke.

In the videos Eve liked best, the women were friends or neighbors or former romantic partners. Some of the other scenarios were a little more problematic, playing on age and power differentials that would have raised serious red flags in real life. A teacher doesn't think a pupil's been working up to her potential. A homesick foreign exchange student needs a little cheering up. A cougarish stepmother puts the moves on her sullen, but very persuadable, stepdaughter.

In the porn world, no one seemed to have heard of sexual harassment. Doctors went down on their patients. Personal trainers fondled their clients. Underperforming employees found creative ways to save their jobs. Eve would have objected strenuously to these scenarios if a man had been involved. But with two women, it was different somehow — a little more playful, and not nearly as creepy. Just a harmless fantasy, rather than something that reminded you of an infuriating article you'd read in the paper, or a bad experience recounted by a friend.

"There was a girl in my dorm who transitioned," Amanda said. "It was an amazing thing to watch. When she showed up freshman year, she was so plain and quiet nobody even noticed her. Then she cut her hair and started dressing like a boy. Sophomore year she began the hormone therapy. Junior year her voice got deep, and it was like, *I'm not*

199

Linda anymore. Please call me Lowell. That summer Lowell got the top surgery. By the end of senior year he was this buff, handsome dude with a scruffy beard and a motorcycle. Lots of girls I knew dated him. It got to be sort of a thing, you know? Like, cross that one off the bucket list."

Eve nodded, but the story sounded so foreign to her. When she'd been in college, there was a woman on campus with patches of dark hair on her face, but nobody thought she was cool or intriguing. People mostly just felt sorry for the poor girl, and did their best not to stare. Eve assumed she was suffering from a medical condition or some kind of cosmic misfortune. It had never even occurred to her that the bearded woman might be making a choice, moving in the direction of happiness.

"So these girls who dated Lowell," Eve said. "Were they straight or bi or what?"

"All kinds." Amanda lowered her gaze, adjusting the napkin in her lap. "I asked him out for coffee one afternoon. We had a pretty good time. When it was over, he drove me home on his motorcycle, and we made out a little outside my apartment. It got pretty heavy, but when he asked if we could go up to my room, I chickened out. I guess I wasn't ready for whatever that was gonna be, which is saying something, 'cause I was pretty much up for anything back then. But he was totally cool about it. The next time I saw him, he was dating this beautiful Turkish girl from my Milton class."

"That's so amazing," Eve said. "It's like a modern-day Cinderella story. You change your body and your name, and all your dreams come true. I wish I could do that myself."

"Really?"

"Not the man part. Just the chance to leave your old self behind. To take all your mistakes and regrets and erase them from the story. Who wouldn't want that?"

Amanda nodded, as if that made a lot of sense.

"So who would you be? If you could start over?"

"I don't know. I haven't given it a lot of thought."

"What about your name? What would you call yourself?"

"Let's see." Eve closed her eyes, and a name appeared to her unbidden, blue letters stamped on a gift shop license plate. "*Ursula*. I'd call myself Ursula."

"That's a strong name. What's this Ursula like?"

"Braver than me," Eve said. "She does

what she wants. Doesn't worry so much about what everybody else thinks. Doesn't settle for less than she deserves, or apologize unless it's absolutely necessary. She just wants to live and have adventures."

Amanda smiled. "I like this person."

Eve knew she'd said more than enough, but she was on a roll.

"Ursula probably doesn't work at the Senior Center."

"I'm sorry to hear that," Amanda said, but she didn't sound sorry.

"She does something a little more exciting. Maybe she's a travel writer. She wears sunglasses and has lots of affairs."

"She sounds pretty sexy."

Eve scratched at a yellowish stain on the tablecloth, hoping her face wasn't as pink as it felt. She was a little drunk, a little embarrassed, but also strangely exhilarated.

"What about you?" she said. "Who would you be?"

"Juniper." Amanda spoke without hesitation. "I'd be petite and graceful. Maybe a dancer. No tattoos. Just my own beautiful skin. And I'd be naked every chance I got. I'd leave my window shades up, let the whole world look."

"Good for you."

Amanda laughed a little sadly, like she was

unworthy of her own fantasy. Eve wanted to tell her she was beautiful already, but instead she made a toast.

"To Ursula and Juniper."

"Juniper and Ursula," Amanda replied, and they clinked their tiny glasses.

By the time they left the restaurant, Eve had come full circle, back to the idea that this *was* a date, and a pretty good one at that. They'd talked for hours without hitting any dead spots, they'd drunk a little too much wine, they'd laughed and told the truth about their lives.

It was quiet as she walked Amanda to her car, a bracing autumnal chill in the air. The fluttery feeling in Eve's chest was even stronger than it had been before.

"Thanks for dinner," Amanda said. "I really enjoyed it."

"Me too."

Instead of getting in her car, Amanda just stood there, smiling shyly, like she was waiting for something else to happen. Eve wanted to kiss her, but she was paralyzed, unsure about which one of them was the confident one.

It has to be me, she thought.

She was older. She was the boss. But she didn't feel confident at all. She felt lost and scared, like she was floating in space, completely untethered.

And then, almost as if she were reading Eve's mind, Amanda stepped forward, opening her arms and tilting her chin at an inviting angle. Eve swooped in and kissed her on the mouth.

"Whoa!" Amanda stiffened and pulled away with a shocked expression, raising both hands in self-defense. "What are you doing?"

"I'm sorry." Eve was mortified. "I just thought —"

"Wow." Amanda laughed nervously, wiping her wrist across her mouth. The gesture seemed a little excessive — the kiss had only lasted a second, no tongue or saliva involved. "I just wanted to give you a hug."

"Oh, God." Eve hid her face in her hands. "I'm so stupid. I drank too much. I'm so so sorry."

"It's okay," Amanda told her, still sounding a little shocked. "It's no big deal."

"Yes it is," Eve muttered into her palm. "I shouldn't have done that. It wasn't right."

"Really. It's okay."

Eve uncovered her face. "Are you sure?"

"Don't worry." Amanda touched her gently on the arm. "I won't tell anyone. I promise."

Eve felt a little sick. She hadn't thought about the possibility of Amanda *telling* anyone.

"Thank you," she said. "I would really appreciate that."

She drove home in a fog of regret, wondering how she could have done something so irresponsible, so unlike herself. Was she that lonely, that desperate for sexual contact? It made no sense, taking a risk like that — jeopardizing her job, her home, her son's college education — just to pretend for a night that she was living in a porn video.

You are so stupid, she told herself, trying not to think about the bitter disappointment she'd felt when Amanda's lips had failed to open.

She was normally a careful person — careful to a fault — and now she'd gone and put her livelihood in the hands of a young woman she barely knew, a girl with a grenade tattooed on her chest, probably not the best decision-maker in the world. It was a terrible thing to hand someone that kind of power, even someone who claimed to be your friend.

She wanted to call Amanda and repeat her apology, let her know that it would never happen again, that their relationship would be cordial and professional for however long Amanda remained at the Senior Center. But maybe a call wasn't the best idea, not so soon. Maybe that would only aggravate the situation, make it seem like a bigger deal than it already was. But she had to say *something,* for her own peace of mind, so she sent the blandest text she could think of:

You okay?

Yeah, Amanda replied, almost immediately. *Fine.*

Are we still friends?

Totally, Amanda replied, with a smiley face added for reassurance.

A moment later, another text arrived, a single word trapped in a separate bubble.

Ursula

Just the name, no exclamation mark. It looked sad like that, all alone, dead on arrival.

"This is Ellen." The freckly redhead handed her phone to the hipster Asian dude sitting next to her. "She's twenty-two and fairly high-functioning. She has a GED and works full time at CVS. She's a really good cashier, as long as the customers don't ask a lot of questions or try to use an expired coupon. She used to freak out when people made small talk, but she's trained herself to handle the common stuff."

The Asian guy took a quick glance at the screen, then passed the phone to Amber, who made a point of staring at it for a long time, because everybody's autistic sibling was uniquely wonderful and important. It was easy to see why she'd been elected president of the club as a sophomore.

"She looks so serious," Amber said. "I bet she's really smart." She passed the phone to her veep, a petite sorority girl named Cat who kept a jumbo dispenser of Purell in her purse and squirted it on her hands every five minutes. The whole room reeked of it. "What was it like for you, having a big sister like Ellen?"

The redhead's smile wilted a little.

"It was hard," she said. "For a long time I didn't understand that everybody's big sister wasn't like mine. But then I started to realize something was wrong. When I was in first grade this girl named Tierney came to my house to play Barbies. It was her first visit. Ellen barged into my room and asked Tierney what her birthday was, and then she asked about Tierney's mother's birthday, and her father's birthday, and the birthdays of her siblings. And then she said, *What about your dog? What's your dog's birthday?* And Tierney — I'll never forget it — she just looked at me, totally matter-of-fact, and said, *Why's she so stupid?* I didn't know how to answer that, so I threw my Barbie at Ellen and screamed, *Leave us alone, stupid!*"

The redhead took a moment to collect herself.

"This is a safe space," Amber said. "No one's judging you. It's a challenge to have a sibling on the spectrum. That's why we're here. To listen and support each other."

The redhead looked relieved. "The weird thing was, Ellen didn't even care that I called her stupid. I'm not sure she even heard it. She just kept talking in this robot voice she uses sometimes: *I know three people who were born on March 10th who aren't triplets and two people who were born on March 2nd who aren't twins. I've never met anyone who was born on November 8th, not even a dog or a cat.* I was just sitting there, dying inside. I looked at Tierney and I said, *She can't help it, she was born that way,* and Tierney said, *I feel sorry for you.*"

"That Tierney sounds like an ice-cold bitch," said the veep, going to town with the Purell.

"She's actually my best friend," said the redhead. "She's really nice to Ellen now. She just didn't know any better."

By that point the phone had made its way to me. The photo on the screen had been taken at the redhead's high school graduation. She was wearing a cap and gown, and Ellen was standing next to her in a shiny green dress, holding her arms way out from her body, like maybe the material bothered her skin.

"That's great to hear," Amber said, and for some reason she was staring straight at me. "That's how we change the world. One person at a time."

■ ■ ■ ■

We were about an hour into the meeting at that point, and already I was itching for it to be over. There are only so many stories you can listen to about somebody's autistic brother or sister.

I was only there for Amber, who I hadn't seen since the night we protested in the library. I'd texted her a bunch of times in the past week, trying to get her to meet me for coffee or pizza or whatever, but she kept putting me off, saying that she'd see me at the October meeting of the Autism Awareness Network and we could make a plan then. She was so insistent about the meeting that I started to wonder if she saw me more as a new recruit than as a guy she might want to hook up with, but I liked her enough that it was worth a couple hours of my time to figure out which it was.

So far things were looking pretty good on the hookup side of the equation. She had let out a happy little squeal when I walked through the door, and then led me around the room, introducing me to her friends like I was some kind of VIP.

"This is Brendan," she told the veep. "He's the first year I was telling you about.

Brendan, this is Cat."

"Hey, Brendan." Cat looked me up and down, like she was thinking about buying me. "Amber was hoping you'd come."

"Shut up!" Amber told her, her cheeks a shade pinker than normal. Instead of her usual sweats and hoodie, she was wearing skinny jeans and a tight top and sexy platform sandals, the kind of clothes you'd wear to a party, or on a date. She had nice small boobs — I hadn't really gotten a good look at them before — that went really well with her athletic build.

"All I meant is that we need more men in the group," Cat said with a smirk, reaching into her purse for the Purell. "I wasn't trying to insinuate anything."

"It's true." Amber glanced at the Asian hipster, who was standing in a circle of girls, basking in the attention. "Usually it's just Kwan. I'm sure he'll be happy to have a bro."

"I don't know," I said, because Kwan was giving me the stink eye, like I'd crashed his party. "Looks like he's doing fine without me."

Cat headed over to the refreshment table, leaving me alone with Amber.

"I'm so glad you came," she said, placing her hand on my forearm, super-casual, like she didn't even know she was doing it. But I knew. I felt it way down in my balls, a warm surge of power, like someone had just turned a key and started the engine.

After the break, a girl named Nellie told us about her brother, who was really smart but flapped his hands and grunted a lot, which made it hard to take him anywhere. Three girls in a row said they had siblings with Asperger's. This other girl, Dora, said she was the only normal kid out of four siblings. The other three were all diagnosed PDDNOS, and one of them was totally nonverbal. Amber suggested that Dora stop using the word *normal* and substitute *neurotypical* instead.

"It's less hurtful that way," she explained. "And besides — in your family, it actually seems like autism is the norm, right?"

Dora shrugged. "My mom always calls me her normal one. That's how she introduces me to strangers. *This is Dora. She's my normal one.*"

The hipster, Kwan, had a brother named Zhang who acted out too much to go to a regular school. He was totally hyper and would run around in circles whenever he got worked up. The only thing that calmed him down was playing the piano. When he was seven years old, he sat down and played "The Entertainer," from that old movie *The Sting.* It came out of nowhere. No one in the family had seen the movie, and Kwan's parents were first-generation immigrants who only listened to European classical music. But Zhang totally nailed it.

"My parents were so happy that day," Kwan said. "It was like, *Oh my God, our son's a genius!* They were really proud of Zhang, which was amazing to see, because they were usually pretty ashamed of his condition, and didn't know how to help him. They hired a piano teacher who specialized in kids with special needs, and did everything they could to encourage his gift."

Kwan stopped talking and looked around, in case anyone had any questions. He was wearing cuffed jeans, a tight plaid shirt with the sleeves rolled up to his biceps, and a beige fedora, but I liked him anyway.

"That's so cool," Cat said. "Does he play classical or jazz?"

Kwan shrugged. "He plays 'The Entertainer.' Over and over and over. Every fucking day of his life. Every time I call home I hear him in the background, banging it out: dada dada DA DA da DA DA! I hate that song."

My little half brother was autistic, but I hadn't grown up with him. I was already in high school when he was born, and I wasn't getting along with my father at the time, or with my stepmother, Bethany, who I liked to think of as The Evil Bitch Who Ruined My Life. I realize now that it was stupid to blame her for the divorce; it wasn't like she brainwashed my dad and kidnapped him from my mom and me. Whatever my dad did, he did because *he* chose to do it. Because he *wanted* to. I still remember the day he explained that to me. He took me out for ice cream, put his arm around my shoulders, and said, *Look, Brendan, if you have to hate somebody for what happened, hate me, okay? Don't take it out on Bethany. She's an innocent bystander, just like you.*

The custody agreement said he'd get me two weekends a month, but he didn't complain if I blew him off for a sleepover at a friend's house, or even if I just needed to stay home and catch up on my schoolwork. I was playing three sports at the time — football, basketball, and lacrosse — so mostly he just came to my weekend games and took me out to dinner afterward. That was pretty much our relationship right after the divorce — my dad and me at Wild Willie's or Haddington Burrito Works, talking about whatever game I'd just played, acting like everything was perfectly normal, like this was how it was supposed to be.

I saw him even less right after Jon-Jon was born. There wasn't one specific day when he sat me down and said, *There's something seriously wrong with your brother.* It was more like a steady drip of bad news. They didn't know why he wasn't talking, why he ignored his toys, why he wouldn't look his father in the eye or smile at his mother. The doctors had concerns about the severity of his tantrums.

By the time they were openly using the word *autistic,* I was getting along better with my dad, and even with Bethany, who had turned out to be a nicer person than I'd given her credit for. She was a lot younger than my mom and had been pretty hot when my dad married her, but she'd aged a lot in the past few years. You could see in her eyes how hard it was, having a kid like Jon-Jon, and you couldn't help but feel a little sorry for her.

There was a brief period during my junior year when we tried to be a two-weekend-a-month family. I'd pack my bag, and my dad would pick me up on the way home from work and bring me to his new house.

The only problem was that Jon-Jon freaked out whenever I showed up. He didn't just get upset — he totally fucking lost it. Bethany would be all fake cheerful when I got there, like, *Hey, Jon-Jon, look who's here. It's your big brother! Can you say hi to Brendan?* Jon-Jon wouldn't even look at me. He just waved his arms around and screamed like I was a monster who was coming to eat him. Sometimes he'd throw himself on the ground or start punching himself in the head, which was a terrible thing to see, because he wasn't fooling around. Once he got going on a meltdown like that, he could keep it up for hours. When he finally wore himself out and fell asleep, the rest of us would have a little time to hang out in peace, except it wasn't really peace, because we were all so rattled by what had just happened. We'd play a game or two of Yahtzee and then Bethany would head up to bed, and my dad and I would watch an episode of *Scrubs,* which we both loved. Those were some of the best father-and-son times I can remember, the two of us sitting on the couch, cracking up about something completely ridiculous that J.D. said to Turk. It felt really good, just being in the same place, enjoying the same thing. When the show was over, he'd kiss me good night — something he never used to do before the divorce — and we'd both go up to bed. Then I'd wake up the next morning, head downstairs for breakfast, and Jon-Jon would start screaming all over again.

It was hard on everybody, so we eventually gave up and went back to the old way — me and my dad getting together for the occasional dinner, talking about sports and TV shows and college and girls. He was easy to talk to, a lot easier than my mom, though that was probably just because he was a guy, and because he never gave me the feeling that he was judging me, or wishing I was a different person than I actually am. I always made sure to ask him about Jon-Jon, and he always said something positive, like *He's getting big,* or, *He really likes his new teacher,* but I never pressed for details. Jon-Jon's life was a mystery to me. I had no idea what he did all day, what he thought about, or why he hated me so much. Mostly I just lived my own life without thinking about him at all.

I wasn't planning on going into my whole family history at the meeting, but Amber just sort of coaxed it out of me. After a while

I forgot about the other people in the room. It was just me talking and Amber listening.

I told her how my father had invited himself to Parents Weekend, catching me totally off-guard. I thought that was a great idea — I hadn't seen him since the week before I left for school — but said he'd have to work it out with my mom, because she was planning on coming, too, and they didn't usually do stuff like that together.

I'll talk to the boss, he said. *Throw myself on the mercy of the court.*

I have no idea how he managed it, but he called a week later and said he'd gotten the thumbs-up. The plan was for my dad to come on his own, because it didn't make any sense to bring Jon-Jon to an event like Parents Weekend. He hated long car rides, responded badly to new environments, and was often freaked out by unfamiliar faces. It would be easier for everybody if he stayed home with his mom and followed the usual routine. Easier for everybody except Bethany, I guess.

It'll just be us guys, my dad said. *Maybe we can go to the football game. If Zack wants to join us, he's more than welcome.*

Zack was totally up for that. He and my dad had talked on the phone a few times, and Zack told everybody what a chill guy he was, way chiller than his own parents, who, he was happy to report, were staying home in Boxborough for the weekend. His little sister was competing in an Irish step dance competition, and that was a big deal in his house.

You ever see that shit, bro? It's like these girls are all dancing with a stick up their ass, and smiling like it's the best feeling in the world.

We had the whole day planned. Commandos game in the afternoon, barbecue on the quad for dinner, and then this student talent show that people raved about. They did it like *American Idol,* with these smart-ass professors acting as judges. Apparently, one of them was a total dick, just like Simon Cowell, and everybody loved him.

Who knows? Zack said. *Maybe your dad'll get drunk with us.*

Yeah, right.

I'm serious, bro. You think he still smokes weed?

Dude, he's not gonna smoke weed with us. Trust me.

We should take him to a party, Zack said. *Maybe we could get him laid.*

Don't even go there, I said.

For the whole week leading up to Parents

Weekend, that was the big joke in our room, all the wild shit we were gonna do with my dad. I knew none of it would happen, but it was fun to think about, and put us both in this goofy, stoked-up mood, like something big was about to happen.

And then, the day before Parents Weekend, I got the phone call.

Change of plans, he said. *I'm really sorry.*

You're not coming?

No, no. I'm still coming. But I'm bringing the gang.

The gang?

Bethany and Jon-Jon.

Oh. What was I supposed to say? You couldn't tell your dad not to bring his wife and kid. *All right. Sure.*

You okay with that?

I guess. I mean, I only have three tickets for the football game, and one of 'em is for Zack.

Yeah, he said. *I'm not so sure about the football game. Think I can take a rain check?*

They showed up around eleven on Saturday morning. I hadn't seen Jon-Jon in about six months, and I almost didn't recognize him. He was a lot bigger than I remembered. He was really cute, blond hair and blue eyes, and those long eyelashes that everybody who met him commented on. Bethany had dressed him in khakis and a button-down shirt and a little denim jacket. He looked like a model in a Gap Kids catalogue, but that wasn't the main thing. He just seemed more together than the kid I remembered. He was actually looking in my general direction and not screaming his head off.

Look, Bethany told him. *It's your big brother. Brendan's in college. This is where he lives. Why don't you say hi to Brendan.*

Jon-Jon took this all in.

Hello, he said, addressing the word to my knees. His voice was soft and mechanical, and the word sounded almost foreign, but still, he fucking said it.

Wow, I said.

I know. Bethany looked so happy. *He's doing great. We finally found the right school.*

He was pretty good in the car, my dad added. *Hardly complained at all.*

They came in and I introduced them to Zack, who totally rose to the occasion, making small talk like an Eagle Scout. Jon-Jon was standing in the middle of the room, lost inside his head, while the rest of us chatted about how nice the dorms were compared to the ones my father and Bethany had lived in back in the day. It was the usual story — they got treated like shit and we got treated like kings.

I saw the lounge on the way in, my dad said. *That's a big TV!*

And that communal kitchen, Bethany said. *Jeez. I wouldn't mind living here for a few months.*

At some point, Jon-Jon took a couple of steps in my direction. I thought he was maybe gonna hug me or sit on my lap, but he was just coming to examine the fabric of the couch I was sitting on, the one Zack and I had found on the street at the beginning of the semester. It had a weird texture, kinda fuzzy but also a little slick — almost greasy — and Jon-Jon seemed fascinated by it. He reached out his hand, very slowly, and started stroking the armrest, as if it were a living thing. For a while, the conversation stopped, and we all just watched him.

I think he likes it here, Bethany told us.

Before lunch we went for a walk. Zack stayed behind, claiming he had work to do, so it was just me, my dad, Bethany, and Jon-Jon. There were lots of official tours available throughout the weekend, but my dad and Bethany didn't think Jon-Jon was ready for something like that. Better to go at our own pace and not bother anyone else, even if that meant they had to listen to my feeble attempts to impersonate a college student

222

who actually knew what he was talking about.

Uh . . . I think that's a science building. Maybe Chemistry. I'm really not sure. Could be Sociology.

Yeah, so this is the new gym. It's a lot nicer than the old one. That's what everybody says. I guess the old one smelled really bad.

So those are bike racks. Maybe I'll bring my bike next year. I just need to inflate the tires.

I'm not sure who that statue is. Some dude from the nineteen hundreds. Guess I should read the plaque.

I felt like a dumbass, blathering on like that, but my dad and Bethany seemed happy enough. Whatever I said, one of them would repeat it to Jon-Jon in simplified language. *Look at the bicycles . . . Look at the statue . . . That's where people go to exercise.* Sometimes Jon-Jon would look where they were pointing, but most of the time he would stare at whatever he felt like staring at. A tree. His own hand. Nothing at all.

I could see why they were in such a good mood. Given the way things usually went with Jon-Jon, it was a minor miracle to be outside on a beautiful day, walking around a public place like a relatively normal family. I met Bethany's eyes a couple of times, and she gave me this shocked, excited look, like, *Oh my God, can you believe this?* I felt pretty good about it myself. It wasn't the fun day that I'd planned, but it was still kinda nice in its own way.

We were walking toward the library, Bethany and Jon-Jon trailing behind my dad and me. I was telling him about my Econ class, leaving out the part about my D average, when he turned to check on his wife and son.

Oh shit, he said.

It didn't seem like a big deal at first. Jon-Jon had stopped walking. He was just sort of frozen in place, staring up at the sky. Bethany stood right beside him, looking at my dad with a worried expression on her face.

What's wrong? I asked.

My dad shook his head and starting walking toward Jon-Jon, moving slowly and carefully. He spoke his son's name in a soft voice, but Jon-Jon didn't seem to hear it. His attention was focused like a laser beam on the small plane that was flying overhead at a low altitude, trailing a banner that read, *WELCOME PARENTS!*

He hates airplanes, Bethany explained. *It's one of his things.*

The plane was directly overhead, buzzing like a giant insect. Jon-Jon let out a yelp, quick and shrill, like someone had jabbed him with a pin. Then he did it again, this time even louder. I could see people turning in our direction, squinting in confusion. Jon-Jon slapped himself in the head.

I'm sorry, Bethany told me. *He was being so good.*

It was hard enough to deal with one of Jon-Jon's meltdowns in the house, but it was way worse with all those strangers around. A gray-haired lady in a BSU sweatshirt wandered over, asking if the poor thing was okay. Bethany fished a business card from her purse and handed it to the woman. They'd gotten the cards printed up the year before, after an epic tantrum at Target.

Please don't be alarmed, it said. *Our son Jonathan has been diagnosed with autism and sometimes needs to be physically restrained to avoid injury to himself and others. We love Jonathan very much and only want to keep him safe. Thank you for your understanding.*

The plane banked away from us, moving toward the football stadium, but I don't think Jon-Jon even noticed. He was rocking from side to side, moaning and clutching his head. And then he punched himself.

225

Hard, right above his ear. Like it was somebody else's head he was punching, somebody he hated.

Please don't do that, Bethany told him.

My father sat down on the grass and hugged him from behind, trying to pin his arms, but Jon-Jon fought like crazy to break free, thrashing and screaming like a trapped animal.

The struggle only lasted a few minutes, but it felt a lot longer. Every time it looked like my dad had Jon-Jon under control, one of his arms would slip free, and he'd start punching himself again. And then my dad would have to grab that arm without losing control of Jon-Jon's other limbs. It almost looked like a game, except that Jon-Jon was drooling and my father's nose was bleeding from a backwards head butt. Even so, he just kept speaking quietly the whole time, telling his son that he loved him and that everything would be okay. A pretty good crowd had gathered by then, and Bethany was handing a card to each new arrival, apologizing for the disturbance.

"They sound like great parents," Amber said, when I'd finished with the story.

"Yeah," I said. "They're really patient with him."

"What about you?" she asked. "How did

you feel while that was happening?"

"I just felt sorry for them," I told her.

That part was true. I really did feel bad for my dad and Bethany, and even for Jon-Jon, because I knew he couldn't help himself. What I didn't tell her was how sorry I felt for myself, and how jealous I was of my little brother, even though that was totally ridiculous. Jon-Jon had a hard life, and I would never want to trade places with him. But that whole time, while he was screaming and thrashing around, I kept thinking how unfair it was that my father loved him so much and held him so tight — way tighter than he'd ever held me — and wouldn't let go no matter what.

THE HUMAN CONDITION

At the end of the Tuesday night seminar, white-bearded Barry raised his hand and invited the whole class to reconvene for a nightcap at his sports bar.

"I don't know about you guys," he said, "but all this talk about gender makes me thirsty!"

The initial response to Barry's overture was lukewarm — it was late, people had work in the morning — but public opinion shifted when he added that drinks would be on the house.

"Now that you mention it," said Russ, the fanatical hockey fan, "I could definitely go for a free beer."

"That's the spirit," said Barry. "What's the point of being in college if we don't socialize outside the classroom? That's like half your education right there."

"Does that include hard liquor?" Dumell ruefully patted his mid-section. "I'm watching my carbs."

"Within reason," Barry told him. "I'm not breaking out the Pappy Van Winkle."

"Don't worry about that," Dumell assured him. "I'm a cheap date. Just ask my ex-wife."

Eve had no intention of joining the party. She'd been dodging Barry's invitations to get a drink after class for the past two months and didn't want to offer him the slightest encouragement, not that he needed any. Barry was one of those guys who didn't know the meaning of rejection; he just kept trying and trying and trying. His persistence might have been flattering if it hadn't felt so smug and entitled — so steeped in male privilege — as if there was no possible way she could outlast him in a battle of romantic wills.

Hoping to avoid any unpleasantness in the parking lot — Barry sometimes lurked outside the exit and then attached himself to Eve as she walked to her car — she ducked into the ladies' room and killed a few minutes in the stall, playing several turns on Words with Friends (random opponent, not very good) and then peeing, not because she needed to, but because she was already sitting on a toilet and it seemed foolish not to. She washed her hands with

229

excessive diligence and checked her face in the mirror — an unbreakable, though less and less rewarding, habit — before leaving the rest room and almost colliding with Dr. Fairchild, who was standing outside the door, her lanky basketball player's frame augmented by businesslike heels.

"Eve." She sounded concerned but vaguely reproachful. "Are you okay?"

"Fine. Why?"

"You were in there for quite a while." The professor heard herself and grimaced, mortified by her own rudeness. "Not that it's any of my business."

"Great class tonight," Eve said, trying to cut through the awkwardness.

Dr. Fairchild gave a distracted nod and then asked, with some urgency, "Are you going? To the bar?"

"I wasn't planning on it."

"Oh." Dr. Fairchild couldn't hide her disappointment. "I was hoping you were."

"Are *you*?"

"I was thinking about it. Might be fun, right?"

Huh. Eve hadn't given a lot of thought to the professor's idea of fun, but it hardly seemed like drinking at a sports bar with guys like Barry and Russ would be high on her list.

"It's been a long day," Eve explained. "I'm kinda wiped out."

"I just —" Dr. Fairchild flipped her hair over her shoulder, first one side, then the other, her favorite nervous gesture. "I really don't want to go there by myself."

"You won't be by yourself. Sounds like a bunch of them are going."

"I know." A pleading note had entered the professor's voice. "It's just a lot easier to walk in with a girlfriend. Especially at a place like that."

Eve was puzzled, but also touched, by the professor's use of the word *girlfriend.* Until this moment, they'd never even had a conversation outside of class.

"I guess I could get a drink," she said. "Just one, though. Tomorrow's a workday."

"Thank you." Dr. Fairchild leaned down and gave Eve a hug. "I really appreciate this."

"No problem. So I guess I'll see you over there?"

Dr. Fairchild's smile was also an apology. She knew she was pushing her luck.

"Could you maybe give me a ride?" she asked. "That way I can't chicken out."

Ten minutes later, they were parked outside of Barry's bar, a squat brick building that had the unappealing name of *PLAY BALL!* emblazoned on the front awning, with a baseball bat standing in for the exclamation point. Dr. Fairchild didn't seem in any hurry to leave the car.

"I have very big feet," she said. "It's not easy to find cute shoes in my size."

"Those are nice," Eve observed. "You can't go wrong with black pumps."

"You should see my red stilettos. I can barely walk in them, but they look really hot. I just don't have many opportunities to wear them at the moment."

"I've pretty much given up on heels," Eve told her. "At my age, I'd rather be comfortable."

"You're not that old."

"Forty-six. Not young, that's for sure."

"I'm not that much younger than you," Dr. Fairchild pointed out. "I guess I'm trying to make up for lost time. I missed out on my best years."

In the bright public sphere of the classroom, Eve never had a problem accepting Dr. Fairchild as a woman. In that context — a teacher interacting with students, deconstructing outmoded concepts of masculinity and femininity — she seemed like an embodiment of the curriculum, her theory and practice a continuous whole. In a minivan outside a sports bar, however, the professor's gender identity seemed a little more precarious, as much wish as reality. It was partly the timbre of her voice in the darkness, and partly just the size of her body in the passenger seat, the way she filled the available space.

I can see who you were, Eve thought. *One self on top of the other.*

As soon as this uncharitable image occurred to her, she did her best to erase it from her mind. She wasn't the gender police. Her job — her *responsibility* — was to be kind and supportive, and not to judge the success or failure of somebody else's transformation.

"You look really pretty," she said.

"I'm trying." Dr. Fairchild's chuckle was tinged with anxiety. "Every day's an adventure, right?"

"I wish."

"At least that's what my therapist tells me. I think she's just trying to cheer me up."

"Is everything okay?"

Dr. Fairchild stared out the windshield while she considered the question. The only thing in front of them was a brick wall.

"It was my daughter's birthday last weekend," she said. "Her name is Millicent. She just turned eight."

"That's a sweet age."

"We threw her a party, my ex-wife and I. And some of the other parents came by at the end, and it wasn't like they were mean to me or anything. But I could see I made them uncomfortable, and my daughter saw it, too. They stood as far away from me as possible. Like whatever I had might be contagious."

"I'm sure they didn't mean anything by it," Eve said. "It just takes people time, you know?"

Dr. Fairchild examined her manicure. "If it wasn't for Millie, I'd probably just move to New York or L.A. Just get far away from all this suburban bullshit."

"If that's what you want to do, you should do it. New York's not that far."

"It's too expensive," Dr. Fairchild said. "And it's not like it's gonna make any difference. Doesn't matter where you live. You're always just kind of alone with your shit, you know?"

"It's the human condition," Eve told her.

Dr. Fairchild turned away from the wall.

"You're as bad as my therapist," she said, but it sounded like a compliment.

Julian Spitzer wasn't old enough to drink legally — not even close — but none of the adults objected when he poured himself a glass of beer from the communal pitcher, and then another one after that. That was the upside of going out to a bar on a Tuesday night with a bunch of middle-aged people. You just sort of slipped in under the radar. Nobody bothered to check your fake ID or otherwise give you a second glance, especially if you happened to be sitting with the owner of the bar, which, he had to admit, was pretty fucking cool.

The downside of this situation was that he was stuck at a dump called PLAY BALL!, surrounded by people twice his age who were talking among themselves about the kind of unbelievably boring crap people that age liked to talk about — dental benefits, kale, lower back pain. He might as well have been hanging out with his parents, except that his parents never would have seated him directly in front of a pitcher of Bud Light or whatever weak-ass beer this was and then pretended not to notice while he imbibed to his heart's content.

This wasn't the kind of news you could ethically keep to yourself, so he snapped a pic of the half-empty pitcher and shot it off to his friend Ethan, who was having a blast at UVM.

Dude I'm getting WASTED with a bunch of

*old farts from my Gender and Society class!
How fucked up is that?*

Until he typed this message, Julian was unaware of the fact that he was in the process of getting *WASTED*. But once he saw the word *WASTED* throbbing like a prophecy inside the green text balloon, it struck him with the force of undeniable truth. Because, really, why shouldn't he get *WASTED*? He'd been in college for almost two months and this was the first time he'd partied with his fellow students, or with anyone else, for that matter. It had not been a very exciting fall.

His phone pinged right away: *That's what you get for going to community college, asshole!*

Dumell, one of two black guys in the class — he was the African-American, not the Nigerian — heard the chime and elbowed him in the arm.

"Message from your girlfriend?"

"One of 'em," Julian replied.

Dumell chuckled. "How many you got?"

"Hard to keep count."

"Listen to you, player. I bet they love it when you roll up on your skateboard."

"What can I say?" Julian told him. "I'm a fuel-efficient lover."

Dumell considered the metaphor.

"Guess that makes me a gas-guzzler," he said. "Old-school Detroit. Ten miles to the gallon highway. But it's a smooth ride, if you know what I'm saying."

Barry, their host, pounded on the table, sparing Julian the need for further banter.

"Welcome, fellow scholars," Barry said. "I'm glad you all could make it. And I'm especially delighted that our esteemed professor has decided to grace us with her presence. Dr. Fairchild, it's a privilege to have you in my humble neighborhood tavern. You really class up the joint."

Dr. Fairchild blushed and waved off the compliment as the students drank a toast in her honor. Julian made a point of clinking glasses with everyone at the table — Barry, Dumell, Russ, the professor, Eve (Brendan Fletcher's mom, weirdly enough), the hilariously named Mr. Ho (who spoke very little English), and Gina (the chatty motorcycle dyke). Aside from Barry, who was one of those *I'm-an-asshole-and-proud-of-it* guys, Julian liked them all just fine, and he was even feeling okay about Barry, considering that he was picking up the tab.

Fuck you, he texted Ethan. *These are my people.*

Julian knew he was too smart for Eastern

Community College. Everybody said so — his parents, his teachers, his friends, his former guidance counselor, who was a bit of a dick, but still. He had the GPA and the SATs to get into a good four-year school, and his parents had the money to pay for it, or so they said. It was just that senior year of high school had been a total bust — he'd been seriously depressed for most of it — and he hadn't been able to complete his applications in a timely fashion.

He didn't start feeling better until the beginning of summer — they'd adjusted his meds for the fourth or fifth time, and finally stumbled on the magic formula — and by then it was way too late to get in anywhere decent. His parents and shrink agreed that it would be wise for him to take a few classes at ECC, *to get his feet wet,* as they insisted on putting it. If he liked it and got good grades, he could transfer somewhere better for sophomore year, somewhere *more commensurate with his abilities.*

Julian hadn't expected much from community college, and for the most part ECC had lived up to his low expectations. His Math class was a joke, way easier than high school. He regularly dozed off in Bio and still got A-pluses on the first two tests. Gender and Society was the only exception to this general rule of mediocrity. It was a wild card, a night class full of rando adults, taught by a female professor who'd been born a male and had *transitioned,* as she liked to say, in her late thirties, which definitely enhanced Julian's academic experience. It was one thing to have a professor tell you that gender was socially constructed, and another to hear it from a person who had actually done construction work.

There was a lot of funky jargon in the reading assignments — *cisgender* and *heteronormative* and *dysphoria* and *performativity* and on and on — but he didn't mind. It was one of those classes that actually made you *think,* in this case about stuff that was so basic it never even occurred to you to question it, all the little rules that got shoveled into your head when you were a kid and couldn't defend yourself. Girls wear pink, boys wear blue. Boys are tough. Girls are sweet. Women are caregivers with soft bodies. Men are leaders with hard muscles. Girls get looked at. Guys do the looking. Hairy armpits. Pretty fingernails. This one can but that one can't. The Gender Commandments were endless, once you started thinking about them, and they were enforced 24/7 by a highly motivated volunteer army of parents, neighbors, teachers, coaches, other kids, and total strangers — basically, the whole human race.

Any hot chicks? Ethan texted.

Ha ha, Julian replied.

Sad to say, it was slim pickings in Gender and Society. The only halfway hot female close to his own age was Salima, the Muslim babe, and she wore a fucking headscarf. The rest of her clothes were normal enough, and she had a cute round face, but that headscarf was black and forbidding. When they'd interviewed each other, she told him she didn't drink, date, or dance — which explained her unfortunate but totally predictable absence at the bar — and was saving herself for marriage to a good Muslim guy. She said she was happy being a woman, except that just once she'd like to know what it felt like to punch someone in the face.

Only three ladies at the table. A dyke, Brendan Fletcher's mom, and my professor

The tranny? Ethan texted back. *Holy shit!*

Julian snuck a guilty glance at Professor Fairchild, who was deep in conversation with Mrs. Fletcher. Early in the semester, he had unthinkingly used the word *tranny* to describe his teacher, before she'd had a chance to explain how offensive it was, and now his friends wouldn't stop using it, no matter how many times Julian asked them not to. They insisted that *tranny* was just a harmless abbreviation, and called Julian a pussy for scolding them about it.

She's a nice person, he wrote.

Hot?

They'd been over this ground before.

Not especially

Professor Fairchild wasn't a freak or anything, far from it. She was what his mother would have called an *attractive older woman.* She wore tasteful conservative suits like a lady lawyer on TV, always with a colorful scarf tied around her neck. Lots of makeup and nice perfume. A little manly around the jaw, but otherwise pretty convincing.

What about Fletcher's mom?

This was a harder question. Mrs. Fletcher actually *was* kind of pretty, as much as he hated to admit it. Not in a young woman way, but *pretty-for-her-age,* which he didn't know exactly, beyond the obvious fact that she was old enough to be his mother. She had a nice face, maybe a little sad around the eyes, or maybe just tired. There was some gray in her hair, and she had a little belly, but she had a decent body overall. Excellent boobs, and she still looked pretty good in jeans, which was a lot more than he could say for his own mom, despite her Paleo diet and yoga addiction.

She's okay, he texted back. *Except that she gave birth to a raging asshole*

The bar wasn't all that crowded on a Tuesday night, but it was pretty noisy, with classic rock blasting in the background, songs that Eve remembered from high school — Aerosmith and Led Zeppelin and "Little Pink Houses" — more than a few of which inspired Barry and Russ to trade high fives or break out their air guitars. Eve hated most of those songs — *cock rock,* her college friends used to call it — but the lyrics were permanently engraved in her memory, courtesy of every boyfriend she'd ever had.

Snot running down his nose! Greasy fingers smearing shabby clo-hoes!

That awful Jethro Tull song came on while Professor Fairchild told Eve about her mother's death, which happened just a few months after Margo — they were on a first-name basis now — had completed her transition. It was one of those freak things, a stubborn cold that somehow turned into drug-resistant pneumonia. Her mother went to the emergency room, complaining of a nagging cough and shortness of breath, and twelve hours later she was on a ventilator, unable to speak, drifting in and out of consciousness. She rallied a little right before she died, just long enough to scribble a final message to the daughter who had once been a son.

You are confused, she wrote, in a weak and trembling hand. *You need to wake up and smell the coffee!*

"Those were her dying words." Margo tried to smile, but couldn't complete the mission. "Right after I told her how much I loved her. *You need to wake up and smell the coffee!* I'll never forgive her for that."

"You should try," Eve told her. "It's unhealthy to resent the dead."

Margo knew this was true. "I wish I could talk to her one more time. Just to make her understand that *this* is me. Not that sad little boy living inside the wrong body. But she'd probably just hurt my feelings all over again. She used to say such horrible things."

"I know how that goes," Eve said. "I work with older people. You wouldn't believe the stuff that comes out of their mouths."

"Oh, I believe it," Margo said. "But my mother was a schoolteacher. She was not an ignorant woman. She just refused to accept my experience and acknowledge my pain."

"She loved her little boy." It was strange

how clear this was to Eve, though she'd never even met the woman. "She didn't know how to think about you any other way."

Margo drank the last sip of wine in her glass.

"She never really knew me. My own mother. Isn't that terrible?"

Margo buried her face in her hands. After a moment of hesitation, Eve reached out and began rubbing the professor's shoulder, aware as she did so that everyone else at the table was watching them with a mixture of concern and discomfort.

"Something wrong?" asked Dumell.

Eve shrugged — of course something was wrong — but Margo raised her head and told him that she was fine.

"Don't mind me," she said, wiping her eyes and mustering an embarrassed smile. "I just get emotional when I drink."

"There's only one cure for that." Barry waved his hand, signaling to the bartender. "Yo, Ralphie! Another round for my friends."

Russ had switched to Diet Coke, and everyone else at the table was drinking wine or hard liquor — trying to get the most bang from Barry's buck — so Julian had the second pitcher all to himself. It was a lot of beer for one person, but he was approaching a level of intoxication where finishing it on his own seemed like a matter of personal honor. To make it official, he texted a pic to Ethan before he poured the first glass: the sweaty plastic vessel filled to the brim, his own liquid Mount Everest.

60 oz bro wish me luck!!!

"You texting or listening?" Dumell asked.

"Both," said Julian, but he put down his phone and turned his full attention back to his real-life companion, who was telling him about Iraq, which was not a subject Julian got to hear about every day, at least not from someone who'd actually been there.

Not that it was all that exciting, apparently. Dumell said it was mostly boring as shit, due to the fact that he was an auto mechanic, not a combat soldier. He spent most of his tour sweating in a repair shop, changing oil and brake pads, replacing spark plugs and rotating tires, the same routine tasks he now performed every day at Warren Reddy Subaru in Elmville. Every once in a while, though, he got sent out in a tow truck to pick up a disabled vehicle that had been hit by an IED or an RPG.

"That's when shit got real," he said. "You're driving through that desert, totally fucking exposed, just waiting for something to explode. Every pothole feels like the end of the world, know what I'm saying?"

Weirdly, Julian thought he did, though he'd never been near a war zone, and had never seen anything blow up that was bigger than a firecracker, except on a screen.

"Anything bad happen?"

"Not to me. Just did my job and came home."

"Must've been a relief."

"You would think so. But I didn't . . . *readjust* too good. Couldn't sleep, couldn't hold a job. Marriage fell apart. Scared all the time. Like I was still out in the desert, driving through a minefield."

"That sucks."

"PTSD," Dumell explained. "That's what the doctors say. But it doesn't make any sense. I was lucky. Came home in one piece. Ain't got shit to complain about."

Julian was intimately familiar with this line of thinking. It had played on a loop during the black hole of his senior year. *My life is good. People love me. I have a promising future. So why can't I get out of bed?*

"Doesn't matter," he told Dumell, surprising himself with the conviction in his voice. "You feel what you fucking feel. You don't have to apologize to anyone."

246

Dumell squinted for a few seconds, as if he was trying to get Julian into focus. But after a moment, his expression softened.

"Guess you know what I'm talking about, huh?"

"Kind of," Julian told him. "I got PTSD from high school."

Eve stopped drinking after her second glass of the house white — a watery pinot grigio — but Margo happily accepted Barry's offer of a third.

"What the heck," she said. "I'm not teaching tomorrow."

It was close to eleven, and Eve started thinking about the logistics of a graceful exit. It would have been simple, except that she felt responsible for getting Margo back to campus, where she'd left her car. She was about to broach the subject when Margo turned to her with a wistful smile.

"This is nice," she said. "It's just what I hoped it would be."

"What do you mean?"

Margo gestured vaguely, sculpting a roundish object with her hands.

"Just *this.* Going out with a girlfriend and talking about . . . stuff." She laughed sadly. "I always thought I'd have more women friends after I transitioned. I mean, don't get me wrong. I have friends. But not too many of them are cis women."

"It's hard," Eve said. "Everybody's so busy."

Margo tapped a manicured fingernail on a damp cocktail napkin. "I think I watched too much *Sex and the City,* and read too many novels about amazing female friendships. These women who talk about everything, and help each other through the hard times. I never had friends like that when I was living as a guy."

"My ex-husband didn't have any friends like that, either. Men just don't need that much from each other."

"But you do, right? You have friends you can confide in. Talk about your love life or whatever. Share your secrets."

"A few," Eve said, though she hadn't done a great job of maintaining those friendships in recent months. She hadn't told Jane or Peggy or Liza about her porn problem, and she certainly hadn't mentioned her crush on Amanda. The only person she could imagine confiding in about her feelings for Amanda was Amanda herself, and that wasn't possible at the moment. They hadn't really talked since their fateful dinner at Enzo, even though they saw each other every day at work. When they did communicate, they were both a little guarded, very proper and professional, as if neither one wanted to venture into any gray areas, or get anywhere near the other's personal boundaries.

"You know what the problem is?" Margo said. "I missed out on the bonding periods. I didn't grow up with a tight group of girls, didn't have any women roommates in college, didn't get to swap sex stories with co-workers at lunch. No Mommy and Me classes, no hanging out with a neighbor while our kids had a playdate. The only woman I could ever talk to like that was my ex-wife, and she refuses to be my girlfriend. She wants me to be happy, but she doesn't want to go clothes shopping or hear about the cute guy I have a crush on. Can't really blame her, I guess."

"That's gotta be complicated," Eve said.

Margo nodded, but her mind was elsewhere.

"When I was a guy, I used to get so jealous when women went to the bathroom together. One of them would get up, and then her friend would get up, too. Sometimes two friends. It was like a conspiracy. And I'd be like, *What's going on in there? What kind of secrets are they telling each other?*"

"Nothing too exciting," Eve said, though she'd actually had some interesting bathroom experiences over the years. Sophomore year of high school, Heather Falchuk pulled up her shirt and showed Eve her third nipple, a little pink island at the bottom of her rib cage. Her college friend Martina, a recovering bulimic, used to have Eve accompany her to the bathroom so she wouldn't be tempted to purge after a big meal.

"I know it's stupid," Margo said, running her finger over the lip of her wineglass. "It's just one of those things I always wanted to do."

Julian had made it through two-thirds of the pitcher when the extent of his inebriation made itself clear to him.

"Oh, shit," he told Dumell.

"What?"

Julian's laughter sounded hollow and faraway in his own ears. "I'm pretty fucking wasted, man."

"I can see that. You been sucking it down pretty good."

"Can I tell you a secret?" Julian leaned toward Dumell. It felt to him like something important was happening. "I never had a black friend before. You think that makes me a racist?"

Dumell thought this over, scratching the corner of his mouth with the tip of a thumb.

"I hope you're not driving home," he said.

Julian shook his head and pointed to the floor.

"Got my trusty skateboard."

"Where you live?"

"Haddington."

"That's five miles away."

"Yes, sir."

"You really commute on that thing?"

"It's better than nothing."

Dumell didn't dispute this. "Is it fun?"

"Fuck yeah. You know that hill on Davis Road? Over by Wendy's? Sometimes I'm going faster than the cars. Feel like a superhero."

"Ever have an accident?"

"Nothing bad. If I see trouble coming, I just hop off."

"I get that," said Dumell. "But you can't always see it coming, right?"

Julian picked up his glass — it was half-full — and then put it down without drinking.

"Only bad thing that ever happened, some jock assholes from my high school kidnapped me."

"Kidnapped?"

"They threw me in their car, drove me to a park, and duct-taped me inside a Port-A-Potty."

Dumell's eyes got big. "You shitting me?"

"Nope."

Julian shot a venomous glance across the table at Mrs. Fletcher, but she didn't notice. She was too busy sucking up to the professor, who was apparently her new best friend. Mrs. Fletcher's dickwad son had been one of the kidnappers.

"Why would they go and do that?" Dumell asked.

"Why? Because one of these jocks was being an asshole at a party, so I threw a drink in his face."

"Crazy motherfucker," chuckled Dumell. "How long were you stuck in there?"

Julian shrugged. It had only been a couple minutes — his house key cut right through the tape — but it felt like forever. The stench of that open toilet had been seared into his nostrils for months afterward. He could still smell it now if he tried hard enough.

"Too fucking long," he said.

Julian shot another hateful look at Mrs. Fletcher. He wanted to say something mean, to let her know what a horrible bully she'd brought into the world, but she was standing up now, not even looking in his direction as she headed off to the rest room with Dr. Fairchild in tow.

"Damn," said Dumell, who was watching the women walk. His voice was low and appreciative. "She looks good."

"Which one?" asked Julian.

"Damn," Dumell repeated in that same soft voice, which wasn't really an answer.

With only one stall and limited standing room, the women's rest room at PLAY BALL! wasn't ideal for girl talk. Eve made a magnanimous *after you* gesture, inviting Margo to avail herself of the facilities. She checked her phone while she waited — there were no texts or emails of note — and reminded herself that it was rude to speculate about the particulars of the professor's anatomy.

It's not important, she thought. *Gender's a state of mind.*

Margo flushed and emerged with a slightly tipsy smile on her face.

"Mission accomplished," she announced in a singsong voice, turning sideways so Eve could slip past. "Your turn."

Eve really did have to pee, but she was overcome with a sudden attack of shyness the moment she sat on the toilet. She had no problem going with strangers nearby, but it was harder when people she knew were within hearing range. It was all because Ted, in the early days of their relationship, had once teased her about the force of her stream.

Jesus, he said. *Who turned on the faucet?*

Years later, when their marriage was falling apart, Eve had mentioned this incident in a couple's therapy session, to which they'd each brought a list of unspoken grievances. Ted had no recollection of making this comment, and was mystified that it could have bothered her for so many years. *It was a dumb joke,* he told her. *Just let it go already.* But here she was, seven years divorced, and still brooding about it.

"Eve," said Margo. "Can I ask you something?"

"Sure."

"What do you think of Dumell?"

"Dumell?" Eve repeated, trying to buy some time. The truth was, she hadn't given a lot of thought to Dumell. They hadn't interviewed each other yet, and he didn't talk much in class. She didn't even know if Dumell was his first name or his last. She mostly just thought of him as *Worried Black Guy,* though she'd been impressed tonight by how attentive he was being to Julian

Spitzer, who looked like he was getting pretty drunk.

"Yeah," said Margo. "Do you like him?"

"He seems nice." Eve discovered to her relief that it was easy to pee while holding a conversation. "Kinda low-key."

"I think he's handsome," Margo said. "He's got really nice eyes."

Eve wiped and flushed and exited the stall. She understood her role now.

"So," she asked, washing her hands in that slightly theatrical way she adopted when other people were watching. "Do you have a crush on him?"

"Maybe." Margo was gazing into the cloudy mirror, applying her lipstick with the concentration of a surgeon. "And by *maybe* I mean *definitely.*"

"Wow."

"I can't stop thinking about him."

"Is that allowed?" Eve inquired. "The teacher-and-student thing?"

"Who cares?" Margo scoffed. "Do you have any idea what they pay me? Anyway, we're all adults, right?"

If they were going to swap secrets, this would have been the time for Eve to mention Amanda, to bond with Margo over their illicit crushes, but she wasn't drunk enough to say it out loud.

"I'm just glad he's tall," Margo said. "I don't think it would work with me and a short guy. I mean, there's no reason why it shouldn't, but a lot of men get freaked out by tall women."

"They're such babies," Eve said. "What doesn't freak them out?"

Margo nodded, but without much conviction.

"I've never actually been with a man before," she confessed.

"Oh," said Eve. "Wow."

"I liked women when I was a man. At least I tried to. But now . . . that's not really working for me anymore. I think I'm ready to branch out."

"Good for you." Eve gave her an encouraging squeeze on the arm. She wanted to say, *I know exactly how you feel,* but once again the words stayed put.

"So what should I do?" Margo asked. "How do I seduce him?"

"Maybe you should just talk to him first. Get to know him a little."

"I was afraid you'd say that."

"Or you could sit on his lap and stick your tongue in his ear. That works, too."

Something happened to Julian in the men's room. He wasn't exactly sober going in —

nowhere near it — but he could still walk and think straight. But when he came out, he was totally fucking *WASTED*. It was like that whole second pitcher caught up with him in the course of a single piss.

Getting back to the table was an adventure worthy of a video game, and Dr. Fairchild seemed to have taken his seat.

" 'Scuse me," he told her. "No offense, but that's my spot."

Dumell pointed across the table. There was an empty chair next to Mrs. Fletcher.

"Why don't you sit over there?" Dumell told him. "Spread the love."

Dumell was giving him a badass military stare, like, *Just do it, motherfucker.* Julian wasn't so hammered that he couldn't take a hint.

"Chillax, bro." He winked at Dumell and then gave him a thumbs-up, which he realized, even as he was doing it, was a little too much of a good thing. "I got your back."

There was something else he wanted to say, but he couldn't remember what it was, and the next thing he knew Mrs. Fletcher was standing next to him with her arm around his shoulders, offering to drive him home. Julian didn't want to leave just yet, but Barry said he didn't have a choice.

"You overdid it, kiddo. It's time to go."

"I'm not drunk," Julian protested, but even he didn't believe it.

They escorted him out to the parking lot like a criminal, Barry on one side, Mrs. Fletcher on the other. It was actually a relief to get out of the bar, to breathe some fresh air.

"I drank that whole pitcher," he told them. "All by myself."

"You're a champ." Barry helped him into the passenger seat of Mrs. Fletcher's mini-van. "You're not gonna get sick, are you?"

"No way, Jose."

"All right." Barry nodded solemnly before he shut the door. "Don't let me down."

Mrs. Fletcher smiled at him as she slid the key into the ignition. Not a happy smile, but one of those *What are we gonna do with you?* smiles. It was weird being in the van with her. Like she was his mom. Or maybe even his girlfriend. Why the fuck not?

Brendan would not like that, he thought.

"How old are you?" he asked.

"Buckle your seatbelt," she told him.

He felt okay at first, except that the world kept lurching at him through the windshield. Too many trees and headlights and store-fronts. It was better to focus on Mrs. Fletcher's face. She had a nice profile.

"You think they're gonna hook up?" he asked.

"Who?"

"Dumell and Dr. Fairchild. I think he likes her."

Mrs. Fletcher turned and looked at him, as if he'd said something interesting.

"Did he tell you that?"

"Kind of."

"Well," she said, after a brief hesitation. "It's none of our business if they do. They're both adults."

Julian nodded. He liked the sound of Mrs. Fletcher's voice. And he liked the tight shirt she was wearing, the way her boobs swelled against the buttons.

"What about us?" he said. "We gonna hook up?"

"You're drunk," she told him.

"You're really pretty. Do you even know that?"

"Julian," she said. "Let's not do this, okay?"

"Why not?"

"I'm forty-six years old," she told him. "You're not even old enough to drink."

He wanted to tell her that age didn't matter, but something went badly wrong in his stomach, and he had to ask her to pull over.

"Right now! *Please.*"

She heard the urgency in his voice and swerved to the side of the road. He jumped out of the van, hand clamped over his mouth, and puked into a nearby storm drain, which was better than leaving a disgusting puddle on the sidewalk for dogs to sample in the morning.

"Oh, fuck."

He was down on all fours, gazing through the metal grate into the dark abyss below, when he realized that Mrs. Fletcher was crouching next to him, rubbing his back in a slow circle, telling him to relax, that he'd feel better when he'd gotten the poison out of his system.

"Poor baby," she said.

"You have great boobs," he told her, right before he puked again.

■ ■ ■ ■

PART THREE:
GENDER AND
SOCIETY

■ ■ ■ ■

A Bouquet of Red Flags

For the most part, Amber and her mom got along really well. They texted each other several times a day and spoke on the phone at least twice a week. And these weren't short calls, either. Once they got started, they could talk for an hour straight without coming up for air.

Unless there was something urgent to discuss, their conversations followed a well-worn path. They always began with an update about her brother — what he was eating, how he was sleeping, how things were going for him at school, how many new Matchbox cars he'd acquired — because Amber missed him a lot and still felt guilty about going away to college, leaving her mom to care for him as if she were a single parent, even though her father lived in the house. He'd never really bonded with Benjy; he acted like there was no point in even *trying,* and everybody let him get away with it, including Amber.

When they'd exhausted the topic of Benjy, her mom would ask a few questions about Amber's schoolwork, and then Amber would reciprocate, giving her mom lots of room to ramble on about anything that occurred to her, no matter how trivial — the weather, a story in the news, the quality of the produce she'd bought at the supermarket. There was always some discussion of her mom's allergies and a segment devoted to any unusual activity in the neighborhood: who got a new car, whose dog was in a clown collar, who had switched from oil heat to natural gas. Amber listened patiently, because she knew how lonely her mother was, and how small her world had become.

It was the least she could do.

At the same time, Amber dreaded these phone calls, because they inevitably drifted to the awkward subject of boyfriends — specifically, her mother's inability to understand why Amber didn't have one. It made no sense: Amber was pretty, she was smart, she had a big heart and a warm personality. Yes, her mother understood that she had a demanding schedule — academics, softball, the various clubs and organizations she belonged to — but young people could always make time for a little romance. Amber's mother certainly had, when she was her daughter's age. She'd been a very popular young lady, if she had to say so herself.

You should go on some dates, her mother would say, as if this were a brilliant idea that had just occurred to her, rather than a suggestion she'd made a hundred times before.

Trying to keep her frustration in check, Amber would explain, for the hundredth time, that no one went on *dates* anymore, that it wasn't a thing people her age actually did.

I literally do not know a single person who's been on a date, she would protest. This wasn't *literally* true, but she didn't want to muddy the waters of the argument with a more nuanced position.

And then came the Big Significant Pause. Every frigging time.

Amber, honey? Is there something you want to tell us? You know your father and I will support you no matter what.

It was all because she'd gone to her senior prom with Jocelyn Rodriguez, a softball teammate and one of the few out kids in her high school. Neither one of them had a date, so they decided to go as friends. Lots of girls did that. But they looked so good together, so totally *plausible* — Joss in a tux, with her short hair slicked back, Amber girly in a pink dress — that everyone simply assumed they were a couple, Amber's parents included. Even Joss seemed to think so, because she was pretty disappointed when Amber wouldn't make out with her during the slow dances.

Jesus, Mom. How many times do I have to tell you? I like guys. There just aren't any good ones here.

Well, that's your problem right there, honey. You're going in with a bad attitude. You have to give them a chance.

At that point in the conversation, Amber was tempted to list all the guys she'd hooked up with during freshman year — eight or nine, depending on how you looked at it, and every one an asshole in his own special way — but she didn't want to be slut-shamed by her own mother. And besides, she was done with all that. No more drunken hookups. No more getting naked with sexist jerks who had no interest in her as a human being.

Maybe if you dressed a little more feminine, her mother would say. *You look really pretty in dresses. Those skinny jeans aren't always so flattering.*

It was like they were actors in a play that never ended, doomed to keep performing the same depressing scene over and over again. But that was about to change, Amber thought, as she took a deep breath and reached for her phone.

Becca was supposed to visit that weekend. It was all set. She'd arranged for a ride from Haddington with a girl in her class who had an open invitation to crash at the Sigma house, and Zack had agreed to sexile himself for a couple of days, not that it was much of a sacrifice on his part. His on-and-off relationship with the mystery girl (who was supposedly not fat, though that's how I always thought of her) was back on again, and he hardly ever slept in our room anymore anyway. Most of the time it felt like I was living in a single, which would have been great, except that I missed having him around. Even when he was there, things weren't the same. I mean, we got along fine, but we didn't joke around or laugh as much as we used to. He seemed a little distant, way more interested in whatever text he'd just received than in anything I had to say. It was pretty fucking annoying.

Dude, I asked him one night. *Are you in love or something?*

What? he said, chuckling to himself as he tapped out a reply.

Forget it, I told him. *It's not important*

I was excited about seeing Becca after all this time, but also kinda nervous. She was the one who'd been pushing for a weekend visit — I was fine with waiting until Thanksgiving — but now that it was a done deal I figured I'd make the best of it. I was juiced about getting laid, because after almost two months at BSU, I'd had exactly zero sex (except solo), which did not seem like an auspicious start to my college career.

But fucking a girl is one thing, and spending a whole weekend with her is another, and Becca and I had never been one of those couples that hung out together very much, or had a lot to talk about when we did. So I can't say I was all that crushed when she Skyped me on Wednesday with her eye makeup smeared from crying and told me that the visit was off. Her parents had talked it over and decided that she was too young to be spending the weekend with a college guy — even if the college guy was actually her high school boyfriend — and wanted to know why, if I was so keen on seeing their daughter, I didn't just come home for the weekend and hang out with her there.

"Damn," I said. "That really sucks."

"I know. I wanted to sleep with you so bad."

"Yeah, me too."

She sniffled and wiped her nose, staring at me with this wounded bird expression.

"It's not such a terrible idea," she said.

"What?"

"You could take the bus, right? And your mom would be really happy to see you."

"You want me to come home?"

"Why not? I'll split the cost with you, if that's what you're worried about."

"It's not the money."

"Then what's the problem?"

I knew I was in dangerous territory. There was no non-asshole way to tell her the truth, which was that I was happy enough to see her if I didn't have a choice, but even happier not to if I did.

"Let me think about it," I said. "I'll text you tomorrow."

And then, like ten minutes after we hung up, Amber called. I hadn't heard from her since the meeting of the Autism Awareness Network, where I'd humiliated myself by crying like a little bitch.

"What are you doing on Saturday night?" she asked.

"I'm not sure."

She made a sound like the buzzer on a game show.

"Wrong," she said. "We're going on a date."

Amber was painfully aware of the mismatch between her politics and her desires. She was an intersectional feminist, an advocate for people with disabilities, and a whole-hearted ally of the LGBT community in all its glorious diversity. As a straight, cis-gender, able-bodied, neurotypical, first-world, middle-class white woman, she struggled to maintain a constant awareness of her privilege, and to avoid using it to silence or ignore the voices of those without the same unearned advantages, who had more of a right to speak on many, many subjects than she did. It went without saying that she was a passionate opponent of capitalism, patriarchy, racism, homophobia, transphobia, rape culture, bullying, and microaggression in all its forms.

But when it came to boys, for some reason, she only ever liked jocks.

It kind of sucked. She wished she were more attracted to men who shared her political convictions — the tree-huggers, the gender nonconformists, the vegan activists, the occupiers and boycotters, the Whiteness

Studies majors, intellectual black dudes with Malcolm X eyeglasses — but it never seemed to work that way. She always fell for athletes — football players, shotputters, rugby forwards, heavyweight wrestlers, even an obnoxious golfer, though he was definitely an outlier — almost all of them hard-drinking white guys with buff, hairless chests, marinated in privilege, unable to see beyond their own dicks. And of course they used her like a disposable object, without regret or apology, because that's what privilege *is* — the license to treat other people like shit while still getting to believe that you're a good person.

What was it her father always said? The definition of crazy was doing the same thing over and over and expecting different results? Well, that was the story of Amber's love life so far, and she'd had enough. She'd vowed over the summer to stop the madness, to either start choosing her partners more wisely or, if need be, to opt for celibacy and self-respect over empty sex and the self-hating sadness that came with it.

And then, as if the universe were testing her resolve, she met Brendan at the Activities Fair on the very first day of her sophomore year. He was a bouquet of red flags — a handsome, self-confident, broad-shouldered, inarticulate, politically oblivious lacrosse player — the exact type of guy she'd sworn to avoid. But it didn't matter: her heart did its usual, incorrigible somersault and gave the middle finger to her brain. It amazed her how weak she was, like a smoker who'd vowed to quit, but couldn't get through a single day without lighting up.

To her credit, she put up more resistance than usual. Freshman year, she would have texted him right away, inviting him to hang out, maybe smoke some weed and watch a movie. At the time, it had seemed like the feminist thing to do — why shouldn't a woman pursue sex as freely as a man? — but for some reason it always ended up with her staring pathetically at her phone, wondering why Trent or Mason or Royce (the asshole golfer) hadn't even sent her a *thanks for the blowjob!* text, as if that would have made her feel any better.

With Brendan, she hung back, playing hard to get, as her mother would have quaintly put it, waiting for him to make the first move. She didn't text him, didn't orchestrate a "chance" meeting in the Higg, didn't even friend him on Facebook, though she did do a fair amount of stalking. He posted lots of shirtless pictures of himself, and, she had to admit, he looked really good without a shirt.

It turned out to be an effective strategy for not hooking up, especially since Brendan made no attempt to contact her, either. But even at a big school like BSU, they couldn't avoid each other forever. About a month into the semester, she'd walked into the library with the newly formed Student Coalition Against Racism and Police Brutality, and there he was, cute as ever, reading a book about climate change.

He'd surprised her in the best possible way. She couldn't imagine any of her former hookups joining her to protest the shooting of Michael Brown, or weeping in front of a roomful of strangers at a meeting for people with autistic siblings. He seemed like a decent guy, and maybe even boyfriend material, definitely worth taking a chance on.

What are you going to do on your date? her mother had asked.

We're going to a movie. After that we'll probably go to a party where everyone gets naked.

Ha ha, her mother said. *Very funny.*

I didn't *hate* the movie. It just wasn't the kind of movie you were meant to *like,* and not the kind you normally went to on a date. But Amber was really into feminism, and one of her good friends, a Vietnamese girl named Gloria, was in charge of the Women's International Documentary Film Festival, so there we were.

It was an eye-opener, that's for sure. The movie focused on a bunch of depressing third-world hellholes where women were treated like garbage. In one African country, young girls got raped all the time and nothing ever happened to the men who did it. There was this one victim — she was twelve, but looked older — who was raped by her "uncle" who was not actually her uncle. He was a family friend, and a very important man in the village. The white people who were making the film convinced her to press charges, but it backfired. She and her mom ended up getting kicked out of their house and the rapist denied everything.

I am not that kind of person, he said, like the accusation had hurt his feelings.

There were other stories — girls sold into prostitution by their own parents, girls forced into sweatshops to support their families, girls who were "engaged" to be married to disgusting old men before they'd even reached puberty, girls who were genitally mutilated while their own mothers held them down. I could hear Amber sniffling next to me and I reached for her hand. She turned and gave me this sad little smile.

After a while I just kinda zoned out. There's only so much misery you can take in one sitting. Normally, in a situation like that, I would've checked my texts or played a game of Hitman, but the girl who introduced the film had made a big deal about asking everybody to turn off their phones and devote their full attention to the screen.

Please, she said. *This is important. Please don't look away.*

The movie was long, which meant I had a lot of time to think. I thought about my mom, and how happy she would've been to know that I was watching a serious documentary like this, getting educated about the world, which to her was the whole point of being in college. And I thought about Becca, who wouldn't have lasted five minutes in that theater, because why should she pretend to care about stuff that happened to people she didn't know in places she'd never heard of? I understood why she felt that way — part of me even agreed with her — though I knew it was selfish, and not the kind of thing you were allowed to say out loud, especially not at the Women's International Documentary Film Festival.

Amber was quiet after the movie ended.

We left the lecture hall and headed outside. It was a chilly night with a light drizzle coming down, but I think she was as grateful as I was for the fresh air. We were still holding hands, and I wondered if I should try to kiss her. But then I looked at her puffy eyes and stunned expression and realized that it probably wasn't such a good idea.

"What did you think?" she asked.

"About the movie?"

That made her laugh just a little.

"Yeah," she said. "About the movie."

If I'd been totally honest, I would have told her that the movie had made me realize just how lucky I was. To be a guy. To be an American. To have a healthy body and enough money that I never had to wonder where my next meal was coming from, and to know that I would never have to sacrifice my own happiness and freedom for anyone else's. To wake up every morning knowing that something fun could happen. The movie made me want to get down on all fours and kiss the ground. But I knew that was the wrong way to go.

"It fucking broke my heart," I told her.

Amber had been looking forward to the party all week. A lot of her friends from the Feminist Alliance were going to be there, and everybody was excited. It was one of those rare situations where you could have fun and make an important point at the same time, at least that's what they were all telling themselves. But now, after the movie she'd just seen, the party suddenly seemed ridiculous, a bunch of privileged college kids pretending that they were making a political statement, fighting the patriarchy by getting drunk and taking their clothes off.

"You okay?" Brendan asked, laying his hand gently on her shoulder. They were standing out on the quad, getting rained on.

"Just sad," she said, touched by his concern. He'd sat through the grueling film without a single complaint, and had held her hand through the worst of it. "The world's so fucked up."

"Tell me about it."

Amber didn't regret watching the movie. You couldn't turn away from the truth just because it ripped your guts out. You had to look cruelty and injustice in the eye, to acknowledge the humanity of people less fortunate than you, and accept your obligation to help improve their lives. It was the least you could do.

But it was so little. It was almost nothing.

Some part of her just wanted to say *Fuck*

it — drop out of school, say goodbye to softball and Women's Studies and Autism Awareness and Slut Walk and her hilarious roommate, Willa — say goodbye to *America* — and get a job with some NGO that built schools for girls in Afghanistan, or fought human trafficking in Thailand, or provided free surgery for African women with obstetrical fistula. Do something useful, instead of wasting her time reading books and watching movies and liking meaningless shit on Facebook. It would be hard on her mother, though, and she'd really miss Benjy, who would only understand that she was far away, not why she'd gone. Her generous motives would be lost on him.

"You want to get a drink or something?" Brendan asked.

Before she could answer, her phone buzzed. It was Cat again. She'd texted three times during the movie.

Where rrrrrr uuuuu???? You better get that big fat booty over here so I can spank it bitch!!!!

Amber smiled in spite of herself. Cat was the only person in the world who could talk to her like that and get away with it. And besides, it was ten thirty on a rainy Saturday night, and she had to accept the fact that, right now, there was nothing she could do to help anyone but herself lead a better and happier life.

"I know where we could get a drink," she told him.

The party Amber took me to wasn't a full-blown naked party. It was an underwear party, sponsored by the Feminist Alliance, so of course it had an uplifting name, which in this case was EVERY BODY IS BEAUTIFUL! — a statement that is totally not true.

When we arrived, a feminist at the door handed us nametag lanyards. Instead of your name, you were supposed to write down something about your body that you didn't like. The idea was that you were supposed to celebrate your flaws and not be ashamed of them. Just get it out in the open, so people could tell you you were beautiful anyway.

Amber didn't hesitate. She uncapped the Sharpie and wrote *DISTURBINGLY LARGE SHOULDERS* on the card as easily as if she were signing her name. Then she handed the marker to me. I was stumped for a second, because I'd been working out and felt pretty good about my body. All I could think to write was *CALVES COULD BE BIGGER,* even though they were perfectly fine, too. Amber laughed when she saw what I'd written.

"That's it?" she said. "Your calves could be bigger?"

I shrugged. The only other thing I could have gone with was *SMELLY FEET,* because I did have an occasional problem in that direction, though I didn't really think it qualified as a physical flaw.

"Mine's not that different from yours," I pointed out.

I could tell she didn't agree, but she nodded anyway and pulled her dress over her head in this totally matter-of-fact way, which gave me an instant half-boner. I had to turn away and stare at a chubby dude in tightey whities until it was safe to start undressing. Weirdly, the chubby dude had listed his flaw as *TWITCHY EYELID,* which seemed a little beside the point. When I was done, we put our shoes and clothes into a trash bag and shoved it behind a couch.

"You think it's okay there?" I asked. "I don't want to walk home in my underwear."

Instead of answering, Amber grabbed my wrist and pulled me into the crowd. She was wearing regular cotton panties, black with a white border, and a V-neck black top that looked like a sports bra but was lacier in the front. Her body was just like I'd imagined it, strong and sleek, no hourglass but a nice round ass I was happy to follow wherever it led.

The house was pretty dark. Some rooms were lit by candles, others had lava lamps, and the dance floor had these swirling disco lights and flashing strobes. It made being half-naked a lot less problematic than it otherwise would have been. In a funny way, you ended up paying more attention to people's lanyards than their actual bodies. It was really interesting to see what people were ashamed of — *MUFFIN TOP, UNI-BROW, HUGE NOSE, MAN BOOBS, ASS ACNE* — and then kind of casually try to check out whatever flaw they were talking about. Sometimes you could spot the problem right away, and other times you had to take their word for it.

Amber knew a lot of the people there, so mostly I just nodded and smiled while she introduced me to her friends — *ECZEMA, TOENAIL FUNGUS,* and *RIGHT ONE WAY BIGGER,* among others. Most of the people I met were nice enough, though a bunch of them seemed skeptical that my non-bulging calves qualified as a bona fide problem. The only person I'd met before was Cat from the Autism Awareness Network, who was alarmingly skinny with her clothes off — all ribs and elbows and hip bones — though, I had to admit, kind of sexy in her leopard-print bra and panties. She was also wearing blue flip-flops and white surgical gloves, all of which added up to an eye-catching package.

"Hey Brendan." The sign around her neck read, FURRY ARM HAIR. "Good to see you again."

"You too," I said, squinting at her completely hairless forearms.

"I wax," she explained. "A *lot*. Otherwise I'd look like an orangutan."

"What's with the gloves?"

She shrugged and drank some jungle juice from a solo cup.

"Too many bodies." She gave a small shudder of revulsion. "Way too much skin and sweat and . . . *ugh*."

We smiled at each other for a couple of seconds, stumped for conversation. She turned and looked at Amber, who was talking to a black girl who had amazing abs and suffered from ASHY SKIN. The black girl was wearing gym shorts and a bikini top, which seemed like cheating to me, since neither one qualified as actual underwear.

"Amber really likes you," Cat told me.

"I like her, too."

"You better not hurt her," she said, poking her latex-covered finger into my sternum. "Otherwise you'll have to answer to me."

Amber's room was on the sixth floor of Thoreau Hall. It was even smaller than her first-year double in Longfellow, but at least it wasn't in the basement.

"We're in luck," she told Brendan. "Willa's away for the weekend."

"Cool." He was busy checking out the posters on the pale green walls: Malala, the Dalai Lama, Andy Samberg. "Nice place."

She hadn't planned on bringing him home after the party. She'd meant to take it slow, maybe just make out a little, plant a seed for the future, but dancing with someone in your underwear turns out not to be the best strategy for taking it slow. They'd gotten into some pretty heavy grinding toward the end, and it had been an amazing feeling, to be that close to fucking with so many people around.

She dumped her coat on Willa's bed and then took off her dress, because why not? She'd already undressed in front of him, and he'd clearly liked what he saw. The party had done wonders for her mood — totally turned the night around — and given a welcome boost to her self-esteem. It had been so moving to be part of that community, one imperfect human among many, all those people admitting to their vulnerabilities, making one another feel safe and loved and beautiful. She took her bra off, and tossed it to Brendan.

"Heads up!"

His reflexes were a little slow — it must have been the weed they'd smoked on the upstairs balcony, their bare skin steaming in the night air — but he managed to make a one-handed grab after it bounced off his chest. Then he just stood there for a second, staring at the bra like it was an object he'd never encountered before.

"You okay?" she asked.

"Yeah," he said. "Awesome."

He was such a *boy*, she thought — sweet and clueless and weirdly passive. Amber was only a year older, but she was a woman, and had been one for a long time. She didn't mind the imbalance. She liked being in charge, the only adult in the room.

"I have one question," she said. "Why are your pants still on?"

It should be a big deal the first time you hook up with someone new. A momentous occasion. I remember it felt like that the first time I fucked Becca. My hands were literally shaking when I put on the condom.

What you don't want is for your mind to be elsewhere, stuck on something stupid that has nothing to do with the girl you're with, especially if she's down on her knees, giving you a blowjob that you didn't expect, and didn't even have to ask for.

What you don't want to be thinking about just then is your asshole roommate, and the way he'd dissed you at the party.

In a funny way it was Amber's fault. She'd been grinding on me so hard on the dance floor, I thought I was gonna bust a nut right there. I told her I needed to pee, but she knew exactly what the problem was and thought it was pretty funny.

"You do what you have to do," she told me. "I'll be right here."

To calm myself, I took a solo lap around the house, upstairs and down, with my hands crossed — casually, I hoped — in front of my crotch. It was a pretty big place, with a balcony on the second floor and a rickety deck off the kitchen. There was also a small sunporch off the living room, and that was where I found Zack, playing quarters with two people I didn't know. One of them was a girl in a wheelchair.

"Yo, dude," I said. "Didn't know you were

coming to this."

"Oh, hey." Judging from the look on his face, he didn't expect to see me there, either. "Brendan, wow."

He put his hand on the wheelchair girl's arm — she was sitting right next to him — and whispered something in her ear. She turned to me, a funny little smile forming on her face.

"Holy shit." She sounded pretty drunk. "The famous roommate."

"That's me," I said. "The famous roommate."

"I'm Lexa." She had straight dark hair and a cute face, though one eye seemed kinda squinty or something, like it had frozen mid-wink. The sign around her neck read, *LEGS DON'T WORK.*

"I'm Brendan."

"Riley," said the other dude at the table. He was short and angry-looking, with ridiculously big biceps, pimply shoulders, and a tag that read, *VERY SMALL BLAD-DER.*

"Riley and I went to high school together," Lexa explained. Her skin was golden-bronze all over, like she'd just gotten a spray tan. "Up in North Ledham."

"Go Raiders," said Riley, without much enthusiasm.

We all shook hands, and then I turned to Zack, whose nametag read, *UNCONTROLLABLE FARTING.*

"At least you're honest," I told him.

"Tell me about it," said Lexa, who was wearing a shiny maroon bra and matching panties. She had a nice body — big boobs and a tiny waist — though I was distracted by the clear plastic tube that snaked out of her underwear and around her back. I couldn't tell where it went and didn't want to look too hard.

"You love it," Zack told her.

"Yeah," she said. "Your uncontrollable farting is a huge turn-on."

"It's a popular fetish," he said. "You should google it sometime."

"Already have," she told him. "You take a nice picture."

Zack high-fived her — *Good one!* — then looked at me. "Where's Becca?"

"She couldn't come. I'm here with that other girl, Amber?"

"The softball player?"

"Yeah, we went to a movie and —"

"We playing or bullshitting?" Riley grumbled.

"Shut up," Lexa told him. She smiled at me and pointed at the shot glass on the table. "Wanna join us?"

Her invitation was totally sincere, and I would have been happy to play a round or two. But I could tell Zack didn't want me there. He didn't shake his head or give a warning glance, nothing that obvious. He just kind of looked down and away, like there was something on the floor that required his full attention, a dead bug or a speck of dirt.

"Not tonight," I told her. "Maybe next time."

Amber felt a familiar vacancy taking shape in the pit of her stomach, an empty space that, if something didn't change, would soon be filled with regret.

It didn't make sense. Things had been so hot on the dance floor. Their hands all over each other, the easy way they'd moved to the music, the sweet dirty things he'd whispered in her ear.

And now . . . *this*. No connection at all. Just a strange dick in her mouth and fingers drumming impatiently on the top of her head, like he wanted to get it over with. She glanced up at him, checking in, hoping for a little guidance, but he didn't notice. He was lost in thought, staring straight ahead at nothing, his expression frozen somewhere between confusion and anger.

She wondered if maybe she'd moved too fast. They'd only made out for a minute or two before she'd decided to go down on him. The kisses had been uninspiring — stiff and distant — and she thought she needed to try something a little more drastic to change the energy.

She was just about to call for a time-out when his fingertips tightened suddenly on her scalp. He pushed into her and gave a soft grunt of approval, his first real sign of life.

Finally, she thought.

She picked up the pace and he responded to the new rhythm, thrusting to meet her. It was encouraging, but also a little worrisome, because she didn't want him to come just yet. She wouldn't have minded if she'd thought he might reciprocate with any degree of skill or patience, but Brendan didn't seem like the type. She'd only ever been with one guy who gave decent oral, and that had been a onetime deal. When it was over, the guy — a wrestler named Angus — never responded to any of her texts, and acted like he didn't know her when they bumped into each other on campus.

"You like that, don't you?" Brendan asked in a soft, dreamy voice.

Amber made an affirmative noise, the best

she could do under the circumstances.

"You like that big cock in your mouth?"

Ugh. She ignored the question. For some reason, she detested the word *cock.*

"Suck that cock, slut."

Whoa, she thought. That was not okay. She tried to tell him, but his hand had slid down the back of her head, and his grip had tightened.

"Suck it, bitch."

She couldn't move, couldn't pull away. Couldn't even breathe. He thrust forward again, and Amber started to gag.

I mean, I would have understood if it was just Zack and Lexa on the sunporch, but that kid Riley was already there, so it wasn't like I was spoiling some big romantic moment. I tried to tell myself that Zack was embarrassed by Lexa, but that didn't make any sense, either. They were at a party together, out in public in their fucking underwear, and they looked like they were having a great time. No, the only person Zack was embarrassed by was me, and I'd done nothing to deserve it, not a damn thing.

Fuck him, I thought.

It wasn't fair to me, and it wasn't fair to Amber. She'd been down on her knees for quite a while, giving it a hundred and ten percent, and I could see that she was starting to sweat a little.

Focus, I told myself. *Get your head in the game.*

Amber was doing a great job, don't get me wrong, but for some reason I wasn't feeling it, not the way I had with Becca on the day I left for college. I could almost hear her voice, the way she looked up at me and said, *This is your going-away present,* and we just kept talking like that the whole time, saying whatever crazy shit popped into our heads.

I know it's a little sketchy, thinking about one girl while you're with another, but you can't control what goes through your head at a time like that. And it worked, you know? I went from zero to sixty in a couple of seconds, and there was no stopping after that. I kept my foot on the gas, the highway wide open in front of me, not a car in sight.

And then Amber punched me in the nuts.

It was no accident. She hammered me in the scrotum — a short, brutal uppercut — when I was about ten seconds away from the finish line.

My knees buckled and I hit the floor, curling into the fetal position, waiting for the agony to subside.

"What the fuck?" I said, when I was finally able to talk. "Are you crazy?"

Amber was standing now, hugging herself so I couldn't see her chest.

"You were choking me," she said.

"No, I wasn't."

"I couldn't breathe, Brendan. I couldn't even move my head."

The pain had faded a little, but it returned in a sickening wave. I looked around for a wastebasket in case I had to puke.

"I don't know what you're talking about."

"And don't you ever call me a slut." She lifted her foot like she was gonna kick me, but then she put it back on the floor. "I don't know who you think you are."

"I was just talking dirty. I thought you liked it."

"Why would you think that?" Her face was really pink. "You have no idea what I like."

I forced myself to sit up.

"I'm sorry. I just got carried away."

"Get the fuck out," she told me.

"Come on, Amber. Don't be like that."

"Like what?" She grabbed my pants off the floor and threw them at me. "Like a person with self-respect?"

She'd been pretty calm up to that point, but then her mouth stretched out and she started to cry. I could tell she didn't want to do it — didn't want to show that weakness in front of me — and she just kind of sniffled really hard and pulled herself together. The tears just stopped. I'd never seen anyone do that before.

"Can't we talk about this?" I said.

But Amber was done talking. She stood there in her black-and-white panties, hugging herself and shaking her head no, like there was no point in discussing anything with me, like I wasn't worth the effort.

ONE WOMAN'S STORY

Amanda waited by the main entrance, doing her best to tune out the usual lecture day jitters and focus instead on her own sense of personal accomplishment, a feeling she rarely got to enjoy in her post-college life.

I did this! she reminded herself. *I made this happen!*

Technically, this was the third monthly lecture she'd overseen, but she'd felt no ownership stake in the September or October offerings — dry-as-dust tributes to the Queen of England and the Versatile Soybean, respectively — both of which she'd inherited from her predecessor. They'd been such demoralizing experiences that Amanda had seriously considered quitting her job after each of them, or at least writing a heartfelt letter of apology to everyone who'd attended, herself included.

But instead of quitting, or poisoning her

work life with bitterness and negativity, she'd behaved like an adult. She'd gathered her courage and discussed the situation with her boss, and together they'd found a way to effect constructive change. Eve deserved a lot of the credit, of course. She was the one who'd floated the possibility of inviting her professor to deliver the November lecture, but she'd only done so in response to Amanda's pitch for a more edgy, out-of-the-box approach.

Bringing a transgender guest speaker to the Senior Center was exactly the sort of bold move Amanda had been advocating, an announcement to the entire town (and beyond) that the monthly lecture series was under exciting new management, and people might want to start paying attention.

Eve was excited, too, and their shared sense of anticipation had brought them closer together, helping them to get past any lingering awkwardness related to the surprise kiss outside the restaurant. It was a relief to Amanda, and not just for professional reasons. She'd been feeling bad about the way she'd reacted that night, flinching as though Eve had been attacking her, rather than making a slightly clumsy but not completely unwelcome overture. It wasn't that Amanda wished she'd gone to bed with her, or even kissed her back, because she knew it was a terrible idea to get involved with your boss. She just wished she'd been a little nicer about saying no, because she really liked Eve, and had actually been flattered, and even a little turned on, at least in retrospect — at the time she'd simply been flustered — because she sometimes found herself replaying the kiss in her mind when she was bored, and occasionally using it as fuel for more fully developed fantasy encounters that totally got her off, not that Eve needed to know about that.

"Excuse me," said an elderly woman in a dark green tracksuit with pale green piping. Amanda had met her a couple of times, but couldn't remember her name. Bev or Dot or Nat, something truncated and nearly extinct. She wore her hair in a cap of tight white curls and had a Halloween-themed Band-Aid pasted on her cheek. "What is this?"

Bev or Dot or Nat jabbed her finger at the hardback poster resting on an easel near the front desk. It featured a blown-up head shot of Margo Fairchild, smiling blandly, like an upscale realtor.

NOVEMBER MONTHLY LECTURE
WEDNESDAY, 7 PM

"She's a local professor," Amanda explained. "A very inspiring person."

The woman with the three-letter name squinted at the poster for a few seconds — long enough for Amanda to be engulfed by a powdery floral cloud of perfume — and then shook her head. She looked deeply irritated, though Amanda had spent enough time with old people to know that their expressions didn't always match up with their moods.

"What's it *about*?" she demanded.

Amanda hesitated. She'd wanted to use the word *transgender* somewhere on the poster and in the press release, but Eve had overruled her, on the grounds that it might alienate or frighten potential audience members.

Let them come with an open mind, she'd advised. *Margo will win them over.*

"It's about taking control of your life," Amanda replied. "Finding happiness on your own terms."

The woman thought this over.

Viv, Amanda suddenly remembered. *Her name is Viv.*

Viv nodded, apparently satisfied.

"Better than soybeans," she said, and headed on her way.

The music was so loud, Margo barely heard the *ding!* of the incoming text, another message from Eve Fletcher, who was, understandably, starting to get worried.

On my way, Margo texted back, after a brief strategic delay, because it was less embarrassing than the truth, which was that she'd been sitting in the parking lot of the Senior Center for the past fifteen minutes, hiding inside her Honda Fit, listening to "Shake It Off" over and over again. *There in 5.*

She could imagine how silly she looked, a middle-aged transgender woman — with a Ph.D.! Tonight's guest speaker! — singing along to a teen anthem as old people hobbled past, heading toward the lecture hall where Margo would soon address them. But the thing was, she didn't really feel middle-aged. In her heart, she was a teenager, still learning the ins and outs of her new body. Still hoping for her share of love and happiness and fun, all those good things that the world sometimes provided.

Her phone dinged again, but this time it wasn't Eve. It was Dumell.

You go, girl!

Margo smiled. He was so sweet. Such a kind, gentle, fragile man. And handsome, too. He scared her a little. Not in a bad way, but because she liked him so much, and didn't want to screw things up. They'd been on two dates so far, the best dates she'd had in her entire life. They'd talked about everything — Iraq, basketball, families, the pros and cons of various antidepressants and anti-anxiety meds, and how strangely normal it felt when they were together, despite the fact that they were a peculiar couple on so many levels. They'd kissed — there'd been quite a bit of kissing — but they hadn't slept together, not yet. It was coming, though, right around the next corner, if one or both of them didn't chicken out.

Will I see you later? she asked.

Unless you go blind, he replied, signing off with a winky face. She shot him a smile in return.

It was past time to get out of the car, but she couldn't help herself and pressed play for one final encore. She felt safe in the car, and the song was so good. She loved the video, too, all those people dancing at the end, not only the lithe, gifted professionals, but the regular folks, bald and chunky and self-conscious and plain, with their eyeglasses and cardigan sweaters and perfectly ordinary bodies, all of them trying to rid themselves of whatever it was that held them back and knocked them down and made them wonder if they would ever find what they were looking for. They were Margo's people.

Taylor Swift wasn't actually one of them — she was just pretending, the same way Jesus had pretended to be a man. That was why she stood in front of the line, ahead of the others rather than among them. Because she was the teacher, the role model. She'd already shaken off the haters and the doubters and activated her best self. She was there to show the world what happiness and freedom looked like. You glowed with it. You did exactly what you wanted to. And whatever costume you wore, you were still yourself, unique and beautiful and unmistakable for anyone else.

Someday, Margo thought. *Someday.*

Eve's office was small and functional — pale walls, metal desk, industrial gray carpeting — the kind of office you got when taxpayers were grudgingly footing the bill. Even so, it was the biggest office at the Senior Center, and the sign on the door said *Executive Director.* Margo was duly impressed.

"Wow," she said. "Look at you. The big cheese."

Eve chuckled dismissively, but she appreciated the phrase. She *was* the big cheese in this little pond, and she was glad that Margo had a chance to observe her in her natural habitat.

"That's right," she said. "I'm not just a part-time community college student. I'm also a mid-level municipal bureaucrat."

"Don't listen to her," Amanda said. "Eve's a great director. Everyone loves her."

It was a pro forma compliment — an employee sucking up to her boss — but Eve felt a blush coming on anyway. Her relationship with Amanda was still a little unsettled, every interaction colored by the memory of that misguided after-dinner kiss and the awkwardness that had followed. Amanda had been nothing but gracious about it — mostly, she acted as if it had never even happened — but Eve had been unable to banish it from her mind, or find a way to behave normally in Amanda's presence.

"I'm not surprised," Margo said. "Eve's a sweetheart."

"Okay, okay," Eve murmured. "Enough already."

She was about to suggest that they head over to the lecture room, but Margo had

shifted her attention to Amanda's outfit —
a black-and-white polka-dot dress over
lime-green tights.

"I love your dress." She stroked Amanda's
sleeve, getting a feel for the fabric. They
were a striking pair — Margo tall and
angular in a conservative navy suit, a colorful silk scarf knotted around her throat;
Amanda short and voluptuous, deeply
feminine, despite her aggressive tattoos and
lace-up Doc Martens. "Where'd you get it?"

"Thrift store," Amanda replied, with the
smugness of the successful bargain hunter.
The dress was adorable, with a Peter Pan
collar and big white buttons down the front.
"Fourteen dollars."

"You're kidding."

"Nope. A little shop called Unicyle. Best-
kept secret in Haddington."

"I need some fun clothes," Margo said, a
little wistfully. "I just hate shopping alone.
Sometimes it's nice to have a second opinion."

"I'll take you," Amanda said. "Anytime
you want."

"Watch out," Margo laughed. "I might
take you up on that."

Eve was happy to see them getting along
so well. It was always gratifying when
friends from different parts of your life hit it

off, a reflection of your own good taste. She just hoped she'd be included if they ever did go on a shopping adventure. She hadn't done anything like that in a long time, a group of friends wandering through the mall or checking out the shops in a quaint suburban town, stepping out of changing rooms with dubious or hopeful expressions. Then they'd stop at Starbucks or a wine bar for a postmortem, shopping bags resting by their tired feet. It was such an appealing fantasy, exactly the sort of innocent female camaraderie Eve needed in her life. But it was hard to reconcile with the guilt she was feeling toward both of the women in her office, the suspicion that she was unworthy of their friendship.

Her offense against Amanda was clear-cut, easy to define: it was sexual harassment, as much as it pained her to use the term — a violation of trust, a misuse of authority, the kind of thing you could rightfully lose a job over. With Margo, the betrayal was a bit murkier, more private and indirect and possibly more forgivable, though it didn't actually feel that way at the moment, probably because the transgression was so fresh in her mind.

It had happened the night before, right after she'd come home from class. All she'd done was google the phrase "transgender woman." She'd told herself she was acting out of simple curiosity — a perfectly reasonable impulse — except that she didn't end up clicking on the sober informational links that would have led her to helpful articles on hormone therapy, Adam's apple surgery, antidiscrimination laws, or anything else decent and aboveboard. Oh, no. She'd gone straight to the smut, as usual, to the Hot Brazilian Trannies and the Slutty Thai Ladyboys and the Dirty Chicks with Dicks, insisting to herself the whole time that she was disgusted by what she saw — the exploitation of vulnerable people, the reductive sexualization of something that went way beyond sex — though not so disgusted that it stopped her from sampling several videos, and then watching an eight-minute clip called *Tranny Seduces MILF* three times in a row, despite the fact that the characters were speaking Portuguese with no subtitles, though in Eve's defense, they weren't saying much besides *Oy!* and *Deus!*

It was pretty hot, she had to admit, though in a very uncomfortable way. A true jolt to her system, one of those mind-expanding moments when you found yourself aroused by something that had never even been on your erotic radar. A beautiful dark-haired woman with an erect penis speaking a mysterious foreign language. There was something almost mythological about it.

On a moral level, Eve was pretty sure that she hadn't done anything truly wrong. She was just a human being watching other human beings do what humans sometimes did. She'd wanted to *know,* and now she did. *Oy!* It was nothing personal. *Deus!* It had nothing to do with Margo, and nothing to do with herself.

And yet, at the same time, she knew it did. *Tranny* and *MILF. MILF* and *Tranny.* They were just labels, a shorthand to organize the chaos of the world. But the labels have a funny way of becoming our names, whether we agree with them or not. *Margo* and *Eve. Me* and *you.* She must have looked puzzled or upset, because she was suddenly aware of a strange silence in the room. She looked up and saw both of the friends she'd wronged staring at her with concerned expressions.

"Eve?" Amanda said. "Are you okay?"

"Fine." Eve mustered a businesslike smile and clapped her hands once, softly. "Guess we better get this show on the road."

Julian was worried. November always felt like a setback, what with the clock change and the sudden onset of darkness, the bitter wind and that ominous sense of *falling behind.* It reminded him too much of last year, the paralyzing sadness that had set in with the cold weather, day after day when he saw no reason to get out of bed, not even to take a shower. That was rock bottom, flopping around like a hooked fish in the tangled sheets, smelling his own sour stink and not caring enough to do anything about it. He didn't think it was going to happen again, not with these new meds, but you never knew. That was the scary part. *You never knew.*

It was a chilly night to be out on a skateboard, with a damp headwind that made the air itself feel like an obstacle. By the time he rolled into the parking lot, his face was pretty much frozen in place. He hesitated for a moment, exhaling vapor clouds and staring at the front of the building, which was bigger and more impressive from this angle than it was from the road. Several old people were making the arduous journey from the parking lot to the well-lit front entrance, moving in super-slow motion.

Julian picked up his skateboard and joined the herd. He understood just how pathetic this was — he had no intention of mentioning it to Ethan or to anyone else, even as a joke — but he also accepted the sad truth of his life: *he literally had nothing better to do.* He was eighteen years old and had come to the fucking Senior Center in search of a good time. Only fifty years ahead of schedule.

Dr. Fairchild had mentioned the lecture yesterday, and invited the whole class to come out — it was free and open to the public — if they weren't already sick of the sound of her voice. *It'd be nice to see some friendly faces in the crowd,* she'd told them. Mrs. Fletcher would definitely be there — she ran the Senior Center and had organized the whole thing — and Dumell said he was hoping to make it, too, but only at the tail end, because he had a class on Wednesday nights.

Julian was hoping that maybe they'd all go out for a drink afterward, though he promised himself that he wouldn't get sloppy drunk like the last time, when he'd ended up on all fours on Haddington Boulevard, barfing into the sewer while Mrs. Fletcher rubbed his back and told him to let it all out. He'd emailed her the next day, apologizing profusely for the inappropriate comments he'd made about her body — not untrue, but totally out of line — and she'd assured him that there were no hard feelings.

He entered the lecture room behind a bulky old man in a windbreaker and baseball cap. The poor guy had a bum leg that he dragged along behind him. Every step he took, it was like he was drawing a new line in the sand.

The room was pretty full, probably close to a hundred people. Julian glanced around, hoping to spot one of his classmates — Russ or Barry, or even Mr. Ho — but all he saw was a bunch of white-haired geriatrics craning their necks and squinting in his direction, as if they'd ordered a pizza an hour ago and were wondering if he might be the goddam delivery guy.

The man in front of him limped into a row with two empty seats on the aisle and Julian followed, because an aisle seat seemed like a smart idea, in case he felt the need to make a quick exit. He bent down and stashed his skateboard under the folding chair. Straightening up, he noticed that his neighbor was watching him with an amused expression.

"Don't see too many of those things around here," the old guy observed. His nose was swollen and veiny, and his baseball cap said *U.S.S. Kitty Hawk.*

Julian nodded politely, not wanting to get into a big discussion while they waited. The old guy stuck out his hand.

"Al Huff," he said. "I live on Hogarth Road."

Julian was sorry he'd sat here.

"Julian Spitzer. Sanborn Avenue."

They shook. Al's hand was soft and dry, weirdly puffy.

"You here for the lecture?" he asked.

Julian couldn't help himself. He glanced around, then spoke in a confidential tone.

"Who cares about the lecture? I came for the ladies."

Al's laugh was loud, but a little wheezy, half cough.

"Me too," he said. "Maybe one of us'll get lucky."

Julian said the odds were on their side, but Al wasn't listening anymore. He was twisting in his seat, trying to look over his shoulder. Julian followed his gaze and saw that Dr. Fairchild had entered the room, along with Mrs. Fletcher and a younger woman, and the three of them began moving toward the stage in single file. Except for the absence of music, it felt almost like a wedding procession, the audience watching in rapt silence as the guests of honor made their way down the aisle. Mrs.

Fletcher nodded to Julian as she passed, and Dr. Fairchild's face blossomed into an expression of happy surprise at the sight of him. The younger woman — she was short and a little heavy, but kind of sexy — gave him a puzzled glance, as if she wondered what the hell someone his age was doing there. When Julian turned back around, he saw that Al Huff was scowling and shaking his head.

"What a shame," he said. "What a goddam shame."

Margo took a deep breath and forced herself to smile. It was a good crowd, bigger than she'd expected, at least two-thirds women. She hadn't even begun her speech and one elderly gentleman was already snoring in the second row, making a soft gargling sound that came and went at random intervals.

"Good evening." She tapped her fingernail on the bulb of the handheld microphone. "Can everyone hear me okay?"

The response was mostly affirmative, though there was some disgruntled murmuring scattered through the room, probably due more to individual hearing impairments than any problem with the sound system. Margo glanced at Eve, who gave her a thumbs-up from the front row.

"I'll try to speak slowly and clearly," she said, scanning the crowd for allies. She was glad to see Julian Spitzer — extra credit, not that he needed any — but she made a conscious decision not to look in his direction for moral support. He was an outlier in this group, totally unrepresentative of the demographic she was hoping to connect with. Instead she found an equally encouraging face to focus on — it was a trick she'd learned in public speaking class — in this case, a plump, pleasant-looking woman in a lavender turtleneck, sitting in the fourth row, dead center. She wasn't smiling, exactly, but she had a patient, benevolent expression, like a proud grandmother at a piano recital.

"Thank you so much for coming out tonight. You're the first group of seniors that I've ever addressed."

Usually Margo spoke to young people, mostly high school students, because they needed to be exposed to transgender role models, and if not her, then who? She remembered how lonely she had been as a teenager, detached from the world by a secret that she could barely admit to herself, let alone her parents or teachers or friends. What she wouldn't have given back then to hear a trans adult tell her that she wasn't alone, that happiness and wholeness were possible, that you could find a way to become the person you knew in your heart you truly were, despite all the undeniable evidence to the contrary.

The teenagers she spoke to were usually on pretty good behavior. They laughed at her jokes and applauded politely when she was done. But Margo wasn't fooled. She knew the bullies were out there, smirking and muttering insults under their breath, hating her because hating was so much fun, and feeling superior was its own reward. It always took something out of her to stand in front of them, to offer herself up for their condescension and mockery, but she did it. She did it because those kids were the future, and even the worst of them could have a change of heart, or at least be shamed into silence.

But these old people in front of her tonight, they weren't the future. They belonged to the past, and Margo had learned from bitter experience — not just with her mother, but with a whole generation of aunts and uncles and family friends and neighbors and acquaintances — that very few of them were willing to examine their fundamental beliefs about gender, let alone revise them so they could make room for trans people in their hearts and minds. It had gotten to the point where she had stopped even trying to argue with her older relatives; it just wasn't worth the effort and the heartache. You just had to wait them out. They'd be gone before too long, taking their narrow-minded, uncharitable ideas along with them.

That was why she'd initially declined Eve's invitation to speak at the Senior Center. But then Eve had performed some tricky PC jujitsu, calling Margo out for ageism and hypocrisy, for doing to seniors what society had done to LGBT people for so long. She reminded Margo that older people were a vulnerable and often stigmatized part of the community, and that it was both morally wrong and politically counterproductive to write them off as a lost cause. After all, they vote. And they have children and grandchildren, the power to give or withhold their love and approval.

Margo looked directly at the woman in the lavender turtleneck. The woman didn't resemble Margo's mother — she seemed soft and easygoing, where Donna Fairchild had been sinewy and judgmental — but she was about the same age, and shaped by the same social forces. She could have been her mother's friend or co-worker. It was close enough.

I'm talking to you, Margo thought. *I hope you'll listen.*

"Good evening, everybody."

She stepped out from behind the podium, letting the crowd take a good look at her body, giving them time to register all the particulars — her unusual height, her pretty hair, her full breasts and narrow hips, her long muscular legs. It was something she was still getting used to, this need people had to scrutinize her from head to toe, as if all of life were a beauty pageant, and every woman a contestant. She even did a little twirl, because the judges liked to see your back as well as your front. It wasn't fair, but Margo knew better than anyone that fairness and gender rarely intersected.

"My name is Margo Fairchild," she announced, "and I used to be a man."

Julian was trying to concentrate on the slide show, a series of photos that documented Dr. Fairchild's early life — baby pictures, the bright-eyed toddler, birthday hats and Halloween costumes and presents on Christmas morning. Cub Scouts and Little League and a smile with a missing tooth.

"I was an adorable little boy and a very

good son," Dr. Fairchild explained. "Everyone said so."

Al Huff let out a groan of despair.

"It's a mental illness," he said.

Al had been delivering this sort of com-
mentary for the entire lecture, in a loud
voice he seemed to think was a whisper. It
was a huge disruption, but no one in the
nearby rows seemed to mind. They acted
like it was perfectly normal, like Al had a
God-given right to express every single
thought that passed through his mind, no
matter how stupid or offensive.

Julian glanced around, checking for empty
seats. A few were available, but none of
them were near the aisle, and he wouldn't
be able to move without forcing a bunch of
old people to stand up and let him pass,
drawing a ton of attention to himself in the
process.

"I had a growth spurt in seventh grade,"
Dr. Fairchild announced, and you could see
it in the pictures. All at once, Mark was a
gangly adolescent with pimples, braces, and
a mortified smile. "There were times when
I woke up in the morning and could tell
from my pajama pants that my legs had gotten longer while I slept. It was a nightmare.
People kept telling me, *You're turning into a
handsome young man,* which was the last

thing I wanted to be. But there didn't seem to be any way to stop it from happening. It had a biological momentum of its own, like my body was telling me, *You'll be a man whether you like it or not.*"

Julian's phone vibrated in his pocket. He pulled it out and saw that it was a text from Ethan, who'd been bugging him to come to Burlington for the weekend to smoke some weed and check out the campus, in case he wanted to transfer sophomore year.

Julian put the phone away without responding. It was cool that Ethan had invited him, and it should have been a no-brainer to say yes. Why wouldn't he want to go away for the weekend, sleep on a dorm room floor, get a taste of real college life? But for some reason the thought of the trip made him anxious, all that pressure to be normal and have a good time with kids his own age. In Julian's experience, guaranteed fun usually just left him more depressed than he'd been in the first place.

"Good Christ," said Al. "I can't even look at this."

The picture on the screen showed young Mark in a basketball uniform, looming over his scrawny teammates.

"The only good thing that happened to me in junior high was that I started playing basketball in a serious way," Dr. Fairchild observed. A flurry of images followed, documenting Mark Fairchild's career as a high school superstar. Some of the photos came from newspapers and yearbooks; others were candid shots taken at school or home. In every one of them, even those taken in classrooms or on a living room couch, Mark was wearing a basketball uniform or a warm-up suit with long pants and a zippered top.

"I felt like myself on the court. That was the only place. Everywhere else I felt like a big mistake."

To illustrate this point, a prom photo appeared, Mark Fairchild tall and handsome in a classic black tuxedo, his arm around a pretty girl in a shiny pink gown. The girl was beaming with happiness, Mark not so much.

"I remember that night so clearly. I was miserable in my tux. I wanted to be in a gown like the one my date was wearing, to feel the skirt swish against my legs while I danced. I just wanted to feel pretty on my prom night, to be seen for who I truly was."

"That's wrong," Al muttered. "It's unnatural."

Julian had finally had enough.

"Dude," he snapped. "Could you please

be quiet? People are trying to listen."

Al wasn't offended. In fact, he seemed genuinely interested in Julian's opinion.

"Do you think that's natural?" he asked.

"There's nothing natural about gender," Julian informed him. "It's a social construction."

Al shook his head. "I don't know what that means."

Julian was sorry he'd opened his mouth. Luckily his phone buzzed, saving him from further explanation.

"Excuse me," he said, reaching into his pocket.

It was Ethan again, reminding him to bring a sleeping bag.

I'm not coming, Julian wanted to write, but he couldn't think of a good excuse.

I have plans?

I hate the bus?

I don't want to sleep on the floor?

He was still staring at the empty text bubble when he noticed that someone was crouching beside him in the aisle. It was the young woman in the polka-dot dress, Eve Fletcher's employee. She was looking at him with a sour expression, as if he were the troublemaker who was ruining the lecture for everyone else.

"Excuse me." She nodded toward Al, who

was ranting about a man being a man and a woman being a woman. "Could you please tell your grandfather to keep it down?"

Eve was trying not to cry; it didn't seem like something the executive director should do at a public event. It was hard, though — the slide show was breaking her heart, the inexorable progress of a child moving through time, changing with every picture, yet somehow remaining the same person. Mark Fairchild had been a beautiful boy — so confident, so *happy,* or so it seemed. But there was Margo standing right beside the screen, insisting that it had all been a lie and a more or less constant torment, a nightmare she didn't know she could escape until much later in her life.

Of course Eve's thoughts turned to Brendan — how could they not? She was overcome by an almost desperate longing to see her son's face, to put her arms around him, to hear his voice, to assure herself that he was okay. She'd been a fool to surrender Parents Weekend to Ted, to volunteer for her own deprivation. She could feel her only child slipping away from her, and understood that she'd been complicit in the process. They hadn't spoken on the phone in almost two weeks, and their text exchanges had been brief and unrevealing, just the usual banalities and apologetic requests for money. It wasn't that she'd forgotten him, but she had allowed him to fade in her mind, to become peripheral. And it had happened so quickly, with so little resistance from either of them. She'd justified it by reminding herself that a little distance was good, that he was growing up, becoming independent, and that she was reclaiming a little of her own life, and maybe some of that was true, but the expanding lump in her throat suggested otherwise.

"This is my mother," Margo said, as an old high school yearbook photo filled the screen, a pretty young woman with dark hair and an enigmatic smile. "Her name was Donna Ryan when this picture was taken. A few years later she became Donna Fairchild."

A wedding-day picture replaced the yearbook photo, the bride admiring herself in an oval mirror. And suddenly the bride was a bald, emaciated woman in a hospital bed, staring at the camera with a bleak, defeated expression.

"If she were alive today, she'd be seventy-four years old. She died too young."

Donna washed the dishes. She fed a baby with a tiny spoon. She stood beside Mark on the day of his high school graduation. Her head only reached to his shoulder.

"I fooled a lot of people," Margo said. "But I never fooled her."

Another picture appeared, this one an overexposed snapshot from the late seventies or early eighties: Donna Fairchild, neither young nor old, standing on the beach in front of an empty lifeguard chair, wearing dark sunglasses and a blue bathing suit with a ruffled skirt. Her face was blank, unreadable.

"I loved that bathing suit," Margo said. "I loved it a little too much for my own good."

Donna remained frozen on the screen throughout the entire anecdote that followed. It happened when Margo was in fifth grade, and still thought of herself as Mark. One day Mark pretended to be sick so he could take a day off from school. Previously, his mother, a second-grade teacher, had stayed home to care for him when he was feeling ill, but on this particular day, Donna decided he was old enough to stay home alone, which was exactly what he'd been hoping for. As soon as his mother left for work, Mark went straight to her bedroom and found the blue bathing suit with the ruffled skirt. It was right where he'd expected, in the second drawer from the top.

"I thought I just wanted to touch it. But touching it wasn't enough."

Mark was only eleven and hadn't begun his big growth spurt, so the suit fit surprisingly well, everywhere except the chest, which had a droopy, deflated appearance. It looked a lot better once he stuffed the padded bra cups with paper towels. In fact, it looked amazing.

"I'm pretty sure I hypnotized myself. I must have stared at my reflection in the mirror for fifteen or twenty minutes. It was like I was seeing *me* for the first time."

Mark eventually left his mother's bedroom, but he didn't take off the swimsuit. He went downstairs, opened a bag of potato chips, and turned on the TV. He figured he had at least four hours before he had to worry about anyone coming home and finding him like that.

"It was such a luxury," Margo said. "Just being alone in the house. That *never* happened."

It was a beautiful hot day, late September or early October, and Mark headed out to the back deck to do a little sunbathing, an activity very popular among the girls at his school. He brought a portable radio and some Bain de Soleil, and he tugged down the shoulder straps of the bathing suit to avoid an unsightly tan line.

"It was so relaxing. The sun and the music. I guess I just let my guard down and fell asleep."

It must have been a deep sleep, because he didn't hear the car pulling into the driveway or his mother entering the house and calling his name. She'd been worried about him, and had come home on her lunch break to see how he was doing. What she found was the daughter she didn't know she had, wearing a matronly bathing suit that did her no favors.

"For a long time, my mother didn't say a word. She just kept staring at me and shaking her head. *No, no, no.* I remember how pale she looked, like she'd just received terrible news about someone she loved, an illness or an unexpected death. When she finally did manage to speak, she asked me if this was my idea of a joke, if I thought it was *funny* to wear her clothes. It's clear to me now that she desperately wanted me to say, *Yes, Mom, it was just a stupid joke.* But I was so scared and ashamed, all I could do was tell the truth. *I love this bathing suit. It's my favorite.* She ordered me to go upstairs, take it off, and never touch it again. Or any other article of her clothing, for that matter."

They never discussed the incident, at least not directly; they weren't that kind of family. But Donna had seen what she'd seen, and it had frightened her.

"She had a code word," Margo explained. "She called it my *nonsense*. Whenever my parents left me home alone — and believe me, they didn't do it very much — my mother would say, *You better not get up to any of your nonsense!* If she ever caught me looking sad, she'd say, *Is this about that nonsense?* And when I finally got engaged to be married, she said, *I hope this means you're done with all that nonsense.*" Margo shook her head, amazed by her mother's stubbornness. "Even on her deathbed, after I'd transitioned and was living as a woman, she looked at me and said, *Are you ever gonna stop with this nonsense?*"

Eve knew it was rude to text in the middle of a presentation, but she couldn't stop herself. She pulled out her phone and sent a quick message to Brendan.

I miss you.

"I'm sorry, Mom," Margo told the photograph. "I can't stop my nonsense. I'm your daughter and I love you very much."

I couldn't wait for Thanksgiving. I just

wanted to go home, sleep in my own bed, eat some decent food, sneak onto the golf course with Troy and Wade, polish off a couple of blunts and a bottle of shit vodka, just like the old days. We'd get completely annihilated on Wednesday night and then drag ourselves to the homecoming game on Thursday morning, where we could brag about our hangovers to people we hadn't seen in three months, though it felt *way* longer than that. Becca would be cheering on the sidelines — the last football game of her career — and I was hoping maybe I could catch her in a sentimental mood and convince her to give me another chance. I loved the way she looked in that stretchy little dress they all wore, red with a big white H on the front.

H is for hot, I used to tell her.

H is for ho, I used to tell my friends.

The only thing I dreaded about going home was having to talk about my *college experience,* pretending it was the greatest thing ever, parties on top of hookups mixed in with challenging classes and inspiring professors and lots of cool new friends, when the truth was, it had pretty much all turned to shit in the past couple of weeks. I was on the road to failing Econ and Math, Amber wasn't responding to my texts, and

Zack was hardly ever around. He was spending all his time with Lexa, sleeping in her room, pushing her wheelchair all over campus, like he was her fucking caretaker instead of her boyfriend. One day I bumped into him at the Student Center Chick-fil-A and asked him point-blank if he was pissed at me, but he said he wasn't. I told him it didn't feel like that, and asked why he'd never said a word to me about Lexa.

"I thought we were friends."

"We are," he said, though he didn't sound all that happy about it. "But honestly? The way we talk about girls? The shit we say? I didn't want to do that to her. She deserves better."

"What are you talking about? I would never make fun of a disabled person."

"It's not you, bro. It's me."

"What's that supposed to mean?"

He took a while to answer. I could see him thinking it over, trying to get it right.

"No offense, dude, but the person I am when we're together? I just don't want to be that guy anymore."

All right. So he was in love or whatever. Good for him, I guess. It didn't really bother me, except that I hated being alone in our double, especially at night, when I had work to do, and I always had work to do, not that

I ever did any. When Zack was around, we would procrastinate for hours, trash-talking and playing video games, and it would feel great, exactly like college was meant to be. But on my own it just seemed kinda pathetic, like I was a loser with no friends who was failing half his classes. I started keeping the door wide open, in case somebody I knew walked by and felt like saving me from my solitary confinement.

That's what I was doing that boring-as-shit Wednesday night, sitting on the ratty couch Zack and I had found on Baxter Avenue, playing Smash on auto pilot — I was Captain Falcon — just killing time, waiting for *something* to happen that would give me an excuse to get off my ass and out of that depressing room. I remember how my heart jumped when the phone buzzed — I was thinking, *hoping,* Amber, Becca, Zack, Wade, in that order — and how disappointed I was when I paused the game and realized it was just a text from my mother.

I miss you.

I mean, it was sweet, don't get me wrong. I was glad she missed me. But it didn't really help with my situation.

Miss you too, I texted back.

And then I looked up and saw Sanjay standing in my doorway, staring at me with his big sad eyes. Somehow, just from that look on his face, before he even said a word, I could tell that bad news was coming.

Somewhere in the middle of the slide show, Margo felt the audience slipping away from her. No one laughed at her jokes; a handful of spectators were behaving badly, disrupting her talk with loud whispers and possibly derisive comments, some of which drew appreciative snickers from their neighbors. The applause at the end of the main presentation barely rose to the level of basic politeness.

But it wasn't until the lights came back on for the Q&A that she realized the extent of her flop. She could see it in the faces staring back at her — some blank, some icy, many others disgusted or confused.

"Go ahead," she said. "Ask me anything. There's no such thing as a stupid question."

The silence that followed took on an embarrassing density. Then, mercifully, she noticed a hand inching upward in the center of the crowd. It belonged to the woman in the lavender turtleneck, her imaginary ally, whose face no longer seemed quite so sweet or supportive.

"Some of us ladies were wondering," she said in a frail voice. "Which rest room do you use?"

Really? Margo thought. It wasn't just the question that depressed her, it was the loud murmur of approval that followed it. *After everything I just told you,* that's *what you want to know?*

"I use the women's room," she said, forcing herself to smile. "I think I'd cause quite a stir if I wandered into the men's room."

The seniors took a moment to discuss the matter among themselves. Margo noticed another hand jabbing into the air, offering her a lifeline.

"Next question. Over there."

The words were already out by the time she realized that she'd called on Julian Spitzer's neighbor, the loudmouth who'd made such a ruckus during the slide show. He rose with some difficulty and gazed at her for a long time with a weirdly expectant expression, his arms spread wide, as if he himself were the question.

"Mark," the man finally said. "Don't you recognize me?"

Margo winced, but maintained her calm. "I'm sorry, sir. I don't go by that name anymore. Please call me Margo."

"You really don't know who I am?" He removed his baseball cap, giving her a better look at his face, but it didn't help. Margo had spent so much time trying to forget so many things that huge swaths of the past were lost to her. And that was okay.

"I'm sorry. You'll have to help me out."

"Al Huff." The man's tone was reproachful, as if he shouldn't have been forced to say his name out loud. "*Coach* Huff. From St. Benedict's? We played you twice in the state tournament, '88 and '89? You were such a great player, Mark. Best pure shooter I ever saw at the high school level."

"Oh, wow." Margo nodded in fake recognition, trying unsuccessfully to connect the Coach Huff she remembered — former Marine, lean and athletic, a motivator and disciplinarian — with the old man standing in front of her, his face bloated with alcohol and disappointment. If she remembered correctly, Al Huff had resigned under a cloud, some kind of recruiting scandal, ten or maybe even fifteen years ago. "It's good to see you."

"You killed us with that buzzer beater in the semis." He shook his head, as if the memory still stung. "Just broke our backs. I'll never forget that."

"Coach Huff is a local legend," Margo informed the crowd. "St. Benedict's was our arch-rival and always one of the best teams in the state."

A few people clapped for the local legend, but Al Huff didn't seem to notice. He opened his arms a little wider.

"Mark," he said. "What the hell happened? Why would you do this to yourself?"

Margo tried to smile, but she couldn't quite pull it off. Moments like this always knocked her off-balance, times when she realized that other people — some of them near-strangers — were more invested in the young man named Mark Fairchild than she herself had ever been.

"Coach," she said. "This is who I am."

Al Huff looked at the floor and shook his head. When he spoke it sounded like he was close to tears.

"You need help, son. You can't live like this."

"Thanks for your concern," Margo said, a little frostily. "But I'm doing just fine. I'm happier right now than I've ever been in my life."

As if to underline this declaration, Dumell chose that moment to arrive. He entered through the back door, unzipping his leather jacket in slow motion as he glanced warily at the old white people in the audience, and then at Margo. He grinned when their eyes met, and gave her a sheepish little wave, apologizing for his tardiness. She wanted to blow him a kiss, but settled on a fleeting smile before returning to her duties.

"Any other questions?" she asked.

Sanjay had warned me about what to expect on the way over, so I wasn't exactly surprised when I walked into the Student Center and saw my face up on the wall. But it still felt like a kick in the gut.

It was crowded in there, lots of kids milling around, checking out the paintings and sculptures, all of them made by undergrads in the Visual Arts Program. Most of it was the standard crap you'd find at any high school art show — still lifes with fruit and wine bottles, self-portraits of hot girls, black and white photographs of poor people. What made it a college art show were the little cards that accompanied each item, which listed the name of the artist and the title of the piece, along with a brief Statement of Intent.

The "project" I was part of was the biggest and most eye-catching work in the show. It took up an entire wall of the gallery and was the first thing you noticed when you walked in: two rows of bigger-than-life portraits, each one with a little caption underneath. The card identified the artist as Katherine Q. Douglass, class of 2017, and the title of the work as *My Call-Out Wall.* The Statement of Intent read, *I asked a few of my friends to call someone out for behavior that damages our community and threatens our safety. This is an interactive project. Feel free to add your own call-out to the Call-Out Wall!*

The portraits themselves were pretty good — acrylic on canvas, according to the card — not perfect, but I recognized myself without any problem. There were ten faces in all, nine of them dudes, along with one unlucky blond girl, who was actually pretty cute. Two of the guys were black; one was Asian. There were no names attached to the faces, only a brief description of the offense the person supposedly committed. A ginger-haired dude *GROPED ME ON THE DANCE FLOOR.* The Asian kid *THINKS HE'S WHITE.* The blond girl *LIES RIGHT TO YOUR FACE.* A fat kid I'd seen around was a *CULTURAL APPROPRIATOR.* One of the black dudes — I'm pretty sure he was a football player — was an *EXTREME HOMO-PHOBE.* A bro in a knit cap was a *GAS-LIGHTER,* whatever that was. Three guys were labeled *RAPIST.*

"I'm not sure this is legal," Sanjay told me. "It's got to be a violation of due process or something."

"Whatever," I said, because I really didn't give a shit about due process.

"You want to get out of here?" he asked.

I knew I should leave, but I couldn't stop staring at my face on the wall. It looked so *real* up there, just as real as the one I saw in the mirror every day. Even worse, I was grinning like an idiot, as if I were thrilled to be included in the art show and had no objection to the words written beneath the painting, a brief summary of my entire life: *HUGE DISAPPOINTMENT.*

I smelled a sharp, medicinal odor and turned to see Amber's friend Cat standing right beside me, rubbing sanitizer into her hands.

"Wow," she said. "Look who's here. You've got some nerve."

I was surprised by the coldness in her voice. Cat had always been pretty nice to me. She nodded toward the wall.

"I had a hard time with your eyes. They're a little asymmetrical."

"You did this?"

She shook her head, like I should have known better.

"I told you not to hurt her."

Eve hadn't planned on company, but she

was relieved to see that the living room looked fine. The throw pillows on the couch were plump and perfectly spaced, one per cushion, exactly as God had intended. There were no slippers abandoned on the rug, no mug of yesterday's tea or crumpled kleenex marring the pristine surface of the coffee table. Even the TV remotes — all three of them — were resting in front of the flat screen in perfect alignment, arranged in descending order of size. It was, if anything, a little too neat and fussy, as if she'd stepped inside a museum exhibit documenting the uneventful life of a woman of exactly her age and circumstances. But better that than a dirty sock on the arm of the wingback chair or a beige bra slung over the newel post.

"What a lovely home." Margo surveyed the décor with what seemed like sincere admiration, and maybe even a touch of longing. "Thank you so much for inviting us."

Dumell and Amanda echoed this sentiment, while Julian Spitzer lingered near the door, skateboard tucked under his arm, nodding in dubious agreement.

"You're welcome," Eve told them. "Make yourselves comfortable."

Shifting into hostess mode, she ducked

into the kitchen to see what she could round up in the way of snacks and beverages. The answer, unfortunately, was not a whole lot. On the plus side, there was an unopened bottle of Australian Shiraz on the counter; wine was one thing she rarely forgot at the grocery store. On the minus side, the refrigerator held only a single beer, a Dos Equis Amber she couldn't remember buying, along with a bottle of Hard Lemonade that must have been over a year old. The food situation wasn't much better — half a sleeve of not-quite-fresh Stoned Wheat Thins, a block of cheddar that had hardened around the edges, a handful of baby carrots that seemed okay if you didn't look too close, and a tub of hummus she wouldn't have foisted on her own worst enemy.

She found a platter and arranged the crackers in a semicircle around the brick of cheese, which looked a lot better after some minor cosmetic surgery. If nothing else, the carrots added a splash of color. The hummus went straight into the garbage, where it should have gone days ago. Removing the cork from the Shiraz, she heard a reassuring burst of laughter from the living room, and realized that it had been a long time since she'd had this many people in the house.

She'd made the invitation on an impulse,

after the lecture room had cleared out. The five of them were standing around, trying to figure out where to go for dinner. It was a frustrating conversation — Dumell didn't like Thai food, Amanda avoided fish whenever possible, Julian wasn't hungry — without any resolution in sight. Margo, the guest of honor, wasn't even participating. She looked tired and rattled — who could blame her? — and it suddenly occurred to Eve that she might not be in the mood for a big night out.

I have an idea, she said. *Why don't you all come to my house? I can order some pizza and we can decompress.*

And now here they all were, laughing and making themselves comfortable.

How about that? she thought, as she grabbed the wine and the snack platter, and went to join her friends in the living room.

Amanda didn't mind taking one for the team. Somebody needed to go to the liquor store, and it might as well be her. Dumell had been the first to volunteer, but Margo had looked so happy, snuggling up to him on the couch — she kept patting his leg and poking him in the shoulder, as if checking to make sure he was real — that it seemed like a shame to separate them. And besides, this was still kind of a work thing, even if she was technically off the clock.

She was glad to get out for a bit, to leave the others to their wine and chitchat. She wasn't in a super-social mood, not after the debacle at the Senior Center. It was just so disheartening, to get yourself all pumped up with optimism — a sense of ownership and personal fulfillment — and then have to sit there and watch your One Big Idea crash and burn.

She glanced at Julian, her fidgety but mostly silent passenger.

"Want some music?"

"Whatever," he said. "You're the driver."

Come on, dude, she thought. *Help me out here.* He'd seemed happy enough to accompany her on the liquor run but apparently didn't feel obligated to contribute anything in the way of conversation.

"You like Prince?" she asked.

"He's okay."

Whatever. She pressed play, and the atmosphere inside of the car was instantly transformed by the spare, sultry sound of "When Doves Cry," possibly the sexiest song ever written. It seemed a little too intimate for the circumstances, but there was no way she was gonna turn it off.

"I've been going through a Prince phase

lately," she told him. "I sort of forgot what a genius he is. So many great songs."

Julian gave one of those noncommittal therapist nods, like it was interesting that she felt that way, not that he necessarily agreed with her.

"What kind of music do you like?" she asked.

"I don't know. All kinds, I guess."

Jesus. It had been a long time since Amanda had hung out with a college freshman, so she wasn't sure if this was standard behavior or not. Maybe terse, grudging replies were the most you could hope for. At least he was cute.

"Is this weird for you?" she asked. "Hanging out with a bunch of old people?"

"You're not that old."

"Ha ha," she said. "You seemed a little uncomfortable back there. I thought you might need a break or something."

"It wasn't the people," Julian explained. "It just kinda freaked me out to be in that house."

"Why's that?"

"You know her son? Brendan?"

"Not well."

"I went to high school with him." Julian gave a shudder of disgust. "Such a fucking asshole. It gave me the creeps, walking in there and seeing his picture on the wall. Felt like I could *smell* him."

"I get that." Amanda had only met Brendan once, but that was enough. "I didn't like him much myself."

"Nothing against Eve," Julian assured her. "She's really nice."

"Eve's great," Amanda agreed. "Everybody loves Eve."

Sanjay really needed to go. He had work to do, a big problem set in CS and a dense chapter in his Architectural History textbook. Sitting in a coffee shop listening to someone else's problems was not a productive use of his time.

"This totally sucks," Brendan said. "I don't know what to do."

Sanjay wasn't sure how to respond. He had no experience with a situation like this, and absolutely nothing of value to contribute, which made it even crazier that he'd gotten himself stuck in the role of advisor.

"Maybe you should apologize," he suggested.

"I already did," Brendan said. "She won't even answer my texts."

The worst part of it was, Sanjay didn't even like Brendan, or any of those other guys he'd met for dinner his first night of college. His roommate, Dylan, was okay, but the rest of them were jerks. It would have been fine with Sanjay if he'd never spoken to any of them ever again.

But then he'd walked into the art show after dinner, and had seen Brendan's portrait up on the Call-Out Wall. It seemed wrong to publicly shame someone like that, and Sanjay thought Brendan should know about it. That's what he would have wanted if it had been his own face up there, not that it ever would have been. The problem was, you incurred an obligation when you made yourself the bearer of bad news. You couldn't just stand up and walk away whenever you felt like it.

"I didn't even do anything," Brendan muttered. "She punched me in the nuts, and I'm the bad guy?"

"She punched you?"

Brendan shrugged, like the details didn't really matter. "You wanna get drunk? I got some vodka back in my room."

"I don't drink."

"We could smoke some weed."

"I don't do that, either."

Brendan looked perplexed. "What *do* you do? I mean, for fun. On the weekends?"

"My sister's a senior," Sanjay told him. "She has a car and she drives home every weekend to see her boyfriend. I usually go with her."

"So you hang out with your buddies?"

"They're all away at school. I just do my work and watch movies with my parents. They like having me there. And the food is way better than the crap we get at the Higg."

"Sounds pretty chill," said Brendan. "I haven't seen my mom since the day I got here."

"I bet she misses you."

"Yeah. She just sent me this."

Brendan picked up his phone and did some swiping. When he found what he wanted, he held up the screen so Sanjay could see his mother's text and his own reply.

I miss you

Miss you too

Sanjay nodded. "Moms are the best."

"Totally," said Brendan.

He stared at the phone for a few more seconds before putting it back in his pocket. Sanjay took advantage of the lull to scoot his chair away from the table.

"I hope you don't mind," he said, rising from his chair. "I really need to go to the library."

"It's cool," said Brendan. "Do what you have to do."

■ ■ ■ ■

Sometimes, Eve thought, a casual gathering like this just sort of gelled into a spontaneous party, which was, by definition, better than a party you had planned, precisely because no one saw it coming. It was a tribute to the people involved, the chemistry of their individual personalities combined with a collective desire to salvage *something* from what otherwise might have seemed like a wasted evening, not to mention a big assist from the pitcher of margaritas Amanda had whipped up in the kitchen, using a jug of cheap tequila and a pre-made, neon-green industrial mixer that was tastier than it looked.

It was a conveniently small group — maybe a little *too* small — and they all seemed to be vibrating on the same wavelength, cracking jokes and laughing a little too loudly, toasting Margo for her excellent scarf collection, Dumell for service to his country, Amanda for the alcoholic beverages, and Julian simply for showing up, representing the millennials. There was a palpable sexual charge in the air — you couldn't have a decent party without it — mostly generated by Margo and Dumell, who, as the night went on, had graduated from hand-holding and whispered endearments to a full-on make-out session on the couch.

Eve knew it was rude to stare at the lovers, but she found it difficult to avert her gaze. Ever since she'd been aware of herself as a sexual being, going all the way back to middle school, she'd been aroused by the sight of people kissing in public, and the familiar effect was intensified in this case by the fact that Amanda was sitting only a short distance away in the wicker chair, and their eyes kept meeting in the awkward interludes that occurred while the happy couple was going at it. Most of these glances felt completely innocent — two friends rolling their eyes, sharing a moment of amused solidarity — but a few of them went deeper than that, lingering moments of silent, searching connection that made Eve wonder if a door she'd thought was closed might have swung open again.

I should kiss her, she thought, even though she'd vowed never to go down that road again, never to embarrass or expose herself the way she had that last time. *I bet she'd let me.*

This reverie was disrupted by the sudden realization that she was being watched, that

Julian was staring at *her* with the same sort of longing that she herself was directing toward Amanda. She turned in his direction, raising her glass in a silent toast, not wanting him to feel left out. He returned the gesture, gazing at her with soulful drunken sincerity.

Things were starting to get a little awkward when Margo finally extracted herself from a marathon kiss, brushing the hair from her eyes and blinking like she didn't quite know where she was. She let out a long, slow, calming breath and straightened her skirt.

"Enough of *that,*" she said, fanning her face with one hand. "Anyone feel like dancing?"

Amber went to a house party with Cat and some of her artist friends, but she left on the early side, unable to connect with the festive mood. Everybody there was really excited about the Call-Out Wall — they thought it would be great to make it a permanent installation in the Student Center — and they found it hilarious that Brendan kept texting her, begging for a moment of her time, sounding more and more pathetic with each successive message.

Amber could appreciate the poetic justice

of the situation — let him see how it felt to be silenced and powerless for once in his life, to be defined by other people — but it wasn't as gratifying as she'd hoped it might be. In fact, the more she thought about Brendan the guiltier she felt, as if she'd done something bad to him, which was totally frustrating, because he didn't deserve her sympathy or anyone else's. It was just like her — just like a girl — to feel sorry for a guy she had every right to despise, and then to turn the blame back on herself.

She could have taken Cat's advice and blocked his calls. That would have solved the problem of her constantly buzzing phone, and spared her his manipulative cries for help. But it seemed kind of harsh, and even a bit cowardly, to call someone out and then cut off all possibility of communication, as if they had no right to respond, as if they were dead to you.

Amber was tired and a little depressed. She just wanted to go to bed and forget this day had ever happened. But there was only one way she was going to be able to do that, and there was no use pretending otherwise. With a small shudder of resignation and distaste, she picked up her phone and touched her finger to his name. He answered in the middle of the first ring.

"Wow," he said. "Took you long enough."

"What do you want, Brendan?"

"I don't know. Just to talk, I guess. I've been having a rough night."

"Well," she said, a little defensively. "I've had some rough nights lately myself."

A nicer person might have picked up on her cue and asked what was wrong, maybe even expressed a little sympathy, but this was Brendan she was talking to.

"The art show," he said. "That was really fucking brutal."

"I'm sure it was. But you have to —"

"Do you really think that about me?" He sounded genuinely curious. "That I'm a huge disappointment?"

Amber hesitated. She'd known that Cat had been working on the Call-Out Wall all semester, but she hadn't realized that Brendan was a part of the installation until two days ago, when she'd helped transport the paintings from the art building to the Student Center. She was startled when she pulled off a sheet of bubble wrap and saw his happy face with the words *HORRIBLE HUMAN BEING* written beneath it like a final verdict.

What the hell is this?

It's my gift to you, Cat told her.

He's not a horrible human being. He's just —

Those were your words, Cat reminded her. *That's a direct quote.*

Amber didn't deny it. She'd said that about Brendan on the morning after their disastrous date, when she felt raw and betrayed, and Cat had been there for her, the way she always was, offering support and validation when Amber needed it most.

I was pissed. I just needed to vent.

You spoke your truth, Cat said. *Don't take it back now.*

It doesn't feel right, Amber had insisted.

Reluctantly, Cat proposed some alternate captions — *DATE RAPIST? MISOGYNIST?* — but Amber didn't think those were accurate, either.

He was just a . . . huge disappointment, that's all.

All right, Cat said. *You're being way too nice, but I'll change it if that's what you want.*

That's what I want, Amber had said, and she wasn't about to retract her words a second time, or give Brendan a reason to think he'd been forgiven. She couldn't even think about that night without feeling sick and degraded.

"Dude," she told him. "You got off easy. It could have been a lot worse, believe me."

"Amber," he said. "I'm really sorry."

"It's a little late for that."

"I know. I'm just saying."

"All right," she sighed. "I should go. I'm wiped out."

"Wait, Amber. I was just wondering —" His voice turned small and hopeless. "Could I come over and hang out with you for a while?"

"Are you fucking kidding me?"

"Not to hook up," he assured her. "I just don't want to be alone right now."

She almost laughed, but she could hear the pain in his voice.

"I'm sorry, Brendan. Our hanging out days are over."

"Yeah," he said. "I kind of figured that."

Amber ended the call and wiped away an embarrassing tear. It was so stupid and unfair that someone could treat you so badly, and still make you want to hug them. She thought she might call Cat and commission a portrait of herself for the Call-Out Wall:

JUST WANTS EVERYONE TO BE HAPPY, EVEN THE PEOPLE WHO DON'T DESERVE IT.

Dumell hated to be the bad guy, but it was a weekday and he had to work in the morning.

"Last dance," he whispered in Margo's

ear. "Then I got to take you home before I turn into a pumpkin."

"I believe it's your car that turns into a pumpkin," she told him.

They were glued together like prom dates, swaying under the spell of "Sexual Healing," which felt just then like an uncanny coincidence, a not-so-subtle message from the universe, even though it was just another song on Amanda's iPhone, part of a crowd-pleasing soul- and Motown-heavy playlist that had kept them going for the past hour and a half.

"That's even worse," he said, making unsolicited eye contact with Julian, who was very drunk, lurching around the room with his hands up, like the music had placed him under arrest. "I still owe money on that car."

Margo laughed and kissed him again. The woman loved to kiss. It was dark and she smelled good and her warm body felt just right pressing up against him. Dumell reminded himself that nothing else mattered.

Don't be scared, he thought. *There's nothing to be scared of.*

Fear was tricky, though. It had a way of sneaking up on you, making you question yourself and worry about the future. *What would people say? What would they think?*

Do I really want this?

They rotated a little, and now he was looking at Eve, who was dancing with Amanda, though they weren't actually touching each other. Eve had one hand in her hair and the other on her hip. Amanda had her eyes closed and her mouth open, head tilted upward like a blind musician. Dumell wondered if maybe something was going on there, 'cause it sure felt like it.

Good for them, he thought.

He slid his hand down Margo's back, tracing the ravine of her spine all the way to the gentle swell at the bottom, the beginning of a different landscape. He tucked his thumb inside the waistband of her skirt, tugging down a little bit, a promise for later.

"Mmmm," she said, like something tasted good.

He'd had only one bad moment the entire night, right when the music started up. Margo was normally a graceful person, with the physical control of an athlete, but you wouldn't have known it from watching her on the dance floor. In motion, she seemed bigger and more masculine than she'd been on the couch, uncomfortable in her own body, not the person Dumell wanted her to be. It must have shown on his face, because she stopped and asked him what was wrong.

She had a slightly spooky ability to read his expressions, to register every flicker of doubt or hesitation.

"Nothing," he told her. " 'Cept you dance like a white girl."

Margo had laughed with relief, as if that were the sweetest thing anyone had ever said to her. She loosened up after that and so did he. But he was still a little off-balance, unsettled by the knowledge that his feelings could — and sometimes did — turn on a dime, that he might not be able to follow through with what he'd started, that his courage would fail in the clutch the way it had so many times before, that he might hurt someone who'd trusted him. All he had to do was think himself outside of this room and this little group of people, to imagine the faces of his family, his ex-wife, his co-workers, the guys in his unit, some of them smirking, others shaking their heads, as if they had a right to judge. Who the fuck were they? They didn't know Margo, or what she'd been through, or how she made him feel. Shit, most of them didn't even know Dumell. Not really.

He felt her stiffen in his arms. She tried to smile, but her face was pale and defenseless.

"Everything okay?" she asked.

The song was still playing, but they weren't moving anymore. They were just standing there, looking at each other from across a very narrow divide.

"It's all good," he said, right before he kissed her.

The only problem with hosting a successful party, Eve thought, was the letdown you felt at the end of it, when the music stopped and the lights came on and the guests started asking for their coats. Margo and Dumell were the first dominoes to fall. Eve hugged them goodbye with a smile that was the product of pure willpower.

Amanda was already busy in the kitchen, rinsing dirty glasses and loading them into the dishwasher, preparing for her own departure. Hoping to postpone the inevitable, Eve asked her to mix one last batch of margaritas, only to be reminded, by her own employee, that they had to work in the morning.

Eve winced. "Let's not talk about work, okay? Work is sooo boring. All I ever do is work."

Amanda opened her mouth, but no words came out. She looked so cute in her polka-dot dress, her face all flushed and glistening.

"You're such a great dancer," Eve told her. "Really sexy."

"So are you. I had no idea."

Eve waved off the compliment. "I'm out of practice. I have to get out more. I spend way too much time at home, staring at my computer screen. It's not good. I need to live in my body, you know? Just get out of my head a little."

"We all do." Amanda placed the last glass in the rack and closed the dishwasher door. "It was a great party. I think Margo really enjoyed it."

Eve agreed, but didn't want to be diverted from her purpose.

"Just one more drink. What's the big deal?"

Amanda exhaled a skeptical breath. "I'm gonna be pretty hungover as it is."

"Call in sick. I won't tell the boss."

Before Amanda could respond, Julian wandered in from the living room, phone in hand, his long hair tucked girlishly behind his ears.

"What's up?" he said, with just a hint of a slur. "You guys talkin' about me again?"

"I should drive you home," Amanda told him. "You're way too drunk to ride a skateboard."

"What?" Julian looked offended. "You're

drunker'n I am."

"Not even close, dude."

"Really?" He squinted at her. "You're not drunk?"

"Maybe a little," Amanda conceded. "I would say I'm mildly inebriated."

Julian smirked. "Tell that to the breathalyzer."

"I live like five minutes away. I'm not gonna get pulled over."

Skateboards. Breathalyzers.

"Why don't you just sleep here?" Eve said. "There's three bedrooms upstairs. I have spare toothbrushes if you need them. My dentist gives them out free with every checkup."

"Mine too!" Julian was excited by the coincidence. "You go to Dr. Halawi?"

The bed in the guest room was perfectly comfortable. There were more than enough blankets, the windows weren't drafty, and the shades blocked out the moonlight much more effectively than the flimsy curtains in Amanda's own bedroom. The pajamas Eve had loaned her were soft and fit reasonably well, despite the difference in their body types. There really was no good reason why she couldn't fall asleep, especially after all the tequila she'd drunk.

It was just nerves, the by-product of a long and sometimes stressful night — the lecture, the party, new people, more dancing than she'd done in a long time. She was all wound up, her senses on high alert. It didn't help that she was also super-horny, a condition that afflicted her whenever she slept in a strange place — a hotel, her grandmother's house, a friend's apartment in the city, a bare-bones Airbnb, a tent in the woods, even a sleeper car on a train, which was something she'd experienced exactly once in her life. Being in a bed that wasn't her own instantly flooded her brain with thoughts of sex.

Or, in this case, the absence of sex.

She'd really believed that something was going to happen with Eve. They'd been flirting all night, lots of meaningful glances and not-quite-accidental contact on the dance floor. And then Eve had convinced her to sleep over, encouraging her to get even more drunk than she already was, and to go ahead and play hooky from work in the morning. It had felt like a pretty straightforward seduction, one person pressing, the other resisting, then wobbling, then giving in.

And then . . . Nothing.

Why'd you make me stay if you weren't go-

ing to do anything?

They'd had their opportunity. Right after Amanda had brushed her teeth, Eve had knocked on the guest room door and presented her with a little bedtime care package — a bath towel, a pair of clean pajamas, a bottle of Tylenol. Eve had already changed into her sleeping clothes, sweatpants and an oversized T-shirt that said, *Haddington Youth Lacrosse.* It felt so intimate seeing her boss in that context, her face tired and sweet, softer without makeup. *I thought you might need a few things.* Julian was in the bathroom — they could hear the water running — so it would have been easy for Eve to slip into the room and stay for as long as she wanted. But for some reason, she lingered shyly in the doorway.

Sleep tight, Eve told her. *I'll see you in the morning.*

Right now, though, the morning felt like an eternity away, and Amanda was dreading the thought of it. It would be so awkward, waking up hungover in Eve's house, heading downstairs with bad breath and a splitting headache, dressed in yesterday's clothes. A walk of shame, but without any shameful fun to make it worth the embarrassment. And then what were they gonna do? Eat breakfast together?

I can't, she thought. *I just can't.*

Better to just slip out now, leave a note on the kitchen table so Eve wouldn't worry. She wondered if she should knock on Julian's door on the way out, see if he was awake and wanted a ride home as well.

He was a sweet kid. He'd really opened up to her on the way back from the liquor store, telling her about his clinical depression, his hatred of high school, his fears of going away to college, the difficulty he had talking to girls his own age.

She knew exactly what was weighing him down: that helpless feeling that you were wasting your precious youth and it was your own damn fault. It was something you never quite recovered from, and it usually led to some stupid mistakes down the road, many of which were worse than a few regrettable tattoos. She wished she could climb into a time machine and make herself twenty again, just so she could be his girlfriend for a while, let him know how great he was, build up his confidence for the future. It sounded like a good idea for a TV show, a modern-day feminist superhero:

Amanda Olney, Agent of Sexual Justice.

Brendan's room was a jock shrine. Trophies from a lifetime of athletic excellence —

Little League baseball (All-Star!), Pop Warner football (County Champs!), middle school swimming (2nd Place, Backstroke!), Haddington Youth Lacrosse (Most Valuable Player!) — were crowded on top of the dresser, right below a framed photo collage that must have been assembled by Brendan's ridiculously hot cheerleader girlfriend, Becca DiIulio, since it included two different images of Becca looking fine in a bikini (one orange, one pink), the latter of which was actually autographed in silver marker, as if she were a fucking movie star: *Luv ya, Becca xxxooo!* There were three pics of Brendan with sunglasses and no shirt. He was the kind of dick who made muscleman poses for the camera and wasn't being ironic about it. Just to rub it in, he had a roll of LifeStyles condoms stashed in his sock drawer — Julian couldn't help taking a peek — eighteen in all, because you never knew when the whole cheerleading squad might show up and beg to be fucked, one right after the other.

Eighteen condoms. A little whimper of defeat leaked from Julian's throat. He hadn't bought eighteen condoms in his entire life. For a minute, he thought about searching for a sharp object — a safety pin or some nail scissors — and poking a few strategic holes in Brendan's lifestyle, but he quickly detected the flaw in this plan: all it would do was populate the world with more little Brendans, which would not be doing the world a favor.

It would be doubly weird if Brendan had a kid, because that would make Eve a grandma, and Eve didn't look like anyone's grandma. Julian had been lusting after her all night — she was wearing a snug gray pullover, just a hint of cleavage, and a fuzzy light blue skirt that he badly wanted to touch. She and Amanda were so into each other on the dance floor that Julian had expected them to start making out, though they never actually did, which was too bad.

After he finished his depressing inspection of the room, Julian turned off the light and climbed into bed. Eve had assured him that the sheets were clean, but even so, it was kind of disturbing — this was Brendan Fletcher's mattress and Brendan Fletcher's pillow, the soft place where Brendan Fletcher rested his empty head and dreamed his vapid dreams. Julian wasn't sure whether to feel disgusted or triumphant. It had to count as a small victory just to be here, to have penetrated so deeply into enemy territory.

Did it qualify as revenge to jerk off in

Brendan's bed while fantasizing about his mother? At the very least, it was fun to imagine Brendan's reaction to the news.

Hey Brendan, your mom is sucking my dick.

Hey Brendan, your mom's got amazing boobs.

Hey Brendan, your mom's a really nice person.

No, wait . . .

Hey Brendan, your mom likes it doggie style.

Hey Brendan, I'm going down on your mom.

That was the one he settled on. He was going down on Eve, and she was totally into it, doing the whole porn star moaning thing, like the whole world needed to know how good he was making her feel. He imagined that she was shaved down there, though he had no idea.

Hey Brendan, your mom tastes like strawberries.

There was a soft knock at the door.

Oh shit.

He let go of his dick just as the door creaked open.

"Hey Julian," Amanda whispered. "You asleep?"

Eve woke with a vague sense of unease. She held her breath and listened. There was something unfamiliar — even slightly alarming — about the silence that surrounded her.

Calm down . . .

She had these night frights every now and then — the panicky suspicion that an intruder had broken into the house — and they were always false alarms.

It's probably nothing . . .

And then it came back to her, a tiny explosion of relief.

She had company.

Thank God.

Maybe Amanda needed a glass of water. Maybe Julian was sick. They'd all had too much to drink, never a recipe for a good night's sleep, though Eve herself had managed to doze off without too much trouble.

It was nice to have guests in the house. Comforting, and also validating — this was exactly what she'd hoped for after Brendan left for college, during those first melancholy and disorienting days in the empty nest. She'd made a vow to create a new life for herself, to meet some interesting people, to make some new friends and have a little fun. And the miracle was, she'd actually done all these things, and it hadn't even taken that much time or effort. She'd signed up for one class. She'd accepted an invitation. She'd thrown a party. She'd opened her heart, and the world had responded.

How often does that happen?

Not very often, she knew, which was why she hadn't pushed her luck with Amanda, though she'd very badly wanted to. New friends were rare and valuable, worth a lot more than a fleeting sexual adventure that would only cause pain and confusion down the road. She could tell that Amanda was disappointed — she'd looked so bereft, standing in the guest room doorway — but Eve knew she'd made the right decision — the *adult* decision — the one that would be best for both of them in the long run. Someday they'd have to talk about it, when they weren't drunk and sleeping under the same roof. She was sure that Amanda would understand.

There was that noise again. It wasn't loud, but it was followed a second later by a groan of distress that sounded like it had come from Brendan's room. Eve threw off the covers. It was a familiar feeling, padding down the hallway in the darkness. Standing outside her son's door, straining her ears for the sound of slow, steady breathing that would let her know that everything was okay. But that wasn't what she heard.

"Ooooh fuck! You're amazing!"

"Shhhh."

"Sorry."

"Shhhh."

You've got to be kidding me . . .

The last time this happened, Eve had retreated in horror. But that was her son, not her friends. This time she opened the door — just a crack — and peered inside.

It was dark, but she could see pretty well.

Amanda was on top of Julian, her polka-dot dress unbuttoned to the waist. Her breasts were shockingly large, her tattoo a blotchy shadow. She turned and looked at Eve. She seemed oddly calm, not the least bit embarrassed.

"Sorry," she said. "We didn't mean to wake you."

"It's not your fault." Eve opened the door a little wider. "I'm a light sleeper."

Amanda continued her gentle rocking. It was beautiful to watch, and weirdly familiar, like a memory from a dream or a video. Eve took a step forward.

"Is this okay?" Julian asked.

"It's okay with me," Amanda said.

Eve moved closer. Her foot landed on something strange, a snakelike object that turned out to be a roll of condoms. She was glad to know they were being safe.

Amanda reached for Eve's hand.

"Ursula," she said, as their fingers intertwined.

Eve bent down and kissed her; this time there was no confusion, no rejection, no need to apologize. It was a long, slow, welcoming kiss, and it didn't stop until Julian lifted his hand and placed it, very tentatively, on Eve's breast.

"Is this okay?" he asked again, gazing up at her with a worried expression.

Eve thought for a second.

"I hope so," she said.

Julian looked relieved.

"You're a really nice person," he told her.

I was going out of my mind, drinking alone in my room, scrolling through my useless contacts. I left two messages for my dad, but I guess he'd already gone to bed, and my mom didn't pick up, either. Becca ignored my invitation to Skype. Wade had a midterm he needed to study for, and Troy's phone was running out of juice. Will and Rico had dropped some acid, and they weren't making any sense. Dylan's phone went straight to voicemail, so I finally tried Sanjay, because I couldn't think of anyone else, and he picked up right away.

"What are you doing right now?" I asked him.

"Just working."

"Let's go get some pizza or something."

"I'm not hungry."

"Come on," I said. "Please? Just one fucking slice."

"Brendan, are you okay?"

"No, dude." I tried to laugh, but it came out weird. "I am not okay."

He told me I should find my RA, or maybe go to Health Services. He said it might help if I talked to someone. But I didn't feel like talking to anyone.

"I hate this fucking place. I just want to go home."

It felt good to say it out loud, but then I started to cry. It took me a while to get it under control.

"I'm sorry," I said. "I'm a fucking mess."

Ten minutes later we were in Student Lot C, buckling ourselves into his sister's Subaru wagon, which wasn't really his sister's. It belonged to their parents and Sanjay had his own set of keys.

"You really don't have to do this," I told him.

"It's okay," he said. "I know how it feels. I get homesick all the time."

The highway was pretty clear at that time of night, mostly big trucks barreling along

366

in the right lane. Sanjay was a decent driver, not as timid as I thought he'd be. He was also pretty easy to talk to, and knew a lot more about sports and music than I'd thought he would, which was a relief, since it was a long way to Haddington. Talking helped pass the time and kept my mind off the fact that I was a *Huge Disappointment.*

He told me about his girlfriend, this Korean-American math whiz named Esther. She was a senior in high school, applying early decision to Harvard. Sanjay was hoping she'd get rejected and end up at the Honors College at BSU so they could finally be together like normal people.

"Her parents are super-strict," he explained. "She's not allowed to date or go to parties. She would go to the movies with her friends, and I would go to the same movie with mine, and then the two of us would go sit by ourselves and make out. But then some girl from her church saw us, and after that she wasn't even allowed to go to the movies. I could only see her at school."

They kept things on the DL until the end of Sanjay's senior year, when it was time for the prom. Sanjay organized this crazy stunt where one of his friends dressed up as a UPS guy and came into Esther's AP Calc class with this big box on a hand truck. He said, *Special delivery for Esther Choi!* And then Sanjay burst out of the box with a rose in his teeth and the word *PROM?* scrawled across his forehead. Everybody clapped, and Esther hugged him and said yes, of course she'd be his date. But then she called him in tears that same night and said her parents wouldn't let her.

"That sucks," I said.

Sanjay nodded. "It sucked so bad."

I must have dozed off after that, because the next thing I knew we were off the highway, driving through Haddington, past all the familiar landmarks I hadn't seen in such a long time. I directed Sanjay to Overbrook Street and we pulled up in front of my house. I unbuckled my seatbelt and gave him an awkward one-armed hug.

"Thanks, dude."

"Take care of yourself," he told me. "Maybe I'll see you in a couple days?"

"Yeah," I said. "Maybe."

I got out of the car and watched him drive away. Then I stood on the sidewalk for a while. My house looked sleepy and peaceful, the way it always did when I got home late. I hadn't told my mom I was coming home, so I was surprised to see that she'd

left the porch light on, almost like she was
expecting me.

■ ■ ■ ■

PART FOUR:
THE MILF

■ ■ ■ ■

That Happened

Eve was deeply relieved, and not at all surprised, when Amanda gave her notice in late January. The only real surprise, given the mess they'd made of their friendship and work relationship, was that she'd lasted as long as she had.

"I got the library job," she said. "Director of Children's Events. I'll be in charge of story time, arts and crafts, author visits, holiday celebrations, stuff like that. Kind of like here, just with kids instead of old people. It pays a little better than what I'm making now, so that's a plus."

"That's great," Eve told her, but then she caught herself. "I mean, I'm really sorry to be losing you. That goes without saying. You're a valued member of our staff. Everybody's going to miss you so much."

"I'll miss you, too. You were such a great boss."

She sounded completely sincere, though

nothing, Eve knew, could have been further from the truth. She'd been a terrible boss — completely irresponsible, not to mention legally culpable — and she'd put Amanda in an impossible position, giving her no choice but to leave.

"Thanks again for the recommendation letter," Amanda continued. "I think it made a big difference."

"I meant every word. You have a bright future ahead of you."

She'd used that exact phrase in her letter: *Amanda Olney has a bright future ahead of her.* She was also *a model employee* and *a beacon of good cheer in the office,* not to mention a *self-starter who revitalized the Lecture Series during her brief but eventful tenure.* And now she was looking for *new challenges more commensurate with her exceptional abilities,* opportunities the Senior Center *regrettably couldn't provide.* Eve had understood, even while composing the letter, that she was laying it on a little thick, but she figured it was the least she could do.

"My last day is February 13th," Amanda told her. "That's a Friday. Just my luck."

"Day before Valentine's," Eve added, unhelpfully.

Amanda nodded, well aware of this fact.

"You doing anything? For the holiday?"

Eve shook her head. "You?"

"Nothing." Amanda shrugged, as if it were no big deal. "Just whatever. I'm not a big fan of Valentine's Day. It's always kind of depressing."

That was when it descended, the gray cloud that followed them wherever they went, the Big Awkward Thing that couldn't be discussed or undone. It seemed completely impossible that it had even happened, except that she could — and all too often did — visualize it with mortifying clarity, though only in choppy fragments, involuntary bursts of memory that made her wince and blink, as if a flashbulb had gone off a little too close to her face: Amanda whimpering through gritted teeth; Julian moaning *oooh fuck, oooh fuck* over and over; all three of them breathing hard, encouraging one another, working together as a team.

It was so stupid and frustrating. They should have been able to get past the weirdness, to find a way back to being friends and coworkers who could meet for an occasional drink, go to the movies on Sunday afternoon, or keep each other company on the loneliest night of the year. Maybe there were women somewhere who could have done that, friendly colleagues who'd blundered into an ill-fated sexual adventure and then found a way to laugh it off, people who just shrugged and said, *Well,* that *happened,* and went back to being the way they were before. That would have been a healthier way to deal with it, instead of dying a little inside every time you saw the other person, as if the two of you had buried a body in the woods or something.

And it wasn't like they were in any danger of repeating their mistake. Whatever desire they'd felt for each other had consumed itself in that single, regrettable burst of flames, and now there was nothing left. They'd learned this the hard way after the staff Christmas party, when they tried to spark it back to life with a tipsy kiss in Eve's office that had left them both empty and discouraged.

I don't know, Amanda said. *I'm just not feeling it.*

Eve nodded, conscious of a sad taste in her mouth. *Let's pretend it never happened.*

Unfortunately, they weren't good pretenders. They couldn't remember how to talk to each other like normal human beings, or find a way to build a fence around their error. In the end, it was easier not to have to see each other at all.

"Good luck," Eve said from behind her desk. "I hope you like your new job."

Amanda scowled at the floor for a moment, as if troubled by what she saw there. Then she looked up.

"I'm not ashamed of what we did," she said. "I want you to know that."

"That's good," Eve told her. "Because you have nothing to be ashamed of."

Unlike Amanda, Eve didn't have the luxury of a clear conscience. She had no problem absolving her partners of responsibility — they were young (Julian was barely legal, for God's sake), they'd been drinking, they were free to do as they pleased, no responsibility to anyone but themselves. That wasn't true for Eve: she was the boss, the homeowner, the host, the adult in the room. The one who should have known better. Nothing but selfishness and bad judgment had compelled her to walk down the hall, barge in on Amanda and Julian's private moment, and turn their duet into a threesome. And no, she hadn't been checking up on Julian to make sure he was okay. Maybe she'd started out worrying that something might be wrong, but by the time she poked her head into the bedroom, she already knew what was going on. She'd *heard* them in there.

She just didn't want to be left out.

That was all it was — simple loneliness. She couldn't bear the thought of retreating to her room, shipwrecked again on the desert island of her bed. Didn't want to lie there feeling sorry for herself — she'd wasted so much time feeling sorry for herself — while they had all the fun. So she'd behaved like a child and invited herself to the party, without a thought for the consequences.

It had taken her a while to understand how badly she'd screwed up, mainly because it could have been *so* much worse. By the time Brendan showed up, with no warning whatsoever — he'd let himself in with the spare key they kept hidden in a fake rock beneath the azalea bush — the main event was over, thank God. Amanda had gone home, too embarrassed to spend the night, and Eve had returned to her own bedroom to process what had just occurred. Only Julian remained at the scene of the crime, and that was all Brendan saw when he turned on the light: a kid he vaguely knew from high school sleeping naked in a tangle of sheets and blankets, a roll of condoms unfurled on the floor, two wrappers torn and empty. Brendan seemed more confused than upset, calling out, *Mom? Mom?* over and over, until Eve finally emerged from her room, clutching the lapels of her fuzzy pink robe. By that point Julian was already tugging on his jeans, talking to Brendan in a calm but frightened voice, assuring him that everything was cool, though it obviously wasn't. Eve felt terrible about sending him home on his skateboard in the middle of the night, but it seemed like the best thing for everyone to get him out of the house as quickly as possible.

Then she lied to her son — what else could she do? — telling him that she'd thrown a little party for her fellow students, and that Julian had hooked up with one of the other guests, a girl named Salima from their Gender and Society class. This was a ridiculous, deeply unfair story — Salima was a modest young Muslim woman who would never have gone to a party where alcohol was served, let alone had sex with Julian — but Brendan was mercifully uninterested in the plausibility of her alibi. He waited for her to finish, and then announced in a matter-of-fact voice that he was dropping out of college, which Eve assumed was a melodramatic way of saying that he was homesick or had failed a test. They were both exhausted and embarrassed, for their own individual reasons, and agreed to postpone further conversation until they'd gotten some sleep and could think more clearly. But first Eve went back up to his room and changed the sheets on his bed, even though he insisted it wasn't necessary, because she knew that it absolutely was.

The closeness of that call — the dizzying, weak-kneed feeling of disaster barely averted, of having been spared an unspeakable humiliation — had thrown her off her game in the days that followed, kept her from being as firm with Brendan as she should have been. She should have insisted that he return to school *immediately,* that he buckle down and study hard and finish what he'd started. She should have made it clear that quitting wasn't an option. But she couldn't locate her inner tiger mom, couldn't find a good-faith way to access the voice of parental authority at the moment when she needed it most.

Instead she listened and sympathized — as if she were his friend instead of his mother — letting precious days go to waste while she gently interrogated him about what had gone wrong at school, and why he was refusing to go back. They spent hours hashing it over, but he never managed to give her a convincing explanation. His laundry list of grievances always struck her as vague and insufficient: his classes were boring, this one professor had a crazy accent, everyone was so PC, Zack was never around anymore, the food sucked, he didn't have any friends. There had to be more to the story, but Brendan was a master at shutting down the conversation. If she pressed him too hard for specifics, he'd pull out his phone and start swiping at the screen with an expression of surly impatience, as if he were a busy corporate executive who didn't have time for this nonsense.

Desperate for professional guidance, Eve called BSU and spoke to an academic dean named Tad Bramwell. He told her what she already knew — the university offered counseling services for students who were struggling emotionally and tutoring for those who were having trouble with their course work — but he reminded her that it was Brendan's responsibility to avail himself of these resources. At Bramwell's urging, she also spoke to her son's faculty advisor, Professor Torborg of the Anthropology Department, who didn't seem overly concerned about her son's plight.

"Freshman year's a tough adjustment," he

told her. "Not every incoming student is willing or able to meet the challenges of college work."

Eve bristled at his tone.

"Brendan's very intelligent. He's just a little lazy sometimes."

"Well," Torborg said, after a diplomatic pause. "You know him better than I do."

"You're his advisor," she reminded him. "Maybe you have some advice?"

Torborg gave the matter some scholarly contemplation. "I think it's totally up to Brendan."

"That's it?"

"It's his choice. If he wants to be in college, he should probably start acting like it. And if he doesn't, he should probably find something else to do."

"What if he doesn't know what he wants?"

"Then he should take some time off and figure it out," Torborg told her. "That's my recommendation. I took a gap year after high school and it was one of the best experiences of my life. I went backpacking all over Southeast Asia — Thailand, Vietnam, Cambodia, Nepal . . ." He paused for a moment, savoring the memory. "God, Nepal was beautiful."

"Sounds nice," Eve said, right before she hung up. "I hope you took some pictures."

■ ■ ■ ■

Ted came over the following evening for an emergency family dinner, the three of them gathered around the kitchen table for the first time in seven years. It felt unexpectedly normal — comforting, even — to have him back in the house, everyone in their assigned seats, order temporarily restored in the universe.

At the same time, for all the familiarity of his presence, Ted seemed like a different person, not just older and heavier — Eve was pleased to note these changes, though both things could also be said about her — but calmer, too, no longer radiating the impatience that had always seemed like such an essential part of his personality. He even chewed more slowly than he used to.

"This is delicious." He jabbed his fork at Eve's sausage mac and cheese. "I don't get to eat like this at home."

"I forgot about the gluten," she said. "I hope you don't mind."

"Do I look like I mind?" Ted grinned at Brendan. "Your mom's a great cook. Always was."

As gratified as Eve was by the praise — he hadn't always been so effusive — she was a little irritated by his air of relaxed good cheer, as if this were a pleasant social occasion rather than a family crisis. It was a part of their marriage she remembered all too well — that feeling of being out of sync with Ted's moods, of always having to swim against his tide.

"How's Jon-Jon?" Brendan asked.

"He's okay." Ted nodded thoughtfully, affirming his own statement. "Doing a lot of drawing at school. He's very interested in circles. Other shapes, not so much."

"He seemed pretty good," Brendan said. "On Parents Weekend."

"That was fun," Ted agreed. "Just bad luck with that plane."

Eve had heard about Jon-Jon's tantrum on the BSU quad. She couldn't imagine what that would feel like, to see your child in such pain and not know how to help him, and all those strangers watching.

"You know what I did last week?" Ted said. "I went to an indoor batting cage. Haven't done that for years."

"I used to love that," Brendan said.

"Let's do it," Ted told him. "We can go to Five Guys afterward. Make a night of it."

"Cool," said Brendan, though Eve doubted it would ever happen. Ted was great with the plans, but less impressive with the follow-through.

It went on like that for a while, Ted and Brendan talking football and debating the finer points of *The Walking Dead,* a show they both loved that Eve refused to watch. She couldn't help feeling a little jealous of their connection. The conversation rarely flowed like this when it was just her and Brendan at the table.

"Well," she said, when everyone's plate was clean. "Can we maybe talk about the elephant in the room?"

"Really?" Brendan muttered. "The elephant in the room?"

Ted accepted the parental baton with obvious reluctance.

"Tough semester, huh?"

Brendan nodded, unable to hold his father's sympathetic gaze.

"You want to go back and finish up?" Ted posed the question in a soothing voice, as if he were addressing a child. "It's only another month or so."

Brendan shook his head.

"Any particular reason?" Ted asked.

Brendan closed his eyes and shrugged, a gesture more suited to an eighth grader than a college student.

"I hate it. I'm not learning anything."

"Well, whose fault is that?" Eve snapped.

Ted silenced her with a cautionary hand. Somehow he always got to be the good cop.

"You sure about this?" he asked.

Brendan nodded. Ted sighed and looked at Eve.

"All right," he said. "I guess that's that."

"That's that?" Eve repeated the phrase in disbelief. "That's all you have to say?"

"I don't know what else —"

"So it's just sixteen thousand dollars down the drain?"

"Eve," he said. "Don't make this about the money."

"I'm sorry to be so mercenary. What do you think this is about?"

"Our son," Ted told her. "It's about what's best for our son."

Eve nodded, as if impressed by his superior wisdom.

"Wow," she said, knowing even as she spoke that she wasn't helping anyone. *"Our son* is lucky to have such a devoted father."

Ted ignored the barb — it was as if she hadn't even spoken — which was another thing he did that drove her crazy.

"Look," he said, doing his best Mr. Reasonable. "It's a big school. Maybe it's just a bad fit."

This was a valid point, Eve knew, but that didn't make it any less irritating.

"Don't blame me," she said. "I wasn't the one —"

"Nobody's *blaming* you," Ted told her. "Jesus. I'm just saying, people don't always make the right choices in life. That doesn't mean they have to be stuck with them."

Eve tried to laugh but nothing came out.

"Do you even hear yourself?" she said, but the question went unanswered.

Ted had shifted his attention to Brendan, who had one hand clamped over his mouth, as if he were about to be sick.

"You okay?" Ted asked. "Are you choking?"

Brendan shook his head and burst into tears.

"I'm sorry," he sobbed through his fingers. "I fucked up."

Eve couldn't remember the last time she'd seen him cry. At least five years, she thought. Maybe longer. But the sound was instantly familiar, like an old song on the radio. Ted reached across the table and patted him on the arm.

"Take it easy," he said.

Brendan struggled to catch his breath. "I'm sorry I . . . disappointed you."

"Hey, hey." Ted shook his head. "Don't say that. Nobody's disappointed."

Speak for yourself, Eve thought. Ted was

staring at her with raised eyebrows, requesting a little support.

"It's okay," she said after a moment, reaching out to pat Brendan's other shoulder. "Everything's gonna be okay."

The next morning, Brendan filled out the paperwork to formally withdraw from BSU. The day after that they drove to campus and moved him out of his dorm room. Zack wasn't around to help, didn't even show up to say goodbye. It didn't take long to load Brendan's stuff into a big orange bin, take it down in the elevator, and cram it into the maw of the van. It barely fit, just like at the beginning of the semester — the oscillating fan, the lacrosse stick, the toiletries, the laundry bin, the rolled-up rug, the suitcase and the garbage bags full of clothes. It had all looked so hopeful back in September, an emblem of the future. But now it just looked shabby and depressing, like they'd found a bunch of crap on the sidewalk and decided to take it home.

SOMEBODY LOVES ME

Valentine's Day felt like just another Saturday in winter, which was bad enough in itself. Eve kept herself reasonably busy during the daylight hours — food shopping, laundry (there was so much more to do now that Brendan was home, especially since he'd gotten into CrossFit), bill-paying, a solo afternoon walk around the half-frozen lake. When she got home, she roasted a chicken with fingerling potatoes and brussels sprouts, a delicious, lovingly prepared meal that she ended up eating by herself, because her son had plans he'd forgotten to mention.

"Sorry," he said. "Thought I told you."

"Nope."

"My bad."

Yeah, she thought. *Your bad.*

"Who are you going out with?"

"Chris Mancuso," he said. "I don't think you know him."

"Why can't you eat here and then go out?"

"We're gonna get pizza and watch the hockey game. Is that a problem?"

"Fine. Do what you want."

"Jeez, what's the big deal?" he asked. "When I was away at school, you ate by yourself every night."

It was true, of course. She'd happily eaten alone in the fall, because that was how it was supposed to be. His absence was part of the necessary and proper order of things. His *presence* now was the problem — a huge backward step for both of them — along with his uncanny ability to take up more than his share of space in the house while giving so little in return.

"You're right." She waved him toward the door. "Go have your fun. Don't drink and drive."

"I know, I know," he said in a weary voice, as if he were a mature adult who could be counted on to make good decisions. "Enjoy your chicken."

She lingered at the table for as long as possible — she owed herself that much — and then dragged her feet on the cleanup, doing her best to stave off that troubling moment when there was nothing left to do, the official beginning of what she already knew would be a melancholy and restless night.

It had been like this all winter long. She found it difficult to relax after dark — couldn't curl up with a book, or settle down long enough to watch a movie from beginning to end. She was full of nervous energy, a nagging, jittery feeling that there was somewhere she needed to go, something else — something urgent and important — that she needed to do. But that was the catch: there was nowhere to go, and nothing to do.

All the freedom she'd experienced in the fall, that giddy sense of new horizons, all that was gone. She wasn't a student anymore, puzzling over feminist theory, drinking and dancing with her friends, exploring her sexuality, making stupid but sometimes exhilarating mistakes. She was just plain old Mom, chopping onions, feeling neglected, cleaning lint from the filter. Her life felt shrunken and constricted, as if the world had shoved her back into an all-too-familiar box that was no longer large enough to contain her. Except that the world hadn't done any shoving. She'd volunteered for her confinement, climbing in and pulling the cardboard flaps down over her head.

She told herself that she'd done it for Brendan's sake. After all, *he* was the college student in the family, not her, despite the fact that she'd completed her first semester with flying colors, earning a solid A in Margo's class, and high praise for her final paper, which explored the fraught relationship between radical feminism(s) and the transgender movement.

This is excellent!!! Margo had scrawled on the back of the essay, in sloppy, barely legible cursive that Eve couldn't help but think of as manly, even though she knew it was a faulty mental reflex, a kind of residual transphobia. But Brendan came first: he was the one who really needed to be taking college classes during the spring semester, and ECC was the logical place for him to do it. Eve understood that it was a tricky moment in his academic career — his confidence at an all-time low — and it had felt right to give him some space, to spare him the embarrassment of attending the same college as his mother, of possibly bumping into her at the library — if he ever actually *went* to the library — or having to compare his grades to hers.

It had seemed like a minor sacrifice at the time — a brief hiatus from her continuing education — but it turned out to be a much bigger loss than she'd anticipated. Without a class to get her out of the house — to focus her thinking and provide her with a community of like-minded people — her intellectual life ran out of steam and her social life went into a coma. She felt like a teenager, grounded indefinitely for one stupid mistake, though she was also the parent who had imposed the punishment, which meant that, as usual, she had no one to blame but herself.

Chris wanted the last wing in the basket. I told him to go for it.

"These are pretty good," he said.

I agreed, and had a big pile of bones on my plate to prove it. But I felt kinda guilty, too, because my mom had cooked a whole chicken at home, and here I was eating hot wings at the Haddington House of Pizza.

"There was this place at my school, Pennyfeathers? Their wings were fucking awesome. Dude, they'd deliver until like two in the morning on weekends." He got this faraway look in his eyes and nodded for a long time. "I miss those wings."

Chris missed a lot of things about college. His frat brothers, his rugby teammates, this amazing ice cream place that had waffle cones dipped in chocolate, all the bars on 12th Street that didn't care if you had a fake

ID, and now these wings from Pennyfeathers.

"Those were good times," he told me.

Chris and I knew each other a little from the Haddington High football team, but he was two years older, a varsity starter back when I was still warming the bench. I'd heard he'd gone to one of those small colleges in Pennsylvania, so I was pleasantly surprised to spot him in the hallway at ECC, where I hardly ever saw anyone I knew from high school (the only exception was Julian Spitzer, who seemed to pop up every time I turned a corner, though we always walked right past each other like we'd never met, like I hadn't found him sleeping in my fucking bed that night, a memory that still gave me the creeps). Chris explained that he was home for the semester due to some disciplinary bullshit and said we should grab a beer sometime. I thought he was just saying it to be nice, but he repeated the offer when we bumped into each other at CrossFit, and it wasn't like I had anything else going on.

"I guess you'll be happy to get back there," I said.

"I don't know if I'm going back." He wiped his mouth with a napkin, but he missed a greasy streak on his chin. "It'll suck without the frat."

"What do you mean?"

"They shut us down. Five-year suspension."

"Why?"

"Because of the kid. You didn't hear about it?"

"I don't think so."

"Huh." He seemed surprised that it wasn't a matter of common knowledge. "This freshman pledge died of alcohol poisoning at our house. It was all over the internet."

"Holy shit. Were you there?"

"Kind of. I mean, I was playing air hockey in the game room, just minding my own business. I saw this kid staggering around, but he wasn't the only one. All the pledges were shitfaced." He pulled the visor of his baseball cap lower, like a celebrity who didn't want to be recognized. "I guess he went outside to puke and everybody forgot about him. My buddy Johnny found him in the yard the next morning."

"Jesus. How much did he drink?"

"A shitload of vodka shots."

"Like how many?"

"I don't know." Chris sounded pissed. "It was a fucking drinking game. Everybody makes it sound like it was our fault, like we poured it down his throat. But he was totally into it. Screaming and high-fiving everybody. Having the time of his life."

He stopped himself, like he realized that probably wasn't the best way to put it.

"We had to write apology letters to the parents, which was brutal. And then there were hearings, and the whole frat got suspended. Didn't matter if you were involved or not. And now if I want to go back I have to reapply. For my senior year. Can you believe that shit?"

"Wow," I said. "I just thought you failed a class or something."

"That would at least make sense."

"So what are you gonna do?"

Chris took another napkin from the dispenser. Instead of wiping his face, he unfolded it very carefully and laid it over his plate, like he was covering his bones with a blanket.

"I might join the Marines," he said. "Just get the fuck out of here, you know?"

Facebook wouldn't let her forget what day it was for a second, flooding her news feed with images of hearts and flowers, a seemingly endless torrent of saccharine memes, happy couple photos, and loving tributes to loyal partners.

Thank you, Gus, for twenty-two years of
red roses!
A romantic dinner for two at the Hearth-
stone Inn. So blessed . . .
This wonderful man didn't just make my
DAY! He made my LIFE! I love you,
Mark J. DiLusio!!!
Snuggling by the fire with my handsome
hubby on V-Day
Somebody's gonna get a little surprise
tonight . . . #feelingnaughty

She tried her best to be a good sport, is-
suing a handful of half-hearted likes and offering a supportive comment when she
could, but she gave up after a few minutes
of resentful scrolling. It wasn't that she
begrudged her friends their happiness —
she wasn't that kind of person — she just
wished they'd be a little quieter about it, a
little more private.

You won, she thought. *There's no need to
gloat.*

She knew that the winners didn't *think*
they were gloating — in their own innocent
minds, they were just celebrating the holiday, sharing a sweet sentiment with people
who cared — but it was hard for Eve not to
take it personally, not to feel like a weepy
high school girl stuck at home while every-

one else was slow-dancing at the prom. It had been a lot easier to be a loser back in the days before social media, when the world wasn't quite so adept at rubbing it in your face, showing you all the fun you were missing out on in real time.

I wasn't crazy about the idea of partying with a bunch of high school kids — it's kinda awkward once you graduate — but Chris really wanted to go. He was friends with the girl who was hosting and said she was totally chill and down-to-earth, despite the fact that she went to the Hilltop Academy, a local prep school that cost almost as much as an Ivy League college.

"How do you even know her?" I asked. Kids from Haddington High and kids from Hilltop didn't usually mix.

"Summer camp. She was my junior counselor. We flirted a lot, but we never hooked up. I'm hoping to take it to the next level."

"That's cool," I said. "You mind if I just drop you off? I'm not really in a party mood."

"Dude," he said, like I'd failed to live up to his expectations. "Just come in and have a beer. If you don't like it, that's fine. But don't be a pussy about it."

■ ■ ■ ■

His friend's name was Devlin and she lived up in Haddington Hills, in what looked like a fairly normal house, except that it was like four times bigger than any house I'd ever been in. She was half-Asian and very cute, dressed in a short black skirt and white knee socks. A construction paper heart on her shirt said, *Are You My Valentine?*

"Oh my God." She gave Chris a fierce hug, like he'd just returned from the dead. "It's so good to see you."

"You too," he said. "This is my buddy Brendan."

She gave me a stern look, her heart all crooked from the hug. "You're going to have to help me talk him out of it."

"Out of what?"

"Joining the Marines. It's crazy."

"Good luck with that," Chris told her. "Brendan's joining up with me."

She squinted in dismay. "Really?"

"Why not?" I said. "Somebody's gotta do it."

I was just goofing around, following Chris's lead, but Devlin didn't know that. She told some of her friends, and pretty soon it spread through the whole party. That was all anybody wanted to talk about, which was fine with me, because it spared me the embarrassment of having to explain that I'd flunked out of BSU and was currently living at home with my mom and taking classes at community college.

Most of the girls I talked to were firmly opposed to my enlistment — a couple said they were pacifists, and others just thought it was too dangerous, or that it made more sense to join the Peace Corps, to help people instead of trying to kill them. Some of the guys were more gung ho, and wondered if I'd given any consideration to the Special Forces, because those dudes were the true badasses, the Rangers and the Seals and Delta Force.

The best conversation I had was with this light-skinned black kid named Jason, a middle-distance runner who was heading to Dartmouth in the fall. He'd taken a summer school class on Contemporary War Literature and told me about a bunch of books he liked — the only one I'd heard of was *The Things They Carried,* which I'd read in English class junior year — and then we switched to movies. Our tastes were pretty similar — we both liked *Lone Survivor* and *The Hurt Locker* and also *Tropic Thunder,* which wasn't really a war movie but was still hilarious.

"Not very PC, though," he said. "I know I'm not supposed to laugh at Robert Downey Jr. in blackface, but damn. Funny is funny, right?"

"Absolutely," I said, and we clinked our bottles.

Jason was one of the few guys at the party with a paper heart pinned to his chest. His said, *Somebody Loves Me!* He tapped it with two fingers.

"All right," he said. "Gotta get back to my girl before somebody steals her."

After that I danced with Devlin's friend Addison, whose heart said, *Make Me an Offer.* I hadn't been out on the dance floor since my date with Amber, and it felt really good to be moving in the dark, getting all sweaty and goofy with a bunch of cool people I'd just met. It was almost like I was back in college, except that it was a better college than BSU, and I was a better person, too, a thoughtful guy with interesting opinions and a solid plan for the future.

I'd only had two beers, so I wasn't close to drunk, but I did need to find a bathroom. Addison told me it was down the hall, just past the den.

I got a little distracted on my way. It was a

long hallway, and the walls were lined with photographs of Devlin and her little brother and her mom and dad, a good-looking family who seemed to live their lives near water — beaches, lakes, swimming pools, fountains — and were always laughing about something when the picture got taken.

The first room I stuck my head into was a home office, and the second had a yoga mat on the floor, along with a big red exercise ball. I found the den on the third try — bookshelves, fireplace, leather chairs.

"Sorry," I said, because there was also a couch, and it was occupied by Jason and the girl he was making out with. They were going at it pretty good, and my arrival had startled them. "I was just trying to . . ."

"Trying to what?" Jason said, after an awkward moment of silence.

I didn't answer. I was staring at the girl. She was staring right back, looking just as confused as I was.

"Becca?" I said. "What are you doing here?"

Eve closed her eyes and let out a heavy sigh, the way she always did before she started watching porn. It was somewhere between an admission of defeat and an attempt to clear her head, to create a mental space free of judgment and open to erotic suggestion.

She had cut way down on her porn consumption in the past few months — that was one upside of Brendan's return — but she still found herself visiting the Milfateria from time to time, usually on nights like this when she was bored and lonely and looking for something to cheer her up, or at least distract her for a little while.

I deserve some pleasure, too, she reminded herself, which wouldn't have been such a terrible status update — not to mention an epitaph on her fucking tombstone — if only she'd had the courage to post it.

She didn't think Brendan would be home anytime soon, but she went upstairs and latched the bedroom door behind her, just in case. Then she took off her jeans, got into bed, and started searching, clicking on any thumbnail that caught her eye.

In the Milfateria, at least, no one knew it was Valentine's Day. The people in the porn videos just did what they did, all day, every day, with boundless energy and unflagging enthusiasm, regardless of the calendar. They fucked on Christmas; they fucked on Earth Day and the Fourth of July and Thanksgiving; their fucking was not affected in the least by wars or terrorist attacks or natural disasters. They never got sick, never got tired, never got old. Some of them were probably dead, Eve realized, not that she'd have any way of knowing which ones. But here they were on her screen, going at it with abandon, having the time of their lives.

Good for you, she thought. *Keep on doing what you're doing.*

She was happy for them, but she wasn't especially aroused, which was not an uncommon occurrence in recent weeks. She just didn't know what she wanted anymore. The lesbian MILF stuff made her nervous, and she hadn't been able to find a new category to take its place. Some items on the menu seemed a little too familiar, while others were *waaaay* too specific. Usually she ended up sampling the Homemade MILFs, ordinary women having fairly straightforward sex, mostly with their husbands, if you could believe the brief descriptions that accompanied the videos.

The problem was, Eve had become a lot more interested in the women than she was in the sex. She kept trying to figure out who they were, and how they'd ended up on her laptop. Had they volunteered, or had their partners pressured them? Did it occur to them that their kids might someday watch the video? Their parents? Their neighbors and co-workers? Were they in denial, or did they simply not care? Or maybe they were proud, like they were finally getting a chance to show the world their best selves.

She must have clicked on twenty different videos, looking for something that would get her out of her head and into her body, but nothing worked. It was sad to fail at masturbation — again, no one to blame but herself — but at least it was better than failing with a partner. You didn't have to fake anything, or apologize, or offer comfort, or pretend it was no big deal. You could just close your computer, shake your head, and call it a night.

I tried to find Chris before I left the party, but someone told me he'd gone upstairs with Devlin. I figured he was all set, so I headed to the mudroom to grab my coat. That was where Becca caught up with me.

"I'm sorry, Brendan." She was standing in the doorway, looking like her usual put-together self — all her buttons buttoned, every hair in place — which was not how she'd looked in the den. "I should have told you."

The coats were in a big pile, and half of them were black ski jackets, just like mine.

"Whatever," I said, tossing aside a girl's red parka. "I guess you weren't as busy as you expected."

I had tried to start things back up with her in early December, a few weeks after I came home from BSU, but she claimed she was swamped with schoolwork and college applications, and didn't have time for a relationship.

"I've been meaning to text you," she said.

It was hard to look at her just then, not only because I'd kinda forgotten how hot she was, but also because she was wearing a paper heart that said the exact same thing as Jason's: *Somebody Loves Me!*

"How do you guys even know each other?" I asked.

"Instagram," she said. "He's a really nice guy."

I found my coat. I knew it was mine because my mom had written my initials on the inside label before I left for college.

"I know," I said. "I talked to him before."

I tried to slip past her on my way out, but she grabbed my arm.

"Brendan?" she asked. "Are you really joining the Marines?"

"I'm thinking about it."

She stared at me for a few seconds, like she was trying to picture me in my dress blues.

"You know what?" she said. "I think that

would be really good for you."

I didn't feel like going home, so I drove around for a while. When that got boring, I went to the high school and sat on the top row of the bleachers, looking down on the football field. Wade and Troy and I had done that a few times over the summer. It was kind of a nostalgia thing, a way to remember our glory days.

It wasn't very cold for February, I guess because of climate change, though maybe it was just a weather pattern, the Gulf Stream or whatever. I didn't know as much about that stuff as I should have. I'd read a chapter for my Comp class that made it sound like the end of the world, but it didn't feel like that in real life. It just felt like a pretty nice night.

Now that the shock had worn off, I realized that I wasn't that upset about Becca. I wanted to be mad at her for lying to me back in December, but I knew she was just trying to be nice, letting me down easy with that bullshit about being too busy for a relationship. And I couldn't blame her for hooking up with Jason, though I did wish she'd found someone a little more ordinary, who didn't make me feel like such a loser by comparison.

The only girl I was really upset about was Amber. I'd sent her a bunch of texts in December and January, just checking in, trying to start a dialogue, but she threatened to block me if I kept bothering her. I hadn't tried to contact her since then, so I figured maybe she'd calmed down a little. I thought about telling her I was joining the Marines — that would at least get her attention — but there was no way I was actually going to enlist. I had zero interest in shaving my head, and even less in going to Afghanistan.

I had a hard time thinking of what to say. I'd already apologized to her a bunch of times, and it hadn't gotten me anywhere. I couldn't think of anything funny or charming or even interesting, so I just wished her a Happy Valentine's Day and left it at that. She didn't reply, but my phone said she'd looked at the message, which I figured was better than nothing.

Eve was fast asleep when her phone dinged, shocking her back into consciousness. She sat up and threw off the covers, her groggy brain sorting through disaster scenarios as she tapped in her security code.

The text came from a number she didn't recognize. It was three words long, a sad little joke from the universe.

Happy Valentine's Day!

She took a moment to breathe, and get her heart rate under control.

Who is this?

There was a brief pause, and then a pleasant *bloop!*

Its me Julian

The glow from the screen was painfully bright. Eve's fingers felt fat and clumsy as she typed.

How did you get this number?

Class list . . . last semester

Was that possible? Eve couldn't remember putting her cell number on a class list. But maybe she had. In any case, another text had already arrived.

Am I bothering you?

She wasn't sure how to answer that. It was sweet of him to remember her on Valentine's Day. But not in the middle of the night. That wasn't okay. Except it wasn't the middle of the night, according to her bedside clock, just a few minutes after eleven. In any case, Julian had already moved on to the next question:

R u in bed?

And the next:

R u naked?

Eve tugged on the blankets, covering her bare legs. She wasn't naked, but she was pretty close. Just underwear and a T-shirt, not that it was any of his business.

Julian . . . please don't do this.

There was a longish pause.

Dont you miss me?

This was an easier question. Of course, she missed him, just like she missed all her new friends from the fall — Amanda, Margo, Dumell, the whole short-lived gang. And she owed him an apology, too, for everything that happened on that night in November, and for ignoring the emails he'd sent her in the days that followed. But this wasn't the time or place for either of those conversations.

Have you been drinking? she asked.

Im kinda wasted

Where are you?

His reply arrived in multiple parts, a rapidly accumulating stack of bubbles.

Vermont

Visiting my friend at UVM

This girl was hitting on me at a party

and I kept thinking

Id rather be with u

Eve laughed, because it was so crazy for him to be thinking of her under those circumstances. Except it wasn't completely crazy.

Not crazy at all, come to think of it.

This girl, Eve wrote, because she suddenly needed to know. *Was she pretty?*

I guess

What did she look like?

Julian took another moment to gather his thoughts.

u r hotter . . .

Waaay fucking hotter

That's sweet, she told him, adding a smile emoji. *I'm flattered.*

Two more messages arrived just as she'd sent hers off.

I jack off all the time

thinking of u

Eve grimaced. A murky sound escaped from her throat.

Julian . . . This isn't a good idea.

Im so fucking hard right now

She closed her eyes and tried not to think about that.

I could send u a pic, he added.

Good night, Julian. I'm turning off my phone now.

He didn't protest, didn't even try to change her mind.

night eve

She didn't really turn off her phone, but he didn't text her again, which was too bad in a way, because she really did miss him, and thought he would've liked to know —

not that she ever would have told him —
that she was touching herself and thinking
about his body. The orgasm that had eluded
her before was suddenly within easy reach
— right there at her fingertips — and a lot
more intense than any she'd had in recent
memory.

Thank you, she would have liked to tell
him. *Thank you for that.*

DIRTY MARTINI

Eve knew it was time to start dating again — it was one of her top three New Year's resolutions — but it was hard to get motivated, to convince herself that she'd have any more success this time around than she'd had in the past.

Feeling the need for moral support, she invited her closest friends — Peggy, Jane, and Liza — for a pep talk/brainstorming session at the Haddington Brasserie and Lounge. It had been months since they'd had a girls' night out — everyone had been so busy in the fall — and they all jumped at the opportunity to escape their houses on a weeknight in late winter, to drink a few glasses of wine, and put their collective romantic wisdom to work on behalf of such a good cause.

As excited as they were to strategize about the revival of Eve's love life, they began where they always did, with a quick update on their kids, which was how they'd all become friends in the first place: young mothers in the schoolyard, on the sidelines at soccer games, at school plays and award ceremonies and graduations, a whole era of their lives — it had felt so permanent while it was happening — suddenly behind them. Just a chapter, and not the story itself.

Jane was missing her daughters, the smart, sweet-natured twins, both of whom were thriving in college. Liza's son, Grant, had just embarked on a semester at sea, and the pictures looked amazing. Peggy was thrilled to report that Wade had survived the fall term, buckling down after a couple of disastrous midterms, and earning Bs and Cs on all his finals, which was better than anyone had expected.

"That's great," said Eve. "You must be so proud of him."

Peggy nodded reluctantly, apologizing for her pride. Jane and Liza regarded Eve with identical sympathetic expressions.

"Brendan's *fine,*" she said, deflecting their pity. "He just had a hard time. He was partying too much and . . . I don't know. Something didn't click. He still has some growing up to do."

"He'll get it together," Liza said.

"On the bright side," Jane added, "at least

he's back home. That must be nice."

"I guess. But I was just getting used to having my own life again. I don't want to lose that. I just want to get out and have some fun, you know?"

Eve's friends were full of encouragement, confident that she would find love on the internet, or at least meet some appealing prospects. You just had to go into it with a positive attitude.

"My sister's friend, Denise, met a great guy on Match.com," Jane said. "They just got married. The husband's a little older, a retired dermatologist. They travel all the time. Couldn't be happier."

"When you say a little older," Eve inquired, "are we talking late fifties, early sixties?"

"More like mid-seventies," Jane replied. "But he's in good shape."

"Stop right there," Eve said. "I don't want to date a guy in his mid-seventies. I don't care *how* active he is."

"The point is, Denise hired a dating coach, and that was why things worked out so well. The coach helped her write her profile, recommended a professional photographer to take her pictures, and advised her on how to respond to the men who reached out. She held Denise's hand every step of the way." Jane looked at Eve. "Just something to consider."

"Out of curiosity," Eve said. "Do you know what that would cost?"

"A lot," Jane admitted. "But Denise said it was the best investment she ever made."

Peggy patted Eve's wrist. "You don't need a coach. You've got us."

"I could definitely use some help with my profile," Eve said. "I always sound so boring. I mean, what am I supposed to say?"

"Just be honest." Jane counted on her fingers. "You're a good mom, a great friend, really good at your job . . ."

"See?" Eve slumped in her chair. "You're making my point. I'm falling asleep just thinking about me."

"Don't stress about the profile," said Liza, who'd been divorced longer than Eve, and had tried every internet dating site in the known universe, to no avail. "Trust me. The only thing that matters is your picture. You need to find a good photographer, and wear something tight and low-cut. That's what I would do, if I had a figure like yours."

"She's right," agreed Peggy. "Go to a salon and get a blow-out. Maybe hire a stylist to do your makeup. You only get one chance to make that first impression."

■ ■ ■ ■

Broadly speaking, Eve was happy with her hair. It was thick but manageable, and unlike some other parts of her body, it had weathered the transition into middle age without losing too much of its youthful bounce and luster. She had to color it, of course, but that was her only serious intervention. In her mid-thirties, she'd briefly experimented with a sassy, athletic bob, but it didn't work, probably because she wasn't a sassy, athletic person. She'd quickly returned to her tried-and-true collegiate hairstyle — long and straight, parted in the middle, a folk singer at the coffeehouse — unless she was at work, in which case she opted for the professional discipline of a bun or a scraped-back ponytail or a tortoise-claw clip.

It was a safe and familiar look, and she'd begun to wonder if that might be a problem. Because she understood on some level that Liza was right, that you needed to make a bold impression if you were going to succeed in the cutthroat world of online dating, especially once you'd crossed the Rubicon of forty. And Eve had a growing suspicion that the Joan Baez/social worker hairdo she'd been sporting for most of her adult life wasn't going to do the trick.

"All right," she announced, settling into the salon chair. "Let's try something new for a change."

Her haircutter — he went by Christophe, though his given name was Gary — was pleased. "What would you like?"

"You're the expert. You tell me."

He studied her in the mirror, nodding with quiet confidence, like he already had a plan.

"Nothing crazy," she warned him.

He began by changing her hair color — it was naturally dark, mahogany bordering on black — to a luminous shade of golden brown that really brought out the hazel in her eyes. Then he shifted her part from the middle to the side and began to snip away, first crudely, to adjust the length, and then with more deliberation, framing her face in a series of artful layers that looked deceptively simple and natural, highlighting the graceful oval of her face and the elegant curve of her jawline — she'd had no idea that her jawline was elegant — while also concealing some of the less fetching regions of her neck. When he'd completed the blow-dry, Eve stared at herself in amazement.

"Oh my God," she said, as Christophe

undid the velcro fastener on her smock. "You're a genius."

He waved off the compliment.

"This was you all along," he told her. "You just needed to come out of your shell."

All that afternoon, Eve kept returning to the mirror, waiting for the usual post-haircut remorse to set in, but instead of the sinking feeling she knew so well — *What was I thinking? Why do I even bother?* — all she experienced was a renewed sense of pleasant surprise.

Just to make sure she wasn't crazy, she took a selfie and posted it on Facebook, along with the matter-of-fact caption *New Do.* The response was instantaneous and overwhelmingly positive, twenty plus likes in the first ten minutes, and lots of supportive comments from her female friends.

It was gratifying, but only for a little while. Her mood darkened as evening set in, another Saturday night with nothing going on. What was the point of getting a fabulous new haircut if no one was going to see it except Brendan, who didn't even notice until she hung a sign around her neck?

"I got my hair done this morning," she said. "What do you think?"

He assessed her for a second or two, then

gave a curt nod of approval.

"Nice," he said. "Did what's-his-name do it? The French dude?"

"Christophe."

"He's gay, right?"

"I think so. Does it matter?"

"Not in a bad way," he said. "It's just, the guy has a gay name and a gay job. It would be kind of confusing if he was straight. This way's better for everyone."

Brendan left around eight, climbing into a battered Toyota driven by one of his Cross-Fit buddies. As soon as he was gone, Eve went upstairs and changed into a tight skirt and tailored blouse and the one pair of special-occasion high heels she still owned. She took a selfie of her reflection in the full-length bedroom mirror, her mouth set in a sultry pout that didn't look as ridiculous as she'd thought it would. Just for laughs, she undid two more buttons on her blouse and took a photo with the edge of her black bra showing, not that she would ever post an image like that on social media. It was just for herself — an ego boost, irrefutable proof that she could still be sexy if the occasion called for it.

Now that she was all dressed up, it seemed crazy not to go out — just for a quick drink, a little human contact. Nothing fun or interesting was going to happen if she stayed home, that was for sure.

The Lamplighter Inn was a lot busier than it had been on her previous visit, the Saturday crowd younger and louder than she'd expected. Feeling instantly self-conscious, Eve took the last open stool at the bar and ordered a dirty martini from a baby-faced bartender who looked like she'd just graduated from college.

"Is Jim Hobie working tonight?" Eve asked.

The bartender gave her a suspicious look. She was wearing a cropped shirt, and Eve could see a tattoo of a black rose peeking out from the waistband of her jeans.

"Hobie only works weeknights. You know him?"

"Not that well. Our kids went to school together."

The girl nodded and swiped Eve's twenty off the bar. When she returned with the change, she frowned like there was something on her mind.

"I know it's none of my business," she said, "but you should be careful. Hobie's a nice guy, but he says a lot of shit that he doesn't really mean. And then he acts like he never said it in the first place."

"Okay." Eve took a sip of her cocktail. "Thanks for the warning."

The girl laughed sadly and rubbed her tattoo, as if it were a sore spot.

"I don't know what I was thinking."

"Join the club," Eve told her.

"What do you mean? Did you and him . . . ?"

"No," Eve said. "I just meant, you know, you're always hoping for the best and . . ."

The girl laughed. "You get Hobie."

"Exactly." Eve shrugged. "But it doesn't mean you were wrong for hoping."

It wasn't a bad night in the end. She stuck it out for two drinks, and chatted with a couple of not-completely-horrible guys around her own age — a divorced home inspector and an ex-cop who'd retired on full disability, though he seemed to be in perfect health — both of whom were reasonably attractive and had nothing of interest to say. But at least she'd tried, that was the important thing.

She left the bar a little after ten and got into her car. While she waited for the engine to warm up — it was another frigid night — she took out her phone and looked at the pictures she'd taken earlier in the evening. They were really good — not just the haircut and the clothes, but the look on her face, and even the way she was standing, with her hand on her hip, and her head canted at the perfect, self-possessed angle. Everything felt right and true, just the way she wanted it.

There I am, she thought.

She selected the second photo — the sexier one — and texted it to Julian. She'd been wanting to do it all night. It was exciting to finally press Send, to turn the fantasy into action.

He didn't answer right away, so she pulled out of the parking lot and started toward home. She'd only gone a couple of blocks when her phone chimed. Eve was adamantly opposed to texting and driving, so she forced herself to wait until she'd pulled into her driveway to read his reply.

Great pic! But you missed a few buttons

Just a minor oversight. I thought you might like it.

She got out of the car and went inside, her heart beating at a rapid clip. There was nothing quite like the suspense of waiting for a flirty text — as if the whole world was on pause, holding its breath until the next little *ding!* started it up again. She'd just locked the door behind her when he replied.

I fucking love it!

She sent him a blushing-face emoji that must have crossed with his follow-up:

Could u take one with your shirt off?

Eve laughed out loud, a melodic, two-martini chuckle.

Don't get greedy, she told him.

An Invitation

As always, it was work that kept her grounded, reminding her that she could still make a positive impact in her community, and in the world. It was hard to feel sorry for herself at the Senior Center, where she encountered so many people who were dealing with problems that made her own seem trivial — chronic arthritis, early-stage Parkinson's, severe hearing loss, the death of a beloved spouse, a Social Security check that didn't cover even the most basic monthly expenses. The resilience of the elderly — their sense of humor and reluctance to complain, their determination to make the best of a bad (and almost always worsening) situation — was both humbling and inspiring.

That winter, Eve threw herself into the day-to-day life of the Center with renewed energy and commitment, delegating fewer tasks to her staff and playing more of a hands-on leadership role than usual. She personally revived the Mystery Novel Book Club — it had faded away after the death of its founder and guiding spirit, a retired English teacher named Regina Filipek — selecting *Gone Girl* as the first title and leading a lively, if occasionally frustrating, discussion of the book's many byzantine twists and turns with a group of seven mostly enthusiastic readers.

She was also drafted into the Tuesday morning bowling league, joining a team called the Old Biddies as a temporary substitute for Helen Haymer, who was suffering from a severe case of vertigo that had left her housebound. None of the Biddies' opponents minded that Eve was a ringer, thirty years younger than the woman she'd replaced. This was partly because they were tickled by her presence at the bowling alley — as executive director, she was a bit of a celebrity — but mainly because she was such a weak bowler compared to Helen, a former school bus driver with a 150 average, one of the highest in the league (Eve was lucky to break a hundred on a good day). She hadn't played organized sports in high school — she'd grown up right before the golden age of girls' athletics — and was surprised by how much fun it was to be part of a team, cheering on her fellow Biddies when they rolled a strike, bucking them up after the gutter balls, patting them on the back and reminding them that it didn't matter, that there would always be a next time.

Tuesday mornings quickly became the highlight of her work week. She came into the office in her most comfortable jeans, took care of her email and any other business that couldn't wait, and then filed onto the Elderbus along with her fellow bowlers. They trash-talked the whole way to Haddington Lanes, where the seniors pretty much had the place to themselves. It was an invigorating break from the daily routine, full of laughter and high fives and soft drinks.

Right before her fifth outing, Eve's teammates presented her with an extra-large T-shirt with the words *FUTURE BIDDY* emblazoned on the front. Eve wore it proudly, and bowled her highest game ever, a completely respectable 117. Later that day, she called to check on Helen Haymer, and was sorry to hear that the vertigo wasn't getting any better, though not quite as sorry as she probably should have been.

Eve was thinking about Amanda as she left work on a rainy Wednesday evening in early

March, curious to know how she was doing at the library. She wondered if it would be okay to reach out to her with a brief, friendly email, just to say hi and let her know that she hadn't been forgotten. It was probably a bad idea, but the silence between them felt wrong and unfinished, like a phone left off the hook.

Amanda had been on her mind a lot in the past few days because Eve needed to find her replacement ASAP — in an era of tight municipal budgets, you had to fill a job opening quickly or risk having the position eliminated — and the hiring process was in full swing. More than fifty applicants had submitted their résumés, many of them seriously overqualified for the low-paid, entry-level post. At least a dozen had master's degrees — mostly in Social Work or Nonprofit Administration — and two had completed law school, only to realize that there were already too many lawyers in the world.

Eve had drawn up a short list of five candidates, and had interviewed three so far. They were all perfectly fine — competent, professional, appropriately dressed. They had relevant experience and impressive letters of recommendation. Hannah Gleezen, the young woman she'd spoken to that afternoon, was fresh out of Lesley College, and had spent the past six months doing an unpaid internship at an assisted living facility in Dedham, where she'd called out Bingo numbers, organized a hugely successful Scrabble tournament, and led a holiday sing-along that had been a real morale booster for the residents. She was earnest and bubbly, and Eve had no reason to doubt her sincerity when she said that she really *liked* old people and believed that her generation had a lot to learn from their elders.

"I don't see it as me helping *them,*" she'd said. "It's more of a two-way-street type of thing."

Eve could have just hired her on the spot. The seniors would love her, and so would the staff. She was the complete antithesis of Amanda, who'd confessed in her interview that old people freaked her out, not only because of their casual racism and homophobia and their love of Bill O'Reilly — though all that was bad enough — but also because of their broken-down bodies, and the terrible clothes they wore, and even the way some of them smelled, which she knew was unfair, but still.

It had been a gamble to hire her — Eve knew that from Day One — and it hadn't paid off in the end, but that didn't mean it had been a mistake. She was proud of Amanda for trying to shake things up at the Senior Center, and proud of herself for taking a chance on such a wild card. She didn't want to settle for a replacement who didn't have that same spark, a bland, safe choice that would look like an apology — or worse, a betrayal of everything Amanda had stood for — so Eve had shaken Hannah's hand and said she'd get back to her in a week or so, after she'd met with the remaining candidates.

The rain was cold and insidious — she could feel it snaking under her collar and rolling down her back as she made her way across the parking lot — but she thought she detected a faint undercurrent of spring in the air, the faraway promise of something better. It was late, almost six thirty, and the lot was deserted except for her minivan and a car she didn't recognize — a newish Volvo sedan — parked right beside it, so close to the white divider line that it felt like a violation of her personal space.

The Volvo's lights and wipers were on, which seemed a little ominous, and made it hard for Eve to see through the windshield. Squinting into the glare, she squeezed into the narrow space between the two vehicles.

As she clicked her key fob — the van's dome light flashed on to greet her — the passenger window of the Volvo slid down.

"Eve." Julian was leaning across the interior console, wearing a green army coat with button-down epaulettes, his head and shoulders torqued at an awkward angle. "What's up?"

As she turned to face him, her shoulder bumped into the van's side-view mirror.

"Jeez," she said. "Did you have to park so close?"

"Sorry." Julian looked embarrassed. "I'm out of practice. I don't drive very much."

It was true, she realized. She'd never seen him behind the wheel before.

"Can I . . . *help* you with something?" Her tone was frostier than she'd intended. It was disorienting to see him here, at her place of work, without any advance warning. Not a practice she wanted to encourage.

"Not really," he said. "I was just hoping we could talk."

A car drove by on Thornton Street, and Eve felt suddenly exposed, as if she'd been caught in the middle of an illicit transaction. She cupped her hands around her face and leaned in closer.

"It's raining out."

"Come in." He nodded at the passenger

seat. "The heater's on."

Eve knew this was her own fault. She never should have sent Julian that picture the other night. It was a stupid, reckless thing to do. And now she had to deal with this. With *him.* And talking to him — clearing up his understandable confusion, apologizing for the mixed messages she'd sent — was the least she could do.

"Just for a minute," she said. "I need to get home and make dinner."

The door didn't open all the way, on account of his terrible parking job, so it took some doing for Eve to slip into the Volvo. She felt calmer once she was inside, no longer visible from the street.

"I missed you," he said.

Eve nodded, acknowledging the sentiment, but not quite returning it. They examined each other for a little too long, reacquainting themselves after the winter-long separation. He'd grown out some stubble on his cheeks and chin, a scruffy hipster look that added a couple of years to his face.

"I like your hair," he said. "It's really pretty that way."

"Thank you."

"I liked it before," he added quickly, in case she'd taken his compliment the wrong way. "But this is better. You look really hot."

Eve let out a cautionary sigh that was directed more to herself than to Julian, a reminder not to drift off course, to wander into a conversation that would be a lot more enjoyable (and dangerous) than the one they needed to have.

"Julian," she said. "That's really kind of you. But I'm old enough to —"

"I don't care," he told her.

"Look." She shook her head in weary self-reproach. "I know I've done some things that have muddied the waters between us, and I'm really sorry about that. But we're not a couple. We can never be a couple. I think you know that as well as I do."

He conceded the point without a fight.

"I totally get that."

"Okay, good." Eve smiled with relief. "I'm glad we're on the same page."

Julian stared through the windshield — the wipers were still arcing back and forth — with a brooding intensity that reminded Eve of her high school boyfriend, Jack Ramos, a sad-eyed baseball player with an explosive temper. Jack had burst into tears when she broke up with him, and then ordered her to get the fuck out of his car, a yellow VW bug that smelled like dirty socks. There were no cellphones back then, and it had taken her an hour to walk home in the dark. But that had seemed like a reasonable price to pay, because the breakup had been her choice, and she was relieved to be done with him.

Julian reached across the console and took her hand. She was so surprised that it didn't occur to her to resist.

"I was just hoping we could hook up sometimes," he said, stroking her knuckles with the pad of his thumb. It was a nostalgic sensation, a memory made flesh. "Nobody has to know but us."

Eve laughed. She hadn't seen *that* coming. Belatedly, and with some regret, she extracted her hand from his.

"Julian," she said. "That's not gonna happen."

"Why not?"

She groaned in disbelief. "I don't even know where to start."

"Just give me one reason."

"Are you kidding me? I mean, really. How would we even —"

"My parents are on vacation."

Eve didn't understand him at first. She thought he was changing the subject, conceding defeat.

"They'll be gone all week." He paused, giving her a moment to catch up. "Come by any night you want. Early, late, I don't care. Just text me and come on over."

Eve couldn't even imagine it. What was she supposed to do? Walk up his front steps and ring the doorbell? Stand there in full view of the neighbors and wait for him to let her in? But it was almost like he read her mind.

"I'll leave the garage door open. You can just pull right in. There's a string with a key on it hanging from the ceiling. You can reach it from the driver's-side window. Give it a tug, the door goes down automatically. No one'll even see you."

Eve didn't know what to say. It sounded like a good plan, simple and totally plausible, if the person pulling the string had been anyone other than herself.

"You've given this some thought," she muttered.

Julian looked at her. His face was serious, full of adult longing. It was like she could see right through the college boy to the man he would one day become.

"It's all I fucking think about," he told her.

COYOTE

Eve had no intention of sneaking out for a tryst with a nineteen-year-old boy whose parents were away on vacation. Leaving aside the difference in their ages, which was a deal-breaker in and of itself, everything about the scenario felt tawdry and vaguely demeaning — the open garage door, the ticking clock (*offer valid for one week only!*), the whole booty-call/friends-with-benefits aspect of what he was proposing. It smelled like a surefire recipe for regret, if not disaster. Even the memory of their semi-illicit rendezvous at the Senior Center — the cold rain, the car and the van side by side in an otherwise empty parking lot, the brief interlude of hand-holding — made her feel foolish and a little uneasy in retrospect.

She remembered reading an advice column a few years back in which the expert suggested the following rule of thumb: *If you're thinking about doing something you won't be able to confess to your spouse or best friend, then DON'T DO IT! YOU ALREADY KNOW IT'S WRONG!* This was solid, unimpeachable advice, and it definitely applied to her current dilemma. With the possible exception of Amanda — to whom Eve wasn't currently speaking in any case — there was no one she could imagine confiding in, no responsible adult she knew who wouldn't be horrified to hear what she'd already done with Julian — *to* Julian? — let alone the proposition that was now on the table.

Luckily, this wasn't a major problem, because there was nothing she needed to discuss. She wasn't going to drive to his house and pull into the garage, nor was she going to tug on a string (the key on the end was a nice detail, very Ben Franklin) and wait for the door to descend so she could sneak inside and compound her previous mistake — which at least had the virtue of being unpremeditated — with a more serious and deliberate error, stupidity in the first degree.

She simply wasn't going to do that.

And yet, for something that was totally out of the question, she found herself thinking an awful lot about it in the days that followed. His desire — the simple fact of it — exerted a kind of gravity on her that she hadn't anticipated, and found surprisingly difficult to resist.

He was waiting for her.

Nobody else was.

That had to count for something.

It would be so easy to make him happy, which also had to count for something, because it wasn't like she was making anyone else happy, least of all herself. Besides, what was the alternative? Updating her Match.com profile and getting some professional photos taken? Wading through hundreds of boastful profiles of guys she wouldn't want to meet in a million years? And the ones she did want to meet, *those* guys probably wouldn't give her a second look, if they ever condescended to give her a first. Months could go by before she got asked on a date. Years could pass before she went on a good one. Maybe even a lifetime.

And the thing was, these men on the internet, the ones she was hoping to someday maybe just possibly meet, they were purely hypothetical. Julian was real. *He was waiting for her.* Yes, he was young — *way too young,* she was well aware of that unfortunate fact — but there was something to be said for youth, wasn't there? The stamina, the gratitude, all the clichés that were clichés because they were true. Even his lack of experience was touching, because it wouldn't last forever. And he was beautiful — there was no other way to put it — at a time when there wasn't nearly enough beauty in her life.

It was painful, to be offered a gift like that, and have no choice but to return it unopened.

Julian was a gentleman; he didn't press too hard, but he didn't let her forget, either. He texted her a question mark on Thursday night, and *all alone* on Friday. At midnight on Saturday, he sent a photo of himself sitting up in bed, narrow-shouldered and shirtless, with a comically forlorn expression on his face.

No one came to my party

She couldn't stop thinking about him on Sunday. She thought about him on her afternoon walk — it was a mild day, and she took a rare second lap around the lake — and she thought about him while cooking a hearty dinner of roast pork, scalloped potatoes, and kale with white beans. She wished she could invite him over, set a heaping plate in front of him, and watch him while he ate. With his parents out of town, he was probably subsisting on ramen noo-dles or yesterday's pizza.

Instead it was just Eve and Brendan at the table, and Brendan seemed a little down. She wasn't sure what was bothering him. They'd barely spoken in the past week — their schedules were out of whack — and she felt guilty about neglecting him, allow-ing her attention to drift into more selfish channels.

"Did you work out today?" she asked.

"Yeah," he said. "Mostly cardio."

Eve took a bite of the pork. It was perfectly cooked, tender and garlicky.

"Were your friends there?"

"A few."

"I'd love to meet them sometime."

"Sure." He took a sip of water and set his glass back on the table. Then he picked it up again and took another sip. "I mean, I mostly just see them at the gym, so . . ."

"No pressure," Eve assured him. "What about school? How's that going?"

Brendan gave a listless shrug. He'd regis-tered for two spring-term classes at ECC — Accounting Basics and Intro to Political Sci-ence — but he hardly ever talked about them, and claimed to do all his homework in the library, which supposedly explained why he never had any studying to do at home.

"It's kinda boring, to be honest."

"What is? The textbooks? The professors?"

"I dunno," he mumbled. "The whole place. It's like I'm back in high school, just with all the losers. The ones who weren't smart enough to get into a real college."

And whose choice was that? Eve wanted to ask him.

"It's not a bad school," she said. "I had a great class there last semester. The professor was excellent, and some of the other students were really smart."

Brendan looked up from his plate. His face was blank, but she could sense some hostility in it nonetheless.

"I know. You only told me a hundred times."

He was probably right about that, Eve realized. And guilt-tripping him wasn't going to help. That had never worked with Brendan.

"You know who I saw at the supermarket?" she said. "Becca's mom. I guess Becca's got her heart set on Tulane."

"Am I supposed to care?"

"She was your girlfriend. I just thought —"

"I'm done with Becca," he said.

441

Eve was curious about their breakup, and its role in his disastrous fall semester. It seemed like an important missing piece of the puzzle.

"What happened to you two? Did you have a fight or something?"

"Not really." Brendan shrugged. "We just . . . I don't know. We never got along that great."

"Well," Eve said. "You weren't very nice to her."

"Me?" Brendan looked offended. "What did I do?"

Eve had been waiting for this opening for a long time.

"Remember the day you left for college?" she began. "When Becca came over to say goodbye?"

Brendan gave a cautious nod, but before she get could any further, her phone emitted a loud chirp, alerting her to an incoming message.

"Somebody just texted you," Brendan said. He seemed grateful for the interruption.

Eve felt a warm blush spreading across her face. The phone was lying facedown on the table, right next to her plate. She wanted to pick it up, but she couldn't, not if it was Julian.

"Aren't you gonna check?" he asked.

Luckily, it was just a harmless group text from Peggy — a picture of her next-door neighbors' chocolate lab puppy with a slipper in its mouth — so she didn't have to lie. She showed Brendan the puppy, and replied with a heart emoji. Her phone chirped again almost immediately; it was Jane, adding a photo of her late and much-loved beagle to the thread.

R.I.P. Horace, Eve wrote. *He was a sweet dog.*

By the time she looked up, Brendan was already at the sink. He rinsed his plate, and stuck it in the dishwasher.

"Good dinner," he said, and then he was gone.

Julian didn't text her at all on Sunday night. Eve tried to tell herself she was relieved, that he'd finally gotten the message implicit in her silence, but she couldn't stop checking her phone, and had an unusually hard time falling asleep.

Monday's silence was even worse. She wondered if something was wrong — if she should maybe give him a call, make sure he wasn't sick or depressed — but the clearer part of her mind understood that this was exactly the reaction he was hoping for. They were in a battle of wills now, and Eve just needed to hold out for a little while longer, until the window of opportunity closed, and they could both get on with their lives.

Stay strong, she told herself. *Don't do anything stupid.*

She followed this wise counsel until about eleven thirty that night, when she slipped out of bed and tiptoed downstairs in her nightgown and slippers. After a brief stop in the kitchen, she grabbed a fleece from the coat rack and pulled it on as she headed out to the van.

The back streets of Haddington were desolate at that hour, uninhabited except for a lone coyote prowling on Lorimer Road. It was scrawny and dejected-looking, all ribs and tail. The animal stared forlornly at Eve as she passed, as if it would have appreciated a ride across town.

She'd only been to Julian's house once before, on the night she drove him home from Barry's bar. It was a nice place, a brick-fronted ranch with a picture window and a wide front lawn. All the lights were off.

The garage door was open, just like he'd promised, but Eve parked in front of the house, right behind the Volvo. Leaving the engine running, she grabbed a small, red-

and-white picnic cooler off the passenger seat and carried it across the lawn and up the steps to the front door. The cooler had two Tupperware containers inside — one with leftover pork, the other with potatoes — along with an ice pack and a post-it note telling him to have a great day. She left it on the welcome mat, where he'd be sure to find it in the morning.

Eve struggled at the bowling alley on Tuesday, regressing from an unspectacular 98 in the first game to a truly abysmal 77 in the second. Her teammates patted her on the back, telling her that she would bounce back next time, because everyone had bad days and you never stayed down for long.

"I hope so," Eve said. "I don't think I can do much worse."

As the afternoon wore on, she found herself glancing at her phone with embarrassing frequency, and feeling deeply resentful of Julian. How could you not acknowledge a gift of food left on your doorstep? It seemed a little rude, and totally unlike him (more like something Brendan would do, now that she thought about it). She wondered if her original intuition had been right — maybe Julian *was* sick and bedridden. Or maybe he'd left the house through the garage, and hadn't even noticed the cooler, though that seemed unlikely, given the location of the Volvo. Unless he'd gone out on his skateboard; that was another possibility to consider. She kept on telling herself that she had better things to think about, but her mind refused to believe it.

The mystery was resolved that evening, when she got home from work and found the picnic cooler resting on her welcome mat. It seemed like a sweet, thoughtful gesture until she slid back the lid and saw that the food was still there, untouched inside the Tupperware. Even her post-it note had been returned, its banality and fake good cheer impossible to miss now that it was directed back at her:

Have a great day!

She hadn't meant to offend him. She'd thought of the food as a peace offering, a clever way of breaking her silence — letting him know that he was on her mind — without actually saying anything that would get her into trouble. But to him — she could see it so clearly now — it had been a taunt. She'd walked right up to his front door — so close, *right there* — but hadn't gone inside. She'd withheld herself, and given him some greasy leftovers instead. No wonder he was upset.

My bad, she thought.

Eve couldn't sleep. Her brain was foggy. She stared at her message for a long time before pressing Send.

I'm sorry. I shouldn't have done that.

It was 2:14 in the morning, but Julian answered right away.

Why didn't you come in?

Lights were out. Didn't want to wake you.

I'm awake now

It's late. I have to work tomorrow.

I cant stop thinking about u

Then, because she didn't respond:

My parents get home on Thursday

Then, in case she hadn't done the math:

Tomorrow's our last chance

Then, because she *still* hadn't responded:

I want you so fucking bad I'm going crazy

Eve stared at her phone. She could feel his desire all the way from outer space, bouncing off a satellite, beaming straight into her hand.

He was still waiting.

He'd been waiting all week.

That had to count for something.

All right, she told him. *You win.*

I do??? What's the prize???

Eve was suddenly exhausted.

Go to sleep, Julian. I'll see you tomorrow.

447

GARAGE DOOR

Eve felt surprisingly alert and well rested in the morning. She'd only slept for a few hours, but it had been a deep and restorative sleep, the best she'd had in days. All the agitation she'd been feeling — the cumulative weight of her indecision — had fallen away. What remained was a fizzy, almost buoyant feeling of anticipation.

I'm doing this, she told herself. *It's going to happen.*

She knew she'd be working late, so she chose her underwear with care, in case she decided to head straight to Julian's from the Senior Center. It wasn't too elaborate — just a red lace bra and matching panties — but it looked pretty on her. She knew he'd approve.

You win, she thought.

She could see it in her head, a romantic scene from a foreign movie. A beautiful woman of a certain age pulling into a dark garage, the door sliding down behind her. She tiptoes through the silent house, heading upstairs, into a candlelit bedroom where a sensitive young man awaits her. She stands in the doorway, basking in his appreciative gaze, and slowly begins to unbutton her blouse . . .

This is the prize.

Her clothes on the floor. Their bodies coming together.

But then what? What would happen when it was over, when she got dressed and went home? That part of the movie was a black hole, the one thing she couldn't afford to think about if she was going to make good on her promise — to do the thing she badly wanted to do — because he was waiting for her, and it was their last chance, and she was the prize.

It helped that it was the second Wednesday of the month — the day of the March lecture — which meant that she was a lot busier than usual, taking care of the last-minute tasks that were normally the responsibility of the events coordinator. She had to run to Staples to pick up the hard-backed poster to place near the main entrance — she'd forgotten all about it — and stop at the supermarket to buy cookies and soft drinks for the reception. She had to set up the folding chairs in the lecture room and make sure the sound system was working, all the while fielding several calls from the guest of honor, a New Hampshire–based journalist named Franklin Russett, who'd written a book called *Sweet Liquid Gold: In Praise of Maple Syrup.* Mostly, though, she was trying to drum up an audience, button-holing every senior she saw, reminding them of the start time, and talking up the speaker, who was in high demand on the regional lecture circuit.

She was glad that Amanda wasn't here for this. Franklin Russett and maple syrup represented everything she'd hated about the lecture series, and had hoped to disrupt. But they'd tried it Amanda's way, and it hadn't worked. A lot of seniors had been upset by Margo's presentation — they'd found it *disturbing* and *inappropriate* and even *appalling* — and the complaints had made it all the way to the Town Council. Eve knew the entire program was under the microscope; she needed to repair the dam-age that had been done to its reputation and protect the funding that had allowed it to become such a beloved institution in the first place. All she wanted was a return to form — an upbeat talk about an insipid subject, a reasonably pleasant evening that no one would ever have to think about again.

There were four rest rooms at the Senior Center — the main men's and women's rooms, an employees-only facility, and a spacious, wheelchair-accessible bathroom that was in almost constant use throughout the day. It was the go-to spot for diabetics to inject themselves with insulin, and for people with ostomy pouches to attend to their sanitary needs. Sufferers of constipation or diarrhea also appreciated the privacy afforded by a single toilet and a locked door, as did a large group of people (mostly men) who liked to hunker down with a crossword puzzle while nature worked its leisurely, unpredictable magic.

This popularity had a downside, however. The toilet in the accessible bathroom was notoriously temperamental — easily blocked and prone to overflow — and it had been malfunctioning with increasing frequency in recent months. Eve had formally requested funding for a replacement, but the council was dragging its feet, as usual. So she wasn't exactly surprised when Shirley Tripko — a grandmotherly woman who looked like she wore pillows under her clothes — approached her a couple of minutes before seven to let her know there was a "problem" with the handicap rest room.

"Would you mind informing the custodian?" Eve asked. "I have to introduce our guest speaker."

"I already informed him." Shirley's voice was tense, a little defensive. "He needs to talk to you."

"All right," Eve sighed. "I'll be there in ten minutes."

"He said *right now.*"

"Are you serious?"

Shirley bit her lip. She looked like she was about to cry.

"I didn't do anything wrong," she said. "I just *flushed.* That's all I did."

Eve stood in the doorway of the accessible bathroom, trying not to breathe. The toilet hadn't simply overflowed; it appeared to have erupted. The custodian, Rafael, was gamely trying to mop up the mess.

"Did you try the plunger?" she asked.

Rafael stared at her with dead eyes, his face partially concealed by a surgical mask. He was also wearing rubber boots and dishwashing gloves, the closest the Senior Center came to a hazmat suit.

"No good," he said in a muffled voice.

"Better call the plumber."

Eve groaned. An after-hours emergency call was a huge — and expensive — pain in the ass.

"Can it wait until morning?"

Rafael cast a wary glance at the toilet. It was filled to the brim with a nasty-looking liquid, still quivering ominously.

"I wouldn't," he said.

A wave of fatigue passed through Eve's body. A phrase she'd never spoken out loud suddenly appeared in her mind.

Shit show, she thought. *My life is a shit show.*

"All right," she said. "I'll take care of it."

She calmed down a little once she got the introduction out of the way and returned to her office. On the bright side, there was a full house in the Lecture Room; her advance work had paid off. And the toilet thing was manageable. All she had to do was call the plumber and get the problem fixed.

It's okay, she told herself. *It's under control.*

Her usual contractor — the ironically named Reliable Plumbing — didn't return her call, and Veloso Brothers said they couldn't get anyone there until ten at the earliest. Eve didn't want to wait, so she tried Rafferty & Son. She made the call with some trepidation, fully aware of the thinness of the ice she was standing on, asking a favor of a man whose late father she'd banished from the Senior Center not so long ago. Luckily, George Rafferty wasn't a grudge-holder. He was cordial on the phone, and said he'd be right over.

"Thank you," she told him. "You're a lifesaver."

Eve barely recognized him when he appeared at the main entrance fifteen minutes later, toolbox in hand. He'd shaved off the reddish-gray beard that had been his most prominent feature for as long as she could remember. He looked younger without it, not nearly as imposing.

"You're lucky you caught me," he said. "I usually go to yoga on Wednesday night, but I got hungry and ordered a pizza instead."

Eve was impressed. He didn't seem like a yoga guy.

"Bikram?" she asked.

"Royal Serenity." He rolled his shoulders and massaged his trapezius with his free hand. "Doctor recommended it for my back."

"Does it work?"

"Sometimes. Gets me out of the house."

Eve nodded, murmuring sympathetically. She remembered that George's wife had died in the fall, just a month after his father. She'd meant to send him a note, but hadn't gotten around to it.

"I'm sorry," she said. "About Lorraine."

"That was hard," he said, shifting the heavy toolbox from one hand to the other. "Really tough on my daughter."

"How's she doing?"

"She's back at school. It's gonna take her a while." He gave a vague shrug, and then put on his game face. "So what do you got for me?"

Eve led him down the hall to the shit show. Rafael had made it more or less presentable — the walls had been scrubbed, the floor carpeted with paper towels — and had even posted a warning note on the door, complete with skull and crossbones: *Broken Toilet!!! Do NOT Use!!! You WILL Regret!* George peered inside and nodded with an air of professional melancholy.

"All right," he said. "Lemme get to it."

Eve slipped into the auditorium and caught the tail end of the lecture. Russett was explaining the difference between Grade A and Grade B maple syrup, which was a matter of color and sweetness and the time of year in which the sap was gathered. Paradoxically, many syrup connoisseurs preferred the cheaper and darker Grade B to the more refined Grade A.

"It's a heated controversy," Russett explained. "But whichever kind you buy, you can't really go wrong. In my humble opinion, real maple syrup always gets a grade of D . . ." He paused, letting the audience wait for the punch line. "For Delicious." He grinned and held up his hand. "Thank you very much. You've been a wonderful audience."

The post-lecture receptions never lasted long. Most of the seniors just grabbed a cookie or two on their way out the door; only a handful stuck around to chat with the speaker. By eight thirty the room was empty, and Russett was on his way back to New Hampshire.

Eve tidied up a bit — she decided to leave the folding chairs for the morning — and went to check on the plumbing situation.

"All set," George told her, drying his hands on a paper towel. "You're good to go."

"What was the problem?"

"Adult diaper." He tossed the crumpled towels in the trash can and wiped his hands on his pants. "Someone must have shoved it down, really wedged it in good. Maybe with a coat hanger or a stick or something. I don't know. It's way too big to flush."

"They get confused sometimes," Eve said. "Or maybe just embarrassed."

"Poor bastards." George shook his head. "That's gonna be us one day."

Eve locked up and walked across the parking lot to her minivan. The sight of it annoyed her — the bulging, shapeless body, the cavernous interior, all those seats that never got used.

I need a new car, she thought. *A tiny one.*

She sat in the driver's seat for a minute or two and tried to compose herself, wondering why her nerves were so jangled. The lecture had been a success, the toilet was fixed, and it wasn't even nine o'clock.

Everything's fine, she told herself. *Right on schedule.*

It was just hard to switch gears, to make the superhero transition from her responsible, professional self to the beautiful older woman in the foreign movie, the one with the lacy red underwear beneath her sensible outfit.

What she really needed was a drink. Just a quick one to clear her head, to get herself into a more relaxed and open frame of mind. She thought about stopping at the Lamplighter for a martini, but a detour seemed like a bad idea.

Just go, she told herself. *He's been waiting all week.*

Maybe his parents had some alcohol on hand. It was probably good quality, too, given the neighborhood they lived in and the car the father drove. She could pour herself a tall glass of vodka over ice, Absolut or Grey Goose. They could sit at the kitchen table and talk for a while before heading upstairs.

Nice, she thought. *Raid their liquor cabinet before you sleep with their son . . .*

It was a bad idea to think about the parents. Mr. and Mrs. Spitzer, enjoying themselves in St. Barts, not a clue about what was happening in their lovely home.

This had nothing to do with them.

It was between her and Julian, and it was their last chance.

She turned the key. The engine hesitated for a moment — it was long overdue for a tune-up — and then sputtered erratically to life. She shifted into reverse and started moving.

She circled his house twice — the first time she got spooked by a passing dog walker, the second by nothing at all — before finally working up the nerve to pull into the driveway. She sat there for a while with her foot on the brake, staring straight ahead, gathering her courage.

An overhead light was on inside the garage, which made her a little uneasy. She was pretty sure it had been dark in there on Sunday night when she'd dropped off the cooler. But then it struck her that Julian was being polite, welcoming her into his home, rolling out the red carpet.

The garage in Eve's house was a disaster area, a jumble of broken and rusted and outgrown objects, the relics of Brendan's childhood and her life with Ted. The Spitzers' garage was enviably clean and well organized by comparison — bare cement floor, assorted tools hanging from a peg board, wall-mounted bicycles, shop vac and lawnmower, water heater with shining copper pipes.

Julian's skateboard, wheels-up on a workbench.

The famous string with the key on it.

Just reach up and give it a tug.

The interior was spacious, the entrance wide. You could just glide right in, no worries about clipping your side mirrors or pulling up far enough for the door to close behind you.

She would have done it, too, except that

something smelled a little off inside the van, and she'd begun to wonder about the source of the odor. She brought the back of her hand to her nose and gave it a quick sniff, but all that registered was the sweet chemical tang of liquid soap — not a great smell, but nothing to worry about.

Continuing her investigation, she tucked her chin and tugged at her shirt collar, sampling the air trapped between her skin and her blouse. A familiar, dispiriting fragrance wafted up, a distinctive compound of sweat and worry mixed with sadness and decay.

Ugh, she thought. *I smell like the Senior Center.*

Of course she did. That was where she'd spent the past twelve hours. It was always on her skin at the end of the workday, trapped in the fabric of her clothes. But today there was something else on top of it, the subtle but unmistakable scent of a plumbing emergency, a rotten cherry on the sundae.

She told herself she was just stopping at home for a quick shower, that she'd return to Julian clean and refreshed in fifteen or twenty minutes, smelling the way a seductive older woman was meant to smell. But this conviction faded as she drove across town. By the time she walked through her own front door and saw Brendan playing a video game on the couch, she knew she was defeated. All her courage was gone, replaced by a sudden wave of anger.

"Don't you have any homework?" she asked.

Brendan didn't answer. He was totally engrossed in his stupid game, flinching and tilting his body from side to side as he banged away at the controller, trying to kill all the bad guys.

"Turn that off," she snapped.

"Huh?" He looked up, more surprised than annoyed.

"Now."

He obeyed. The gunfire ceased, but the silence that followed was just as unnerving.

"You need to treat women with more respect," she told him.

Brendan blinked in confusion.

"What?"

"I'm not deaf. I hear the way you talk sometimes, and I don't like it. We aren't sex objects and we're not *bitches,* do you understand? I never want to hear that word in this house again."

"I never —" he protested.

"Please," she told him. "Don't insult me.

461

Not tonight. I'm not in the mood."

He stared at her for a long time, still clutching his useless controller. And then he nodded.

"Sorry," he said. "I don't mean anything by it."

"Life's not a porn movie, okay?"

"I know that." He sounded genuinely hurt that she might even think he thought it was. "Jesus."

"Good," she said. "Then please start acting like it."

Julian texted three times while she was in the shower, wondering where she was and what was wrong. Eve didn't know what to tell him.

I smelled bad.

I'm a coward.

I'm way too old for you.

All these things were true, but none of them would make him feel any better. She remembered how awful it was at that age — at *any* age — to get your hopes up and then to come up empty.

Poor kid.

She lay down for a few minutes, but she wasn't tired anymore. She got up and stood in front of the full-length mirror in her fuzzy pink bathrobe. Then she undid the belt of the robe and let it fall open.

Not too bad, she thought.

Her body wasn't what it used to be, but she looked okay. Her stomach not so much, but it was easy enough to frame the image so only her head and chest were included.

Not bad at all.

The first picture was too dark, so she turned on her bedside lamp and tried again. This one was much better. Her hair was wet and her eyes were tired, but she looked like herself, which was a fairly rare occurrence.

In real life, her breasts were a bit droopier than she would have liked — no longer *perfect* or *amazing* — but the way the robe fell alongside them, you couldn't really see that.

In the photo, her breasts were lovely.

In the photo, she was smiling.

This is just for you, she told him. *Please don't show it to anyone else.*

After she sent the text, she went to her contacts and blocked his number, so she could never do anything like that again.

■ ■ ■ ■

PART FIVE:
LUCKY DAY

■ ■ ■ ■

RED CARPET

Eve got married in early September, around the beginning of what would have been Brendan's sophomore year of college, if Brendan had still been going to college. The day dawned gray and drizzly, but the sky cleared in late morning and brightened into a glorious afternoon, which was a huge relief, because the ceremony was taking place in her own backyard.

A few minutes after four o'clock, she stepped out onto the patio, wearing a pale yellow dress and clutching a bouquet of peonies and garden roses. The guests were gathered on the lawn, standing on either side of a narrow, slightly wrinkled red carpet that had been unfurled on top of the grass.

She paused for a moment to savor the tableau, to imprint it on her memory. There weren't a lot of people in the yard — only forty or so, with more on the groom's side than the bride's — but the faces turned in her direction formed a map of her life, old and new. Her sister and mother had made the drive up from New Jersey in the morning and had done nothing but complain about the traffic since their arrival. Jane and Peggy had come with their husbands; Liza completed the friend group, the self-proclaimed fifth wheel. She'd been sweet and supportive over the past few months, repeatedly congratulating Eve on her good fortune, though it clearly pained her to see her best divorced buddy rejoining the ranks of the married, leaving her to face the harsh world of middle-aged dating on her own.

Don't forget me, she'd whispered at the end of the previous week's bachelorette dinner, after too many glasses of wine. *Promise?*

I won't, Eve told her, and it was a promise she intended to keep.

Ted and Bethany had surprised her, not only by RSVP'ing an enthusiastic *Yes!!!,* but also by bringing Jon-Jon, who looked adorable in his little blue blazer, eyes wide, arms rigid at his sides. He was doing okay, observing the scene with some apprehension, but no outbursts or tantrums so far, knock on wood. And if he did start screaming, Eve thought, then so be it. She wasn't some starry-eyed twenty-five-year-old who expected everything to be perfect on her

Special Day.

Aside from Jon-Jon, the only other child present was Margo's eight-year-old daughter, Millicent, who'd come to the ceremony straight from a soccer game, in cleats and a blue-and-white jersey with *HUSKIES* on the front. She was tall for her age, with toothpick legs and long blond hair, wedged between Margo and Dumell. They looked happy and very much together, though Eve knew that they'd gone through a rough patch and had been broken up for most of the summer.

There was also a small contingent from the Senior Center, among them Hannah Gleezen, the popular new events coordinator, whose energy and positivity felt like a force of nature, and the Gray-Aires, an a cappella group she'd created and coached over the course of the spring and summer. Eve had heard them from inside the house, serenading the guests during cocktail hour, harmonizing on "Going to the Chapel" and "Walking on Sunshine," as well as an out-of-left-field version of "Beat It" that got a big round of applause.

The only person on Eve's list who'd sent her regrets was Amanda, but she'd been so touched by the invitation that she took Eve out for a celebratory lunch the week before the wedding, the first time they'd seen each other since January. She was thriving, happy with her new job, and deeply in love with one of her co-workers, an excommunicated Mormon research librarian named Betsy.

Unlike Eve, Amanda had kept in touch with Julian. She reported that he'd transferred to the University of Vermont and was really excited about starting the next chapter of his life, and especially about living away from home for the first time.

"Good for him," Eve said. "He's a sweet kid."

Amanda did something sardonic with her eyebrows — just a subtle lift-and-lower, a brief acknowledgment of the inadequacy or absurdity of the bland phrase Eve had used — but it was enough to bring it all back into the open, the strange and intense half hour the three of them had spent together in Brendan's bedroom, and the impossibility of integrating that episode into any sensible narrative of her life. Mostly she dealt with it by not thinking about it at all, or treating it like an erotic dream she'd had, an embarrassing one that refused to dislodge itself from her memory.

"So this is a little weird." Amanda leaned forward, dropping her voice into a more confidential register. "Julian and I . . . we kinda hung out for a while. Back in the springtime."

"Hung out?"

Amanda's face had turned a pretty shade of pink.

"It was totally casual. He came over once or twice a week, after his night class. Just for a month or two, when I really needed the company. But then I started to get to know Betsy . . . Anyway, he was really cool about it."

Eve was surprised to feel a slight pang of jealousy, or maybe just possessiveness, as if Amanda had gotten hold of something that rightfully belonged to her. But it was a ridiculous, greedy feeling, and she banished it from her mind.

"I'm just curious," she said. "Did he ever show you any pictures of me?"

Amanda opened her mouth, mock scandalized.

"Ursula! Did you send him some pictures?"

"Just one. I asked him not to show anyone."

"Well, I never saw it." Amanda shrugged, as if it were her loss. "Not that I would have minded."

Eve wasn't sure if she was relieved or

disappointed.

"Next time you talk to him," she said, "tell him I said hi."

"I'll do that," Amanda promised.

Hannah Gleezen tooted on her pitch pipe and held up one finger, as if she were about to scold the singers. Then she brought it down and the Gray-Aires launched into "Here, There and Everywhere," the song that had been selected as the wedding processional. Eve thought it was a little excessive, as if the woman in the song were a goddess — *making each day of the year/ changing my life with the wave of her hand* — but George had put his foot down.

Please humor me on this, he'd said, and of course she'd agreed, because she was flattered, and because he didn't ask for much.

Eve still marveled on a daily basis at the speed with which her own life had changed. A year ago, she'd been lost and flailing, and now she was found. She wanted to call it a miracle, but it was simpler than that, and a lot more ordinary; she'd met a kind and decent man who loved her. He was standing there at the end of the red carpet, handsome in a dark blue suit, a tear rolling down his cheek as he smiled at her and mouthed the words, *You're beautiful.* His best man,

Brendan, was standing right beside him, supportively squeezing his shoulder. It was almost like a fairy tale, Eve thought, a little too good to be true, and certainly more than she deserved.

Of course, she hadn't exactly *met* him. It was more accurate to say that she'd tracked him down, engineering a "chance meeting" at Royal Serenity Yoga a week after he'd fixed the toilet in the accessible bathroom. She'd acted like it was an unexpected treat to see him there — as if he hadn't informed her that he was a Wednesday night regular — but he didn't call her on the lie. He just told her how happy he was to see her, and apologized for his baggy gym shorts.

If I'd known you were coming, he said, *I woulda worn my lululemons.*

They went on their first date two nights later. The Hollywell Tavern was booked solid, so they ended up at Enzo, which was just as romantic as she remembered. Only a few months had passed since she'd gone there with Amanda, but it felt a lot longer than that, as if their ill-fated kiss in the parking lot belonged to the distant past, a youthful indiscretion she could look back on with grown-up, head-shaking nostalgia. It felt so much more solid — so much more *real* — to be sharing a meal with an eligible man close to her own age, a man with whom she was already, improbably, beginning to sense the possibility of a future.

George had dressed up for the occasion — khakis, Oxford shirt, tweed jacket — and the outfit gave him a surprisingly academic aura, especially when he put on his reading glasses to study the menu.

"You don't look like a plumber," she said, realizing even before the words were out of her mouth that it was a stupid and condescending thing to say.

"Thanks," he said, though he didn't sound especially grateful.

"I'm sorry." Eve felt like a fool. "All I meant is that normally when I see you, you're —"

"Filthy."

"No, not filthy. Just not quite as handsome as you are right now."

"I clean up nice," he said, forcing a smile. "It's a necessity in my line of work."

He took a sip of the Chilean Malbec he'd selected after an in-depth consultation with the waiter. He clearly knew his way around a wine list, which was another thing Eve hadn't expected. It was humbling and illuminating, coming face-to-face with her own snobbery.

"Actually," he told her, "I'm thinking

about retiring in a couple of years, as soon as Katie graduates. Just sell the business and be done with it. I'd like to travel a little, maybe live near the ocean. I've been doing the same thing for thirty years. I think that's enough."

He said he'd never really wanted to be a plumber in the first place. He'd gone to BU for Communications, but he liked partying a lot more than he liked studying, and had only lasted three semesters. He was nineteen years old, living at home, and of course he drifted into the family business, becoming his father's apprentice, not so much choosing a trade as accepting his fate, which turned out to be not such a terrible way to go.

"The pay was good and I liked working with my dad. I bought a nice house, had a beautiful family. The years go by and all the sudden I'm the boss." He bit the tip of his thumb, then took a moment to inspect the toothmark. "It all made sense until Lorraine got sick."

Her illness was a four-year ordeal — diagnosis, surgery, chemo, radiation, fingers crossed. A brief period of hope, a bad scan, and the whole cycle all over again. His older daughter, Maeve, got married right out of college, moved to Denver with her husband.

She was launched. It was Katie he worried about, a moody teenager, really close to her mom. She was a wreck. On top of all that, George's own mother died, and all the crap started up with his father.

"This past year was a nightmare. I didn't handle it very well. I was trying to keep the business running and take care of everybody else. I wasn't sleeping too well, so I started drinking to slow my mind down, and you know how that goes. It got to be a problem."

"It's hard being a caregiver," Eve told him. "You muddle through however you can."

He said he'd had some difficulty controlling his emotions. He was angry all the time — at God, at himself, at the doctors, all of which was okay, as far as he was concerned. But he was also angry at his wife for being sick, which was unforgivable.

"You know what I was mad about? I was mad because I didn't have a sex life anymore. Like she was inconveniencing me. The poor woman can't eat, she's in terrible pain, but what about me, you know?" He released a soft, bitter chuckle. "I watched a lotta porn while she was dying. I mean, *a lot.* My wife was upstairs, wasting away, and I'm down in the office watching Spring Break Hotties, or whatever they call it." He delivered the bulk of this confession to the tablecloth, but now he looked up with a slightly bewildered expression. "I don't know why I'm telling you all this."

Eve was wondering the same thing. It wasn't the kind of story you expected to hear on a first date. But she was touched by his trust, and relieved to know that their experiences had overlapped in this one peculiar arena, not that she would ever tell him about that.

"You're a good man." She reached across the table and patted the back of his hand. "You took care of your family when they needed you. I remember that day you came to the Center. I saw how much you loved your dad."

He managed a weak smile. "I'm sorry if I was rude to you. That was probably the worst weekend of my life. Up to that point, anyway."

"You don't have to apologize. It was a sad situation. We all did the best we could."

He cheered up after that, told her about the trip to Hawaii he'd been fantasizing about, if he could work up the courage to go alone. He thought he might like to learn how to scuba dive, even though it terrified him.

"It's a whole other world down there. You're like an astronaut on a spacewalk."

She told him about Brendan and the rough patch he was going through, and talked a little about her Gender and Society class at ECC. George was more interested than she'd expected, explaining that Katie was big into all that stuff, queer this and trans that. She'd had a girlfriend her freshman year, but now she was dating a guy.

"She says she's attracted to the person, not the gender. I guess it doubles your chances of getting lucky."

"That's a very enlightened way of looking at it."

"Whatever makes her happy," he said. "That's the only thing that matters to me."

He drove her home and walked her to her front door. He asked if he could kiss her and she said yes. It was a nice kiss, though a little more polite than it needed to be. Brendan was away that weekend, visiting Wade at UConn, and Eve decided to seize the day.

"You want to come in for a drink?"

George wrinkled his brow like she'd asked him to solve a tricky riddle.

"I'd like to. But I think maybe we should take it slow."

He kissed her a second time, an apologetic peck on the cheek, and then headed back to his car. Eve went inside, feeling like she'd somehow snatched defeat from the jaws of victory, and poured herself a glass of consolation wine. She'd only taken one sip when her phone chimed, a text that made her close her eyes and thank a God she didn't believe in.

Is it too late to change my mind?

Things moved quickly after that. Why shouldn't they spend their weekends together? And why wouldn't he drop by for dinner on a Tuesday night, and maybe stick around and watch some TV? And if he got a little sleepy on the couch, which he tended to do, who said he had to go home? Her bed was a queen, and she discovered that she slept a lot better with him lying next to her, snoring very softly, as if he were making an unconscious effort not to disturb her.

Everything was better when George was around. Even Brendan liked him, which was the biggest surprise of all, given how grumpy and territorial her son could be. They bantered easily, employing a half-affectionate, half-mocking style that Brendan had previously reserved for his favorite teammates and closest buddies.

"Oh shit," he'd say, returning home from CrossFit. "This guy again? Don't you have a TV at home?"

"I have a nice one," George would say. "Lot nicer than this piece of crap. But your mom has Netflix and she's really pretty."

"Whatever, dude. I just hope you left me some food this time."

"I finished off the steak, but I left you lots of that zucchini you like."

Eve was deeply frustrated with Brendan in those days — he was the problem she couldn't solve — but George insisted her son was just going through a rough patch, that tricky transition between high school and the real world.

"He'll be fine, Eve. Not everyone's a Rhodes Scholar."

"I'm not asking him to be a Rhodes Scholar. I'm just asking him to do his homework every once in a while."

They'd probably had a dozen versions of this conversation before the night George laid his hand on her stomach and said, "You know, he can always come work for me. Just for the summer. If he doesn't like it, no big deal. He can try something else."

Eve was silent for a while, trying on the idea of her son holding a big wrench, wearing dirty Carhartt pants. It wasn't a life she'd ever imagined for him, but it seemed oddly plausible, certainly easier to picture than Brendan as a financial analyst or CPA.

And she knew George would be a good boss and a patient teacher.

"You should talk to him," she said.

A week later, Brendan withdrew from ECC and started working full-time as a plumber's apprentice. He took to it right away. He enjoyed the physicality of the work, the tools and the terminology, the sense of accomplishment he felt at the end of the day. It could definitely be gross, but he said you got used to that pretty quick. The starting pay wasn't bad — way better than minimum wage — and it would get a lot better in a few years, after he passed his exams and got his journeyman's license. A six-figure salary by the time he was thirty was definitely not out of the question. It was even possible that he could someday take over the business, be the Son in Rafferty & Son.

Eve told him not to get ahead of himself, to just take things one step at a time. She was disappointed by his decision to give up on his education, but she was relieved to see him so upbeat and purposeful, with some of his old confidence restored. It was a huge improvement on the sullen, beaten-down version of her son she'd gotten used to living with over the past winter and much of the spring.

■ ■ ■ ■

I was hungover pretty bad on the day of my mom's wedding, but at least I had a good excuse. After the rehearsal dinner, I went to George's house and stayed up really late, drinking vodka shots with his daughter Katie and her boyfriend, Gareth, this tall, skinny dude who seemed about ninety-five percent gay.

"We're gonna be stepsiblings," Katie said. "Might as well get to know each other."

It was weird that I'd never met her until the night before the wedding, considering how much time I'd spent with her father, way more time than I spent with my own. George and I were like family already. But she'd been living in Ithaca for the summer, tutoring underserved youth, and it was too long a drive to just pop home for the weekend.

"I don't know." She glanced around the living room, which was full of family pictures that included her dead mother, and gave a little shudder. "It's just really hard to be here. I feel like crying every time I walk through the door."

"It's a grief museum," muttered Gareth. He had a goth thing going on, hair that was really short on one side and really long on the other. The long side just kinda flopped over his face, covering one eye.

"Yeah," I said. "I'm sorry about your mom."

"Thanks." Katie tried to smile. She showed me the inside of her forearm, her mother's name tattooed in graceful cursive letters. "She was a great person. You would've liked her. Though I guess if she was alive, you two would never have met."

"Probably not," I said.

Gareth poured shots and we all drank to Katie's mom.

"It's kind of amazing," she said. "She hasn't even been gone for a year, and here's my dad getting married again."

I asked if that bothered her, and she shook her head, no hesitation at all.

"I was worried about him over the winter. He was a real mess. But he's been a lot better since he met your mom. I think he just needs a woman to take care of him. He doesn't do that well on his own."

That made sense to me. I remembered how George had just kinda showed up at our house in the spring and made himself a fixture. Right from the start, it seemed like he belonged there, like he filled an empty space in our lives. But I guess we'd done the same for him.

"You know what?" Gareth said, as if an idea had just occurred to him. "Fuck cancer."

"I'll drink to that," Katie said, and we did.

Cancer was too depressing to think about, so I asked them how long they'd been together. They traded a quick look, like maybe this was a more complicated question than it appeared to be.

"We're, uh . . . not really together together," Gareth said.

"Yes we are." Katie sounded a little annoyed. "We live together."

"Yeah," Gareth conceded. "But we don't have sex."

Katie nodded, maybe a little sadly.

"Gareth is an ace," she told me.

"A what?"

"Asexual," he explained. "I want to *be* with people. I just don't want to *do* anything with them." He made a face, like he was thinking about a food that grossed him out. "I never got what all the fuss was about."

"That's cool," I said. "To each his own."

We drank a shot to that, to people being whatever the fuck they wanted. I was feeling pretty loose by then, so I looked at Katie.

"So . . . are you like that, too? Asexual?"

"Only with Gareth," she said. "If I'm attracted to a person, I tend to mold myself to whatever they are."

They were sitting together on the couch, and she dropped her head affectionately on his shoulder. After a few seconds, he reached up with his hand and started rubbing her back in a circular motion, kind of like he was cleaning a window.

"We do a lot of cuddling," Katie told me. "That's the best part anyway."

She was prettier than I'd expected — in the pictures I'd seen, she looked kinda plain — with her red hair and freckles, and kind of a soft, earth-mother body. Actually, she reminded me a lot of Amber, which was weird, because Amber had just sent me a long email a couple of days earlier, totally out of the blue. It was the first time I'd heard from her since I'd come home in the fall.

She said she'd just gotten back from Haiti, where she'd spent her summer volunteering in a women's shelter in the capital city. It had been an amazing and humbling experience, trying to help women who were so much braver and more resilient than she could ever be. Women who had so little to begin with, and had to struggle just to survive — to feed their kids, to keep them healthy, and, maybe, if they were very lucky, to send them to school so they could learn to read and write and maybe someday have a shot at a better life. It was a transformative experience for her, an experience that made her realize how trivial her own life had been, especially her life at college.

She said she was dreading the thought of going back to BSU, getting sucked into *that meaningless vortex* again — the parties, the softball team, the social media, the dining halls, with all that food getting thrown away every day.

She said she'd been meaning to write to me for a few months, but kept putting it off, because part of her had wanted to apologize and part of her thought that other part was insane. She certainly didn't want to apologize for anything *she'd* done — not for punching me, which I'd totally deserved, or kicking me out of her room, or ignoring the messages I'd sent her — but only for Cat's painting, which didn't accurately reflect her own feelings.

I'm not saying you weren't a disappointment to me, Brendan. But so many guys have disappointed me, I don't think it's fair to single you out.

Also, if you were going to be up on that wall, I should have been up there with you. Because I'm the one who gave you the power to disappoint me. In that sense, I disappointed myself, which is just as bad, if not worse.

I'm not going to let that happen again.

I hope you had an okay summer,

Amber

I didn't really know what to make of the email, though I guess it was somewhat comforting to know that she didn't hate me as much as I'd thought she did. I was tempted to tell Katie the whole story, just to hear what she had to say. I had a feeling she was somebody you could turn to for advice in situations like that. But Gareth had started to give her a neck massage, and she was totally distracted by how good it felt, wincing and groaning like a porn star as he kneaded her traps.

"So Brendan," he said, squinting at me while he worked his magic fingers. "Are you really gonna be a plumber?"

"I'm just an apprentice," I told him. "It takes a long time to get your license."

Katie opened her eyes. "My dad says you might take over the business someday."

"Maybe," I said. "Unless I decide to go back to school."

It was weird — until I said those words, I

hadn't even realized that I was thinking about maybe giving college another try. But I'd been feeling kinda down these past few weeks, listening to Wade and Troy and all my other buddies talk about how excited they were to get back to their dorms, back to their friends and their classes and the parties. It was hard to believe they'd just pack up their shit and leave me stranded in Haddington, doomed to a lifetime of installing water heaters and fixing leaky U-joints.

"You should definitely go back," Gareth said. "I transferred three times before I got to Ithaca. You just gotta find the right fit."

"I don't know what my dad tells you," Katie said, "but he never liked his job. He always said that he wished he'd gotten his bachelor's."

"Maybe I'll fill out some applications," I said. "Just to see what happens."

"You'll get in somewhere decent," Katie said, and we all drank to that, and then to some other stuff, and we kept going until the bottle was empty and everything was pretty much a blur.

The guests continued to smile at Eve, beaming that united front of love and approval, but some confusion had begun to creep into their expressions, a collective unspoken question: *Is something wrong?* The Gray-Aires had been singing for a while now, so why wasn't she moving? Why was she still standing on the patio, strangling that bouquet with her fists? What was she waiting for?

Go, she told herself, but her feet remained rooted in place.

The singers forged ahead with the second verse, though they sounded a little less confident than they had on the first. The quizzical look on George's face had deepened into outright worry, and maybe even fear.

He's a good man, Eve reminded herself.

There had been only one genuinely troubling moment in their relationship, a tiny blip on an otherwise unblemished record of happiness. It had happened a few months ago, maybe the fourth or fifth time they'd slept together, and it was not something she wanted to be thinking about right now, with the sun shining and everyone dressed so beautifully, and the rented minister trying so hard not to look impatient.

The sex had been especially good that night, Eve on top, which was the way they preferred it. They'd found a groove, sweet and slow, and their eyes were locked together. It seemed to her that they'd moved beyond physical pleasure to a place of deeper intimacy, a place where their truest selves connected.

Oh, God, he told her. *I can't believe this is really happening.*

It's amazing, she agreed.

Eve, he said. *I've been dreaming about you for so long.*

About me?

Fuck yeah, he grunted, in a voice that seemed jarring to her. It was harsher than usual, and maybe even a little angry, as if he were speaking through gritted teeth. *You're my MILF!*

Eve stopped moving. A chill spread through her body, the memory of something unpleasant.

Excuse me? she said. *What did you say?*

He opened his mouth to reply, but then caught himself.

Nothing, he told her. *It's not important.*

That was the whole incident, just a few words in the middle of some otherwise great sex. It broke their rhythm for a few seconds, but then they found it again. When they were done, Eve thought about revisiting the matter, but what was she going to do, ask him point-blank if he'd sent her a creepy anonymous text back when they barely knew each other, back when his wife was dying and his father was losing his mind? And what if he'd said, *Yes, that was me.* What would she have done then? Where would she be now?

It was nothing, really, just a passing shadow, and Eve had lived long enough to know that it was foolish to worry about a shadow. Everybody had one; it was just the shape your body made when the sun came out. Her own was visible at that very moment, a familiar dark figure skimming the ground, moving slowly over the length of the shimmering carpet, leading her to the man she loved.

ACKNOWLEDGMENTS

Mrs. Fletcher and I would like to thank Liese Mayer and Nan Graham for their probing questions and excellent advice; Maria Massie and Sylvie Rabineau for their unflagging guidance and support; and Lyn Bond and Carolyn J. Davis for illuminating conversations that gave me momentum when I needed it the most. Nina and Luke Perrotta made the book better with their careful readings and thoughtful comments, and Mary Granfield helped in too many ways to list here.

ABOUT THE AUTHOR

Tom Perrotta is the bestselling author of eight works of fiction, including *Election* and *Little Children*, both of which were made into critically acclaimed movies, and **The Leftovers**, which was adapted into an HBO series. He lives outside Boston.

The employees of Thorndike Press hope you have enjoyed this Large Print book. All our Thorndike, Wheeler, and Kennebec Large Print titles are designed for easy reading, and all our books are made to last. Other Thorndike Press Large Print books are available at your library, through selected bookstores, or directly from us.

For information about titles, please call:
(800) 223-1244

or visit our website at:
gale.com/thorndike

To share your comments, please write:
Publisher
Thorndike Press
10 Water St., Suite 310
Waterville, ME 04901

P9-DMV-046

Praise for *The Green Collar Economy*

"This book illustrates the link between the struggle to restore the environment and the need to revive the U.S. economy. Van Jones demonstrates conclusively that the best solutions for the survivability of our planet are also the best solutions for everyday Americans."

> —Al Gore, former vice president and cofounder and chairman of Generation Investment Management

"As the Earth warms and the oceans rise, the civil and human rights agenda must expand. In the wake of Katrina and Rita, we must focus on equal protection from environmental disasters. And as solar and wind industries take off, our jobs agenda must embrace these new opportunities. No one has worked harder to level the playing field in the rapidly growing green economy than Van Jones."

> —Ben Jealous, president, NAACP

"The baton is passed to climate advocate Van Jones who clearly sees that our future must be green and must include everyone. His powerful new book *The Green-Collar Economy* shows us how to accomplish it."

> —Laurie David, global warming activist, stopglobalwarming.org

"Van Jones reminds us that the worst of times can also be the best of times; that a nation with an abundance of resources it's wasting—beginning with its youth—has an enormous opportunity to stop foolishly bankrupting itself by chasing resources it is running out of, such as oil. We also have lots of ingenuity, engineering talent, wind, and sun—put them together and we have a powerful tomorrow."

> —Carl Pope, executive director, Sierra Club

"With *The Green-Collar Economy,* Van Jones accomplishes the super heroic feat of linking together the solutions for poverty, the energy crisis, and global warming. That's 'silver rights' movement leadership at its best. And Van is the only environmentalist I know who acknowledges the central role of low-wealth communities in creating the green world of the future. Van is a visionary of our times, and one of my personal heroes. Every relevant 21st century leader needs to read Van's book."

—John Hope Bryant, founder & CEO,
Operation Hope

"Van's words echo the sentiments of many indigenous communities, who have endured the effects of coal strip mining, uranium mining and mega dams. We too embrace a green path for the future—indeed this green path is a part of Ojibwe prophecies. There is an absolute mandate in the wealthiest society in the world to create an economy not based on conquest but on survival, and on dignity between peoples and the natural world. *The Green-Collar Economy* outlines industrial society's path towards a just future."

—Winona LaDuke, environmental and
Native American rights activist

"Around the world, people of African descent are creating exciting new environmental movements: from Kenya's Wangari Maathai to the South Bronx's Majora Carter. To that list, we now can add a new name: Van Jones. In *The Green-Collar Economy,* he shows how 'green' can be good for people of ALL colors."

—Kerry Washington, actor

"It's rare that someone with such a gift for speaking is able to convey the energy and excitement of his message equally well in writing. With *The Green-Collar Economy*, Van Jones surpasses all expectations. The country seriously needs his take on the environment and the economy."

—Gavin Newsom, mayor of San Francisco

"In *The Green-Collar Economy*, Van Jones has penned a working folks' manifesto for the solar age. When green solutions finally catch on among everyday people, Van and this book will deserve the lion's share of the credit."

—Rev. Lennox Yearwood, hip hop caucus

"*The Green-Collar Economy* is a both a rallying call and a road map for how we can save the planet, reduce our dependency on budget-busting fossil fuels, and bring millions of new jobs to America. Van Jones shows how climate solutions can turbocharge the ailing U.S. economy. So what are we waiting for?"

—Fred Krupp, president of the Environmental Defense Fund and *New York Times* best-selling coauthor of *Earth: The Sequel*

"Brother Van Jones is a visionary who spells out real solutions in black and white—and, of course, green. Van's vision of a thriving, green economy doesn't have throw-away things or throw-away people. It's the kind of environmentalism everyone can get behind."

—Mario Van Peebles, actor and producer, *Mario's Green House*

"I can think of no one more pertinent to our future than Van Jones and his seamless integration of race, poverty, the environment, and human rights."

—Paul Hawken, author of *Blessed Unrest*

"Out of those seen as today's leaders, I know Van Jones to be one of the most important visionaries, strategists, and voices of our times."

—Julia Butterfly Hill, eco-heroine and author of
The Legacy of Luna

"Every once in a while, in the course of history, someone comes along—often miraculously and just in time—who completely changes the game. Van Jones is that person, and his breathtaking new book, *The Green-Collar Economy* will do exactly that. Van has written an absolutely stunning, astounding, and life-changing book."

—Lynne Twist, author of *Soul of Money*

THE
GREEN-
COLLAR
ECONOMY

How One Solution Can Fix
Our Two Biggest Problems

VAN JONES

with Ariane Conrad

HarperOne
An Imprint of HarperCollins*Publishers*

HarperOne

A portion of the text of Robert F. Kennedy Jr.'s foreword originally appeared in the May 2008 issue of *Vanity Fair.*

The photo that appears in the lower right-hand quadrant of the figure on page 55 was used by permission of the Ella Baker Center for Human Rights. Solar Installation and training by Solar Richmond / RichmondBUILD / GRID Alternatives / Solar Living Institute.

THE GREEN-COLLAR ECONOMY: *How One Solution Can Fix Our Two Biggest Problems.* Copyright © 2008 by Van Jones. All rights reserved. Printed in the United States of America. No part of this book may be used or reproduced in any manner whatsoever without written permission except in the case of brief quotations embodied in critical articles and reviews. For information address HarperCollins Publishers, 10 East 53rd Street, New York, NY 10022.

HarperCollins books may be purchased for educational, business, or sales promotional use. For information please write: Special Markets Department, HarperCollins Publishers, 10 East 53rd Street, New York, NY 10022.

HarperCollins Web site: http://www.harpercollins.com
HarperCollins®, 📖 ®, and HarperOne™ are
trademarks of HarperCollins Publishers.

FIRST EDITION
Designed by Level C

Library of Congress Cataloging-in-Publication Data is available upon request.

ISBN 978–0–06–165075–8

09 10 11 12 13 RRD(H) 10 9 8 7 6 5 4 3 2

This book was printed on paper containing 20 percent
postconsumer recycled fiber.

Contents

green-collar job
\\'grēn-'kä-lər 'jäb\ noun

: blue-collar employment that has been upgraded to better respect
   the environment
: family-supporting, career-track, vocational, or trade-level employment in environmentally-friendly fields
: examples: electricians who install solar panels; plumbers who
   install solar water heaters; farmers engaged in organic agriculture
   and some bio-fuel production; and construction workers who
   build energy-efficient green buildings, wind power farms, solar
   farms, and wave energy farms

Foreword

ROBERT F. KENNEDY JR.

L AST NOVEMBER, LORD (David) Puttnam debated before
Parliament an important bill to tackle global warming. Addressing industry and government warnings that we must proceed
slowly to avoid economic ruin, Lord Puttnam recalled that precisely
two hundred years ago Parliament heard identical caveats during
the debate over abolition of the slave trade. At that time slave commerce represented one-fourth of Britain's gross domestic product
(GDP) and provided its primary source of cheap, abundant energy.
Vested interests warned that financial apocalypse would succeed its
prohibition.

That debate lasted roughly a year, and Parliament, in the end,
made the moral choice, abolishing the trade outright. Instead of
collapsing, as slavery's proponents had predicted, Britain's economy
accelerated. Slavery's abolition exposed the debilitating inefficiencies associated with zero-cost labor; slavery had been a ball and
chain not only for the slaves, but also for the British economy,

hobbling productivity and stifling growth. Creativity and productivity surged. Entrepreneurs seeking new sources of energy launched the industrial revolution and inaugurated an era of the greatest wealth production in human history.

Today, we don't need to abolish carbon as an energy source in order to see its inefficiencies starkly or understand that the addiction to it is the principal drag on American capitalism. The evidence is before our eyes. The practice of borrowing a billion dollars each day to buy foreign oil has caused the American dollar to implode. More than a trillion dollars in annual subsidies to coal and oil producers has beggared a nation that four decades ago owned half the globe's wealth. Carbon dependence has eroded our economic power, destroyed our moral authority, diminished our international influence and prestige, endangered our national security, and damaged our health and landscapes. It is subverting everything we value.

We know that nations that "decarbon" their economies reap immediate rewards. Sweden announced in 2006 the phaseout of all fossil fuels (and nuclear energy) by 2020. In 1991 the Swedes enacted a carbon tax (now up to $150 a ton), closed two nuclear reactors, and still dropped greenhouse-gas emissions to five tons per person, compared to the U.S. rate of twenty tons. Thousands of entrepreneurs rushed to develop new ways of generating energy from sun, wind, and tides and from wood chips, agricultural waste, and garbage. Growth rates climbed to upwards of three times those of the United States. The heavily taxed Swedish economy is now the world's eighth richest by GDP.

Iceland was 80 percent dependent on imported coal and oil in the 1970s, its economy among the poorest in Europe. Today, Iceland is 100 percent energy-independent, with 90 percent of the nation's homes heated by geothermal and its remaining electrical needs met by hydro. The International Monetary Fund now ranks Iceland the fourth most affluent nation on Earth. Geothermal and hydro produce so much cheap power that Iceland has become one of the world's top energy exporters. (Iceland exports its surplus energy in the form of smelted aluminum.) The country, which previously had to beg for corporate investment, now has companies lined up to relocate there to take advantage of its low-cost clean energy.

Brazil, which decarboned its energy over the past decade, is now experiencing the most sustained economic boom in its history. Costa Rica, which is phasing out carbon, is Central America's wealthiest economy. It should come as no surprise that California, America's most energy-efficient state, also possesses its strongest economy.

The United States has far greater domestic energy resources than Iceland or Sweden. We sit atop the second-largest fund of geothermal resources in the world. The American Midwest is the Saudi Arabia of wind; indeed, North Dakota, Kansas, and Texas alone produce enough harnessable wind to meet all of the nation's electricity demand. As for solar, according to a study in *Scientific American,* photovoltaic and solar-thermal installations across just 19 percent of the most barren desert land in the Southwest could supply nearly all of our nation's electricity needs without any rooftop installation, even assuming every American owned a plug-in hybrid car. This is, incidentally, a much smaller footprint than would be required by the equivalent power from coal.

In America, several obstacles impede the kind of entrepreneurial revolutions that brought prosperity to Sweden and Iceland. First, that trillion dollars in annual coal and oil subsidies gives the carbon industry a decisive market advantage and creates a formidable barrier to renewables. Second, an overstressed and inefficient national electrical grid can't accommodate new kinds of power. Third, a byzantine array of local rules impedes access by innovators to national markets. And fourth, state and federal governments have failed to develop efficiency standards and long-promised market incentives for green buildings and machines.

There are four things the new president should immediately do to hasten the approaching boom in energy innovation. A carbon cap-and-trade system designed to put downward pressure on carbon emissions is quite simply a no-brainer. Already endorsed by Senators John McCain and Barack Obama, such a system would measure national carbon emissions and create a market to auction emissions credits. The supply of credits is then reduced each year to meet predetermined carbon-reduction targets. As supply tightens, credit value increases, providing rich monetary rewards for innovators who reduce carbon. Since it is precisely targeted, cap-and-trade is more effective than a carbon tax. It is also more palatable to politicians, who despise taxes and love markets. Industry likes the system's clear goals. This market-based approach has a proven track record.

The next president must push to revamp the nation's antiquated high-voltage power-transmission system, so that it can deliver solar, wind, geothermal, and other renewable energy across the country. Right now, a Texas wind-farm manager who wants to get his electrons to market faces two huge impediments. First, our regional power grids are overstressed and misaligned. The biggest renewable-energy opportunities—for instance, Southwest solar and Midwest wind—are outside the grids' reach. Furthermore, traveling via alternating-current (AC) lines, too much of that wind farmer's energy would dissipate before it crossed the country. The nation urgently needs more investment in its backbone transmission grid, including new direct-current (DC) power lines for efficient long-haul transmission. Even more important, we need to build in "smart" features, including storage points and computerized management overlays, allowing the new grid to intelligently deploy the energy along the way. This backbone would operate at the speed of light and incorporate sophisticated new battery and storage technologies to store solar energy for use at night and to deploy wind energy during the doldrums. Construction of this new grid will create a marketplace where utilities, established businesses, and entrepreneurs can sell energy and efficiency.

The other obstacle is the web of arcane and conflicting state rules that currently restrict access to the grid. The federal government needs to work with state authorities to open up the grid, allowing clean-energy innovators to fairly compete for investment, space, and customers. We need open markets where hundreds of local and national power producers can scramble to deliver economic and environmental solutions at the lowest possible price. The energy sector, in other words, needs an initiative analogous to the 1996 Telecommunications Act, which required open access to all the nation's telephone lines. Marketplace competition among national and local phone companies instantly precipitated the historic explosion in telecom activity.

Construction of efficient and open-transmission marketplaces and a green-power-plant infrastructure would require about a trillion dollars over the next fifteen years. For roughly a third of the projected cost of the Iraq war we could wean the country from carbon. And the good news is that the government doesn't actually have to pay for all of this. If the president works with governors to lift constraints and encourage investment, utilities and private entrepreneurs will quickly step in to revitalize the grid and recover their investment through royalties collected for transporting green electrons.

One investor anxious to fill this breach is Stephan Dolezalek, a managing director of VantagePoint Venture Partners, one of the world's largest green-tech venture-capital firms. Dolezalek scoffs at claims that a carbon-free economy is still decades away. "With the right market drivers and an open-access marketplace, we can completely decarbon our electric system within years," says Dolezalek. He analogizes the grid initiative to the federal Arpanet high-speed

Internet backbone that accelerated the PC revolution and the information-technology boom in the 1990s. "In 1987, there were less than 500 networks," he recalls. "By 1995, there were 50,000. By 1996, there were 150,000. The energy sector has the potential to evolve forward more quickly than most people can grasp today. We're going to see those same quick responses in the renewable-energy sector. As soon as the national marketplace is up, the curves will go vertical."

Energy expert and former CIA director R. James Woolsey predicts: "With rational market incentives and a smart backbone, you'll see capital and entrepreneurs flooding this field with lightning speed." Ten percent of venture-capital dollars is already deployed in the clean-tech sector, and the world's biggest companies are crowding the space with capital and scrambling for position. Says Dolezalek, "The Internet boom caused information flow to increase exponentially, but the price per bit dropped to almost zero. The same thing can happen with energy." Dolezalek reminds us that energy is hitting the Earth for free. We just need to erect the infrastructure to harvest and deliver it to the consumers. Solar and wind plants are far quicker to deploy than conventional power plants because of their simple design and lower environmental-impact concerns. The plants have modest maintenance and operation costs. There are no mining, refining, or transportation costs or the catastrophically expensive environmental and military consequences associated with carbon.

"We have the ability to make clean energy both abundant and cheap," says Dolezalek. Accessible markets will give every American the opportunity to become an energy entrepreneur. Homes and businesses will become power plants as individuals cash in by installing solar panels and wind turbines on their buildings and selling the stored energy in their plug-in hybrids back to the grid at peak hours. "As capital and entrepreneurs rush into this space, the pace of change will accelerate exponentially. As energy production goes up, you could see the price per unit drop to practically nothing."

The president's final priority must be to connect a much smarter power grid to vastly more efficient buildings and machines. We have barely scratched the surface here. Washington is a decade behind its obligation, first set by Ronald Reagan, to set cost-minimizing efficiency standards for all major appliances. With the conspicuous exception of Arnold Schwarzenegger's California, the states aren't doing much better. And Congress keeps setting ludicrously tight expiration dates for its energy-efficiency tax credits, frustrating both planning and investment. The new president must take all of this in hand at once.

We need to create open national markets where individuals who devise new ways to produce or conserve power can quickly profit from their innovations. Open, efficient markets will unleash America's entrepreneurial energies to solve our most urgent national problems—global warming, national security, our staggering debt, and a stagnant economy. Everyone will profit from the green gold rush. By kicking its carbon addiction, America will increase its national wealth and generate millions of jobs that can't be outsourced. We will create a decentralized and highly distributable grid that is far more resilient and safe for our country; a terrorist might knock out a power plant, but never a million homes. We will cut annual trade and budget deficits by hundreds of billions and improve public health and farm production. And for the first time in half a century we will live free from Middle Eastern wars and entanglements with petty tyrants who despise democracy and are hated by their own people.

The Green-Collar Economy is a critical step forward into this brave new world. Van Jones articulates the urgency and importance of the task and the opportunity before us. Let the revolution begin.

Reality Check

F IRST, THE BAD news: the pain at the gas pump is just the beginning. Because our society has remained so dependent on oil
in every aspect of our lives, petroleum prices are the Achilles' heel
of the entire economy. This weakness can and will send the entire
country into a particular kind of a tailspin.

This tailspin has a name, one that sends shivers of horror down
the spine of every economist: stagflation—stagnant economic
growth occurring simultaneously with runaway inflation. We are
already in the early stages of the horrible economic malady that
made the 1970s so dismal for so many. And this time around, everything could get a lot worse.

Stagflation is perhaps the worst possible outcome in a market
economy. It is rare, yet it is almost always fueled by a sharp rise in
energy prices. To put it simply, in a stagflation scenario the prices
keep going up—and the number of jobs keeps going down.

The reason is straightforward. It takes energy to make anything
and everything. So when energy costs go up, all prices tend to go
up. At the same time, those very same steep energy prices eat into

consumer confidence. They depress nonessential spending and discourage hiring. So consumers stop buying, employers hold back on making job offers, and tourists travel much less. As a result, the economy starts to stall—with all the attendant job loss and pain. Yet prices throughout the economy, driven by rising fuel costs, keep going up just the same. The result is that society finds itself stretched on the rack, with soaring costs and plunging jobs pulling the body of the nation in opposite directions.

It is nearly impossible to grow the economy and add jobs when energy prices are going through the roof. And there is no easy way out of this inflationary cycle. Of course, over time, sky-high energy prices will force both individuals and businesses to consume less energy and seek alternatives; a new equilibrium point will be found. But by the time this kind of shift occurs naturally, an oil-dependent economy like ours could be dead as a doornail.

The solution for the economy is simple: deliberately cut demand for energy and intelligently increase its supply. Those two steps will bring supply and demand back into balance, stabilizing energy costs and eventually lowering them. When energy prices settle and come down, all prices settle and come down—and we can begin to grow the economy again.

But all of that is a lot easier said than done. Our economy is powered almost exclusively by fossil fuels, a nonrenewable resource. That means the supplies are limited—by definition. There is only so much oil, natural gas, and coal in the world.[1] The more we use the stuff, the less of it we have—and the more it will cost us over time. The laws of supply and demand tend to make dwindling resources more and more expensive over time.

Unfortunately, our entire economy was designed to function in a world where fossil fuels are forever abundant and forever cheap. Today, as those fuels—and especially oil—become increasingly scarce, prices are rising to reflect that reality.

And they will keep rising. The main reason is that the oil supply can no longer hope to keep pace with demand. On the one hand, global demand is skyrocketing, especially from growing economies such as those of India and China. As both countries blossom into full-blown, economic superpowers, energy demand from the Asian continent will only increase.

However, on the supply side, oil companies are not finding more oil fields.[2] Some experts even fear that global oil production has already peaked and that supplies are headed for a permanent world-wide decline—even as demand goes up. Combine that fact with a weakening dollar, and you have an irreversible spike in U.S. oil and gas prices. In other words, the days of cheap oil and gas are over—forever.[3] So if we want to lower fuel prices by increasing the supply of energy, we must find alternatives to oil—and eventually to coal and natural gas as well.

Of course there are plenty of proposals to keep us addicted to fossil fuels. Some of these ideas are downright scary. Others are bizarre. To keep us hooked on polycarbons, companies are now proposing that we make fuels out of tar sands and oil shale.[4] Or drill off our shores and in our national parks.[5] Or liquefy coal to run our cars.[6] Reputable experts doubt whether these dubious efforts will make more than a small dent in the energy problem, but there seems to be no end to the efforts to find "alternatives" that are actually just a repackaging of the same fossil fuels—with the same problems. What's worse, many of these so-called alternatives come from the polycarbons that are the hardest to extract, costliest to produce, and nastiest to burn. Yet companies are still willing to go out there, dig them up, and try to bring them to market—at the right price.

Further exacerbating the problem, the world's scientists are sounding the alarm that we cannot continue to burn fossil fuels at anywhere near the present rate—let alone introduce even dirtier fuels. Greenhouse-gas levels may have already passed key tipping points, threatening to overheat the atmosphere and unleash climate chaos. The experts posit that we must cut back on burning fossil fuels altogether.[7] That's right. Not only are fuel costs prohibitive and leading us down a path to economic ruin; any attempt to offset those oil prices by burning dirtier fossil fuels would essentially cook the Earth.

And so we find ourselves stuck with a dual crisis and a potentially major dilemma. Should we use even dirtier fossil fuels to rev up the economy and in turn bake the planet? Or should we stop using oil and coal tomorrow and wreck the economy?

Whom do we love and care about more? Our children—and their immediate need for a viable economy? Or our grandchildren—and their long-term need for a viable planet? Go ahead—choose one.

Fortunately, this dilemma is a false choice. It is true that we cannot drill and burn our way out of our present economic and energy problems. We can, however, invent and invest our way out. Choosing to do so on a massive scale would have the practical benefit of cutting energy prices enough—and generating enough work—to pull the U.S. economy out of its present death spiral. But the true benefits would be much greater than that.

A serious shift in our energy strategy would open a new chapter in the story of human civilization. Right now, we are still scurrying about on our planet's surface, eking out our living as part of a vulture society—living off the dead. Out of the Earth we suck the liquefied remains of dead organisms. We burn our ancestors' remains in our engines, without ceremony. Then we go back to the Earth, like vampires, to suck out even more oil. Our coal-fired power plants munch daily on the black bones of the ancients—and belch out death. Today, the climate itself threatens to bring everything full circle: if we keep pulling death from the ground, we will reap death from the skies.

There is a wiser and more civilized alternative. Rather than continuing to base our economy on a finite supply of dead things, we can base it on sources that are practically infinite and eternal: the sun, the moon, and the Earth's inner fire.

Solar energy is as reliable as the sunrise; through solar-thermal and photovoltaics, we can harness the sun's majesty to make abundant, clean energy. Enough solar energy falls on the Earth's surface in one hour to power all of human civilization for a year.[8] The warmth from that same sun creates the weather patterns that also drive the winds; modern wind turbines can turn a gentle breeze into raw power. The interaction between the Earth and the moon creates the tides of the ocean; turbines in the sea can convert their constant rhythm to usable energy, just as wind turbines pull power from the air. And below the Earth's surface, our planet is alive with heat and power. The same drilling technology that once helped us reach pools of dead oil could someday help us tap the living furnace beneath us.

The possibility of an economic recovery based on clean energy (to increase supply) and on wasting less energy (to cut demand) is not a daydream. There is already a huge green economy developing. It is growing despite inadequate and inconsistent support from a public sector that is still easily cowed by the big polluters. In 2006, renewable energy and energy-efficiency technologies generated 8.5 million new jobs, nearly $970 billion in revenue and more than $100 billion in industry profits.[9] This is happening while the government is still giving billions of dollars in subsidies to the oil and coal companies. Imagine what would happen if the public sector fully and passionately supported the shift to clean, renewable power—and gave those supports to the next generation of power producers. Also, energy conservation measures are readily available. If the United States slashed per capita emissions to current California levels, it would cut its output to 1.7 billion tons below the targets set by the international Kyoto agreement.[10]

Most clean-energy technologies are not mature enough and current clean-energy companies are not large enough to carry the full load right away. That's why the government needs to immediately launch a massive initiative like the Manhattan Project (which invented nuclear technology) or the Apollo Mission (which put a human being on the moon) to solve the riddles of clean energy and perfect these technologies. But we do have some technologies—from solar panels to wind turbines—that are ready to go. To break the downward spiral of stagflation and avoid climate catastrophe, we should begin deploying these technologies at the pace of a war-time mobilization.

That option sure beats scraping the bottom of the fossil-fuel bucket for another decade or two. It also beats any of the false solutions represented by corn-based ethanol, nuclear power, "clean" coal, or destroying our protected areas in pursuit of the last drop of oil.

Government-mandated and -subsidized ethanol from corn will go down in history as the "Iraq war" of environmental solutions: ill-considered, costly, and disastrous. In a world full of hungry people, burning food should be criminally punished—not financially subsidized—by the U.S. government. Instead, Washington has granted subsidies and incentives to big agriculture to divert tons of a staple crop into the gas tanks of Americans.[11] As the supermarket and the gas station both fight to get the same ear of corn, the price of that ear goes up and up. And since corn is used in everything—from feeding chickens, pigs, and beef and dairy cows to sweetening sodas—the prices of nearly all food items are also going up. Today food costs are ballooning across the world, causing food riots and pushing vulnerable populations to the brink of starvation and beyond.[12] We should be storing our corn in the stomachs of the world's children, not in the gas tanks of our SUVs. Corn should be food, not fuel.

Nuclear power is also a false solution. Just as there is only so much coal in the ground, there is only so much uranium down there as well. At some point, the laws of supply and demand will catch up to that nonrenewable energy source too.[13] Additionally, mining uranium is messy, destructive, and potentially hazardous for neighboring communities. Highly toxic nuclear waste poses new dangers today; fanatics would love to nuke a Western city. And despite clever attempts at repackaging, nuclear power is not even a good "low-carbon" solution for global warming. Constructing a single power plant requires gigantic amounts of concrete—the creation of which spews tons of carbon into the atmosphere. Besides, most proposed plants won't even come online for decades—long past the window for urgently needed reductions.

"Clean coal" is an oxymoron at this point; the technology for it does not even exist. It is a just a great slogan that conceals the awful fact that the mining and burning of coal are two of the dirtiest activities occurring in the United States. "Clean coal" represents a breakthrough in the marketing of coal, but not in the science of burning coal. Proposals for horizontal smokestacks lined with carbon-eating algae do have some appeal,[14] but such facilities exist only in theory at this point. Each power plant would gobble up tons of freshwater and multiple acres of land. And in cooler climates, they would not work at all. We cannot base our entire energy strategy on this idea. Another notion that also should be eliminated as any kind of magic cure-all is the idea that we can pump all of the carbon dioxide from coal-fired power plants into big holes in the ground. It's simply not an option for the vast majority of the world's power plants; few places on Earth have the right geological features underground to even try the experiment. And even then, no container is guaranteed forever.[15]

Besides, even if we can solve the carbon problem for coal, it is still a nonrenewable resource. At some point, coal supplies will drop, prices will rise, and we will be in the same stagflation mess again. Drilling for more oil is no solution either. Prices might dip for a while, but the underlying laws of economics would push them back up. And then what would we do?

Apparently, the fossil-fuel industry's strategy is to convince the American people that we should just burn all the way through the last of our existing oil and coal reserves. Then we can let our freezing, stranded children figure out how to heat their homes and power their vehicles. This is no solution. At best, we will prolong the problem, not solve it. At some point, inevitably, fossil fuels will run out, and we will have to either power down or switch to something else. Given the climate crisis, we need urgently to begin the transition now. Fossil fuels are a finite resource doing infinite damage. As long as we rely on fossil fuels to power our society, our economy is at risk for stagflation—and our planetary home is at risk too.

Ironically, that's where the good news begins. The generations living today get to retrofit, reboot, and reenergize a nation. We get to rescue and reinvent the U.S. economy. We may as well do it right the first time. We may as well move the society as dramatically as we can, in the direction of a fully clean and renewable system. The more aggressive we are, the better off we will be. There is a better future out there.

SOME OF THE barriers to a real breakthrough are not technological, economic, or political. Even under ideal circumstances, rarely discussed practical barriers could prevent us from implementing the economic and energy solutions that are ready at hand.

For example, let's just imagine for a moment that the U.S. president has just signed the best legislation to reverse global warming that anybody ever imagined. Everyone would be clapping and cheering; supporters at the Rose Garden signing ceremony would be weeping with joy. But tomorrow morning, the president of the United States is not going to go out and put up one solar panel. The senators and representatives who passed the law are not going to go out and weatherize one building or manufacture parts for one wind turbine.

So who will do the hard and noble work of actually building the green economy? The answer: millions of ordinary people, many of whom do not have good jobs right now. According to the National Renewable Energy Lab, the major barriers to a more rapid adoption of renewable energy and energy efficiency are not financial, legal, technical, or ideological. One big problem is simply that green employers can't find enough trained, green-collar workers to do all the jobs.[16]

That is good news for people who are being thrown out of work in the present recession. That is good news for people in urban and rural communities who are suffering from chronic lack of work. That is good news for our veterans coming home from Iraq and Afghanistan. That is good news for people returning home from prison, looking for a second chance. And those opportunities for work and wealth creation can be available to all of them—starting right now. Not twenty years from now. Today.

When commentators evoke the "future green economy" or the "green jobs of the future," our minds sometimes start conjuring up images at the far edge of our imaginations. Perhaps we envision a top-secret California laboratory, where strange and mysterious geniuses are designing space-age technologies to save the world. We see cool and beautiful Ph.D.s wearing fancy goggles and green lab coats, turning the dials on strange and wonderful machines. Perhaps someone in the corner is reworking the equations for a new hydrogen fuel cell—or maybe even nuclear fusion. Or maybe we see a courageous space cowboy in orbit, bravely constructing the solar panels that somehow beam down energy to our cities. The possibilities are endless. Someone says "green jobs," and our minds go to Buck Rogers.

Let's be clear, the main piece of technology in the green economy is a caulk gun. Hundreds of thousands of green-collar jobs will be weatherizing and energy-retrofitting every building in the United

States. Buildings with leaky windows, ill-fitting doors, poor insulation, and old appliances can gobble up 30 percent more energy. That means owners are paying 30 percent more on their heating bills. And it often means that 30 percent more coal-fired carbon is going into the atmosphere. Drafty buildings create broke, chilly people—and an overheated planet.

Another bit of high-tech green technology is the clipboard. That tool is used by energy auditors as they point out energy-saving opportunities to homeowners and renters. This job does not require much training and can be an early entry point into the booming world of energy consultation and efficiency. And one consultation can save an owner hundreds—or even thousands—of dollars annually.

Other green-collar workers can then follow up with other tasks for building owners: wrapping hot-water heaters with blankets, blowing insulation, plugging holes, repairing cracks, hauling out old appliances, replacing old windows with the double-glazed kind. Other pieces of green tech are ladders, wrenches, hammers, tool belts, and nonslip work boots. Those are the space-age gadgets used by solar-panel installers every day.[17]

The point is this. When you think about the emerging green economy, don't think of George Jetson with a jet pack. Think of Joe Sixpack with a hard hat and lunch bucket, sleeves rolled up, going off to fix America. Think of Rosie the Riveter, manufacturing parts for hybrid buses or wind turbines. Those images will represent the true face of a green-collar America.

If we are going to beat global warming, we are going to have to weatherize millions of buildings, install millions of solar panels, manufacture millions of wind-turbine parts, plant and care for millions of trees, build millions of plug-in hybrid vehicles, and construct thousands of solar farms, wind farms, and wave farms. That will require thousands of contracts and millions of jobs—producing billions of dollars of economic stimulus.

And don't think of green-collar workers as laboring only in the energy sector. Though the need for a clean-energy revolution will be the main driver in revamping the economy, we will also need well-trained, well-paid workers in a range of green industries: materials reuse and recycling, water management, local and organic food production, mass transportation, and more.

We will have to completely overhaul not just the economy, but the way we think about the economy. The foundations for most of our economic models, accounting tools, and business practices have their roots in the eighteenth and nineteenth centuries. At that time, there was an awful lot of nature—and relatively few people. Today there are an awful lot of people, but shockingly little nature left. Most Western economic models assume cheap and abundant energy forever. They assume cheap and abundant everything forever—such that we can throw millions of tons of materials into landfills and incinerators every year, year after year, and never run out of anything important.

However, the price signals alerting us to this folly are starting to kick in. Today we live on what author and *New York Times* columnist Tom Friedman calls a flat, hot, and crowded planet.[18] That means there are appreciable and obvious limits to resources that the textbooks once described as inexhaustible. Over the course of this century—out of choice, necessity, or both—we will rework our economic and business models to reflect that reality.

In the meantime, opportunities abound to make things better for everyone. It is not as if the present economy has been so perfect that everyone should cling to it—fingers and toes—for fear of any changes. The U.S. economy and society have been malfunctioning for some time. Green-collar jobs could help us conserve resources, create new sources of energy, and give the nation the power to grow the economy again. What's more, we have the chance to build this new energy economy in ways that reflect our deepest values of inclusion, diversity, and equal opportunity for everyone.

The key to this is setting high standards and expectations for what a green-collar job even is. That starts by baking high quality and good values into the very definition of a green-collar job. My definition of a green-collar job is this: it is *a family-supporting, career-track job that directly contributes to preserving or enhancing environmental quality*. Like traditional blue-collar jobs, green-collar jobs range from low-skill, entry-level positions to high-skill, higher-paid jobs and include opportunities for advancement in both skills and wages. Think of them as the 2.0 version of old-fashioned blue-collar jobs, upgraded to respect the Earth and meet the environmental challenges of today.

Green-collar jobs can and should be good jobs. Like blue-collar jobs, green-collar jobs can pay family wages and provide opportunities for advancement along a career track of increasing skills and pay. We should never consider a job that does something for the planet and little to nothing for the people or the economy as fitting the definition of a green-collar job. A worthwhile, viable, and sustainable green economy cannot be built with solar sweatshops.

Here's more good news. Most green-collar jobs are middle-skill jobs. That means they require more education than a high-school diploma, but less than a four-year degree. So these jobs are well within reach for lower-skilled and low-income workers, as long as they have access to effective training programs and appropriate supports. We must ensure that all green-collar-job strategies provide opportunities for low-income people to take the first step on a pathway to economic self-sufficiency and prosperity.

The green economy demands workers with new skill sets. Some green-collar jobs—say, renewable-energy technicians—are brand-new. But others are actually existing job categories that are being transformed as industries transition to a clean-energy economy: for example, computer control operators who can cut steel for wind towers as well as for submarines, or mechanics who can fix an electric as well as an internal combustion engine. We can identify the specific skills the green economy demands. Then we can invest in creating new training programs and retooling existing training programs to meet the demand.

Even better news. Much of the work we have to do to green our economy involves transforming the places we live and work in and changing the way we get around. These jobs are difficult or impossible to outsource. For instance, you can't pick up a house, send it to China to have solar panels installed, and have it shipped back. In addition, one major group of manufacturing jobs—a sector that has been extensively outsourced—is producing component parts for wind towers and turbines. Because of their size and related high transportation costs, they are most cost-effectively produced as near as possible to wind-farm sites. Cities and communities should begin thinking now about ways their green strategies can also create local jobs.

Both urban and rural America have been negatively impacted over the past decades by a failure to invest in their growth. Green-collar jobs provide an opportunity to reclaim these areas for the benefit of local residents. From new transit spending and energy audits in inner cities to windmills and biomass operations in our nation's heartland, green jobs mean a reinvestment in the communities hardest hit in recent decades.

The "green" in "green-collar" is about preserving and enhancing environmental quality—literally saving the Earth. Green-collar jobs are in the growing industries that are helping us kick the oil habit, curb greenhouse-gas emissions, eliminate toxins, and protect natural systems. Today, green-collar workers are installing solar panels, retrofitting buildings to make them more efficient, refining waste oil into biodiesel, erecting wind farms, repairing hybrid cars, building green rooftops, planting trees, constructing transit lines, and so much more. California has shown that a state can still grow its economy while reducing the rise in greenhouse-gas emissions. The nation can do the same thing.

The green economy should not be just about reclaiming thrown-away stuff. It should be about reclaiming thrown-away communities. It should not just be about recycling materials to give things a second life. We should also be gathering up people and giving them a second chance. Formerly incarcerated people deserve a second shot at life—and all obstacles to their being able to find that second chance in the green sector should be removed. Also, our urban youth deserve the opportunity to be a part of something promising. Across this nation, let's honor the cry of youth in Oakland, California, for "green jobs, not jails."

In other words, we should use the transition to a better energy strategy as an opportunity to create a better economy and a better country all around. In fact, we should see this whole process as a "break-up" situation. When you break up with your lover, it is tough at first. But the next weekend you start going to the gym, you quit smoking, you buy some new clothes. You can use the energy unleashed by one big change to positively transform your life for the better. Well, we in America are about to break up with oil. Why not break up with poverty and discrimination too?

If we decide to do that, we can do something extraordinary. We can connect the people who most need work to the work that most needs to be done—we can fight pollution and poverty at the same time.

We have the chance now to create new markets, new technology, new industries, and a new workforce. Let's do it right—with good wages, equal opportunity, and pathways to success for those whom the pollution-based economy left behind.

We had the opportunity to do all of this decades ago, but we blew it. In the 1970s energy crisis, U.S. president Jimmy Carter and California governor Jerry Brown gave the go-ahead to very aggressive programs in alternative energy.[19] Practically every major breakthrough we associate with clean energy was created or dramatically improved during that short window of time—from solar photovoltaic to wind turbines.[20] For a while, we even had solar panels on the White House. But President Ronald Reagan took them down. Soon gas prices dropped, and we relapsed completely back into our oil addiction. Other countries—namely, Germany and Japan—took our technological breakthroughs and turned them into major economic boons for themselves. Meanwhile, we have fallen behind on the clean-energy revolution that we initiated. We started down the right road, but we turned back. It hurts to think how much stronger our economy would be today, had we continued full bore in the direction we were headed thirty years ago.

Now it is time to head back down the right road again. If the federal government shifts its policy to fully back the green economy, the private sector can create millions more jobs in new clean and green industries. A smart climate bill—which mandates reductions in greenhouse gases and ends our oil dependence—would not wreck the economy, but save it. It would eventually break the back of stagflation. It would be an economic stimulus package on steroids.

But no single group can win that monumental victory in Washington by itself. Certainly, affluent, mostly white environmental lobbying groups cannot win a comprehensive victory on their own. No top-down agenda, dictated to society by a perceived eco-elite, will win acceptance in a country as proud and diverse as ours. Any kind of elitist approach will fuel resentment and generate a "backlash alliance" between polluters and poor people. For the sake of the planet, the effort to green the economy must be owned by a much bigger and broader coalition. Most environmental groups know this, but adjusting to true partnership with very different people may not be easy for some of them.

There is reason to worry. Here we must face honestly some hard and painful truths about a sad history of racial blind spots and class exclusion in some parts of the mainstream environmental movement. I raise the point not to pick at old scabs, but to help avoid new injuries. The truth is that even the greatest ecological victories—from the Wilderness Act to the establishment of the Superfund—could have been better engineered to involve, include, and help more people. As we build this new green wave, the new environmentalists will need to work in partnership with people of all classes and colors—not just because it is the right thing to do, but because it is also the best way to ensure that we are doing things right.

And yet Velcro needs two sides to stick. Working-class people, people of color, religious leaders and groups, and other nontraditional constituencies also need to step up to the plate. The time has come for us to stop letting a small number of groups and leaders carry the load on environment and energy policy. Rather than complaining about the way they do it, all of us must step forward, take responsibility, and say in our own voices: "This is our Earth, too. We are going to be a part of saving it."

If we do that—and if a critical mass of people from all races, faiths, genders, and classes were to see the mutual benefit of cocreating the future economy—a visible and dramatic transformation of the entire economy is entirely possible. And I am hopeful that a new kind of movement will emerge from our joint efforts to save the planet and the people.

Let us all say together: "We want to build a green economy strong enough to lift people out of poverty. We want to create green pathways out of poverty and into great careers for America's children. We want this 'green wave' to lift all boats. This country can save the polar bears and poor kids too."

Let us say: "In the wake of Katrina, we reject the idea of 'free market' evacuation plans. Families should not be left behind to drown because they lack a functioning car or a credit card. Katrina's survivors still need our help. And we need a plan to rescue everybody next time. In an age of floods, we reject the ideology that says we must let our neighbors 'sink or swim.'"

Let us say: "We want to ensure that those communities that were locked out of the last century's pollution-based economy will be locked into the new clean and green economy. We know that we don't have any throwaway species or resources, and we know that we don't have any throwaway children or neighborhoods either. All of creation is precious and sacred. And we are all in this together."

Those words would open the door to a cross-race and cross-class partnership that would change America and the world. The idea of a new "social-uplift environmentalism" could serve as the cornerstone for an unprecedented "Green Growth Alliance." Imagine a coalition that unites the best labor and business leaders, social justice activists, environmentalists, intellectuals, students, and more—all sharing the burdens and benefits, risks and rewards, of the journey to a green-collar economy. The power of that combination would rival the last century's most powerful alliances: the New Deal and New Right coalitions.

Imagine a Green New Deal—with a pivotal role for green entrepreneurs, a strategic and limited role for government, and an honored place for labor and social activists. Such a force would change the direction of our society. It would put the government on the side of the problem solvers in the U.S. economy, not the problem makers—and bring us all together.

The road to unity and ultimate victory will be hard, with many pitfalls. But to understand why such a journey is necessary and vital, we first must understand the true dimensions of the peril we are facing.

ONE

The Dual Crisis

F OR FORTY-EIGHT HOURS, Larry and Lorrie waited for the "imminent" arrival of the buses, spending the last twelve hours standing outside, sharing the limited water, food, and clothes they had with others. Among them were sick people, elders, and newborn babies. The buses never came. Larry later learned that the minute the buses arrived at the city limits, they were commandeered by the military.

Walgreen's remained locked. The dairy display case was clearly visible through the widows. After forty-eight hours without electricity, the milk, yogurt, and cheeses were beginning to spoil in the ninety-degree heat. Without utilities, the owners and managers had locked up the food, water, disposable diapers, and prescriptions and fled the city. Outside, residents and tourists grew increasingly thirsty and hungry. The cops could have broken one small window and distributed the nuts, fruit juices, and bottled water in an organized manner. Instead, they spent hours playing cat and mouse, temporarily chasing away the looters.

Repeatedly, Larry and Lorrie were told that resources, assistance, buses, and the National Guard were pouring into the city. But no one had seen them. What they did see—or heard tell of—were electricians who improvised long extension cords stretching over blocks in order to free cars stuck on rooftop parking lots. Nurses who took over for mechanical ventilators and spent hours manually forcing air into the lungs of unconscious patients to keep them alive. Refinery workers who broke into boatyards, "stealing" boats to rescue people stranded on roofs. And other workers who had lost their homes, but stayed and provided the only assistance available.

By day four, sanitation was dangerously abysmal. Finally Larry and Lorrie encountered the National Guard. Guard personnel said that the city's primary shelter, the Superdome, had become a hellhole. They also said that the city's only other shelter, the Convention Center, was also descending into chaos and squalor and that the police were not allowing anyone else in. They could offer no alternatives and said, no, they did not have extra water to share.

When Larry and Lorrie reached it, the police command center told them the same thing. Without any other options, they and their growing group of several hundred displaced people decided to stay at the police command post. They began to set up camp outside. In short order, the police commander appeared to address the group. He told the group to walk to the expressway and cross the bridge, where the police had buses lined up to take people out of the city. When Larry pressed the commander to make certain this wasn't further misinformation, the commander turned to the crowd and stated emphatically, "I swear to you that the buses are there."

The group set off for the bridge with great hope and were joined along the way by families with babies in strollers, people using crutches, elderly clasping walkers, and others in wheelchairs. It began to pour down rain, but the group marched on.

As they approached the promised location, they saw armed sheriffs forming a line across the foot of the bridge. Before Larry and

Lorrie were even close enough to address them, the sheriffs began firing their weapons over people's heads. The crowd scattered and fled, but Larry managed to engage some of the sheriffs in conversation. When told about the promises of the police commander, the sheriffs said there were no buses waiting.

Larry and Lorrie asked why they couldn't cross the bridge anyway. There was little traffic on the six-lane highway. The sheriffs refused.

Heartbroken and desperate, the group retreated back down the highway and took shelter from the rain under an overpass. After some debate, they decided to build an encampment on the center divide of the expressway, reasoning that it would be visible to rescuers and the elevated freeway would provide some security. From this vantage point they watched as others attempted to cross the bridge, only to be turned away. Some were chased away with gunfire, others verbally berated and humiliated. Thousands were prevented from evacuating the city on foot.

From a woman with a battery-powered radio they learned that the media were talking about the encampment. Officials were being asked what they were going to do about all those families living up on the freeway. The officials responded that they were going to take care of it. "Taking care of it" had an ominous ring to it.

Sure enough, at dusk a sheriff rolled up in his patrol vehicle, drew his gun, and started screaming, "Get off the fucking freeway!" A helicopter arrived and used the wind from its blades to blow away the flimsy shelters. As Larry and Lorrie's group retreated, the sheriff loaded up his truck with the camp's small amount of food and water.

Forced off the freeway at gunpoint, they sought refuge in an abandoned school bus under the freeway, more terrified of the police and sheriffs with their martial law and shoot-to-kill policies than of the criminals who supposedly were roaming the streets.

Finally a search-and-rescue team transported Larry and Lorrie to the airport, where their remaining rations, which set off the metal detectors, were confiscated. There they waited again, along-side thousands of others, as a massive airlift gradually thinned the crowds and delivered them to other cities across the region.

After they disembarked from the airlift, the humiliation and dehumanization continued. The refugees were packed into buses, driven to a field, and forced to wait for hours to be medically screened to make sure no one was carrying communicable diseases. In the dark, hundreds of people were forced to share two filthy, overflowing porta-potties. Those who had managed to make it out with any possessions were subjected to dog-sniffing searches. No food was provided to the hungry, disoriented, and demoralized survivors.[1]

AMONG THOSE LEFT behind after Katrina, they were the lucky ones. Larry and Lorrie are a Caucasian couple who had some re-sources available to them. The whole world knows what happened to the poor, black residents of New Orleans who had none.

I believe stories like this deserve retelling, revisiting, remember-ing. Stories from Katrina's aftermath demonstrate that the issues of poverty, climate destabilization, petrochemical poisons, and the vulnerabilities of an oil-based economy are not just petty obsessions of the politically correct crowd. They are life-and-death issues for real people.

To be clear, it wasn't Hurricane Katrina that wrought that catas-trophe. It was a "perfect storm" of a different kind: neglect of our national infrastructure combined with runaway global warming and blatant disregard for the poor.

The flooding was not a result of heavy rains. It was a result of a weak levee—one that was in mid-repair when the storm hit. And that levee collapsed for one simple reason: fixing it was not a prior-ity for our country's administration. Instead, funds that should have gone for our infrastructure and to the repair of the levee were allocated to the war effort.

The dollars that could have saved New Orleans were used to wage war in Iraq instead, a war undeniably linked to our dependency on that region's oil. Additional funds that might have spared the poor in New Orleans and the Gulf region (had the dollars been properly invested in levees and modern pumping stations) were instead passed out to the rich as tax breaks. The Katrina disaster and what followed clearly point to the fact that overfunding the military and cutting services make us *less,* not more, safe.

Yet that is only one of the lessons. As Pulitzer Prize–winning journalist Ross Gelbspan said: "Katrina began as a relatively small hurricane that glanced off south Florida, [but] it was supercharged with extraordinary intensity by the relatively blistering sea surface temperatures in the Gulf of Mexico."[2] In other words, global warming supercharged the hurricane. Yet American energy policies continue to add even more carbon to the atmosphere, further destabilizing the climate.

The human suffering in the floodwaters was not—and continues not to be—equally distributed. Poor people and black people didn't "choose to stay behind." They were left behind. The evacuation plans required the city's residents to have working private cars—plus gas money and nearby relatives or funds for a hotel stay. If people didn't have those things, tough luck.

Had the responsible agencies valued the lives of the poor, they would have helped the destitute flee in the face of the hurricane—even those who couldn't afford a car or a motel room. But when the face of suffering is mostly black, somehow our high standards for effective action and compassion begin to sag.

The story of Katrina is a rare political circumstance, a genuine teaching moment. We owe it to the dead not to waste it. We cannot allow a messy stew of shame, pain, and racial disdain to prevent us from looking deeply into the heart of this disaster. If we can look into it and not turn away, we learn something invaluable: that we are all living in a floodplain today.

For some of us this is literally the case, like New Orleans's Ninth Ward residents. Poverty has forced many people into homes in neighborhoods that are vulnerable to everything from flooding to mudslides to toxic air—as if it isn't destabilizing enough to have to worry about safety on war-torn streets, get an education in schools with no resources, or hunt for scarce jobs.

Meanwhile, the stability of the relatively affluent is also under threat. The average American family has spent itself out onto a perilous perch. Credit-card debt outstrips savings plans. A sharp economic downturn or the collapse of the U.S. dollar could toss millions overboard into financial crisis.

And of course we are also on the verge of environmental bankruptcy. That big greenhouse-gas bill is fast coming due—in the form of extreme weather events that could overtake more than just the Gulf Coast. Some say it could be Manhattan, and most of our cities are no more ready than New Orleans was. Our levees, dams, schools, and hospitals are crumbling or in poor repair.

On a larger scale, Katrina also shows the flaws of the individualist "sink or swim" philosophy that dominates both major political parties. That political-economic worldview informed New Orleans's free-market evacuation plan, which ensured that only those with private cars and money could get out.

The Katrina story illustrates clearly the two crises we face in the United States: radical socioeconomic inequality and rampant environmental destruction.

CRISIS #1:
RADICAL SOCIOECONOMIC INEQUALITY

Given the skyrocketing energy prices and the specter of stagflation, it will be hard to revive the sputtering U.S. economy. But even before the present energy crisis and economic downturn, the U.S. economy and society were in deep trouble. We will examine in some detail the symptoms of a grave malady.

The country has long been deep in the throes of a socioeconomic crisis, one characterized by contracting economic opportunity for working people, growing disparities between the races, and the hording of immense wealth and privileges at the very top of our society. These features are getting worse, not better.

In fact, the United States is experiencing the greatest economic inequality between its wealthiest and poorest citizens since the Great Depression of the 1930s.[3] While a tiny number of people at the top amass wealth, very little is left for everyone else to get by on; today more than 34 percent of the country's private wealth is held by just the richest 1 percent of people. Their wealth equals more than the combined wealth of the bottom 90 percent of people in this country.[4]

In comparison to their employees, chief executive officers of major corporations are earning ungodly sums of money. Their salaries are four hundred times higher than that of the average worker. That outrageous disparity has been growing exponentially: in 1990 executive pay was (just?!) about a hundred times that of the average worker.[5] Meanwhile Americans are working longer, if not harder, than ever: we have added eighty hours to our work year over the last twenty-five years.[6]

Meanwhile, 15.6 million American households live in extreme poverty (their incomes are below half the amount considered the poverty line, which was $20,650 for a family of four in 2007), the

highest rate recorded since researchers started tracking those numbers in 1975.[7] Since 2000, the country has lost more than 3 million
manufacturing jobs.[8] More than 44 million of us live without health
insurance—a number that continues to grow.[9] In too many homes,
the family health plan is short and simple: "Nobody get sick!" At the
same time, the great majority of Americans are less and less able to
get out of debt or to save money for the rainy days that are coming.

So many folks have needed to declare personal bankruptcy that
the government finally decided to step in.[10] Unfortunately, the government did not move to bail people out (as the Fed did for Bear
Stearns investment bank when it got in trouble in 2008).[11] To the
contrary, Congress saw the tidal wave of bankruptcy petitions as a
sign of threat—not to families, but to the profits of the credit-card
industry. So it changed the laws to make it even *harder* for card
holders to declare bankruptcy and free themselves from usurious
interest rates and outrageous fees.

As painful as it is to acknowledge, factors of race and gender ex-
acerbate the inequities. Even today, female workers earn 77 cents for
each dollar earned by their male counterparts.[12] People of color own
a mere 18 cents for every dollar of white wealth.[13] Median income
levels are lowest among females of all races, and significantly lower
for black, Latino, or Hispanic women.[14] And income levels are related to educational attainment—whether someone graduates from
high school or attends college: compared to the 32 percent of whites
who hold a bachelor's degree, only 19 percent of blacks and 13 percent of Hispanics hold one.[15] About 33 percent of African American
children, 29 percent of Native American children, and 28 percent
of Latino children live below the poverty line, compared to 9.5
percent of white children.[16] In our school system, students of color
often are more likely to be taught by an underqualified teacher; they
are nearly twice as likely as white students to attend overcrowded
schools.[17]

New immigrants and undocumented workers suffer unequal and unfair treatment. Our society profits from the labor of 11 million people[18]—many of whom pick our food, nurse our children, clean up after us—without embracing them fully, without honoring their work, and without extending to them the same rights and respect we would demand for ourselves.

In the area of health and wellness, we see race-correlated differences as well. Infant mortality among black Americans is more than twice the rate for whites. Rates of cancer are 25 percent higher for blacks than for whites. Asthma death rates are more than twice as high for Latinos than for whites. Deaths from diabetes are more than twice as high for blacks than for whites. Tuberculosis and hepatitis B also show up more in communities of color.[19]

Disparities are concentrated in some places. Over the past decades, manufacturing jobs in cities have disappeared. As a result, employment opportunities for young, unskilled men living in inner cities eroded significantly through the 1960s and 1970s. At the same time, anxious whites and affluent climbers fled to the suburbs. In some inner-city neighborhoods, basic services deteriorated—including health care, stores, schools, garbage collection, police and fire protection, and employment options. Poverty, social chaos, and violence ensued. Today the life expectancy for African American men living in places like Harlem and Washington, D.C., (57.9 years) is lower than for men in Bangladesh (58.1) and Ghana (58.3).[20]

In the midst of all that suffering, the incarceration industry saw and seized a huge growth opportunity. In today's criminal justice system, the racial disparity is astounding. The Drug Policy Alliance reports:

Although African Americans comprise only 12.2 percent of the population and 13 percent of drug users, they make up 38 percent of those arrested for drug offenses and 59 percent of those convicted of drug offenses, causing critics to call the war on drugs the "New Jim Crow." The higher arrest rates for African Americans and Latinos do not reflect a higher abuse rate in these communities but rather a law enforcement emphasis on inner-city areas where drug use and sales are more likely to take place in open-air drug markets where treatment resources are scarce.[21]

As a result of these and other disparities, African Americans are seven times more likely to go to jail than whites. Although youth of color represent one-third of the adolescent population in this country, they represent two-thirds of our country's juvenile inmates.[22]

Just to be clear, people of color and the urban poor are not the only ones hurting. In many ways, those suffering in rural and small-town America are even worse off, because their plight doesn't even make the sensationalized evening news. Midsize family farmers are being squeezed—they are struggling to get fair prices for their products and compete on the open market as farm consolidation pushes more of them out of business. High fuel prices are hitting them especially hard. Meanwhile, they have less access to quality doctors; rural schools have a tough time recruiting teachers.

Those small towns that are able to attract businesses often find themselves being converted within a few years into an indistinguishable, cookie-cutter version of every other town in the country. Big-name chains, strip malls, and big-box giants are replacing the mom-and-pop stores that once gave such life and distinctive character to America's hometowns.

Furthermore, the U.S. military draws a disproportionate share of its recruits from low-income families in economically distressed parts of the country.[23] Soon, thousands of young veterans will be coming home from Iraq and Afghanistan. They will have injuries, both visible and invisible, but most will have no visible job prospects. If there is going to be a functioning society into which they can reintegrate, we must work to create a national economy that works better for everyone.

That means we have our work cut out for us. Wages, wealth, health, homes, schooling, fairness in the courts, youth opportunity: the low performance and disparities in these categories are both shocking and shameful. This is a nation that has committed itself to equal protection, equal opportunity, and "liberty and justice for all." We are earning a failing grade on those core values. The totality of these negative outcomes cannot be dismissed as just a blip on the screen or passing problem. They represent a serious system failure— one that we must muster the will and the courage to correct.

But we must do so without worsening the other major crisis we face: the ecological crisis, epitomized by the climate catastrophe that our present economy is courting.

CRISIS #2:
RAMPANT ENVIRONMENTAL DESTRUCTION

I won't take up a lot of space and time attempting to convince you of the reality of climate change and global warming or of human responsibility for these events. There are many excellent books and Web sites that describe the consensus of the most significant and well-respected scientific institutions, including the Intergovernmental Panel on Climate Change (IPCC), the American Meteorological Society, the American Geophysical Union, and the American Association for the Advancement of Science.

Their predictions grow increasingly clear—and frightening—as they compare vast amounts of climate and natural resource–related data and compare them to historical records of temperatures and conditions on Earth. An overwhelming number of experts also agree that human consumption of natural resources and our treatment of the

Earth are largely responsible.[24] It is no longer a question of whether or not climate change is happening; it is a matter of how soon—and how hard—it will hit. When it comes to the looming climate crisis, everything is a question of degrees.

By burning fossil fuels to meet our ravenous hunger for power in our homes, factories, and means of transportation, humanity adds about seven billion tons of carbon (twenty-six billion tons of carbon dioxide) to the atmosphere every year.[25] Meanwhile we keep chopping down trees; those trees are the lungs of the planet, pulling carbon out of the air and breathing out oxygen. Therefore, clear-cutting whole continents undermines the Earth's overall ability to soak up the carbon dioxide. In effect, we are running the carbon faucets at full blast, while we plug up the carbon sinks. As a result, our carbon cup runneth over.

That is why temperatures are rising at unprecedented rates. Over the course of the twentieth century, mean temperatures rose by 1.4 degrees Fahrenheit (.8 degree centigrade). But global temperatures have been quickly accelerating since the 1980s, with the top ten warmest years on record occurring since 1990. The IPCC employs approximately two thousand scientists working on climate models and predictions; their frightening projections plot a temperature increase of 10.6 degrees F (5.9 C) by the end of the century if greenhouse-gas emissions continue unabated.[26]

The temperature shifts have already set in motion many mostly destructive weather changes. Depending on the region, warming causes drought, floods, blizzards, cyclones, and other extreme weather. Deserts are expanding inexorably. Fully one-third of the Earth's land, or seven times today's percentage, according to the British Meteorological Office, will be subject to extreme drought by the end of the century.[27]

The oceans are already rising, because warmer water expands. But if the Greenland ice sheet melts, then untold numbers of coastal settlements, low-lying islands, and croplands will be submerged. All totaled, climate-driven water disasters—storms, floods, and droughts—claimed more than half a million lives between 1991 and 2000, costing the global economy the equivalent of fifty dollars for every human on Earth.[28]

As precious frozen supplies of freshwater melt into the salty seas and rivers dry up in the heat, the demand for water will further outstrip supply. The World Bank predicts that two-thirds of the global population will suffer from lack of access to freshwater by 2025.

Absorption of carbon dioxide has altered the pH balance of the oceans, resulting in the possible extinction of many shell-forming organisms like corals, which in turn impacts the aquatic species that depend upon them. And those are far from the only species we have to be concerned about losing. The most sensitive species—those with narrow temperature tolerances limited to extreme cold (like our friends the polar bears) or tropical climates—are going extinct as their habitats become inhospitable. The IPCC estimates that 30–40 percent of all species are at risk of extinction with projected levels of warming.[29]

Yet warmer temperatures are more hospitable to some. Insects that bring diseases such as malaria, dengue fever, and possibly new tropical viruses thrive. So do insect pests like locusts and corn borers, which can spread to higher altitudes and latitudes, decimating more crops in longer active periods as the winters get milder. Fungal and bacterial plant diseases flourish too. That's life on a superheated planet: if the floodwaters don't get you, the pestilence and plagues will.

Scientists estimate that ecosystems can adapt to a temperature change of only 1.8 degrees F (1 C) over a century. More than that, and the changes in habitat, mass extinctions of species, and disturbances to the predator/prey balance throw off our entire food chain.[30] Some of our key cereal crops fail with increased carbon dioxide levels. But aggressive weed varieties love the stuff. And that's not the worst news for farmers or people who like to eat. Water shortages will make growing food even harder. Topsoil—already badly eroded—loses nutrients even faster at higher temperatures and is more prone to being washed away as it dries out and becomes compacted.

The British Meteorological Office predicts that fifty million additional people will be starving or facing severe food shortages by 2050. Others estimate that, on a hotter planet, *hundreds* of millions will starve.[31] Particularly in Africa, which is considered one of the places most vulnerable to climate change, millions of people will face food and water shortages as early as 2020.[32]

Catastrophic events disproportionately impact the poor. Certainly weather instability and other environmental changes like rising ocean levels can hit any part of the country or the world, but the poor usually have fewer resources to protect themselves. And it is especially ironic—and horribly unfair—that the people who are least blameworthy are likely to suffer the most. Those of us in industrialized countries generate sixty times more carbon dioxide pollution per person than people in the least industrialized countries.[33] So it is *our* lifestyle that is most to blame for the coming troubles.

But the guiltless will bear the brunt and suffer the wrath of an enraged Mother Nature. People in wealthy countries can cushion the blows. That's why, as the 1999 edition of the World Disasters Report concludes, about 96 percent of all deaths from natural disasters happen in developing countries.[34] Our actions—and refusals to act—in the wealthier nations are funneling more disasters and death toward the poorest people on Earth.

Some reputable experts have already given up hope. They say it is already too late and that too much damage has already been done to the climate to avert catastrophe. But there is still widely held scientific opinion that if we radically cut our greenhouse-gas emissions, we can keep warming below 3.6 degrees F (2 C). And at that level, we can avert or manage the worst of the damage to our ecosystem and our lives. In large part, cutting greenhouse-gas emissions means developing clean energy and increasing efficiency.

To achieve the needed reductions, we will need both political and economic transformation—immediately. The necessary solution is to establish the kind of politics and policies that could win over a critical mass of U.S. citizens and inspire them to launch a crash program in conservation and renewable energy—so that we can save our ability to survive on the only planetary home we have ever known.

No matter what we do, however, we can be sure that the economy and the environment will both get worse before they get better. That is why this chapter began with the story of the time that a storm came and this nation left its most vulnerable people—its poor, black, elderly, and disabled people—behind to die. We must sear the moral of that story into the memory of this nation. This catastrophe—and its lessons—must become part of our national legend. Only then can we be assured that the mind-set that permitted it will never again be allowed to lead this country.

Even today, New Orleans still lies demolished. The survivors are scattered; some of them are still living in the toxic trailers provided by the Federal Emergency Management Agency (FEMA). Many sections of the impoverished Ninth Ward still look exactly as they did after the waters receded. The devastation serves as a reminder of the magnitude of the problems we face—both social and ecological.

Is there a way to address both crises simultaneously? Can we help the people without harming the planet? Can we protect the planet, without dooming more people to material poverty?

I believe the answer is yes. And if so, the key to a dual victory is to be found in the heart of the one sector of the U.S. economy that is still thriving and growing: the green part.

The Fourth Quadrant

IN THE LAST chapter, we examined a lot of discouraging data. However, as the picture becomes fuller and clearer, we will see how we can restore confidence and meet the many challenges before us.

One powerful source of hope is the explosion of interest in this country in all things "green." Now, just as the ecological crisis nears the boiling point, our society is entering the third wave of environmentalism. And just in time. The key to solving both the economic and the ecological problems described in the last chapter can be found in the emerging green wave.

Environmentalism's first wave was the "conservation" movement of the early 1900s, which worked to preserve and conserve the best of the natural past. The second wave was the "regulation" wave of the late 1960s and 1970s, which sought to manage the problems of the industrial present. Both of these waves continue to this day; in fact, their work is more necessary than ever.

Now a new wave is emerging alongside them, and it is a fundamentally different phenomenon. It is not focused on saving the beauty and bounty of the past, as important as that work is. Nor is it focused on regulating the problems of the present, as vital as that work is. The new stage is focused, instead, on inventing solutions for the future. The new green wave is an "investment" wave, and it has the power to change the world.

We will trace the origins and dynamics of all three phases. Then we will explore the profound importance of the recent explosion in ecological invention, entrepreneurship, and investment. And I make the case that the entire future of U.S. politics and economics will be bound up with the direction and final fate of the new green wave.

Before we look too far ahead, it is wise to ground ourselves by looking back.

ENVIRONMENTALISM'S FIRST WAVE: CONSERVATION

There was a time when America didn't need an environmental movement. The original human inhabitants of this land, the Native Americans, were geniuses at living in harmonic balance with their sister and brother species. Before Europeans arrived, the entire continent was effectively a gigantic nature preserve. Squirrels could climb a tree at the Atlantic Ocean and move branch to branch to branch until they reached the Mississippi River. So many birds flew south for the winter that their beating wings sounded like thunder; their numbers blotted out the sun. And the Native Americans achieved this feat of land management and sustainability over thousands of years, on a continent that was fully populated by humans.

How did they manage it? The worldviews of indigenous peoples connected them inextricably to the cosmos, the climate, the land— and its plant and animal inhabitants. It still does. Indian's economic and social structures were and are based on their knowledge and understanding of natural processes and cycles like the tides, the phases of the moon, the movements of stars, the seasons, and the reproductive cycles and migrations of animals. In this worldview, nothing is linear; everything is cyclical.

As a result, Native peoples practice reciprocity. They honor the gifts of the Earth and its creatures and give back in return for them. As a basket weaver from the California Pomo tribe instructed, "When you come to dig these basket roots, you don't rush in there and run all over. You don't do that. My mother always approached this grass very slowly. She'd come and stand and say a prayer. . . . She always asked the Spirit to give her plenty of roots. Then she'd say 'Thank you, Father,' before she dug. And after she'd finished and had got what she wanted, she said a prayer, which is like saying 'That's good, you gave me enough. Amen, Father.'"[1] Another tradition might call it "mindfulness."

Perhaps most important, Native Americans traditionally believe in accountability. The Great Law of the Iroquois Confederacy states: "In our every deliberation, we must consider the impact of our decisions on the next seven generations." We humans, being just one component of an interconnected system that also extends forwards and backwards in the continuum of time, inherit a world shaped by the actions of our forbears. And we are responsible for holding that world in trust for all the generations to come.

Environmental stewardship wasn't the only area in which early Native Americans excelled. In contrast to a prevailing image of indigenous peoples as primitive or less evolved, paleoanthropologists have found that tribal peoples in the past had stronger bones, lower rates of infant mortality, and fewer dental cavities and signs of degenerative illnesses than today's "civilized" and immunized people.[2] The leading American indigenous civilizations achieved world-historic heights of political statesmanship; an example is the founding of the Iroquois Federation, a model for the framers of the U.S. Constitution. It is a tragedy of the highest order that

Native legacy and wisdom were almost entirely decimated—along with the environment—when their lands came under new management in 1492.

The European colonizers "discovered" what was to them a "new world," a land of unimaginable beauty and splendor. But they exploited it relentlessly, razing acres of ancient and majestic trees, wiping out whole populations of gullible seals and buffalo, and killing entire societies of indigenous people. In the little more than a hundred years between 1769 and 1890, for example, the population of California Indians dropped from 310,000 (conservatively estimated) to 17,000.[3] The Europeans grew nonnative plants; they hunted animals not to subsist, but to sell the meat or the furs. Their enterprises wreaked havoc on the native ecological systems. The European conquest drove countless species into extinction.[4]

These are hard and ugly facts, but they are a part of the nation's legacy. The sad truth is that the world's most powerful democracy was founded on land stolen from Native Americans. And it was built, in surprisingly large measure, by labor stolen from enslaved Africans. These are two of the birth defects of the republic, and we forget them at our own peril. They set a low mark from which every generation of Americans must actively strive to further distance the country—through repairing the Earth, opposing racism, respecting treaty obligations, and uplifting the disadvantaged of all colors. It is the patriotic duty of all who enjoy this society's bountiful fruits to also face up to its painful roots—and to take intelligent steps, in each generation, to find ways to make things better.

In accepting this responsibility, one places oneself in good company. After all, a movement of white abolitionists eventually rose up to oppose slavery. And the children of European settlers eventually did rise up to defend—if not the red inhabitants of the land—then at least the land itself. Their noblest efforts deserve our eternal respect. Historians call those defenders of the land "conservationists."

They were far from perfect people, but our quest for hope begins, in many ways, with their struggles to preserve and conserve the bounty and richness of these lands.

During the late 1800s and early 1900s, American writers like Ralph Waldo Emerson, Henry David Thoreau, George Perkins Marsh, and John Muir were extolling the sacred qualities and beginning to note the fragility of the natural world. Their words stirred concern in middle-class Americans, influencing public opinion and, ultimately, government policy. Theodore Roosevelt, the twenty-sixth president of the United States, is generally acknowledged as the first president to have prioritized the conservation of natural resources. Rightly so. During his tenure, he spearheaded and accomplished— often by executive fiat—a great number of landmark environmental conservation victories.[5]

What motivated his actions? As it turns out, Roosevelt was an unhealthy youngster. He wrote of his childhood in his *Autobiography:* "I was a sickly, delicate boy, suffered much from asthma, and frequently had to be taken away on trips to find a place where I could breathe."[6] The places he breathed freely were unpaved and green, and it seems likely that he never entirely forgot the debt he owed nature for rescuing his lungs.

Roosevelt said, "The relation of the conservation of natural resources to the problems of National welfare and National efficiency had not yet dawned" before he took office, and no comprehensive data on the scope or condition of the nation's resources existed.[7] In response, Roosevelt established the National Conservation Commission, which completed the first inventory of national resources.[8]

In the early part of the twentieth century, there were two wings of the conservation movement: the more pragmatic wing, symbolized by Gifford Pinchot, a close adviser to Teddy Roosevelt, and the more idealistic wing, the "preservationists," represented by Sierra Club founder John Muir.[9] Pinchot became the chief of the U.S. Forestry

Service and cofounder of the Yale School of Forestry. He held that private interests could utilize forests, in exchange for a fee, so long as certain conditions were met. In his book *The Fight for Conservation,* he wrote:

> The first great fact about conservation is that it stands for development. There has been a fundamental misconception that conservation means nothing but the husbanding of resources for future generations. There could be no more serious mistake. Conservation does mean provision for the future, but it means also and first of all the recognition of the right of the present generation to the fullest necessary use of all the resources with which this country is so abundantly blessed. Conservation demands the welfare of this generation first, and afterward the welfare of the generations to follow.[10]

Muir, a passionate writer, held that nature was divine and must be preserved for its spiritual value rather than developed.[11] The two men were friends until 1897, when Pinchot's stance on development and the commercialization of nature received public attention.[12] At that point, Muir chose to distinguish himself as part of an oppositional camp of "preservationists." An excerpt from Muir's 1911 memoir *My First Summer in the Sierra* showcases his rapturous concept of the land:

> We are now in the mountains and they are in us, kindling enthusiasm, making every nerve quiver, filling every pore and cell of us. Our flesh-and-bone tabernacle seems transparent as glass to the beauty about us, as if truly an inseparable part of it, thrilling with the air and trees, streams and rocks, in the waves of sun—a part of all nature.[13]

Teddy Roosevelt's administration benefited from both men's efforts.[14] Bolstered by the surveys, reports, and the public-relations impacts of Muir and Pinchot, among others, the Roosevelt administration set aside an unprecedented 42 million acres of national forests, 53 national wildlife refuges, and 18 areas of "special interest," including the Grand Canyon, for a total of 194 million acres of preserved natural resources.[15] Among them were the so-called midnight forests, 16 million acres in the West that Roosevelt and Pinchot slyly and heroically signed into protection as national forests in the final hours before an amendment to the agriculture bill made the creation of additional forest reserves illegal.[16]

No one disputes the fact that these men—and yes, it's only *men* who are mentioned in the annals of history, although surely there were female voices too—accomplished worthy gains for the environment. Despite Muir's "preservationist" dissent, the efforts of that era have gone down in history as the launch of the "conservation" movement.

But Muir's more radical legacy was revived some half century later in the figure of David Brower. Also of European descent, Brower tried to move defense of the environment back into the realm of morality and spirituality. During the fight to keep the Grand Canyon from being dammed, Brower collaborated with Freeman, Mander & Gossage, Jerry Mander's innovative social-issue advertising agency, to create the infamous headline: "Should we also flood the Sistine Chapel so tourists can get nearer the ceiling?"[17]

In his book *Let the Mountains Talk, Let the Rivers Run,* Brower advocated for "CPR" for the Earth: conservation, preservation, and restoration. He included this prescient passage:

Restoration means putting the Earth's life support systems back in working order: rivers, forests, wetlands, deserts, soil, and endangered species, too. . . . Human systems also need restoration. Let's rehabilitate the South Bronx, and all the other places like it across the Earth. To accomplish that, we must give the unemployed and the never-employed a stake in the wider restoration process. Let's also put environmental conscience into world trade and into our corporate thinking.[18]

Brower's generation of conservationists won the designation of Redwood National Park and Point Reyes National Seashore in California; it also got the 1964 Wilderness Act passed, which established areas in which humans could not permanently reside.[19]

However, it is neither Roosevelt nor Pinchot, nor even the eloquent purists Muir or Brower, who should be celebrated as the first or truest champions of American conservation and preservation. The fact remains that all of them owed an incalculable debt to the physical and philosophical legacy of indigenous peoples.

Unfortunately, that debt continues to go largely unpaid—and even unacknowledged—by the conservation movement as a whole. It's really a shame. Imagine the good that could be done and the healing that could occur if major conservationist organizations were to fully honor the contributions of this continent's original stewards. For example, the aforementioned 1964 Wilderness Act defined "wilderness" as places absent of humans, where "man is a visitor who does not remain." This language was well-intentioned, but not all of its consequences were benign. In the words of scholar Carolyn Merchant:

> As environmental historians have pointed out, this characterization reads Native Americans out of the wilderness and out of the homelands they had managed for centuries with fire, gathering, and hunting. By the late nineteenth century, following the move to eliminate Native Americans and their food supplies, Indians were moved to reservations. National parks and wilderness areas were set aside for the benefit of white

American tourists. By redefining wilderness as the polar opposite of civilization, wilderness in its ideal form could be viewed
as free of people, while civilization by contrast was filled with
people. Yet this was a far different view of Indians than had
been the case for most of American history, where Indian presence in the landscape was prominent.[20]

Imagine if the 1964 act had carved out an exception to allow
Native Americans greater access to lands the government deemed
"wild." What if it had acknowledged the fact that traditional Indian
lifestyles would not undermine the ecosystems, but enhance them?
Unfortunately, the act—as monumental as it is—failed to make
adequate provisions for the needs or the wisdom of America's indigenous people. In other words, one of the biggest conservationist victories overlooked the needs of the continent's original, indigenous
conservationists.

Even today, in an era when large conservation groups have countless members, hundreds of millions of dollars, and scores of professional lobbyists, their Web sites and publications do not generally
foreground the connection between the beauty of America's land
and the wisdom and rights of its original inhabitants. Thus, when
Native Americans fight poverty, hostile federal bureaucracies, and
the impact of broken treaties, those massive environmental groups
are too often absent. Or silent.

From that perspective, Indian-killing Teddy Roosevelt may have set
the enduring pattern for the racial politics of the conservation movement. Viewed in the harshest possible light, perhaps his goals could be
summed up simply as: "Let's preserve the land we stole, but get rid of
the peoples from whom we stole it." Sadly, many of his own words and
actions indicate that he had this kind of attitude. Such are the limita-
tions and blind spots of even the greatest of human heroes.

And yet it must be said in closing, were it not for the heroic efforts
of the preservationists and conservationists, much of the remaining

natural wonder of North America would already be paved over. Many of the distinctive plants and beautiful animals that define this country and continent would be nothing but photos in a history book. Generations to come will sing the praises of the conservationists—and rightly so—for standing up to the buzz saws and bulldozers, for protecting and defending "America the beautiful."

But history also shows that, for all of those invaluable contributions, environmentalism's early record is marred by a failure to honor the full humanity and contributions of this continent's original stewards. The conservationists stood up for the most vulnerable places—but not always for the most vulnerable people. And decades later, we will see a similar shortcoming in environmentalism's second wave.

THE SECOND WAVE OF ENVIRONMENTALISM: REGULATION

Although active at around the same time as David Brower and also hailed as a conservationist, Rachel Carson was the pivotal figure in launching the next wave of environmentalism in the United States. I call this phase the "regulation" wave. Like the conservation wave that preceded it, this wave accomplished much, but it too stumbled over issues of race, class, power, and inclusion in ways that have much to teach us.

Carson was different from those who came before her. She was a scientist, a marine biologist, and only the second woman to ever be employed by the U.S. Bureau of Fisheries. Although Carson, who came from a white farming family that owned sixty-five acres in Pennsylvania, was able to attend college, she had to help support her family throughout her life.[21]

Like Brower, she maximized the written word in the form of articles and books; she also broadcast, through radio, film, and television, her messages about threats to the environment and the health of humans and other critters. Her most famous contribution was *Silent Spring*, a revolutionary book questioning the advances of the chemical industry and technology—especially pesticides:

> These sprays, dusts, and aerosols are now applied almost universally to farms, gardens, forests, and homes—nonselective chemicals that have the power to kill every insect, the "good" and the "bad," to still the song of birds and the leaping of fish in the streams, to coat the leaves with a deadly film, and to linger on in the soil—all this though the intended target may be only a few weeds or insects. Can anyone believe it is possible to lay down such a barrage of poisons on the surface of the earth without making it unfit for all life?[22]

Her poetic protest helped lead to the eventual domestic ban of the particularly nasty pesticide DDT in 1972, although she and her legacy have had to endure a slew of distorted, personal attacks ever since from chemical-industry giants including Dupont, Velsicol, and American Cyanamid. For example, Carson specifically addressed the use of DDT in combating malaria, although she did not urge a total ban; instead, she insisted that the chemical be used sparingly. Her opponents continued to attack her legacy into the 1990s (Carson died in 1964 of a heart attack, following her battles with breast cancer), blaming her for deaths caused by malaria after DDT was banned. Despite these smears, Carson's standing as the initiator of the modern environmental movement remains intact and undiminished.[23]

By 1962, the year in which *Silent Spring* was published, Americans were palpably experiencing the environmental impacts of the ramped-up industrialization that followed World War II, especially from disposable packaging, the planned obsolescence of an ever increasing number of consumer goods, and the subsequent explosion of waste. As just one of many examples, the Cuyahoga River in Ohio, which travels past the industrial cities of Akron and Cleveland, regularly caught fire because of the amount of floating debris and oil on the water. A June 1969 fire on the river, though, received national attention and combined with *Silent Spring* in ratcheting up public awareness about the interconnectedness of human industry and the natural environment.[24]

The very first Earth Day, in April 1970, brought unity to the diverse grassroots efforts that had begun fighting against polluting factories and power plants, raw sewage and toxic dumps, pesticides, freeway construction, oil spills, the loss of wilderness, and the extinction of wildlife. Campuses across the country rallied in the name of the environment and against polluters.

In 1970, in response to the public's concerns and persistent media coverage of disasters, President Nixon formed the Environmental Protection Agency (EPA)—by cribbing personnel from four other federal entities. From the Department of Health, Education, and Welfare came the heads of Air, Solid Waste, Radiological Health, Water Hygiene, and Pesticide Tolerance; from the Department of the Interior, Water Quality and Pesticide Label Review; from the Atomic Energy Commission and the Federal Radiation Council, Radiation Protection Standards; and from the Department of Agriculture, Pesticide Registration. Legislation passed in the regulation era included the Clean Air Act (1963) and the Air Quality Act (1967), Federal Water Pollution Control Amendments (1972), Environmental Impact Statements required by the National Environmental Policy Act (1970), and the Endangered Species Act (1973).[25]

Just four years after *Silent Spring* was published, another biologist named Paul Ehrlich came out with *The Population Bomb*. This book—and the zero population growth campaigns that followed it—also challenged the status quo in the United States. This time it wasn't industrial pollution, but human reproduction, that was under fire and linked to environmental degradation as well as sustainability, the availability of resources, and poverty. With allies inside the reproductive rights and women's rights communities, zero population growth helped legalize contraception, for both married and unmarried folks, as well as abortion, through 1973's landmark *Roe v. Wade* decision.[26]

And at the end of the 1970s, local parents discovered a toxic chemical dump buried under Love Canal in Niagara Falls, New York. Leaking underground waste was said to be causing myriad nervous disorders, miscarriages, and birth defects in more than half of the children born in the area between 1974 and 1978. The highly publicized tragedy led Congress to pass the Comprehensive Environmental Response, Compensation, and Liability Act, better known as the Superfund law. Superfund assessed a tax on petroleum and chemical industries to create a fund for cleaning up abandoned or uncontrolled hazardous waste sites.[27]

Yet despite the era's multitude of gains, particularly in the domain of legislation, this second wave of U.S. environmentalism had its disappointing aspects as well. And once again the culprits were race, class, and power. The movement to better regulate industrial society was, in its origins, almost entirely the purview of the affluent and white. As a result, it failed to see the toxic pollution that was concentrating in communities of poor and brown-skinned people, even after major environmental laws were passed. In fact, some people of color began to wonder if white polluters and white environmentalists were unconsciously collaborating. At times it seemed that both groups were willing to see the worst polluters and foulest dumps steered into black, Latino, Asian, and poor neighborhoods.

These unjust and unequal outcomes prompted activists representing people of color and low-income communities to speak out—forcefully. In the 1980s, a new movement was born to combat what its leaders called "environmental racism." Those leaders said, in essence: "Regulate pollution, yes—but do it with equity. Do it fairly. Don't make black, brown, and poor children bear a disproportionate burden of asthma and cancer. Regulate, yes—but do it justly." Their battle cry marked the beginning of a serious corrective movement insisting that the regulatory wave protect all people equally. And that corrective movement has now become a force in its own right; it is called the movement for environmental justice.

This aspect of the second wave has a proud history. It was born in 1987, when the Commission for Racial Justice of the United Church of Christ released a landmark report entitled *Toxic Wastes and Race*. Among the devastating findings was that three out of the five largest commercial hazardous waste landfills in the United States were located in predominantly black or Hispanic communities. These three landfills accounted for more than 40 percent of the estimated commercial landfill capacity in the nation. In addition, in communities with a commercial hazardous waste facility, the average minority percentage of the population was twice the average minority percentage of the population in communities without such facilities. Finally, three out of every five black and Hispanic Americans lived in communities with uncontrolled toxic waste sites, while approximately half of all Asian/Pacific Islanders and Indians lived with them.[28]

Racial justice activists also expressed real concerns about other elements of environmentalism's second wave. For instance, some pointed to the fact that zero population growth campaigns can sometimes have racist overtones and implications, particularly when they focus on trying to limit the number of babies born to Africans, Asians, and Latin Americans. Many Latinos and Asian Americans were offended by the fact that zero population growth's founder, Paul Ehrlich, was a longtime board member of the xenophobic anti-immigrant group Federation for American Immigration Reform.[29]

Even the Superfund victory turned out to be a point of pain for communities of color. The *National Law Journal* found that the amount of the penalty paid by the polluter for cleanup was an average of 500 percent higher at sites with majority white populations. Meanwhile, abandoned hazardous waste sites in minority neighborhoods took 20 percent longer to attend to than in white areas.[30] And because Superfund targets the new or current owner of a Superfund-listed site for damages, most businesses choose to develop on virgin, nonindustrialized land. Fearing massive liability, they tend to avoid buying one of the many abandoned industrial sites, known as brownfields, that linger in our inner cities. One result is even fewer job opportunities for the urban unemployed.

None of these consequences were intended, but stronger protections could have been built into these laws. The fact that much of the legislation went forward with minimal involvement from people of color practically ensured that racially imbalanced outcomes would result. And when disparities and negative unintended consequences started to surface, the original champions of change could have been more responsive and enthusiastic about modifying the laws they had passed.

The good news is that the environmental justice movement itself has made significant progress and inroads. It is led in a decentralized way by academics such as Robert Bullard;[31] African American activists like Peggy Sheppard and Beverly Wright;[32] Native American leaders like Winona LaDuke, Tom Goldtooth, and Evon Peter;[33] Latino leaders like Richard Moore and Alicia Marentes;[34] Asian American activists like Peggy Saika, Pamela Chiang, and Vivian Chang[35]—and too many more to possibly name. The community's very diversity has allowed it to make the connection between race and the environment, linking the movement to the civil rights movement, Native American struggles, and the labor movement and including such groups as tenant associations, farmworkers, and religious organizations. Unlike in the traditional environmental movement, churches have played a significant role. For instance, the United Church of Christ published its landmark report and also helped to organize the First National People of Color Environmental Leadership Summit.[36]

Environmental justice activists helped to expand the definition of the "environment" to include neighborhoods and the economic as well as social aspects of communities. They focused on "disproportionate impact": the relatively higher level of exposure to environmental hazards faced by the poor and people of color. They also advanced the concept of "environmental racism": how policies and regulations exclude people of color from decision making. Throughout the 1990s, the movement saw victories such as the ones in South Central Los Angeles against the LANCER, a trash-to-energy incinerator; in Louisiana against a uranium-enrichment facility and a proposed chemical plant; and in Kettleman City, California, against Chemical Waste Management.[37] Bill Clinton signed a 1994 executive order directing the government to address these unjust patterns.

Some members of the environmental justice community, like Carl Anthony of Urban Habitat, realized the need to reach out to bridge the chasm between "mainstream" (white) environmentalism and the opponents of environmental racism. Early in the development of the environmental justice movement, he said: "There must be a massive campaign at the national level explaining the benefits that [the majority white environmental groups] might have from addressing diversity and environmental justice. At the same time, there needs to be a campaign with community organizations to teach them why they should be concerned with the environment. We need to create more ability to see the interconnectedness of things."[38]

But Anthony's pleas went largely unheeded. As a result, since the 1980s, the United States has had a shameful secret: its environmental movement is almost explicitly segregated by race—the mainstream environmentalists are in one camp (mostly white) and the environmental justice activists in another (made up almost entirely by people of color). Without assigning blame to anyone on either side, it is safe to say that the entire second wave of environmentalism has been less powerful, less perceptive, and less transformative than it might have been, if the leaders on both sides had been able to overcome the divisions. Certainly, the major victories—like the Wilderness Preservation Act and the Superfund law—could have achieved more good for more people, had the initial proposals been grounded in the perspective of a broader, more cohesive movement.

The lesson from both the conservation and the regulation waves of the environmental movement is clear: unless everyone is included at the decision-making table, even the best-intentioned proposals miss chances to do good—and may unwittingly even do harm. Our challenge now is to build these hard-won lessons into the very DNA of the next wave of eco-activism. If we fail to do so, the next effort will probably come up short—and possibly doom us all. But if we succeed, the next wave of environmentalism will have the power to carry our whole society through a positive transformation like nothing we have seen in our lifetimes.

INVESTMENT AGENDA: THE THIRD TIME'S THE CHARM?

Given the history of racial apathy, exclusion, and even conflict, is there any reason to expect anything different from the latest upsurge of eco-activism? I believe there is. This new stage is grounded in the dynamics and logic of a big, new economic opportunity. The need to expand markets and secure the favor of government will give the new green leaders a tremendous incentive to pitch as broad a tent possible.

Already, the green wave is taking off as a financial locomotive. We're seeing consumers and investors flocking to carbon-cutting solutions like solar power, hybrid technology, biofuels, wind turbines, tidal power, fuel cells, green construction, and energy effeciency. Reporters and editors are moving their environmental stories from the back of the paper to the first page, above the fold. Corporations compete furiously with each other in showcasing their love of clear skies and lush forests. Venture capitalists are pouring billions into clean-tech and green-tech companies. Organic cuisine and natural products are flying off the shelves. And both the blue Democrats and the red Republicans are suddenly waving green banners.

In other words, solutions to the climate crisis are galloping from the margins of geek science to the epicenter of our politics, culture, and economics. Concern for the Earth and an embrace of ecological values are moving from the eco-freak fringe to the eco-chic mainstream. A sea shift is taking place in public consciousness and concern. As the new environmentalists move to the front of the line in public discourse, only two questions remain: Whom will they take with them? And whom will they leave behind?

This is the great moral challenge facing the movement for climate solutions—and the broader movement for ecological solutions as a whole. For instance, we know that climate activists eventually will convince Congress to adopt market-based solutions (like "cap-and-trade"). This approach may help big businesses do the right thing. But will those same activists use their growing clout to push Congress to better aid survivors of Hurricane Katrina? Black and impoverished victims of our biggest eco-disaster still lack housing and the means to rebuild. Will they find any champions in the rising environmental lobby?

We know that the climate activists will fight for subsidies and supports for the booming clean-energy and energy-conservation markets. But will they insist that these new industries be accessible beyond the eco-elite—creating jobs and wealth-building opportunities for low-income people and people of color? In other words, will the new environmental leaders fight for eco-equity in this new "green economy" they are birthing? Or will they try to take the easy way out—in effect, settling for some version of eco-apartheid?

Eco-Apartheid?

It is not too early to sound the alarm against the possibility of eco-apartheid. In that scenario, on one side of town there would be ecological "haves," enjoying access to healthy, morally upstanding green products and services. On the other side of town, ecological "have-nots" would be languishing in the smoke, fumes, toxic chemicals, and illnesses of the old pollution-based economy.

This kind of morally disgraceful, politically untenable, and ecologically unsustainable result is not far-fetched—at all. In fact, we can already see the early signs of it. As my colleague Majora Carter, award-winning founder of Sustainable South Bronx, explains it:

> The public image of the environmentalist is all about eating organic food, driving a Prius, and buying solar panels. And that's incredibly narrow and alienating. In the South Bronx and other poor neighborhoods, people don't have a sense of belonging to the environmentalist identity. It makes low-income communities of color say, "We can't do it, we can't afford it, it's something that we can never aspire to—nor do we necessarily want to." And that just won't work. Sustainable and green alternatives will really take off only as we reach economies of scale. And to do that, we need everyone's participation.[39]

To have everyone participating and benefiting equally—that's the alternative to eco-apartheid. That's what we call eco-equity: *equal*

*protection and equal opportunity in an economy that respects the
Earth.*

The sad racial history of environmental activism tends to discourage high hopes among racial justice activists. They doubt the
new greens will become enthusiastic champions or reliable partners
in pursuing an eco-equity agenda. Many working-class whites look
at the green phenomenon and shake their heads; all they see are
hippies or snobs. They too doubt whether all the green hoopla will
make a difference in their lives.

However, more optimism is warranted. This new wave has the
potential to be infinitely more expansive and inclusive than previous environmental upsurges. The reason for hope has to do with the
very nature of the present wave: because it is centered on investment
and solutions, it is a qualitatively different phenomenon. Although
they will always remain important topics, discussions of race, class,
and the environment today can go beyond how to atone for past
hurts or distribute present harms.

Today we can also ask: How do we equitably carve up the benefits
of a green future for our children? How do we expand the number
of people who are moving from the old, gray economy into the new,
green one—as workers, consumers, investors, and owners? The new
eco-entrepreneurs need all the customers and supporters they can
get. And that creates a different basis to engage in cross-race, cross-
class dialogue.

That's why working people need to give the green wave a second
look. The green economy is not just a place where affluent people
can spend money. It is fast becoming a place where ordinary people
can earn money. In fact, the only part of the U.S. economy that is
growing—the only part of the economy that *can* grow, long-term—
is the green part.[40] So the green wave's new products, services,
and technologies could mean something important to struggling
communities: the possibility of new green-collar jobs, a chance to

improve community health, and opportunities to build wealth in a sustainable way. Besides gaining dignified and meaningful employment, ordinary people have the chance to become inventors, investors, owners, entrepreneurs, and employers in the new, greener world. Working people will have a powerful incentive to support a green-growth agenda as long as green partisans embrace broad opportunity and shared prosperity as key values.

And the new greens have every reason—and every need—to reach out and be inclusive. To illustrate this point, let me share with you a pictorial graph from presentations I have made to audiences across the country. I use this grid to shed some light on the race and class dimensions of the environmental movements of the past, present, and future.

The horizontal axis charts ecological progress from old, gray problems, on the left, to new green solutions, on the right. The vertical axis maps the human dimension, from poor and mostly people of color, on the bottom, to wealthy and mostly white, at the top.

In quadrant one (upper left), relatively affluent people worry about ice caps melting, rain forests disappearing, oceanfront properties vanishing, and polar bears drowning due to global warming. Their own basic needs are met. Therefore, they have the time to think more deeply about long-term, global ecological problems. They also have the means and capacity to defend the long-term interests of the defenseless species that can't vote or lobby for themselves. This quadrant corresponds to the mainstream environmental movement—in its conservationist and regulatory modes. (Of course, Native Americans traditionally share these concerns, and few of them are materially wealthy. I suppose it is their spiritual and cultural wealth that lets them focus on the big picture and the long term.)

In quadrant two (lower left), Americans of more modest means worry about local environmental problems: dirty air, polluted water, cancer clusters, childhood asthma rates, lack of access to fresh food, and the devastation that might follow a disaster like Hurricane Katrina. Their basic needs are not securely met. Therefore, they tend to focus more on the personal and immediate aspects of the ecological crisis. Even though they may not consider themselves environmentalists, they have the means and capacity to push for important environmental changes at the local level. It is in this quadrant that much of the environmental justice movement is located.

In the third quadrant (upper right), affluent people choose to abandon their SUVs and Hummers. Instead, they buy hybrid cars, solar panels, and other green technologies. This is the quadrant of business opportunities for wealthy people. It is also the quadrant of consumer choices for the affluent (who must pay a premium for the slightly pricier green goods and services). Activity in this quadrant has a double benefit. The wealthy shift their considerable resources away from economic activity that harms the planet—and toward economic activity that helps it. As early adopters, they also create markets and support start-ups—which over the long term bring down costs and let more people participate in the green economy.

In the fourth quadrant (lower right), working-class people are motivated to take on green-collar jobs and start green businesses. This is the quadrant of "work, wealth, and health" for people of more modest means. Here, former brownfields, depressed urban areas, and hard-hit rural towns blossom as eco-industrial parks, green enterprise zones, and eco-villages. Farmers' markets, community co-ops, and mobile markets get fresh, organic produce to the people who can't afford to shop at health-food stores.

All four of these quadrants are important and have tremendous value. One quadrant is no more important than any other in the big picture, but right now, in order to expand the coalition opposing global warming and grow the green economy to include millions more people, the time has come to focus energy on building the fourth quadrant. Once the green economy is no longer just a place for the affluent to spend money, once it becomes a place for ordinary people to earn and save money—nothing will stop it. And this country will meet—and more than meet—the dual challenge of growing the economy without hurting the Earth.

The Case for Eco-Equity

For global-warming activists, embracing eco-equity—and ensuring that as many people as possible concern themselves with the issues of the second and fourth quadrants—would be a politically brilliant move. In the short term, a more inclusive approach will prevent polluters from isolating and derailing the new movement. Opponents of change will actively recruit everyone whom this new movement ignores, offends, or excludes. To avoid getting outmaneuvered politically, green-economy proponents must actively pursue alliances with people of color, and they must include leaders, organizations, and messages that will resonate with the working class.

The real danger lies in the long term. The United States is the world's biggest polluter. To avoid eco-apocalypse, Congress will have to do more than pass a cap-and-trade bill. And Americans will have to do more than stick in better lightbulbs. To pull off this ecological U-turn, we will have to fundamentally restructure the U.S. economy. We will need to "green" whole cities. We will have to build thousands of wind farms, install tens of millions of solar panels, and retrofit millions of buildings. We will have to retire our car, truck, and bus fleets, which are based on combustion engines and oil, and replace them with plug-in hybrids and electric vehicles powered by a clean-energy grid.

Reversing global warming will require a World War II level of mobilization. It is the work of tens of millions, not hundreds of thousands. Such a shift will require massive support at the social, cultural, and political levels. And in an increasingly nonwhite nation, that means enlisting the passionate involvement of millions of so-called minorities—as consumers, inventors, entrepreneurs, investors, buzz marketers, voters, and workers.

Climate-change activists may be tempted to try to sidestep the issues of racial inclusion in the name of expedience—but eco-apartheid won't work. The green sector needs to break out of its elite niche and succeed on a broad scale economically. If the green economy remains a niche market, even a large one, then the excluded 80 percent will inevitably and perhaps unknowingly undo all the positive ecological impacts of the green 20 percent. And that excluded 80 percent will also likely vote down measures to boost green business at the expense of the rest of the economy. So eco-apartheid would represent a self-defeating cul de sac for the green movement; at best, it would be just a speed bump on the way to eco-apocalypse.

Any successful long-term strategy will require that the green wave fully and passionately embrace of the principle of eco-equity.

Now is the time for the green movement to reach out. By definition, a politics of investment is a politics of hope, optimism, and opportunity. The bright promise of the green economy could soon include, inspire, and energize people of all races and classes. And nowhere is the need for a politics of hope more profound than it is among America's urban and rural poor. More important, climate activists can open the door to a grand historic alliance—a political force with the power to bend history in a new direction.

To give the Earth and its peoples a fighting chance, we need a broad, populist alliance—one that includes every class under the sun and every color in the rainbow. By focusing on the fourth quadrant—and ensuring that as many people as possible have a financial stake in the green economy—we have a real shot at that outcome. The key is to ensure that, having learned the lessons of the past, a critical mass commits to ensuring that the green wave lifts *all* boats.

THREE

Eco-Equity

S O HOW DO we move forward when government regulations and subsidies are still weighted heavily in favor of the old, gray economy? The dead hand of "politics past" is blocking humanity's path to a livable economic future.

The U.S. government continues to give huge tax breaks and pay-outs to the oil, gas, and coal industries; meanwhile, the fledgling solar and wind industries are left to beg and plead—just to get extensions of their modest tax credits. Multinational corporations benefit from lopsided trade deals that protect capital and copyrights, but fail to protect workers and the environment. Thus our trade treaties and tax code reward economic titans who abandon their native soil to exploit peoples overseas desperate enough to accept starvation wages and toxic pollution. Sadly, most of the economic power we need to green the Earth is still in the hands of people with a "pillage and pave" mentality. And they have unleashed their lob-byists to further defend their prerogatives, extend their power, and prop up their positions. As a result, between the leather-bound covers of innumerable law books, our lawmakers have written—in ink—all of the assumptions of a suicidal status quo.

Therefore, unless people around the world change their governments' policies, even the best green entrepreneurs and coolest gee-whiz inventions will fall far short—*far* short—of their potential impact. Even legions of conscientious consumers, nonprofit do-gooders, and enlightened local officials won't be able to propel the world's eco-entrepreneurs to victory. At least, not on their own.

To truly take off, the heroes and she-roes of the green economy need the raw power of the public sector to clear the runway. They need government on their side—not on their backs (and certainly not on the other side of the battle lines). Until national policy stops rewarding the despoilers and the downsizers, no green enterprise or industry will be able to reach its full potential as a creator of U.S. jobs or a healer of ecosystems. And this fact should come as no surprise to anyone. After all, no major new set of modern industries—from the railroads, to nuclear power, to the Internet—has ever succeeded without government playing a powerful and supportive role.

Additionally, unless the government helps to steer jobs and investment in new directions, those who most need the benefits of a new, green economy are highly unlikely to get them. If the best of the green wave bypasses the most disadvantaged urban and rural communities, then low-income and marginalized places will miss out altogether on their one shot in this new century at a glorious rebirth.

And smart government action is necessary not only to ensure that the green wave lifts up the poor within the industrialized countries. To survive and thrive during this period of wrenching changes, the Global South also needs wealthy governments to immediately begin making it a priority to assist them. To best develop their own economies while cutting carbon and restoring the Earth, our sisters and brothers in the developing world need the full engagement and cooperation of Western governments.

Therefore, the transition to a green-collar economy is not only a matter of economics and entrepreneurship; it is also a matter of policies and politics. The green-collar economic revolution cannot succeed without a corresponding realignment in the public sector. In addition to the power of business innovators, consumers, and grassroots champions, the green economy must add the might of government.

Turning the world's governments green will not be an easy task. And it will be especially challenging in the United States, given the entrenched political power of the old polluters and the overwhelming "business as usual" inertia inside the D.C. Beltway. To create a pathway to a livable future, a mobilized U.S. citizenry will have to march into the halls of power and rewrite the rules—at every level of government.

We cannot be naïve about the obstacles. A people's movement strong enough to achieve that aim would have to quickly become as big, sophisticated, and morally appealing as the greatest democratic movements of the last century. And yet building just such a movement is the central challenge—and the highest calling—of our time.

Success in this world-historic endeavor will require genius, courage, a Herculean effort—and a great deal of luck too. But we must begin. Fortunately, we have good examples and role models to guide us along the way.

When facing grave dangers in the last century, our parents and grandparents routinely faced up to the peril, overcame cynicism, and beat the odds. Today, as new generations climb onto the world stage, we are blessed to be able to learn from the heroic examples of those in the past who faced down totalitarianism, beat back an economic depression, and ended overt racial apartheid and colonial oppression in most parts of the world.

Their proud histories teach us that a successful movement for change requires three things. First, change must be grounded firmly in moral *principles*. Second, change must move rapidly to reinvent and realign *politics*. And third, change must effectively pursue and implement smart *policies*. Those of us who are concerned about the future must take those lessons as our own instructions and guideposts as we go forward.

What can ordinary people do to support the transition to an inclusive, green-collar economy—not just as smarter consumers, but as fully engaged citizens, informed voters, and active community members?

PRINCIPLES

Any movement that seeks enduring, transformative change must be founded on enduring, transformative principles. For example, the American settlers who led the revolt against British rule announced early on their commitment to a timeless principle, "No taxation without representation." And in 1776, that simple ideal became the anvil upon which ordinary people shattered the shackles of colonialism.

The labor movement also committed itself to timeless ideals: fair wages for all, safe working conditions, the right to bargain collectively, and dignity for all workers. Supported by those four pillars, labor activists were able to invent or help create practically everything good in the world's market economies—from the "middle class" to the "weekend." Labor's struggle continues into the new millennium, guided by those same unalterable principles.

In the United States, the founders of the civil rights movement declared their steadfast commitment to the principle of equality between the races. The women's rights movement devoted itself to the ideal of social equality between the sexes. The movement to liberate lesbians, gays, bisexuals, and transgendered people from the pain of ostracism and persecution is founded on the simple conviction that all persons, regardless of their sexual orientation or gender identity, should be equally free to love and form families without fear. The movement to protect the rights of immigrants is rooted in another simple idea, that all workers and families should be afforded basic rights and respect, no matter where they were born, what color their skin is, or what language they speak.

It should be noted that the political left has no monopoly on social-change movements that are rooted in unwavering principles. For instance, conservative leaders like Margaret Thatcher, Ronald Reagan, and Newt Gingrich helped guide the New Right to political victory over "big state" liberalism in the 1980s and 1990s. Their core principles—upholding lower taxes, smaller government, a strong military, and "traditional" values—continue to be the touchstone ideals of the conservative movement today.

Nor is the industrialized world alone in generating social-change movements grounded in clear principles. For instance, Mohandas Gandhi's independence movement was based on a core belief in equality between the Indian and British peoples—and nations. South Africa's anti-apartheid movement, led by Nelson Mandela, was committed to the ideal of a "free South Africa"—democratic, nonracial, and nonsexist. The clarity of those movements' principles guided their actions over decades, helped to attract global support, and ensured a generally positive outcome in their countries.

History teaches us that it is impossible to guide a complex series of deep changes in culture, economics, and law without first grounding efforts in a set of unchanging ideals. Successful movement leaders often end up employing a dizzying array of tactics; sometimes they are forced to make zigzag shifts in their short-term aims and mid-term goals. Yet their bedrock principles do not change. Their strategies may be complex, but their ideals remain simple and clear.

The movement to create eco-equity in the world will continue, through many ups and downs, for decades. Social-uplift environmentalism will not triumph in one day. So it behooves us to take some time to clarify the principles upon which we must rest our efforts to create an inclusive, green economy: equal protection, equal opportunity, and reverence for all creation.

Principle 1: Equal Protection for All

As we move into this age of ecological challenge and opportunity, our first principle must be "Equal protection for all." This ideal is key because, in an ecological crisis, those individuals, families, and communities without money and status will always be hit first—and worst. When the floodwaters rise, fires rage, droughts parch, or superdiseases attack, the most marginal cannot afford to get out of harm's way. They cannot afford to protect themselves. And still worse, once the crisis has passed, they are least able to bounce back, to rebuild, to recover. Therefore, as dangers multiply, we must revive—as a cornerstone commitment in our national life—the deep principle of equal protection.

Yet for decades our society has been moving in the opposite direction. Starting in the 1980s, it became fashionable to pretend that every social problem could be solved at the individual level. U.S. president Ronald Reagan famously declared, "Government is not the solution; government is the problem."[1] Most voting citizens looked at the practical flaws, bureaucratic dysfunction, and moral quandaries inherent in the liberal welfare state—and found that, in their hearts, they agreed with him.

Soon thereafter, Democrats joined Republicans in sneering at the idea that government should play a strong role in sheltering and shielding the disadvantaged. They even backed away from programs—like funding world-class public schools and affordable college tuition—that helped the middle class. Many leaders from *both* major parties began telling the public that there were few government solutions or collective answers to our problems; what we really needed, they suggested, was a return to strong families and "rugged individualism."

So it was that, throughout the 1990s, the federal government rolled back its commitment to protecting the most vulnerable members of our national family—by undercutting organized labor with global trade deals that favored big corporations, backtracking on affirmative remedies for victims of racial discrimination, and ending the federal right to welfare assistance for low-income mothers. In 1995, Democratic president Bill Clinton himself put it bluntly: "The era of big government is over."[2]

However, all was not well in America. Problems continued to mount in our health-care system, public schools, natural environment, and job market. Homicide and drug abuse continued to cut short young lives in urban America; suicide and meth addiction did the same among rural and suburban youth. Those who could afford it crawled down bright, digital wormholes. In the 2000s, they tried to cover the emptiness in their lives with flat-screen TVs or plug the holes with iPod earbuds. But nothing worked.

Still, our politicians and pundits never flinched. They went on assuring the public that everything would work out just fine. We all just needed to be a little bit more "rugged" and a little bit more "individual." That's all.

And if it turned out that some of the people in our midst just couldn't cut it, well then the government had a moral obligation to simply let those people "sink or swim." In the end, exposure to the harsh discipline of unchecked market power would be good for their lazy, little souls. Yes, indeed, this nationwide "tough love" austerity program was the key to a brighter future for all, even for the poor and disadvantaged.

Those who doubted that this path was morally defensible got a prompt rebuke. The airwaves were soon flooded with "prosperity preachers," each giving God's own blessing to the new, hardscrabble arrangement. Megachurch pastors with megawhite teeth assured their far-flung flocks that, with the right amount of prayer and the right mental attitude, great abundance, tons of wealth, and high profits were sure to be enjoyed by all.

So we ordinary people decided to give it a try. And as problems piled up for the country (and difficulties accumulated in our own lives), we ran after every solo solution we could find. We worked longer hours. We worked extra jobs. We hocked our homes. We bought lottery tickets. We sought shelter under a house of credit cards. And yet our expenses and troubles kept on rising.

Nonetheless, the very idea of a renewed government role in fixing these problems—indeed, the very notion of broadly shared problem solving of any kind—seemed outlandish, outdated, out of the question. Thus when we saw our own relatives and neighbors struggling financially, we blamed them for lacking sufficient pluck and guile to succeed. But we were fair about it. When our own debt and health crises began to threaten our own lives and dreams, we even blamed ourselves.

Then one day, something horrible happened. And that tragedy exposed our folly for all the world to see. In late August 2005, we turned on our television sets—and were shocked to see an American city under water. The aftermath of Hurricane Katrina—which drowned New Orleans and much of the Gulf Coast—left thousands of people dead and tens of thousands homeless. The storm's damage was magnified by faulty levees, which collapsed. Overnight, floodwaters swept away an iconic global city.

It was hard to fathom. But then the truly unthinkable happened. As the survivors struggled to stay alive in the waterlogged ruins awaiting help—none came. Not on the first day. Nor the second. Nor the fourth. Nor the fifth. For days on end, we saw desperate, hungry, and frightened people—crowded into the Superdome, trapped on rooftops, holding babies, waving American flags. They lived in the richest country in the history of the world, yet somehow that nation was unable to deliver to them a drop of water for their tongues or a scrap of food for their children's mouths.

Over time, tragedy curdled into spectacle. The submersion of New Orleans became the world's sickest reality TV show: "Will this woman *drown*? Will these people *starve*? Will this infant *ever* get a bottle of formula? . . . How many of these poor black people are going to *survive* the aftermath of Hurricane *Katrina*? . . . Stay tuned to find out! We'll be right back—*after* these messages!"

The world stared in disbelief. The truth slowly sank in. The citizens of that once proud city had been left to the tender mercies of what could only be called a "free market" evacuation plan. Everyone who owned a functioning car (and who had a working credit card) was perfectly able to flee. But those who didn't own private vehicles, those who didn't have credit cards or savings accounts, those who were two days shy of a pay day that might have let them buy a full tank of gas were left to face the floodwaters, alone. No matter how the TV talking heads tried to spin it or explain it away, the reality was painfully simple: an awful flood had come, and the United States had left behind its poor, its black, its disabled, its infirm—to "sink or swim."

The catastrophe of New Orleans was not the result of a deliberate act of malice by any person or party. In many ways, it was, however, the logical, necessary, and inevitable outcome of the kind of politics that both major parties have been promoting for two decades. It was a concrete manifestation of a mentality that says that we are not, in fact, our sisters' and brothers' keepers. Years of neglect of the nation's infrastructure and inattention to the needs of the poor combined with the colossal distraction of a military occupation of Iraq all added up to one thing: a government too hollowed out to competently perform its basic functions in a crisis.

The revulsion that gripped the country was total. The Bush administration's approval numbers started heading south that week and never recovered. Fifteen months later, U.S. voters walked into voting booths and ended fourteen years of GOP control of Congress—and terminated six years of one-party Republican rule in D.C. Few politicians referenced Katrina directly; the country was too deeply ashamed to consciously dwell on the images from those nightmare days. But the public had had enough of Bush's smirking and shirking—his incompetence and ho-hum contempt for life. The truth is that George W. Bush's presidency drowned in the floodwaters of Katrina.

And yet the hard work of exterminating the overall mentality that led to the abandonment of Katrina's victims still remains. In a time of climate chaos and dwindling resources, our society will have to face many more moments of danger: superstorms, intensifying wildfires, droughts, shortages of food and water, rising sea levels, new pathways for the spread of disease. An energy crunch could lead to global economic turmoil, leaving millions drowning on dry land. In a post-Katrina world, we must remember those left behind in the Gulf Coast disaster and say, "Never again!"

To be sure, all individuals must take full responsibility for their own lives, strive to live up to their full potential, and do their fair share of the work. That much goes without saying in a sane and healthy society. But there are some dangers that are too big for any individual to overcome, especially the most vulnerable among us. So in an age of floods, we must reject any philosophy that would tempt us to tell people in wheelchairs to "sink or swim." We must embrace, instead, the principle that says: "We are all in this together—come what may." On that basis, we can truly honor the principle of equal protection for everyone.

Principle 2: Equal Opportunity for All

The task at hand is not just to win equal protection from the worst of global warming and the other negative effects that go hand in hand with ecological disaster. It is also to win equal opportunity and equal access to the bounty of the green economy, with its manifold positive opportunities.

Wonderful developments in our economy are underway: solar power, wind-generated energy, organic food, improved mass transit, high-performance buildings, and more. All of these developments will deliver benefits to the Earth and society as a whole. If the architects of the green economy honor the principle of equal opportunity, they can also deliver help and hope to those who most need new jobs, new investments, and new opportunities.

Our business and political leaders will launch tens of thousands of new green enterprises and initiatives. Each time they do, they must ask the question: How can we make this effort inclusive, ennobling, and empowering to people who were disrespected in the old economy? How can this effort be used to increase the work, wealth, health, dignity, and power of our society's disadvantaged?

It is not yet fashionable in eco-elite circles to pay much attention to issues of social justice and equity. The potential is there. Living mainly in Hollywood, Silicon Valley, the San Francisco Bay Area, Seattle, and Boston, many of the architects of the green economy have photographs of Mohandas Gandhi on their walls. They consider themselves tolerant and open-minded people. Almost all of them, if asked, would confess to a deep respect for Dr. Martin Luther King, Jr., and the civil rights movement.

So it may be worth pointing out a strange set of facts. Dr. King is a global hero because he marched and died to racially integrate the last century's economy—even though that economy was based on the old pollution- and poison-based technologies. He made the supreme sacrifice; he laid down his life to ensure that the old economy—flawed though it was—had a place for everyone.

And he was not alone. Those buses that the freedom riders risked death to integrate—they were not using biodiesel fuel or hybrid engines back then. Those lunch counters that the civil rights activists risked beatings and arrests to open up to everyone—they were not serving organic tofu. Those schoolhouses, which little black children risked pain and humiliation to integrate—they were not green buildings with solar panels on them. No, the civil rights champions all risked their lives to win equal access to an economy that—in retrospect—was undermining the health of the planet. Their calling and achievements were undeniably among the noblest in human history.

If the crusade to racially integrate the dirty, gray economy represented the height of nobility in the last century, then how morally compelling is the calling to build an inclusive, green economy in this one? If Dr. King and other activists were willing to face attack dogs and fire hoses and murderous mobs to get everyone included in the pollution-based economy, then what should you and I be willing to do today to ensure that the new, clean, and green economy has a place in it for everyone?

It is important that we wrestle with these questions consciously and openly—before the greening of the world's economies proceeds irretrievably along the same lines as the unjust, unequal, gray economy. There is no racist governor standing in the warehouse door, blocking solar-company CEOs from hiring urban youth. There are no white-hooded hoodlums insisting that health-food stores charge prices for healthy food that low-income parents could never afford. On the other hand, there is no Bull Connor preventing African Americans, Asians, Native Americans, Middle Easterners, or Latinos from joining the movement to reverse climate change.[3] The barriers separating us from each other are wafer thin—and largely of our own making.

In pursuit of equity, today's rainbow-colored generations will not have to break into a closed, pollution-based economy. We have the option, instead, of cocreating an inclusive, green economy together. No one can stop us from doing so—except ourselves. The fact is, if we do wind up with some version of eco-apartheid in the United States and the industrialized countries, it will be because good people who knew better simply failed to do better.

We cannot afford that kind of moral shortfall. To solve our global problems, we need to engage and unleash the genius of all people, at all levels of society. Some of the minds that can solve our toughest problems are undoubtedly trapped behind prison bars, stuck behind desks in schools without decent books, or isolated in rural communities. A green economy that is designed to pull them in—as skilled laborers, innovators, inventors, and owners—will be more dynamic, more robust, and better able to save the Earth.

It perhaps goes without saying that our first two principles— equal protection and equal opportunity—go hand in hand. Especially for the most vulnerable, we have a duty to do two things: we must minimize their pain *and* maximize their gain. We are one human family. So on a good day, we should not leave anyone out. And on a bad day, we should not leave anyone behind. We should not accept a world where people of color and low-income people are always first in line for everything bad and then are left to benefit last and least when it comes to anything good.

Everyone must be allowed to share equitably in the benefits and the burdens, the risks and the rewards, of our transition to a more survivable economic system. That ideal must undergird and accelerate our commitment to equal opportunity and equal access in the green-collar economy.

Principle 3: Reverence for All Creation

The traditional environmental movement has wisely impressed upon the public at large the value of nonhuman life and the natural world. It insists that we don't have any throwaway species or throwaway resources. Those of us who labor to build the green-collar economy should affirm that insight and echo that conviction. And we should take it one step farther.

It is true that we don't have any throwaway species or resources. We don't have any throwaway children, throwaway neighborhoods, or throwaway nations either. Therefore, the green economy must do more than reclaim thrown-away stuff. It must also reclaim thrown-away lives and thrown-away places. And it must reclaim the thrown-away values that insist we are all members of one human family, with sacred obligations to each other.

In the United States, especially, we have strayed far from these truths. The following facts are worth repeating. We represent only 4 percent of the world's population, but we are responsible for 25 percent of the world's greenhouse gases.[4] And we now jail more than 25 percent of the world's prisoners.[5] In other words, one out of every four carbon molecules superheating the atmosphere has our name on it, and one out of every four people locked up anywhere in the world is locked up in a U.S. jail or prison. Some say that number is closer to 50 percent. This is a disturbing testament to a profound moral failing: we are functioning as if we have a disposable planet—and disposable people.

We know deep inside us that all beings have value. All people are precious. All of creation has sacred, inherent worth. We must take a stand in defense of the children of all species—including our own.

At some level, this stand is purely self-serving. Obviously, our desire to survive as a species dictates that we become much better stewards of—and partners with—the billions of nonhuman species with which we share this planet. The human family has invaluable friends and irreplaceable allies in the plant and animal worlds. We cannot continue indefinitely abusing those relationships. We cannot continue to tug at the web of life without tearing a hole in the very fabric of our earthly existence—and eventually falling through that hole ourselves.

At the same time, let's be clear. Creation is not to be revered simply because it is useful to the human species. Our commitment must be deeper than a desire merely to maximize the utility of other living beings and ecosystems for our own desires and pursuits. Creation has an independent value beyond and irrespective of us.

For example, imagine that someday our intergalactic viewfinders are able to reveal to us another planet as rich, thriving, and gorgeous as ours. The entire human family would be awestruck. We would stare at the images, endlessly variable and vibrant. We would love the beauty of that planet, wonder at its mysteries, treasure its manifold species. We would name our children, our buildings, and even our sports teams after its wonders. And even if no human ever were able to set foot on that faraway place, even if no corporation were able to extract its resources, even if no intrepid explorer could jump into a rocket ship and open up a McDonald's restaurant there—all of humanity would see the intrinsic worth and celebrate the miracle of such a planet's very existence.

Now imagine a situation in which that distant gem were somehow imperiled—say, by a massive asteroid whose trajectory was sure to destroy it. All of humanity would experience anxiety and foreboding. And even though no human had ever touched its trees' leaves, walked its shores, or cradled its furry offspring, such a planet's sudden obliteration would move the whole world to tears.

Let's take it a step farther. Imagine—on that day of global shock and of mourning—that someone standing at the water cooler in your place of work were to shrug and say, "Well, you know, that planet didn't add anything to Earth's GNP, so what was it really worth to us, anyhow?"

Can you imagine the reaction? Such a person would be exposed, in the eyes of everyone, as a fool—and a dangerous kind of a fool at that. Something deep within us recognizes that the true worth of creation can never be reduced only to its value in the human marketplace. And yet it is precisely the people who think like that watercooler cretin—those who try to reduce every value to a dollar value, those who try to measure beauty with a calculator—to whom we have given great authority in our national life and global affairs.

We need not deny the economic value of the Earth's resources. And thankfully, there are environmentalists who express their love for the Earth by quantifying in monetary terms nature's "services" (the dollar value of bees pollinating plants, of trees filtering water, etc.). In the public debate, they are doing a good thing. But in the quiet of our own souls, let us never forget that the full beauty, value, and the mystery of creation can never be captured on a spreadsheet.

We need a much deeper understanding of exactly what it is that our industrial society, in its present creation, is jeopardizing. We need a more profound perception of what is at stake. Perhaps it is time to humbly confess the wisdom of the Native Americans, from whom our forebears stole these lands. The original Americans knew and tried to teach their conquerors: "We don't inherit the Earth from our parents; we borrow it from our children. The Earth doesn't belong to us; we belong to the Earth." Reclaiming and reaffirming their wisdom—which is truly the wisdom of all indigenous people everywhere—is likely the first step toward discovering a survivable future for our children and grandchildren.

Those of us in the West have tended to limit our reverential awe strictly to the lands surrounding Jerusalem, the crossroads of the great monotheisms. Anyone who has visited that region can attest to its majesty and spiritual power; the world can rightfully call that place the Holy Land. And yet, from another perspective, all land is holy land; every people is a chosen people, divinely loved; and every creature—no matter how humble—is a signature work of the Creator's own genius. Recognition of those facts is the key to showing proper reverence for all creation—and encouraging all humans to tread more lightly and respectfully on what my grandmother always called "God's green Earth."

So those are the three pillars of the new "social-uplift environmentalism": equal protection for all people, equal opportunity for all people, and reverence for all creation. These are the lasting principles upon which we can build a modern movement to birth an inclusive, green-collar economy—here and around the world.

FOUR

The Green New Deal

To BIRTH A just and green economy, our society needs the government to act as an effective midwife. And to get the public sector to play that role, champions of the green economy need a powerful political movement—one that is grounded in the kind of principles discussed in the last chapter.

Yet principles alone do not generate successful movements. Movements for political and social change also need a strategy—with long-term goals, enduring coalitions, and an effective mode of operating. (They also need a concrete policy agenda, which we will lay out in Chapter 7.)

In this case, the transition to an inclusive, green economy must be supported by a political movement that aims to create a "Green New Deal" in the United States and other industrialized nations; forges a "Green Growth Alliance" to unite the best of business, labor, social justice advocates, youth, people of faith, and environmentalists (while paying special attention to the challenges of working across old divisions of race and class); and advances a positive, solution-oriented "politics of hope."

GOVERNMENT AS PARTNER

The time has come to reimagine and re-create the New Deal. The last time a serious economic crisis gripped the country was during the Great Depression. Early in that crisis, President Franklin D. Roosevelt took office and ended a generation of Darwinist social policy—in his first hundred days. With the support of a broad coalition, FDR used the government's power to help the people, stimulate the economy, and restore the environment. His so-called New Deal represented a new arrangement in society with a more balanced division of authority between government, business, and civil society. Up until the mid 1930s, unregulated financial interests had been running amok—to the detriment of all (including, ultimately, much of the business community itself).[1]

Economists still debate the ultimate effectiveness of the New Deal's many programs. But for those who received a warm meal, signed up for Social Security, had their spirits lifted by murals and theater, or formed lifelong friendships while creating our national parks as Civilian Conservation Corps (CCC) members—there was not much debate. There was only gratitude for the sense of solidarity and common purpose in the face of national calamity—and a renewed sense of confidence in the future.

Today, we are entering a new period of national and global challenge; already, our society is being impacted by ecological, social, spiritual, and economic crises. To resolve them, the federal government must act boldly and comprehensively. A temporary tax credit here or there, briefly benefiting one or another clean-energy industry, is not enough to deal with the energy crisis. And a patchwork of job-training programs haphazardly assembled and rarely aligned with actual job opportunities is not going to move the needle on the jobs crisis.

We need an entire suite of programs—intelligently coordinated. We need a complete set of policies and programs that would accelerate a market-led transition to a cleaner, greener, and more just economy—creating jobs, renewing hope, and strengthening community in the process. In other words, the time has come for a "new" New Deal. And this time it should be a green one.

This, however, is not the only difference that we can imagine, as we fashion the New Deal 2.0. This time, we can also imagine a much wiser, smarter role for government overall. After all, despite its positive features, no one can deny the shortcomings of the last century's "welfare state," which the New Deal helped create in the United States. At the same time, no one can argue that this century's "warfare state" has been a vast improvement either. We need a new model, a new role for government in helping society to meet its defining and fundamental challenges.

For too long, political debate has been stale because it has been premised on a false choice. The left—in effect—has argued for big, clunky, compassionate government à la that of Lyndon Baines Johnson. The right—in effect—has argued for big, clunky, warmongering government à la that of George W. Bush. But most of us do not want government as a nanny. Nor do we want the government as a big RoboCop bully. We do not want the government to create a new bureaucracy to fix every problem. We are happy to place our faith in the power of ordinary people to do extraordinary things. We just want government to be a smart, supportive, reliable partner to the forces that are working for good in this country.

We know that society is going to have to meet some huge challenges in the coming period. The individuals, entrepreneurs, and community leaders who will step up to make the repairs and changes are going to need help. As they strive to meet world-class challenges, they will require and deserve a world-class partner in our government.

And that central insight—the idea of "government as partner" to the innovators, the scientists, the eco-entrepreneurs, the neighborhood heroes, the ones who are close to both the problems and the solutions—is the key to understanding how a Green New Deal might function. It would be born out of the knowledge that government can't do everything, but that government can play a key role as a partner to those who are trying to do the right things—namely, the entrepreneurs and community leaders who trying to solve the problems we face.

Government can become a much better partner to the eco-entre-preneurs who are trying to bring world-saving innovations to market by giving them permanent and reliable tax breaks, putting exponen-tially more research money on the table, making polluters pay for carbon emissions, and providing green employers with a well-trained, green-collar workforce. Government can be a better partner to civic leaders and community groups trying to solve neighborhood prob-lems by helping to finance money-saving weatherization and solariza-tion for low-income homes, reinvesting in science and math programs in public schools, supporting vocational and technical training in the green trades, and shifting money from the failed incarceration indus-try to smarter, cheaper programs that get better results by focusing on emotional healing, economic opportunity, and rehabilitation.

The time has come for a public–private community partner-ship to fix this country and put it back to work. In the framework of a Green New Deal, the government would become a powerful partner to the problem solvers of the world—and not the problem makers. Were government to play such a role, it would represent a dramatic turnaround. That's because right now the public sector gives most of its love, respect, and money to the problem makers in our economy: the war makers, polluters, and incarcerators. They all get billions and billions of dollars in tax breaks and direct subsidies, while the renewable sectors—the job creators of the future—still get pennies.

And yet our problems keep getting worse, not better. The wars in Iraq and Afghanistan have cost nearly a trillion dollars—and the government says we are still not much safer. The economic gain from those industries that pollute the air and savage the land will be more than erased by the costly consequences of our destroying our ecological life-support systems and superheating the atmosphere. And evidence is beginning to show that the prison industry (which has more than doubled in size and cost over the past twenty years) is actually making neighborhoods less safe—both by failing to rehabilitate the people it locks up and by diverting money from the community-based programs that could.

For too long, the government has been a partner to the problem makers—and all we have to show for it is more problems. By advancing the idea of "government as a partner to the problem solvers," we can break through some of the stale debates and false dilemmas of the last century, and we can finally move our society from the present raw deal to a Green New Deal.

THE NEW COALITION

We cannot achieve the goal of a Green New Deal just by wishing for it. There is an existing power structure—call it the "military-petroleum complex"—that holds sway over our national economic, energy, and foreign policies. It is unlikely that the present high lords of oil, coal, and armaments will reverse course or give up their power without a struggle. A new force must emerge to realign American politics, transform the political landscape, and supplant the Texas/Pentagon axis.

Therefore "step one" in getting the government to support an inclusive, green economy is to build a durable political coalition— one that aspires, ultimately, to govern. Again, the New Deal period offers an important example. It was the broad, electoral, pro–New Deal coalition that moved the government onto the side of ordinary people, not FDR alone. Farmers, workers, ethnic minorities, students, intellectuals, progressive bankers, and forward-thinking business leaders all joined forces at the ballot box to support FDR and his congressional backers as they worked to revive the economy.

To accomplish our tasks today, we need a similar force: an electoral "New Deal coalition" for our time. Let's call it the "Green Growth Alliance." A Green Growth Alliance would be a broad, coalitional effort—fusing wise, compassionate forces in civil society with the enlightened self-interest of the rising green business community.

Its aim would be to put the government on the side of the people and the planet. The goal would be straightforward: to win government policy that promotes the interests of green capital and green technology over the interests of gray capital (extractive industries, fossil-fuel companies) in a way that spreads the benefits as widely as possible. The idea would be to resolve the economic, ecological, and social crises on terms that maximally favor both green capital and ordinary people.

Some in the environmental and social justice worlds may wince at our explicit inclusion—and even prioritization—of the needs and interests of green businesses. Many activists of all stripes are suspicious of any corporation; they have become hostile to the entire business community without distinction or exception. They say, "Big, greedy businesses led us into this global mess; we can't trust them to lead us out." They eye with deep suspicion a lot of the green advertising being paid for by companies that have historically been big polluters.

Much of their concern is understandable. Abuses of power by many big corporations—both directly against workers and the environment and indirectly through what amounts to legalized bribery in the political system—continue to have profoundly negative consequences.

But there is another side to the business community, rarely seen or celebrated. In recent years, organizations like the Social Venture Network, Business Alliance for Local Living Economies, Co-Op America, Green Business Alliance, Ceres, and the Investors' Circle have been gaining members and momentum. These are groups of financiers, investors, entrepreneurs, and business leaders who are committed—even in advance of any legislation or comprehensive federal support—to conducting their business in a manner that better respects both people and the environment. They have been inspired by visionary entrepreneurs like Paul Hawken and Ray Anderson. Joel Makower's GreenBiz.com has been cheerleading for them and chronicling their efforts for years.

As for how the government will separate the truly green companies from the pretenders—fortunately, the most trustworthy and socially conscious business leaders (not to mention investors, who don't want to be hoodwinked) are already far along in the process of defining tough criteria themselves. We can use their initial standards and definitions as starting points—and springboards.

The numbers are small right now, but the emergence of true "triple-bottom-line" businesses (which balance "profit, planet, and people" in their operations) is a potentially significant development. And it is just beginning. "Green" MBA programs like the Bainbridge Institute and Presidio School of Management are cranking out young business leaders with a different view about how to make money while making a difference. At the same time, increasing numbers of minority-owned enterprises (MBEs) and women-owned enterprises (WBEs) are expressing interest in "going green" and becoming part of the eco-revolution.[2]

These businesses—plus renewable-energy companies, firms selling conservation services, community-based cooperatives, nonprofit social enterprises, organic food companies, recyclers, and others—constitute business sectors with whom people of conscience can and should cooperate. Ordinary citizens and community members should actively help them win maximum support from the government—so that they can displace the despoilers and replace the polluters. And the faster we change the rules to aid the emerging sectors, the faster the old dinosaur companies will retool and get on board.

There will surely be an important role for nonprofit, voluntary, cooperative, and community-based solutions. But the reality is that we are entering an era during which our very survival will demand invention and innovation on a scale never before seen in the history of human civilization. Only the business community has the requisite skills, experience, and capital to meet that need. On that score, neither government nor the nonprofit and voluntary sectors can compete, not even remotely.

So in the end, our success and survival as a species are largely and directly tied to the new eco-entrepreneurs—and the success and survival of their enterprises. Since almost all of the needed eco-technologies are likely to come from the private sector, civic leaders and voters should do all that can be done to help green business leaders succeed. That means, in large part, electing leaders who will pass bills to aid them. We cannot realistically proceed without a strong alliance between the best of the business world—and everyone else.

That said, again, no business should be considered "green" just because it says it is. We need strong standards and clear criteria to weed out those companies that will seek out support while merely "green-washing" their same old bad practices. And society's support should not be unconditional. All legislation to boost green industry should also be strong on labor rights and civil rights. The captains of green enterprises should go beyond the letter of any law, enthusiastically seeking out the full diversity of the country in their hiring, promotions, and contracting. And, without undermining their need to stay profitable, they also should seek to locate their operations in places that need new infusions of jobs and capital. Only companies that work to meet those tough standards should be considered truly "triple bottom line."

On the civil society side, five main partners should make up the Green Growth Alliance:

1. *Labor.* Organized labor has been in steep decline over the past few decades, but it remains the best and most stalwart defender of working people's interests—in the workplace and beyond. Policies that lead to the retrofitting and rebuilding of the nation will give unions a tremendous opportunity to both expand and diversify their ranks. If the unions and green business leaders can identify win-win compromises on wages and other issues, they can work together to pass legislation that will help both sides.

2. *Social justice activists.* Legions of people have committed themselves to broadly shared opportunity for those who were left out of the old economy. They should be on the front lines working to create the new one. Advocates for economic justice, civil rights, immigrant rights, women's rights, disability rights, lesbian/gay/bisexual/transgendered rights, veterans' rights, and other causes should seize the opportunity to ensure that the new, green economy has the principles of diversity and inclusion baked in from the beginning.

3. *Environmentalists.* With their large organizations, broad networks, Beltway savvy, and large budgets, the mainstream environmental organizations have tremendous assets to bring to bear in the effort to green the country. They have a chance

to turn the page on decades of perceived elitism by working as better collaborators with other sectors of society. An exchange of knowledge, experience, and even personnel between the mainstream environmentalists and social justice groups would be healthy and invigorating for everyone.

4. *Students.* Students' energy and enthusiasm have already turned up the heat in the movement to prevent catastrophic climate change. Just a year ago, it was considered outlandish for anyone to call for an aggressive target like an 80 percent reduction in carbon emissions by the year 2050. But student-centered efforts like Step It Up, Focus the Nation, and the Energy Action Coalition[3] have already made "80 by 50" a mainstream demand—accepted by presidential candidates and even energy-company CEOs. As more racially diverse groups like the League of Young Voters, the Hip Hop Caucus, the Environmental Justice and Climate Change Initiative, and Young People For (YP4)[4] join the movement, the sky is the limit for the next generation's leadership role.

5. *Faith organizations.* The moral framework suggested by the three principles of social-uplift environmentalism (equal protection, equal opportunity, and reverence for all creation) should attract faith leaders and congregants. Many are look-ing for alternatives to some of the divisive fundamentalism that has taken up a great deal of airtime lately. The idea of "creation care" is a positive, alternative frame that can help faith communities move into action as a part of the Green Growth Alliance.

These five forces, in alliance with green business, can change the face of politics in this country.

The Importance of Including People of Faith

Just as some may recoil at the prospect of warmly embracing the business community, others may raise their eyebrows at the idea that religious organizations should play a strong and leading role in the greening of the country. Many environmental and social change activists say, "Well, I'm all for spirituality, but I reject religion." This is a perfectly reasonable and respectable personal choice. Yet it can often mask a deep resentment or even a hatred of the totality of organized worship—and a stereotyping of all religious people as stupid, dogmatic simpletons.

Too often those working for change quietly see religion itself as the enemy. They tend to reduce the great faiths of the world to their worst elements, constituents, and crimes—and then dismiss all other facts and features. Nothing pains me more than to hear so-called progressives snarl the word "Christian" as if it were an insult or the name of a disease. I grew up in the black churches of the rural South, listening to the civil rights stories of my elders. As children, we heard about the good and brave people who had poured their blood out on the ground so that we could be free. We learned how police officers had clubbed and jailed them. We learned how Klansmen had shot and lynched them. And how the G-men from Washington just stood by and doodled on their notepads.

We learned of marches and mayhem, freedom songs and funerals. We saw images of black women on their hands and knees, searching for their teeth on Mississippi sidewalks—crawling while still clutching their little American flags. We felt pity for the children who spent long nights in frigid jail cells, wearing clothing soaked by fire hoses, while their untended bones began to mend at odd angles. We saw pictures of black men like our fathers hanging by their necks, their faces twisted, their bodies rigid, their clothes burned off—and their skin too. And we saw photos of carefree killers sauntering home out of Alabama courtrooms—their white faces sneering and proud.

We learned how the very best of humanity had faced off with the very worst of humanity—each circling the other, under the same summer sun. Their epic struggle had elevated Southern backwaters onto the great world stage. And the fate of a people—and the destiny of a nation—hung in the balance, for all to see.

In the end, we cheered, for the righteous did prevail. Our parents and grandparents overcame—and then some. They performed one of the great miracles in human history; they transformed a U.S. apartheid into a fledgling democracy, tender and delicate and new. And today's social change activists proudly and eagerly celebrate the achievements of the civil rights movement. Rightfully so.

But one key fact seems to escape their notice. The champions of the civil rights struggle didn't come marching out of shopping centers in the South. Or libraries. Or high-school gymnasiums. They came marching out of churches, singing church songs. These people, these unimpeachable examples of audacity and accomplishment, were people of deep, deep religious faith. And when they prayed, it was through a long-dead Nazarene carpenter named Jesus Christ.

When progressives dismiss and disdain religious people, they are spitting directly in the faces of their greatest champions. This is why smug activists who treat the word "Christian" as a useful synonym for "dumb, mean bigot" do so much damage. They offend people of faith within our ranks. They needlessly cut themselves off from their own elders, families, and neighbors. And they deny the truth of how meaningful social change has most often come about in this country.

Worse, they leave powerful symbolism in the hands of dangerous practitioners of a less noble politics. It makes no sense to those seeking change to willingly surrender the language of the great faiths. In the end, it is nearly impossible to shrink our message of abundant love, hope, and faith into the tiny straitjacket of a sterile secularism anyway. Many activists are already turning, in the quiet of their own lives, to yoga and meditation, to self-help books, to alcohol and drug recovery programs that invoke a higher power, and even to the organized religions of their childhoods. Of course, no movement should force any particular brand of religious observance or spirituality on anyone else. But even secular activists sometimes seek for a power that is greater than our familiar "power to the people." And it should be okay to acknowledge that.

We do a great disservice to the cause of justice when we pretend that only the hateful represent the faithful. We can oppose theocracy without opposing all theology. We can denounce bias in the Christian church—whether the bigotry appears as sexism, homophobia, racism, or anti-Semitism—without pretending that all Christians are bigots. We can separate fundamentalism from faith in any of the great religions.

The United States is one of the most religious countries in the world. People of faith here have powered much of the social change in our nation's history—from the abolitionists up to the present peace movement. Imagine how powerful the Green Growth Alliance will be when it can claim as one of its pillars the millions of Christians, Jews, Muslims, and others who acknowledge and worship a justice-loving God.

Green Growth Alliance Seeds Already Sprouting

Fortunately, the Green Growth Alliance is not just a theoretical necessity. It is already becoming a practical reality. National organizations such as the Apollo Alliance and the Blue Green Alliance have already come on the scene, promoting good jobs in the clean-energy sector. The Apollo Alliance is an alliance of labor unions, environmental organizations, community-based groups, and businesses;

the Blue Green Alliance is a partnership between the Sierra Club and the United Steelworkers.

Former U.S. vice president Al Gore's Alliance for Climate Protection is also reaching out broadly to engage new sectors in the battle to avert catastrophic climate change. And the new kids on the block—1Sky and Green For All—are engaging important new constituencies like PTA moms and African American ministers. (I serve on the Apollo Alliance board, and I am a co-founder of both 1Sky and Green For All.) The bottom line is that the raw materials for a Green Growth Alliance already exist.

Of course, the very idea of "growth" itself will be challenged over time—whether it is green growth or any other kind. On a crowded planet, the very notion of economic growth itself—with automatic assumptions of increasing resource consumption and consumerism—is something that human society will someday be forced to abandon.

In the future, resource constraints and a growing population will force human society to adopt an even more sustainable model: a closed-loop, "steady state" economy premised on nearly 100 percent recycling of materials and 100 percent renewable energy. This economy will be designed to maximize well-being—not necessarily wealth. The growth we seek will be in steadily improving the quality of life, not steadily increasing the quantity of goods consumed.

However, at this stage, a quick leap to this kind of postgrowth, postconsumerist "eco-topia" is not possible. Let's take a lesson from history on this one point. The day after Rosa Parks refused to give up her bus seat, civil rights leaders could have demanded reparations for slavery, legalization of interracial marriages, and a massive redistribution of wealth. Such demands would have been justifiable—but foolish. "Maximum demands" like those would have created more resistance than support.

Thus early civil rights champions instead pressed "minimum demands"—for integrated buses, kindergartens, and lunch counters. The more militant Malcolm X attacked this approach as too timid. But the more modest demands knocked over the first dominoes, sparking mass movements that eventually tore segregation from U.S. law books, led to the War on Poverty, and helped stop a U.S. war.

Well, today, with Earth itself imperiled, we should be at least as savvy as our grandparents were. It's fine for the "Malcolm Xs" of the environmental and social movements to directly challenge the paradigm of growth and consumption—or to attack U.S. militarism. They are advancing important arguments. But to move large numbers, we also need smart, minimum demands or goals—like the calls for "Green-Collar Jobs for All," "Green Jobs, Not Jails," and "Greening the Ghetto First." Such slogans do not challenge everything that is wrong in the world. They simply point in the right direction. And they can inspire pragmatic, working people to take notice and get involved.

A family-friendly "eco-populism" can mobilize and unite millions who, at this point, would be turned off by a more extreme set of demands. Such appeals can get more people taking the first practical steps toward ecological sanity. The momentum will build, through those early efforts, for more comprehensive solutions. The later, bolder solutions will be even more effective, intelligent, and productive when they arise from the experience of millions of ordinary people who already have been actively engaged.

Meanwhile, the most urgent task remains: to rapidly shift society from our present suicidal, gray form of capitalism to a more viable and just eco-capitalism. Success will mean that the Earth will still be a livable place decades from now, giving those still alive the chance to pursue other improvements and transformations.

MORE ECO-POPULISM, LESS ECO-ELITISM

Although the movement for social-uplift environmentalism is on its way to forging an eventually powerful Green Growth Alliance, the very notion that a politics centered on green solutions could build a muscular, governing majority in the United States seems laughable at the moment. That is because the "green movement" itself seems to be the cushy home of such a thin and unrepresentative slice of the U.S. public.

When most people think of "green solutions," they are not thinking about a massive people's movement that can pick up the Capitol building in D.C., turn it upside down, and dump out all the legislators who are holding back a green economic renaissance. They are not thinking about the next best thing to a full-employment program, led by the private sector, that could put millions of Americans back to work retrofitting the country. They certainly are not thinking about the incredible pioneers—like Winona LaDuke, Majora Carter, and Omar Freilla[5]—who are daily bringing hope and opportunity to people of modest means.

Rather, they perhaps imagine a few Hollywood celebrities eating tofu, doing yoga, and driving hybrid cars. They envision affluent white people who care about nothing but polar bears and can afford to shop at health-food stores and put solar panels on their second home. Their minds leap to a high-priced market niche serving individual consumers who are willing to pay a premium for green goods and services so they can feel better about themselves and their many purchases.

Many of these caricatures are grossly unfair. Many lifestyle greens are actually just health-conscious, community-minded folks who earn middle-class wages. As for the rich ones, it is actually a good thing that wealthier people are now spending their dollars in ways that are healthier for the planet. They have helped to jump-start the market for the products and technologies that may help save the Earth.

Nonetheless, when many ordinary people hear the term "green" today, they still automatically think the message is probably for a fancy, elite set—and not for themselves. And as long as that remains true, the green movement will remain too anemic politically and too alien culturally to rescue the country. Enlightened, affluent people who embrace green values do a great deal of good for the country and the Earth—and they are making an importance difference every day. But nobody should make the mistake of believing that a small circle of highly educated, upper-income enviros can unite America and lead it all by themselves. Eco-elite politics can't even unite California.

If you doubt me, let's examine a recent statewide election in California to see how eco-elitism can actually set back environmental initiatives—even very thoughtful and well-financed ones, even in places where the overall support for environmentalism is relatively high. Everyone loves to praise GOP governor Arnold Schwarzenegger for signing global-warming legislation in 2007. Yet few discuss the fact that just a few months earlier, the majority of California voters rejected a clean-energy ballot measure called Proposition 87. That's right. Elected officialdom might be willing to dictate major green steps—or at least hold major green press conferences. But when Californians got the chance to speak up in the ballot booth in 2006, ordinary people said no.

This defeat holds many lessons for us, going forward. The idea for Prop 87 was brilliant in its simplicity: California would start taxing the oil and gas that oil companies extract from our soil and shores. This state-level oil tax would generate revenues of $225 to $485 million annually. And those dollars would go into a huge "clean-energy" research and technology fund—totaling $4 billion over ten years.[6] Many states and nations have similar extraction taxes.

California, however, would have been essentially alone in dedicating the revenues to inventing alternatives to carbon-based energy sources. Had the measure passed, California would have used money from oil to find a replacement for oil.

It was a brilliant idea. And at first, the measure was polling off the charts. Silicon Valley and Hollywood put $40 million on the table to ensure the measure passed. Al Gore and Bill Clinton campaigned for it. Victory was certain. But in the end, Californians voted the measure down 45 percent to 55 percent. Why? Mainly because big oil convinced ordinary Californians that the price tag would be too high for them to bear. The oil and gas industry spent $100 million warning that the tax would be passed along to consumers. They suggested that it would push gas and home-energy costs through the roof and hurt the poorest Californians.[7]

It was a predictable line of attack. It was also a false argument. Gas prices in California are not determined by oil extraction taxes in any one region or state; they are set mainly by the huge global energy market. Numerous other states and countries already have a similar tax, including Texas, Alaska, and Venezuela. One more teeny levy, in one state, in one country, would have had a minuscule or negligible impact on the overall world price of oil—or on California consumers.

And to the contrary, the benefits of a shift to cleaner energy would have helped the poorest in the state—significantly improving both their health and their chances for wealth. For one thing, disproportionate numbers of low-income people live near oil refineries and other sources of dirty-energy pollution. As a result, they suffer from higher rates of cancer, asthma, and other illnesses. Largely uninsured, they then pay through the nose for inferior medical care. In other words, the dirty-energy economy is literally killing poor people. A switch to cleaner energy could save untold lives.

Beyond that, a clean-energy economy actually is more labor-intensive—meaning, it creates more jobs. After all, somebody has to install and maintain all those solar panels, build all the wind farms, construct the wave farms, weatherize those millions of homes and office buildings. A green economy begins to replace some of the clunking and chugging of ugly machines with the wise effort of beautiful, skilled people. That means more jobs.

So there was a strong, eco-populist argument to be made for Prop 87. Switching to clean energy would have cost individual Californians little—but given working people better health and better jobs. Yet the campaign—led almost exclusively by well-intentioned do-gooders with few financial problems themselves—did not make these eco-populist arguments with any force. Instead, Prop 87 commercials yammered on about "energy independence"—which polling firms said was the best message. Maybe so. But in some demographics, people needed that message to be bolstered by a great deal of reassurance on the kitchen-table issues, and it never was.

Seeing the obvious opening, the polluters pounced. Big oil ran full-page ads in practically every African American newspaper in the state. The ads showed a black mom looking aghast at fuel prices while she tried to fill up her car. An NAACP official vocally opposed the measure, fearing economic damage to her constituency. And the scare tactics didn't alarm only black Californians. Across the state, the initially sky-high poll numbers for the initiative proved surprisingly fragile. The support for the measure was completely hollow. The Prop 87 proponents were not just outspent by the polluters; they were outmaneuvered.

And in the end, the biggest clean-energy ballot measure in the country went down to defeat—in California. That setback didn't just hurt the backers of Prop 87 or the Golden State. It set back the entire world's ability to invent new, clean-tech technologies and beat global warming.

The Eco-Elite Cannot Win by Itself

The defeat of Prop 87 should sound a clear warning for all of us as we work to birth a green, postcarbon economy. We all must recognize and celebrate the fact that well-off champions of the environment will be indispensable to any coalition effort. In fact, it is their business smarts, monetary resources, social standing, and political savvy that have propelled the green wave to this point. But at the same time, the eco-elite cannot win major change alone, not even in the Golden State. After all, if a Prop 87–style collapse is possible in California, what do you think will happen in the other forty-nine states?

To change our laws and culture, the green movement must attract and include the majority of all people, not just the majority of affluent people. The time has come to move beyond eco-elitism to eco-populism. Eco-populism would always foreground those green solutions that can improve ordinary people's standard of living—and decrease their cost of living.

The messaging must make it plain to the country that we envision a clean-energy future in which everyone has a place—and a stake. One way to do that is to speak to the economic and health opportunities that "ecological" solutions will also provide. Another way is to always show the many, many people of color and working-class Americans who are actively engaged in environmental struggles. If nearly every "green" initiative, TV program, or magazine cover excludes them, we are essentially handing millions and millions of people over to the polluters. We are essentially saying to big coal and big oil: "Please organize all of these people against everything green. Thanks!"

The nation has already passed a certain tipping point in eco-consciousness. But we should never underestimate the danger of rapid progress actually fueling a major backlash. Handled badly, green proposals can create the opposite of our much needed Green Growth Alliance. They can actually produce a backlash alliance—between polluters and poor people. The polluters are afraid of losing their immense profits and privileges. And low-income folks are just afraid of losing even more ground. Together they can derail the movement to green this country. We can, however, easily head that off, just by making sure that "green" includes all classes and colors.

NOT JUST HYBRID CARS—A HYBRID MOVEMENT

Bringing people of different races and classes and backgrounds together under a single banner is tougher than it sounds. The affluent have blind spots. The disadvantaged have sore spots. And both pose barriers to cooperation.

For instance, large and powerful constituencies of white, affluent, and college-educated progressives exist and are active in the United States. They are passionate about the environment, fair trade, economic justice, and global peace. Unfortunately, many do not yet work in concert with people of color in their own country to pursue this agenda; they champion "alternative economic development strategies" across the globe, but not across town. These people could be great allies in uplifting our inner cities, if they are given encouragement and a clear opportunity to do so.

On the other hand, the truth is that many groups of people of color do not want to work in coalition with majority white organizations and white leaders. Many fear betrayal; others resent chronic white arrogance. Cultural differences and power imbalances create tensions; some organizations are actually committed to a racially exclusivist ideology. Even though such organizations could benefit from additional allies and outside assistance, the very folks who could most benefit from a green opportunity agenda are loath to get involved.

Taken altogether, this means that the various U.S. social change movements today are still nearly as racially segregated as the rest of U.S. society. This is a moral tragedy. And it is a tremendous barrier to building sufficient power to move forward a positive social change agenda for anyone and everyone. Breaking through this standoff is a critical first step toward building a "New Deal coalition" for the new century—which would be the only thing dynamic, diverse, and powerful enough to overcome the shared obstacles to progress.

I have been trying to bridge this divide for nearly a decade. And I have learned a few things along the way. What I have found is that leaders from impoverished areas like Oakland, California, tended to focus on three areas: social justice, political solutions, and social change. They cared primarily about "the people." They focused their efforts on fixing schools, improving health care, defending civil rights, and reducing the prison population. Their studies centered on "social change" work like lobbying, campaigning, and protesting. They were wary of businesses; instead, they turned to the political system and government to help solve the problems of the community.

The leaders I met from affluent places like Marin County (just north of San Francisco), San Francisco, and Silicon Valley had what seemed to be the opposite approach. Their three focus areas were ecology, business solutions, and inner change. They were champions of the environment who cared primarily about "the planet." They worked to save the rain forests and important species like whales and polar bears. Also, they were usually dedicated to "inner change" work, including meditation and yoga. And they put a great deal of stress on making wise, Earth-honoring consumer choices. In fact, many were either green entrepreneurs or investors in eco-friendly businesses in the first place.

Every effort I made to get the two groups together initially was a disaster—sometimes ending in tears, anger, and slammed doors.

Trying to make sense of the differences, I wrote out three binaries on a napkin:

1. Ecology vs. Social Justice

2. Business Solutions (Entrepreneurship) vs. Political Solutions (Activism)

3. Spiritual/Inner Change vs. Social/Outer Change

The Marin County leaders tended to focus on the left side of the list; the Oakland leaders usually focused on the right side. And for some reason the people on both sides tended to think that their preferences precluded any serious embrace of the options presented on the opposite side of the ledger.

Increasingly, I saw the value and importance of both approaches. I thought to myself: What would we have if we replaced those "versus" symbols with "plus" signs? What if we built a movement at the intersection of the social justice and ecology movements, of entrepreneurship and activism, of inner change and social change? What if we didn't just have hybrid cars—what if we had a hybrid movement?

I came to believe that at the precise place where all these countercurrents converged was where we would find enough power to generate a Green Growth Alliance, displace the military-petroleum complex, and initiate a Green New Deal. But first I had to figure out how to engage African Americans, Latinos, and others from the urban environment who were resistant even to the idea of being a part of something calling itself "green."

I had two main breakthroughs in finding a way to move urban leaders. I call these breakthroughs "The *Amistad* Meets the *Titanic*" and "Crisis vs. Opportunity."

The *Amistad* Meets the *Titanic*

Most people who are committed to racial justice activism see themselves as rebels against racism. Perhaps they would most deeply resonate with Cinque, the hero of the slave-revolt movie *Amistad*. In that film, based on a true story, the righteous, enslaved Africans fight back and take over the slave ship.

The people at the bottom rise up and take over the ship—taking their destiny into their own hands. It's really a metaphor for the last century's version of racial politics. The slave ship is Earth, the white slavers are the world's oppressors, and the African captives are the world's oppressed. The point is for the oppressed to confront and defeat their oppressors. I took that as my mission.

But what if those rebel Africans, while still in chains, had looked out and noticed the name of their ship was not the *Amistad,* but the *Titanic*? How would that fact have impacted their mission? What would change if they knew the entire ship was imperiled, that everyone on it—the slavers and enslaved—could all die if the ship continued on its course, unchanged.

The rebels would suddenly have had a very different set of leadership challenges. They would have had the obligation not just to liberate the captives, but also to save the entire ship. In fact, the hero would be the one who found a way to save all life on board—including the slavers. And the urgency of freeing the captives would have been that much greater—because the smarts and the effort of everyone aboard the ship would have been needed to save everyone.

"*Amistad* meets the *Titanic*" has been an important bridge metaphor to help people who have been committed to an earlier model of racial justice activism understand their expanded leadership role and responsibilities—as the entire planetary ship is threatened with going down.

Crisis vs. Opportunity

A lot of environmental rhetoric remains rooted in "crisis" language. It is evident that people who already have a lot of opportunity are sometimes powerfully motivated to act by tales of a planetary crisis. But people who already live in a constant state of personal crisis are not so moved. In fact, they often have the opposite reaction to hearing about things like global warming. They will shrug, shake their heads, and say: "Well, it's just the end times, I guess. That means Jesus is coming back." And then they will change the subject or walk away.

But if you tell people who are living in a state of constant personal crisis about the economic solutions inherent in the green economy, then they get excited. Nowhere is an eco-populist, opportunity-based message more important than in engaging people of color.

As pointed out above, we should advance more popular slogans that present green solutions to real-life, kitchen-table problems. I have discovered some with real appeal and resonance: "Green the Ghetto" and "Green-Collar Jobs for All" (or "Green Homes for All," or "Solar for All," or "Organic Food for All"). I think we should explore a clean-energy call framed as the desire for "Asthma-free Cities."

One urban eco-populist slogan stands out above the rest, with a power all its own. It speaks to the full range of urban concerns, addressing simultaneously issues of economic justice, criminal justice, and environmental justice. That slogan is "Green Jobs, Not Jails." My hope is that it will someday be adopted and embraced by the entire green movement as the central goal guiding our efforts.

The point is that these eco-populist slogans—and programs to back them up—will be key to engaging people of color and other disadvantaged communities in the struggle for a green-collar economy. To those who have plenty of personal opportunity, speak first about the environmental crisis. But to those who have plenty of personal crises, speak first about the environmental opportunities—and how solutions for the Earth's woes can be solutions for their problems too.

THE NOAH PRINCIPLES

So the direction is set. We seek a social-uplift strategy that creates green jobs, not jails; a politics anchored in a Green Growth Alliance for this century; and a moral framework based on reverence for each other and the planet. It can be done. However, there are many habits of mind and unconscious assumptions that stand in the way, even for those of us who have been lifelong change makers. We need some new distinctions and ways of seeing our work, or we are likely to reproduce some of the same negative patterns in this movement that we have seen in others.

For instance, when I was a young activist, the role model I subconsciously had for making a difference was David confronting Goliath. And that image or archetype served me well—for a while. After all, the David and Goliath story is a beautiful tale, one that foregrounds courage and allows for the possibility of miraculous outcomes, of defeating the bully against all odds. I have come to believe now that there is also a shadow side to the myth. It requires that the protagonist always be small and marginalized, and it requires a politics of confrontation and opposition. Such a politics may serve us poorly as we confront the dangers that will demand cooperation on a massive scale.

So I raise the possibility that we need a new guiding narrative, a new myth, for the new challenges that face us. Our leaders need a different yet familiar story that defines the kind of leadership we need.

With violent storms, rising seas, and financial chaos darkening the horizon, perhaps the best models for the new century will prove to be Noah and his wife. Theirs is a story of leaders who must make plans for a difficult future while trying to save as many people and fellow species as possible. It's also a story about honoring and managing diversity, about making space for everyone from the tiniest termites to the lions and the elephants. Instead of preparing to protest against a giant, as David did, perhaps it is better to prepare to lead a community through a crisis and into the future beyond that crisis, as Noah did.

Of course, there are good people on the other side of important disputes who will not be won over; they will have to be run over. There will be times when we have to fight—in the old "us versus them" mode. But when we do, we want the biggest possible "us"— and the smallest possible "them." I mean, when all life everywhere is threatened, we might even need Goliath to help us build the ark.

A politics in keeping with Noah's principles would focus on creating something new rather than confronting something old. It would be more about "proposition" and less about "opposition." As guideposts to creating that kind of politics, we could advance the following five points. Call them the Noah principles:

1. Fewer "issues," more solutions

2. Fewer "demands," more goals

3. Fewer "targets," more partners

4. Less "accusation," more confession

5. Less "cheap patriotism," more deep patriotism

Fewer "Issues," More Solutions

Organizations working for change usually place themselves into one of two categories: single-issue groups (e.g., fighting against homelessness) or multi-issue groups (e.g., fighting against police abuse, prison expansion, and youth violence). I propose a different distinction: issue-based groups and solution-oriented groups. After all, the word "issue" is just another word for "problem." If you have an "issue-based" group or coalition, you essentially have a "problem-based" organization. And defining any cause based on a negative can lead to a great deal of negativity.

If you doubt me, try this experiment. Approach almost any hardworking activist committed to a cause and say: "Tell me what issue you are working on." The activist will talk to you for an hour, pouring out all the horror stories, pet anecdotes, and shocking statistics that animate and inform her or his work. The minute the activist runs out of breath and you see a chance to get a word in—seize it. Say, "Okay, so tell me what solution you are working for." Most of the time the person will fall silent and then perhaps start yammering and stammering. But I can almost guarantee you that the problem statement will be much sharper and generate much more passion than the solution statement.

Eco-heroine Julia Butterfly Hill has an explanation for this phenomenon. She says of people who have committed themselves to important causes: "Many of us have gotten so good at defining what we are against, that what we are against has started to define us."

And it is true. Many individuals and organizations define themselves solely by what they are against. They are anti-racism, antisexism, anti-homophobia, anti-globalization, anti-imperialism, anti-capitalism, anti-corporation, or anti-war. Many of us on the left define ourselves in wholly negative terms, and then we wonder why people run the other way when they see us coming.

As we build new organizations and networks, it is not enough to know what we are against. Saving the Earth and its peoples requires that we also know—and know with specificity—what it is that we are for.

Fewer "Demands," More Goals

Some people who want to use their talents to make change, rather than money, decide to become community organizers. They sign up with a community-based organization or an environmental campaigning group. And then they go to workshops or even training camps to learn how to do their jobs right.

Invariably, they are taught some version of a three-step process. The organizer is supposed to help aggrieved people come up with a list of "demands," help pick a "target" who can meet those demands, and go with others to "pressure the target" into meeting their demands. This approach constitutes the basic, underlying "operating system" for activism in the United States. It is the literal codification of the David and Goliath approach to social change: the little "we" versus the big "them."

The truth is sometimes that formula works. And sometimes there is no obvious alternative. And yet the problem with always formulating our desires as "demands" is that the word itself assumes (and may reinforce) an adversarial relationship. As the *Titanic* sinks, one has to wonder whether multiplying adversaries is a very good idea— especially for those trapped at the bottom of the ship, who may need more allies than enemies.

One simple option is to reimagine and reformulate our desires as "goals." Goals can be shared—even by people who disagree on many points. Demands can never be shared. One party makes them; the other party must either deny them or capitulate. A victory under those circumstances can feel quite hollow. Sometimes we can win the short-term battle, but lose the long-term aims.

I have often wondered how far I would get if I marched into the offices of some social change groups and made "demands." I don't think they would be very receptive. Sometimes a mere change of language can change the mind-set—on both sides—and possibly yield a much greater outcome. Given the threats we face, it should be worth a try.

Fewer "Targets," More Partners

The other problem with the standard "organizer's" formulation is the constant seeking out of "targets" to pressure. Again, sometimes there is a person in a position of authority who is so obstinate, so biased, and so recalcitrant that one has no choice but to declare him or her an opponent. Also, there are institutions that have acted in bad faith for so long that trust is almost impossible to regenerate. Under those circumstances, the advocates of a righteous cause do need a battle-hardened cadre of well-trained organizers who know how to twist pinkies and otherwise force an adversary into submission. The protectors of the status quo use power tactics all the time. The champions of a better tomorrow should not unilaterally disarm.

Yet this approach can be overdone, overplayed, and overused. Too often activists just assume that any change worth making will always require a big battle with someone. They start preparing for Armageddon every time any issue comes up—even before they have taken the first steps to resolve it using less confrontational means.

Some organizations are like countries run by generals who have an army but no diplomatic corps. Therefore, they spend all their time drilling their troops and scanning the horizon, hoping for an opportunity to declare war on someone or something. Again, sometimes this is justifiable.

However, it comes down to a question of balance. When all you have is a hammer, everything looks like a nail. If all you have is "direct-action organizing," everyone with power looks like a target. It does take real skill, talent, and training to identify targets, challenge them, and get them to do what you want. The time has come for social change and environmental organizations to add another set of skills: the ability to turn would-be "targets" into real, long-term partners for change. And that can be a tougher challenge.

For one thing, it requires that organizers move beyond assumptions, stereotypes, and past hurts. It requires that organizers (and those they organize) invest time in relationship building and trust building across lines of race, class, and authority—trying to surface points of shared interest and concern. Not every grassroots group has the time, capacity, or organizational strength to function in this way. Sometimes it is easier for marginalized activists to just call a press conference and start painting protest signs. I understand that. Yet over the long term, the accumulated results often are not worth all the expended effort.

Here's the truth. If you rush into a situation looking for enemies, you will always find plenty. At the same time, if you go into a situation trying to find friends and allies, you will almost always find at least one. Sometimes they are in surprisingly powerful places—like behind the receptionist's desk in your opponent's front office.

In this age, our main job is to seek out friends wherever we can, not just to defeat enemies. What if, rather than mainly looking for opponents to punish, those of us who are committed to social change spent our time seeking out potential allies to encourage, befriend, and reward. After all, for every scofflaw polluter, there may be dozens of local businesses out there trying to do the right thing ecologically—but getting little support or recognition. What if environmentalists did more to partner with them, celebrate them, and help them? For every racist employer or bigoted beat cop, there are tens of thousands of white people who absolutely abhor racism. And yet civil rights activists like myself rarely ask them to do anything—except to feel guilty. Why not focus on finding better ways to access their time and talent for the good of all?

Our cause needs fewer enemies and more friends. To get through the coming crises, we are going to need each other. Let's start laying the groundwork now, so that—later on—we will be more likely to turn *to* each other, not *on* each other.

Less "Accusation," More Confession

None of this is to say that we won't have to confront and defeat real, implacable, and unyielding enemies on our journey. We will. If we could achieve eco-equity only by defeating external enemies, we would be walking an easier path than the one we're on.

That's because some of the enemies we need to defeat are inside us. We ourselves are a part of the problem. Every day, almost all of us are working and consuming in the pollution-based economy. We are participating in an economy that lacks equity, and yet we each have an understandable aversion to giving up our own money or status. We are trying to change the status quo. But we all have stake in it too. We all rely upon it to live and survive. And so, every day, we end up feeding the very monster we are fighting.

This is a humbling fact. If we are honest, even those of us who desperately want change must admit that we are not just battling the polluter without; we are also battling the polluter within. We can say this not just in the obvious "material" sense. This is not just about how many times we fail to recycle, bicycle, or bring our cloth bag to the grocery store. We all have inner demons that pollute our minds and hearts—that cloud our thoughts and distort our actions.

As we try to work with others, our egos often get in the way. Tempers flare. Suddenly we find ourselves not just battling the warmonger without, but that white-hot warmonger within. Later on, resentment creeps in over some perceived slight and indignity. Eventually, we find ourselves battling not just the punitive, unforgiving jailers on the outside. We end up battling the punitive jailer within, the hurt and angry part of ourselves who can't forgive our coworkers and allies for shortcomings and disappointments. These are the hidden struggles that define our days. Cumulatively, these inner tumults determine and limit the impact of our work itself, but nobody talks about them much.

Instead, we engage in the old politics, naming, blaming, and shaming somebody else while concealing our own faults, flaws, and hypocrisies. However, the cause of pursuing eco-equity does not easily lend itself to that approach. The change we are seeking is too monumental, and our own capacities are too modest.

We would be better off confessing our own weaknesses, our fears, our needs. Doing so will let others see the gaps more quickly, find their rightful places around the growing circle—and come to the campfire with fewer pretenses themselves. If we confess our own struggles to realign our own lives and change our own behavior, we may seem less alien to those we are trying to convince.

Also, the change we seek is so complex that no one person can understand everything that must be done. In that regard, we are all equally ignorant about how to get where we are going. This weakness actually is our strength. If we confess our own uncertainty, we are much more likely to listen attentively to others—and pull others into speaking more honestly and fully. As we move forward, our motto should be: accuse less, confess more.

Less "Cheap Patriotism," More Deep Patriotism

We have gone through a period during which people waving American flags have done great damage to the country, to the people of Iraq, to America's prestige in the world, to the national treasury, to the U.S. Constitution, and to the international rule of law. While force-feeding the country a brand of cheap and mindless patriotism, the "leaders" waving the biggest flags have steered the nation into a ditch. People of conscience should embrace Old Glory—and use the flag to help guide the public back in the direction of sanity.

One begins to fear that this accident was not very accidental. After all, GOP anti-tax operative Grover Norquist had declared openly: "I don't want to abolish government. I simply want to reduce it to the size where I can drag it into the bathroom and drown it in the bathtub."[8] That is not a patriotic statement.

We have an obligation to tell the ultraconservatives who are so rabidly antigovernment: "If you don't love this government, then let it go and hand it over to people who do." Those who would hijack the government and crash it with deficits pose a bigger threat than the terrorists.

And while we are at it, we could make do with a lot less knee-jerk antipatriotism from the left. I know it is hard to make peace with the country's original sins of stolen land and stolen labor. It is hard to forgive its repeated entanglement in unjust wars, up to the present moment. However, the far left's strategy of trying to fix the country by putting it down all the time has been an utter failure.

To paraphrase scholar Cornel West, you can't save a country you don't serve, and you can't lead a country you don't love. And there is much to love in this country. After all, we are talking about the nation that gave the world basketball, iPods, and Beyonce Knowles. (If those three won't get you up stomping and cheering for the red, white, and blue, I don't know what will.)

The United States has the power to be a huge obstacle to planetary survival—or giant springboard to planetary salvation. A better America is the best gift that we can offer the world. Yet caring Americans will never give the world that gift if they are holding their noses and handling the flag like a used tissue.

If we do our work right, the United States will lead the world, again, someday. This next time—not in war. Not in per capita greenhouse-gas emissions. Not in incarceration rates. The United States will lead the world in green economic development, in world-saving technologies, in human rights. We will lead by showing a multiracial, multifaith, rainbow-colored planet how our multiracial, multifaith, rainbow-colored country pulled together to solve tough problems. The United States will go from being the world leader in ecological pollution to the world leader in ecological solutions.

Bruce Springsteen put it best in 2004 when he said: "America is not always right. That's a fairy tale for children. . . . But one thing America should always be is true. And it's in seeking her truth, both the good and the bad, that we find a deeper patriotism, that we find a more authentic experience as citizens, that we find the power that is embedded only in truth to change our world for the better."[9]

It's time for the deeply patriotic to take back the flag from the cheaply patriotic, because, despite the pain of old crimes and recent disappointments, some of us still believe in America. Some of us still believe in "a more perfect union"—and in making it more perfect every day. Some of us still believe in "America the beautiful"—and in defending its beauty from the clear-cutters and despoilers. Some of us still believe in "one nation, indivisible"—and in opposing those who profit by keeping us needlessly divided. Some of us still believe in "liberty and justice for all," and we won't stop until that classroom pledge is honored from shore to shore.

Some of us still believe in America—and in all of those things we learned about it as children. Of course, we know now that America is not the place we live, but a destination to which we all are headed. So we keep faith on the journey. No, some of us haven't given up on Dr. King's dream. There are those of us who yet believe we are going to win.

And when we do, we'll be doing more than just "taking America back." We will be taking America—forward.

FIVE

The Future Is Now

W E HAVE EXPLORED the principles and the politics that could revive the economy on a more inclusive and eco-logically responsible basis. Luckily for us, leaders in far-flung and unlikely places are already moving ahead and creating this future. They are not waiting for federal action to give them the green light to start creating the new economy.

We will examine courageous pioneers who are already helping or-dinary people blaze green pathways to prosperity. I hope that some-day the vast majority of U.S. workers will have jobs in the kinds of innovative enterprises and programs that we explore below. After all, every day, about 145 million people go to work in the United States.[1] Imagine if those jobs—plus new ones created for people who are currently unemployed—were largely working in fields and pro-fessions that uplift human dignity and honor the Earth.

Some are already doing it today. Here are their stories, organized by five major subsystems of sustainability: energy, food, waste, water, and transportation.

ENERGY

The transition from our reliance on fossil fuels to clean and renewable energy is the linchpin of the green economy. If done correctly, it will bring our carbon emissions down to a manageable level. It will free us from foreign oil and its national security risks. It will halt the skyrocketing rates of pollution-based illnesses, and it will revitalize our economy and create millions of green-collar jobs.[2] Here are projects that are simultaneously producing clean energy and creating career paths for the unemployed.

Energy Efficiency

The cleanest energy is the energy that we never have to use—because we were wise enough to conserve it. We waste a lot—in heating, cooling, and lighting our drafty, poorly designed homes and offices. Not to mention driving our cars, with their unimpressive number of miles per gallon. The energy we don't use is cheap, silent, clean. It's measured in "negawatts," instead of megawatts. Improvements in the energy efficiency of buildings (such as weather stripping, replacing fixtures, and insulating hot-water heaters) can simultaneously save property owners money, reduce demand for fossil-fuel-generated electricity, and provide both skilled and unskilled jobs for local workers.[3]

In Los Angeles, the community-based group Strategic Concepts in Organizing and Policy Education (SCOPE) convened the local Apollo Alliance. Campaign Coordinator at SCOPE, Elsa Barboza says the local Alliance's first step was "to collect signatures from black, Latino, Asian, and Anglo working-class families throughout Los Angeles' inner-city neighborhoods for a petition to create a sustainable, equitable, and clean energy economy that will bring quality jobs to their communities, create a healthier and safer environment, and promote community-based land use planning and economic development."[4]

One of the people out knocking on doors with the petition was Oreatha Ensley, a lifelong civil rights activist, a mother and grandmother, a former teacher, and an LA resident for nearly forty years. She says: "I expected some folks to tell me that jobs are number one and cleaning our environment is just a nice wish. Instead, they told me that it's about time we reinvest in our community, because we are slipping away further into poverty and getting sicker because of it."[5]

It wasn't just the poor communities who were in favor of the Alliance's objectives. "Mayor Villaraigosa, a liberal-leaning City Council, and forward-thinking Commissioners have articulated a bold vision to make Los Angeles a national leader in the transition to a sustainable, equitable, clean energy economy," Elsa notes. Indeed, the City of LA has already committed to one of the local Apollo Alliance's proposals: implementation of a pilot program to retrofit one hundred city-owned buildings with energy- and water-conservation technologies.[6]

Nationwide, buildings are responsible for 36 percent of our energy use, 30 percent of our greenhouse-gas emissions, and 30 percent of our waste production. Once complete, retrofits in LA are slated to save the city up to $10 million per year in utility costs.[7]

The City of LA owns and operates more than eleven hundred buildings, many in deteriorating condition, that cover over a million square feet. The work includes audits; energy-efficiency improvements (e.g., sealing around or replacing doors and windows); lighting upgrades (replacing bulbs, installing sensors, and maximizing daylight); water-conservation improvements (fixing leaks, replacing urinals and toilets); healing- and cooling-system updates; and cool- or green-roofing installation Audits—the first step in the process—are under way in LA as I write this.[8]

In the longer term, workers from the retrofit jobs can be transitioned into maintenance and construction jobs in both public and private sectors. According to the California Employment Development Department, employment opportunities in construction in the LA area are projected to increase by 30 percent between 2002 and 2012. The industry's career ladders allow workers earning entry-level wages of $9 to $18 per hour to become advanced skilled workers such as plumbers, sheet-metal workers, and electricians, earning $15 to as much as $50 per hour.[9]

Meanwhile, in the old industrial city of Milwaukee, Wisconsin, an organization called the Center on Wisconsin Strategy (COWS) is exploring how workers in the Rust Belt can move to the center of the clean-energy economy. COWS has cooked up a brilliant scheme to retrofit all of Milwaukee's buildings—and to create a slew of green-collar jobs in the process. To make this work, a new building-efficiency service—Milwaukee Energy Efficiency (Me2)—is being created to offer all of that city's residents the opportunity to buy and install cost-effective energy-efficiency measures in their homes and businesses.

Here's the beautiful part: there will be no up-front payment, no new debt obligation. Customers will have full assurance that their utility costs will be lower, and they will make monthly payments only for as long as they remain at the location and the measures continue to work. Outside of *The Godfather,* that's about as close as you can get in this life to "an offer they can't refuse."

This is how it will work. Owners or renters sign up to have their place retrofitted to save energy costs; a qualified person shows up and does the work; and then the renters or owners pay off the cost of the retrofit a little bit at a time, over the course of years, as a part of their (now radically reduced) electricity or property-services bill. That's it. Everybody wins—including the Earth.

In the policy section that follows, we will go into more detail about how this program works. For now, suffice it to say that the

Me2 program will be great for those community residents seeking jobs. COWS and the University of Florida estimate that every $1 million spent on the effort will generate about ten job-years in installation and construction activities and another three job-years in upstream manufacturing for needed parts. For a roughly $500 million project, that's a lot of job-years: about sixty-five hundred. Residents can start with less-skilled work—like blowing insulation or wrapping pipes—and move up to the more advanced work in plumbing, wiring, and installing new heating and ventilation systems.[10]

Retrofitting work will provide good jobs—family-supporting gigs, with solid opportunities for advancement—that cannot be outsourced. They will feed into the exploding green building industry, and that will simultaneously reduce our emissions and our reliance on foreign oil. Similar energy-efficiency programs should be implemented across the country.

Wind Energy

Winona LaDuke cites a prophecy among her people: "In the future, we've got two paths ahead. One path is well-worn . . . but it's scorched. The other path, they say, is not well-worn, but it's green. It's our choice upon which path to embark."[11] LaDuke is a member of the Anishinaabe tribe, a Native activist, and twice the Green Party candidate for vice president on the ticket with Ralph Nader. She has chosen her path and has spent much of the last decade rallying other Native Americans to embrace the green economy. It's not such a tough argument to make to her people, when the economic implications for Indians are considered.

"Native Americans are the poorest people in the country," notes LaDuke. "Four out of 10 of the poorest counties in the nation are on Indian reservations. . . . Over half of the American Indians on my reservation live in poverty. . . . Unemployment on the reservation is at 49 percent according to recent BIA statistics. And nearly one-third of all Indians on the reservation have not attained a high-school diploma."[12]

At the same time, Native America contains much of the continent's old-school energy resources. One-third of all uranium and two-thirds of all low-sulfur coal come from Native lands. The largest coal strip mine in the world is on a Native reservation. Massive hydroelectric projects in the subarctic are also on Native lands.[13]

One might assume this is good news for Native America. But Indians suffer from the disastrous and toxic side effects of extraction of these resources. Mining operations cause the displacement of communities, destruction of natural habitat, disruption of sacred sites, and water pollution with deadly toxins. Industrial toxic and radioactive wastes accumulate in fish, crops, animals, and soil. Oil drilling and related activities fragment, deforest, and pollute the landscape and fragile ecosystems. Clear-cutting and other intensive logging methods destroy the habitat of animals and fish, cause soil erosion and thermal pollution, and pollute water with both sediment and herbicides. Large hydroelectric projects flood lands needed for crops, disrupt and destroy subsistence-based cultural practices, and forcibly displace entire communities.[14]

Trying to get rich by further devastating the land has little appeal for those committed to traditional ways. Fortunately, it turns out that Native lands are also extraordinarily rich in clean energy, wind in particular. The wind potential of twelve reservations in North and South Dakota alone could meet 41 percent of the U.S. energy demand, and more than half the country's electricity demand could be met by the wind available on all the reservations.

The first turbine on Native lands was installed in early 2003 on the Rosebud Sioux Tribe Reservation in South Dakota. It produces enough clean electricity each year to power over two hundred homes. Another was erected on the Mandan, Hidatsa, and Arikara

Nations' reservation in North Dakota in 2005; six more were set up in 2006 in the Native villages of Toksook Bay and Kasigluk, Alaska (three per village); and many more are under construction. Rosebud alone aims to produce 50 megawatts by 2010.[15]

That's environmental justice—and poetic justice—for you. And there's more poetry in a former steel town in Pennsylvania.

When the U.S. Steel plant on a three-thousand-acre site along the Delaware River in Bucks County, Pennsylvania, shut down the last of its operations in 1991, it brought nearly forty years of manufacturing-based stability to an end. At the height of its operations, in the mid-1970s, the plant had employed more than eight thousand people. "This is a sad day for U. S. Steel, our employees and the communities surrounding," Thomas J. Usher, chairman and chief executive officer of U.S. Steel's parent, USX Corporation, said at the time.[16] Little could he imagine that, just a little over a decade later, the site and some former steelworkers would be in the business of manufacturing components for clean-energy projects.

In 2005, the Spanish wind-energy company Gamesa bought twenty-four acres of that plant. Gamesa is among the largest wind-energy companies in the world. Currently it is the only vertically integrated wind-energy company in the world, meaning it manufactures the parts for wind-energy units and also develops wind farms itself.[17]

Pennsylvania governor Ed Rendell and the head of Pennsylvania's Department of Environmental Protection, Katie McGinty, wooed the Spanish company. They were eager to attract the manufacturing jobs and meet the state's Alternative Energy Portfolio Standard, which dictates that 18 percent of the state's power come from renewable sources by 2020. The state extended Gamesa $10 million in grants, loans, and tax credits from the state's Department of Community and Economic Development and the Bucks County Economic Development Corporation. Because the site is a brownfield (a "Keystone Opportunity Improvement Zone," in Pennsylvania's terms), Gamesa gets breaks on state and local taxes through 2019.[18]

One of Gamesa's thirteen hundred workers is former U.S. Steel worker Jim Bauer. He had been a crane operator for twenty-five years when U.S. Steel laid him off. Now he's back. At Gamesa, he heads up a team that assembles parts for the turbines, and earns $17 per hour, just slightly less than his U.S. Steel wage. The wind workers are even part of the same union they belonged to in the old days, after United Steelworkers of America persuaded Gamesa not to fight an organizing drive. Jim says he's proud of his new work making clean energy—proud to be keeping America safe and free from foreign oil and keeping the planet intact for his children.[19]

Solar Energy

Richmond, California, has been in need of some healing. Its motto is "The City of Pride and Purpose," but in recent decades it's been better known as the city of *violence* and *pollution*. In 2004, it was ranked the eighth most dangerous city in the country, and the second most dangerous in California after Compton and ahead of Oakland. The following year, city-council members declared a state of emergency due to the crime rate.[20]

And the pollution? Chevron USA has a major oil refinery in the city, with a storage capacity of fifteen million barrels. The refinery often releases toxic gases and has had many disastrous chemical spills and leaks, often of chlorine and sulfur trioxide. Driving back from pristine Marin County just on the other side of the Richmond–San Rafael bridge, I've had to roll my windows up more than once to blunt Chevron's stench.

Under the leadership of a Green Party mayor, in 2007 Richmond joined together with neighboring Berkeley, Emeryville, and Oakland to form the East Bay Green Corridor. Mayor Gayle McLaughlin said at the time: "Given the crises the world faces from resource depletion, poverty, and species extinction, a green economy is also the only way to reinvigorate our economy while at the same time addressing environmental destruction and social inequity. Cities generate 75 percent of the carbon emissions. Cities like ours are where the problem must be solved."[21]

Lighting the way in Richmond is a solar-energy initiative organized by a group called Solar Richmond, a coordinating organization that is partnering with solar-panel vendors, City agency RichmondBUILD, and nonprofits Solar Living Institute and Grid Alternatives. Together they aim to create a hundred new family-supporting solar jobs and achieve 5 megawatts of solar energy in Richmond by 2010. The founder and director of Solar Richmond, Michele McGeoy, is on a mission to restore the pride and purpose of its slogan to the city. "Solar is one antidote to pollution, and jobs are one antidote to violence," she says.[22]

In 2006, McGeoy contacted Sal Vaca, Director of Richmond-WORKS, the City's employment and training program. She persuaded him to send three students in the City's vocational program in construction trades, RichmondBUILD, to her home and allow them to spend three days learning—on the job—to install solar panels as a pilot project. The following week, her newly installed panels were slated to be part of a solar tour as a shining example of what Richmond's young people could do in the promising field.

In a great example of innovative civic partnerships, installations for low-income homeowners are made possible through the City's redevelopment agency, which grants loans for the equipment to these homeowners, at cost. The labor by RichmondBUILD trainees for the installations is free. If the homeowners are senior citizens or disabled, it's a deferred loan. The loan for the equipment is perhaps $6,000, but it increases the value of their home by about $12,000. Plus it lowers their utilities bill for the rest of their lives.

Angela Greene is one of the graduates of the training program. Now forty-seven, Greene spent twenty years in the printing industry, working her way up from being a messenger to managing her own store. A single mother of two girls, she was nevertheless able to buy her family a house in Richmond. And then the parent printing company with which she was affiliated shut down, and Greene lost her job. She struggled to make ends meet while on unemployment, had to give up her car, and fought to hold on to her house.

Then she heard that the City of Richmond was offering a construction training program. Figuring she would at least learn skills to save her money around her own home, she enrolled. That's how she was introduced to McGeoy and Solar Richmond.

"I'd never really thought about carbon dioxide emissions before that," Greene says. "I'd been doing recycling and gardening, but the solar training started really making me think about what we were doing to the Earth. I want my children to be on this Earth to see their children." She says she saw the dot-com boom come and go without benefiting from it—this time she was determined to be a part of the boom.[23]

There are a lot of opportunities for graduates. Solar Richmond's immediate goal is to get graduates placed into entry-level installer positions. From there, they can become a project lead, and from there, a project manager—assuming more supervisory roles. McGeoy says, "Right now, the industry's biggest shortage is project leads. What's exciting is that the field is so new that you only need two to three years of experience to be considered an expert. Compare that to the trajectory of a traditional electrician, where you have to have fifteen years under your belt to be considered experienced. That means that three to five years from now, our graduates are going to be doing a lot of the management. The demand is there." In fact, in California, the demand for expertise in the field of solar power distinctly outstrips the supply.[24]

Another graduate of the RichmondBUILD/Solar Richmond training program is Rodney Lee, who found his way to the program after losing his job at the local telephone company due to an extended illness. He had never seen a solar panel before starting the program. Now Lee's an operations assistant at a Silicon Valley–based company called SolarCity.[25]

Founded in 2006 by two brothers, Lyndon and Peter Rive, Solar-City became the fastest-growing solar-power company in California in less than two year's time, with over 250 employees at time of publication and $29 million in sales in 2007. The company expanded to fellow solar-friendly states Oregon and Arizona in 2008 and expects to be on the East Coast soon.[26]

The Rive brothers quickly realized that the major barrier to solar adoption was the prohibitive cost of equipment and installation—anywhere from $20,000 to $100,000 or more. They knew that a successful solar business model would need to be built on making solar more affordable. They felt that if they could convince an entire neighborhood or community to go solar, they could lower the cost for every resident. They even created a financing program called SolarLease, backed by Morgan Stanley, to help more people get panels.[27] As far more residents go solar—and entire communities in some cases—SolarCity has been able to create more installation jobs.[28]

FOOD

At first glance, the food system—how we fuel our bodies—may seem less connected to climate change than how we fuel our cars or how we heat, light, and cool our homes. Yet consider just one random and bizarre fact that drives home the interconnectedness of our systems: as a result of the ten pounds that the average U.S. citizen gained in the 1990s, the airline industry has burned 350 million additional gallons of fuel per year.[29] Although that's among the more obscure correlations you can find, our food system is a major consumer of precious resources and has, between its production processes and global distribution, a significant carbon footprint.

Trade and food-security expert Anuradha Mittal comments on the ridiculous distances that food travels in fossil-fueled transport: "Today 20 percent of California table grapes go to China, while China is the world's largest producer of table grapes. Half of all California's processed tomatoes go to Canada, and the U.S. imports $36 million worth of Canadian processed tomatoes yearly. . . . We are exporting what we are also importing because it is profitable for the companies doing it, not because it is good for the nation or the environment."[30]

The real and often hidden costs of the food system include water pollution from chemical runoff and factory farm waste, poisonings caused by pesticides, greenhouse-gas emissions from livestock and cropland operations, the loss of topsoil and soil deterioration, the operation of multiple federal agencies tasked with regulating the food industry and mitigating damages, federal farm subsidies, the use of oil to develop petrochemical fertilizers and pesticides, the use of petroleum in food processing and transportation, and the use of preservatives and sometimes packaging needed for foods traveling long distances. One estimate places the total of these true costs at $40 billion per year.[31]

Meanwhile, people in our own country are actually going hungry. According to the U.S. Department of Agriculture (USDA), in 2006, 35.5 million Americans lived in "food insecure households," comprising 22.8 million adults and 12.6 million children.[32] Many low-income communities, particularly in urban settings, don't have access to a single real supermarket. They are forced to patronize liquor stores selling Cheetos and Snickers—if they're lucky maybe a potato or a banana—all at 30–70 percent higher prices than regular stores.[33] And of course there are the ubiquitous fast-food chains. Medical costs to treat diet-related ailments like diabetes and heart disease run more than $75 billion a year in the United States.[34]

A final failure of the system is the severe negative impacts on the people who work in the food industry, particularly farm laborers. Nearly seven out of ten U.S. farmworkers are foreign-born, 94 percent of them from Mexico.[35] Although there are devices available that lessen the physical impacts, many workers still engage in backbreaking "stoop labor," as César Chávez termed it, when farm owners won't pay for appropriate ergonomic tools. Our current system also deeply dishonors the work of traditional farmers, who are not only going out of business at record rates—more than seventeen thousand each year, or one farmer every half hour—they are also killing themselves at record rates; suicide is now the number-one cause of death among American farmers.[36]

It is clear that the system has to be reformed. There needs to be a shift to local food that is organic, free of pesticides, fertilizers, and preservatives; that is produced in ways that do not harm consumers, food workers, animals, or our soil and water; and that provides dignity to those who produce as well as consume it.

Happily, a movement for community food security is growing. This movement holds that a local and sustainable food system can not only guarantee nutrition and health; it can maximize community self-reliance and social justice. It can create jobs. Urban and peri-urban (on the edges of cities) agricultural projects are opening new labor markets. And these can be green-collar jobs.

Two of the fiercest catalysts for change in the arena of food-system reform and organic urban agriculture initiatives are LaDonna Redmond, in Chicago, and Brahm Ahmadi, who heads up the People's Grocery in Oakland. Oakland might seem logical. It is so close to the cradle of fresh and seasonal food (as represented by Chef Alice Waters in Berkeley). But Chicago?

LaDonna Redmond's involvement in urban agriculture began in 1999 after her infant son Wade was diagnosed with severe food allergies to a range of items from peanuts and shellfish to eggs, cheese, and milk as well as a host of additives. As a concerned mother, she started researching allergies and, to her horror, learned about the chemicals involved in standard food production: GMOs (genetically modified organisms), preservatives, additives, growth hormones, pesticides, and fertilizers (including toxic sewage sludge). She decided that Wade—and the rest of her family—needed a whole-foods diet with as little processed, packaged food as possible: "I needed to gain access to food unpolluted by genetic engineering and free from pesticides. I needed organic food."

That was easier said than accomplished. Her search for organic food took her out of her Westside neighborhood and through the city of Chicago; her search for *affordable* organic food was entirely in vain. "You could buy two-hundred-dollar sneakers, semiautomatic weapons, and heroin, but you couldn't get an organic tomato," she said. The idea that her community did not desire high-quality organic food was one of the many myths she wound up shattering.

Indeed, once LaDonna and her husband, Tracey, turned their backyard into an urban "micro-farm," as they called it, neighbors started coming by to help and share the harvests. Lettuce, tomatoes, peas, squash, greens, cabbage, onions, and herbs were all part of the early abundance, with more than enough to share. One thing led to another, and today the Redmonds' organization, the Institute for Community Resource Development, secures empty lots from the city, oversees a whole network of lots-turned-gardens, manages a farmers market, provides technical support and nutritional education, and is planning for the opening of a retail store.[37]

City support has been crucial. Income from food sales can pay for maintenance and staff salaries, but start-up costs can be prohibitive, especially since land values in urban centers such as Chicago are relatively costly. Luckily Chicago's Mayor Daly is committed to leaving no stone unturned in the greening of his city.

"LaDonna's projects go beyond mere gardening because the intent is to look at the comprehensive approach to the issue of developing local economies—hiring locally, selling locally," notes fellow Chicagoan Orrin Williams, founder and director of the Center for Urban Transformation. In the eighty thousand vacant lots totaling several square miles, plus the thousands of flat rooftops and backyards, Williams guesses that as much as 40–50 percent of the city's food could be grown. Another estimate puts the number of full-time jobs that would result from cultivating that land at forty-two thousand.[38]

Although it's been the construction trades that have traditionally been most receptive to hiring formerly incarcerated people, agriculture presents opportunities for them as well. Some prisons even smooth the path by offering horticultural training programs. (In the Bay Area, Catherine Sneed's "garden project" at the San Mateo jail still sets the gold standard for this kind of work.)

Williams also works as the employment training coordinator for another organization in Chicago called Growing Home, which fosters life and job skills in a transitional employment program for previously incarcerated, homeless, and low-income Chicagoans. Many are recovering from addiction, suffering from mental illness, or have not held a steady job in years. But more than 65 percent of the folks who go through Growing Home's transitional job-readiness program find full-time work in the retail, landscaping, and food-service industries or placement in further training or educational programs.[39]

Working in the soil is life-affirming. One Growing Home graduate who found the program after spending three years in a correctional facility for using and selling heroin and cocaine, says she "loves seeing little sprouts push up through the ground."

George Washington Carver wisely said: "I believe that the great Creator has put ores and oil on this earth to give us a breathing spell.

As we exhaust them, we must be prepared to fall back on our farms, which is God's true storehouse and can never be exhausted. We can learn to synthesize material for every human need from things that grow."[40] When it is grown and processed in ways that do not harm the Earth or its inhabitants, there is great dignity to the creation of food.

Back in Oakland, Brahm Ahmadi shares this core belief. He's the son of a Midwestern mother descended from generations of farmers in the Iowa-Missouri area and an Iranian father from merchant families in Tehran and Tabriz. Ahmadi understands the deep significance of food and simultaneously believes in the potential for entrepreneurship to create innovative solutions.

Ahmadi started out in the environmental justice community, defending the poorest communities from toxins. Yet that work took its toll. Ahmadi realized that he and his colleagues were good at articulating the problems and being angry about them, but they fell short on inspiring hope and possibility.

So now, as the executive director of the People's Grocery, he's all about solutions, particularly as applied to the community of West Oakland. It's a place facing multiple challenges, where residents' economic as well as mental, emotional, and physical health issues compound one another. The lack of amenities and services (which fled to the suburbs), the police brutality, the environmental toxins—in West Oakland all these have converged to create a crisis situation. Chronic diseases are at epidemic levels. There are severe mental-health challenges. Overall, there are a lot of struggling families and individuals.[41]

"Food is our medium for achieving broader outcomes in community development and public health and addressing disparities in opportunities and quality of life," says Ahmadi. "We chose food as our tool because it's intimate and universal, regardless of differences in culture or personal preferences. On a fundamental level, we all have to eat every day, and we have that in common."

"We've taken risks, in the entrepreneurial tradition, which isn't as common in the nonprofit world," says Ahmadi. The risks are paying off. People's Grocery has expanded from its three urban gardens in Oakland and signature Mobile Market to a two-acre farm in nearby Sunol, growing nearly eighteen thousand pounds of produce. These enterprises not only provide healthy foods and good jobs; they also educate community members.

Ahmadi says:

> We get started with a conversation about individual food consumption, the meaning of what you eat, and the history behind why certain food is or isn't available to you. From there we connect the dots to the structural and systemic issues of the food system: considering the global environmental footprint of food production, how far food travels, and equity issues related to farmworkers and the struggles of small farmers . . . connecting those to the struggles of low-income urban consumers.

Despite its public image, there is significant spending power in the community. People's Grocery has assessed West Oakland as an approximately $50 million food market, of which about 70 percent is not captured locally. That's a lot of money being sent outside the neighborhood and thus not contributing to local jobs and wealth. Ahmadi dreams of

> completely localized food systems that are regionally based, with the majority of the food that consumers consume coming from within a few hundred miles of where they live, so that consumers have direct knowledge of the farms and farmers, and how and where that food is produced. A revolution in terms of environmental stewardship and reducing the carbon footprint in the food system. And finally, dignified job creation

and wealth creation rooted in social justice and environmental sustainability.

The local model is economically viable. When farmers sell directly to local shops and restaurants or through farmers markets or subscriptions ("boxes"), they earn as much as 80–90 percent of the price of food. Anuradha Mittal has calculated the impact on California's economy as one example: "If just 10 percent ($85 per person per year) of Californians' food expenditures were directed toward food produced within the state, an estimated $848 million in additional income would flow to the state's farmers, $1.38 billion would be injected into California's overall economy, $188 million in tax revenue would be generated, and 5,565 jobs would be created."[42]

The political and economic ramifications of localized food systems operating in harmony with nature can be as lucrative as they are beautiful.

WASTE

We humans—especially we Americans—are literally trashing our environment. There's a great twenty-minute film by my friend Annie Leonard, called *The Story of Stuff*, that lays out the whole system by which goods are produced, starting with the extraction of natural resources from the environment and moving along to the factories where stuff is made, to the retailers who move stuff as fast as possible, to us consumers, to the dump. Along this continuum, we're producing mountains and boatloads of trash. Astronauts have looked down on dumps that are visible from space and rival the Great Wall of China in size.[43] There's a 3.5 million ton heap of debris called the Great Pacific Garbage Patch that's twice the size of Texas floating in the Pacific Ocean.[44] Houston, we have a problem.

The average American throws away four and a half pounds of garbage daily. And for every garbage bin of waste an individual puts out, seventy garbage bins come from each factory that makes stuff during the production process.[45] Dumps—and especially incinerators—pollute the air, land, water, and our bodies with toxic chemicals like dioxins. It's an altogether unsustainable situation.[46]

A handful of states and municipalities have adopted zero-waste plans, setting targets for waste reduction in the meantime.[47] Massachusetts, for example, aims to reduce municipal solid waste by 70 percent by 2010. The city of Seattle is recycling 60 percent of all the waste it generates in 2008.[48] Even so, we still have a lot of trash to deal with. And dealing with it in a smarter way could generate hundreds of thousands of jobs.

Unfortunately there's been a persistent (and understandable) stigma in many low-income communities of color about working with waste. There was a time when the occupation of sanitation worker (a.k.a. trash man) was virtually a separate caste, relegated to black or brown men who were treated and paid badly. It's only recently that the dirty, toxic operations of waste management have been complemented by the more uplifting work of recycling and reuse, with its decent, purposeful jobs. If we changed the job title to "recycling technician" and improved the pay, work in material reuse and recycling could be another sector of growth for green-collar jobs.

"In the U.S., on a per-ton basis, sorting and processing recyclables alone sustains eleven times more jobs than incineration does," says Leonard. More than 56,000 recycling and reuse centers across the country already employ over 1.1 million people. Entry-level jobs in recycling include collection, sorting, driving, and loading and can lead to advanced positions like operations manager. Entry-level jobs in materials-reuse operations include salvaging, sorting, driving, warehousing, packaging, and retail sales, after which an employee can move up to warehouse manager or floor manager.

Growth in the sector is being encouraged by measures like California's 1989 Integrated Waste Management Act, which required cities to divert 50 percent of their solid waste from landfills by 2000. California also designated forty Recycling Market Development Zones and provision of low-interest loans up to $1 million for businesses using recycled materials. As a result, in its first eighteen months, the Oakland/Berkeley Zone generated $8.2 million in investment for recycling, creating 155 new jobs and diverting 100,000 tons of new material from landfills.[49]

Specialized types of materials reclamation and reuse are cropping up. Two of the significant areas producing green-collar jobs are computer recycling and deconstruction of building materials.

Computers

At Chicago's Household Chemical and Computer Recycling Facility, students participating in the city's Greencorps job-training program learn warehousing skills; how to refurbish computers for use in schools, community centers, and low-income households; and how to disassemble the computer for individual component-part recycling. A nonprofit called Computers for Schools partners with the city to provide training. They've placed more than twenty-five thousand computers since getting started in 1991.[50]

The Alameda County Computer Resource Center in Berkeley likewise recycles computers—as well as VCRs, televisions, and copy machines. It provides on-the-job training in repairing computers, identifying and extricating computer components, and installing and using computer software. Local rehabilitation programs, homeless shelters, and parole officers refer potential employees, including homeless and mentally ill individuals as well as others with barriers to employment.[51]

Building Materials

The Environmental Protection Agency (EPA) estimates that 136 million tons of building-related construction and demolition waste are generated every year. The debris consists of a wide array of materials including wood, concrete, steel, brick, and gypsum, making for a complex waste stream.[52] Rather than demolishing this material to useless bits, buildings can be *deconstructed*, a systematic process by which valuable materials are recovered in usable form. This conserves landfill space, reduces the need for new materials, and can reduce overall building-project expenses through reduced purchase and disposal costs. The deconstruction process also keeps materials local, reducing the need to transport materials, and provides solid, family-sustaining jobs.

A nonprofit in Baltimore called Second Chance launched its architectural salvage and deconstruction services in 2003. Over the next four years the company grew quickly, filling a 120,000-square-foot warehouse space and engaging more than fifty employees—three deconstruction crews and a retail store crew. The crews consist entirely of local low-income residents who are trained on the job. Second Chance's founder, Mark Foster, explains: "Deconstruction is time-consuming and exacting. The architectural elements must be removed from the building without becoming damaged. Elements that are too large to remove intact must be removed in pieces to be reassembled later."

Foster established contracts with the City of Baltimore that call for workforce-development funds for training and first dibs on government buildings scheduled for takedown. Trainees, who are recruited through the City's workforce-development programs, receive sixteen weeks of training. The program covers a range of carpentry and craftsmanship skills such as sandblasting, painting, and stained-glass and wood repair. Once the training is completed satisfactorily, the worker is guaranteed a permanent job with the company, making between $12 and $25 an hour plus benefits.

Second Chance trainee Durrell Majette says: "As I ride down the streets now, I find myself looking at doors, the way the windows are built, the frames, stuff I used to never even notice. It's like I have a new direction in new life. I feel like I'm part of something bigger."

Foster is running trainings in Philadelphia and Washington, D.C., and hopes to open retail stores like Baltimore's in both of those cities. "We are not just offering a good job, but employment in a growing company and sector of the economy. That's a pathway to a career."[53]

Meanwhile, in the South Bronx, Green Worker Cooperatives might respond: "Employment is great, but ownership is better." Omar Freilla had the idea to found a local green co-op after serving on a coalition of labor and community groups that aimed to get green businesses to relocate to the brownfields that litter many low-income communities of color like the South Bronx.

"But I was never really comfortable with that approach," admits Freilla. "The way I saw it, if history is any guide, the profits generated by businesses—even green businesses—always leave the workers' community and largely enrich the predominantly white, middle-class and upper-middle-class owners. They live somewhere else." Surrounded by dirty waste–transfer and toxic waste–processing facilities in his native South Bronx, Freilla had an epiphany: What if we didn't throw it all away? What if we could sell it instead?

Soon after, his incubator launched its first worker co-op: ReBuilders Source, an 18,000-square-foot retail warehouse for surplus and salvaged building materials recovered from construction and demolition jobs. Among the items for sale are stainless-steel sinks, porcelain toilets, cans of paint, and doors—many of them brand-new, all of them in good shape and available at a significant discount.

There are four worker-owners, Julie Falu Garcia, Yasin York, Gloria Walker, and Carlos Angel, who manage all aspects of the business from soliciting and removing materials to warehousing and selling them. Each of them is making $35,000 a year, a good deal more than the median estimated household income in the district, which was $21,100 in 2006.

Freilla recruited local South Bronx residents by posting flyers around the neighborhood that said "Fire Your Boss" and offering the Co-op Academy. In the evening, once a week for eight weeks, the Academy provided workshops that explained and explored what a worker co-op is and what environmental justice is, along with tips on how to facilitate meetings or run consensus-based decision making. The Academy is becoming a regular event in the community, with the intent of nurturing further cooperative ventures.

"Not only do co-ops have the benefit of keeping wealth in the community; they also make democratic decision making a part of daily life. And true democracy is something that most people don't experience," Freilla says proudly. "We can set up our society so we no longer produce anything that needs to be thrown away, and we don't throw anything away, but keep it in circulation. And when you do that, you reduce waste, create new jobs, and preserve natural resources."[54]

WATER

On this blue planet of ours, freshwater scarcity is an issue of increasing concern. Retooling our society to be smarter about water can help cities save money—and also generate new jobs.

But first, some disturbing facts. Of the Earth's water, just 2.5 percent is fresh, and most of that is ice or snow. Unfrozen, liquid freshwater is mainly found underground as groundwater.[55] Unfortunately, we've covered most of our cities with nonporous materials like concrete. Therefore, a lot of rainfall runs off and becomes "storm water" instead of replenishing the underground reserves as nature intended.[56] As a result, in many of our cities, we are using groundwater faster than the rain can refill the aquifers.

With our growing human population needing to be fed by thirsty crops, freshwater supplies are shrinking fast. Climate change is also taking its toll, melting precious frozen supplies of freshwater into the salty seas and causing storms and floods of ever increasing intensity. Those heavy rains in turn magnify our storm-water problems.

Urban forestation is a key solution to the problem of storm water. This means planting and maintaining trees, yes, but also installing green roofs, which are covered in vegetation that is planted on top of a waterproof membrane. Since 2000, the green-roof phenomenon has been flourishing in cities—especially in Europe and, newly, Chicago—to absorb water that would otherwise run off into storm drains, with the added benefits of absorbing carbon dioxide, cleaning local air, cooling the building underneath (thus lowering its energy consumption), and extending roof life.

Sustainable South Bronx (SSBx), the organization founded by my colleague the MacArthur "Genius" Award–winning Majora Carter, champions urban vegetation as one solution for the pollution-ravaged South Bronx community. It cites not only the above advantages, but also the improvement of public health and building of pride in the neighborhood. Sustainable South Bronx has developed a training and placement program called Bronx Environmental Stewardship Training (B.E.S.T.).

Carter explains: "Nearly all B.E.S.T. students were previously on public assistance, and about half have prison records. They range in age from about eighteen to forty-five, and learn landscaping, green-roof installation, and brownfield remediation. After four years, 85 percent of our graduates have good, steady jobs."[57]

As B.E.S.T. program graduate James Wells explains with regard to his job planting and maintaining trees and green roofs in the South Bronx community: "It's not just transforming the environment, it's also transforming attitudes. If people see someone cares, it gives them hope, and now they care, and change their behavior. When I first started there was a lot of trash and debris, but now residents and business owners assist us. That's the best part."[58]

There's more good news. Just as in the energy sector, conservation and efficiency measures can increase our supply of water. In *Blue Gold: The Fight to Stop the Corporate Theft of the World's Water,* Maude Barlow and Tony Clarke write: "With technologies known and available today, agriculture could cut its demands by up to 50 percent, industries by up to 90 percent, and cities by one-third, with no sacrifice of economic output or quality of life." For starters, gray water (wastewater produced in domestic processes like showering) can often be used in place of clean water. We also need to widely embrace waterless, odorless composting toilets, sophisticated models of which are already available.[59]

In the meantime, there is work to be done: installing low-flow toilets, repairing leaky pipes, and replacing inefficient irrigation with high-efficiency sprinklers and drip irrigation. A regulation requiring all new residential toilets sold since 1994 to be high-efficiency and low-flow has successfully reduced the water used in flushing by 70 percent in U.S. cities.[60] There are jobs for qualified plumbers in installing toilets and repairing leaky pipes, although not necessarily for entry-level workers.

And more jobs are on the way. In the area of urban water planning, the most exciting work in the country is being spearheaded by a man in Los Angeles named Andy Lipkis. His organization, TreePeople, has planted millions of trees and taught thousands of young people the value of trees, recycling, and freshwater.

Because two-thirds of the city is paved, Lipkis explains, all the rainwater rushes into storm drains, picking up gunk from streets and sidewalks, and moves quickly to the concrete-lined LA river and the beach. Not only does the city lose all that valuable water; it has to pay fines for spewing polluted water into the ocean. But Lipkis saw a remarkable opportunity within this skewed system—to work *with* nature, rather than against it, and save the city a lot of money in the process. His idea was to build cisterns to capture the rainwater—and create jobs doing it.

The concept of building structures to catch the rain is an ancient one. TreePeople and its city and county partners have installed six demonstration cisterns in Los Angeles, which on average collect 1.25 million gallons of water for every inch of rainfall. When paired with redirected downspouts, low walls of soil known as berms, and porous ground (which comes from ripping up the concrete and re-placing it with soil and groundcover), virtually none of the precious freshwater falling from the sky is lost.

Officials were so impressed with TreePeople's projects that the city and county gave the green light to build a $200 million cistern project in Sun Valley, a flood-ravaged community mostly populated by low-wage workers. TreePeople predicts that about three hundred jobs will be created, including manufacturing and installation of water-capture systems, adapting landscaping to function as water-shed, and maintaining the landscapes, trees, berms, cisterns, and other elements of the system.

Better still, some city sanitation workers will be transformed into watershed managers. "A watershed manager is a water manager, a waste manager, an energy and resource manager—a job that takes more time and has more dignity," he points out. "The old way of dealing with water—erecting treatment plants or allowing rain-water to escape into drains, for example—actually eliminated jobs after the initial construction was finished. But watershed management creates all kinds of jobs."

Over a period of thirty years, this approach will save city and county an estimated $300 million in water and other costs. That's more than enough to pay for the retrofits, the installations, and the system's ongoing maintenance, which is where a lot of jobs are created.

Lipkis's efforts in LA have been fifteen intense years in the making, but he predicts that similar projects in cities across the country will start moving more quickly as water scarcity hits home. If he is right, many green-collar jobs will have a tinge of aqua blue.[61]

TRANSPORT

As the price of gas continues to skyrocket, we will need to reimagine, redesign, and rebuild our transportation systems and infrastructure. A massive investment in public transportation would immediately help the poor, create long-term jobs, and cut greenhouse gases.

Even with soaring fuel costs, Americans are still in love with their cars. Cars, trucks, and airplanes account for roughly two-thirds of the petroleum we consume. Each gallon of gasoline burned pumps twenty-eight pounds of carbon dioxide into the atmosphere—nineteen from the tailpipe and nine from upstream refining, transporting, and refueling.[62]

The federal government is not helping. "Four times as much federal money goes into roads as goes into transit projects," says Sam Zimmerman-Bergman, project director at the Oakland-based technical assistance group Reconnecting America and the Center for Transit-Oriented Development.[63] As a result, fewer than 3 percent of trips are made by public transit. If we increased that number to 10 percent of all trips (about the European level), we could reduce our dependence on oil by more than 40 percent, which is nearly as much oil as we import from Saudi Arabia every year.

It must be said that our failure to fund public transportation really hurts low-income Americans. The poorest fifth of Americans spend 42 percent of their annual household budget on the purchase, operation, and maintenance of their cars. That's more than twice the national average. Low-income people typically have older cars and more unexpected repair costs. More than 90 percent of former welfare recipients do not have access to a car, and yet three in every five jobs suitable for welfare-to-work program participants are not accessible by public transportation. Better bus service alone would free low-income people from car-related expenses—and expand the number of workplaces they could get to.[64]

Also, big public transit projects could be a tremendous source of jobs. Already, public transportation is a $44 billion industry that employs more than 360,000 people. More than 50 percent of these employees are operators or conductors. Thousands of others are employed in related services such as manufacturing, construction, and retail.[65]

There is no reason not to make this shift. Jobs lost in Detroit's auto industry would be more than offset by new jobs in manufacturing equipment, installing or building transit infrastructure, and maintenance and service for mass transit. Economic studies prove that transit investments actually create many more jobs than highway construction boondoggles: per $1 billion invested only 42,000 jobs are created in highway construction versus 80,000 in transit capital projects and an additional 100,000 jobs in transit operations. And many more local and long-term jobs are created in transit than in highway construction.[66]

If you want proof that communities can increase good jobs while pushing for better public transportation, look no further than the Alameda Corridor Jobs Coalition. It set an important precedent recently through its involvement in a $2.2 billion major rapid-rail project in Los Angeles. By convincing the Transportation Authority to make sure that local residents got at least 30 percent of the work hours, the coalition was able to steer a projected $40–$50 million in wages to local people. The coalition also got the Transportation Authority to require the project's prime contactor to pay for a thousand paid preapprentice training slots, so that local residents would not be excluded for lack of skills.[67]

Other countries have much smarter systems for moving people around. Picture a city of 1.8 million people with a spiderweb of bus lines connecting people to literally every part of town. Each triple-compartment bus can hold up to three hundred passengers. Passengers pay one low price to get anywhere in the city, and pay at the entrance to the bus stops rather than on board. This makes for faster loading and less idling and air pollution. Many of the city's major thoroughfares are reserved for pedestrians only, which draws more community activity into the center and more business to shopkeepers. This is no pie-in-the-sky scenario—it's been up and running in the Brazilian city of Curitiba for several *decades*.[68]

If we want to make a dent in the dual crisis, we will follow that city's wise example in every significant metropolis in the United States. If we want to employ a lot of people, help the poor, and cut back on greenhouse gases, we should cut back on building highways and cars—and invest massively in constructing buses, light-rail cars, and mass-transit projects.

ALL OF THE efforts we just examined are remarkable, in large part because most are moving upward against the force of gravity.

The old rules, regulations, laws, and subsidy schemes of the dying, pollution-based economy are still holding them back. One can only imagine what innovators of projects like these will do, once they have the government on their side.

Fortunately, help is on the way. For instance, in December 2007, President George W. Bush signed the Green Jobs Act as a part of the 2007 energy bill, to train workers for green-collar jobs. The bill was put forward by Hilda Solis (D-CA) and John Tierney (D-MA) and strongly supported by Speaker Nancy Pelosi (D-CA). It authorizes $125 million for green-collar workforce training programs. Twenty percent of those funds are targeted for veterans, displaced workers, at-risk youth, and families in dire poverty.[69] Those relatively modest funds constitute a small down payment on the massive investments that the Green Growth Alliance must someday soon require of the government, but they represent an important step in the right direction.

In the next chapter, we will discuss the full set of specific policies that will be needed to aid the pioneers discussed above—and to accelerate the process by which millions of others can join them.

SIX

The Government
Question

T HE PREVIOUS SECTION demonstrates—and celebrates—
some great news. Even in tough places never associated with
hybrid cars or organic cuisine, an inspiring transition is already
under way. From the South Bronx to South Dakota to South Central
LA, the tender shoots of a new economy are pushing up through
the cracks in the asphalt. The reality, however, remains sobering.
Encouraging and instructive as they are, these early signs of hope
simply are not succeeding at the scale necessary to secure the future
for vulnerable communities—or for the Earth itself.

Government policies can and must play a key role in creating an
inclusive, green economy—by setting standards, spurring innovation, realigning existing investments, and making new investments.
Government action can ensure that we make the transition rapidly,
while protecting and benefiting our most vulnerable populations.

Governments can accelerate equitable green growth in three ways. They can *regulate conduct*—setting the rules of the game, laying down the law, establishing standards, and telling members of society what they must or must not do. They can *invest money*—from direct spending, to offering incentives, to underwriting risk. And they can *convene leaders*—spurring the formation of new collaborative institutions that solve problems by bringing together public, private, and nonprofit stakeholders.

All levels of government—federal, state, and local—will be needed to remove the barriers to green growth. And if you doubt the U.S. government can use its power to help solve big problems, I offer some reminders from the nation's history.

In 2008, old-timers across the country gathered for reunions on the occasion of the seventy-fifth anniversary of the Civilian Conservation Corps (CCC), which FDR created to alleviate the predicament of millions of unemployed people (predominantly white men, it's true) during the Great Depression.[1] When the scope of the economic crisis was understood, President Roosevelt wasted no time. He called Congress into an emergency session to authorize the program virtually overnight. The Departments of Agriculture and the Interior were responsible for planning and organizing work to be performed in every state of the union. The Department of Labor, through its state and local relief offices, was responsible for the selection and enrollment of applicants.[2]

With the CCC, the government engaged more than two million men in protecting—and sometimes developing—America's natural resources. In return for their labor, the corpsmen received monthly checks of $30 from Uncle Sam as well as basic housing and meals. The CCC is estimated to have completed projects that included planting 2–3 billion trees, controlling erosion on 40 million acres of farmland, and providing mosquito control on over 240,000 acres of land.[3]

In launching the program, FDR announced: "It is my belief that what is being accomplished will conserve our natural resources, create future national wealth and prove of moral and spiritual value, not only to those of you who are taking part, but to the rest of the country as well."[4] First-person accounts of corpsmen from that time reveal they didn't value only the money, the regular meals, and the basic literacy skills they received. They also appreciated the less tangible benefits:

> After everything I'd been through, I'd thought I was an adult when I started with the program, but it takes a tempered-steel file to put the edge on an axe. I mean that in two ways. For one, I actually learned how to sharpen an axe and a cross-cut saw. In the second way, I had the edge put on my manhood by learning how to live with others whose background was not mine, the only thing we had in common being our youth. . . . I learned a lot of skills I still use, but more than anything, it gave me my confidence back, made me feel like I was a worthwhile member of our great country, and for that I'll always be grateful.[5]

Soon after FDR's New Deal, our government decided to intervene on a global scale during World War II. A massive war effort was undertaken: a draft of men into armed forces, of women into war-related industries—remember Rosie the Riveter—and of resources into the vehicles, meals, uniforms, and so forth needed by our armed forces. The government raised taxes and strongly encouraged citizens to purchase war bonds, using posters and films and teaming up with Hollywood celebrities to amass popular support. It rationed food and fuel. And—amazingly—it even froze free enterprise, decreeing that business and labor must be subservient to the country's security interests. As one example, FDR told automobile manufacturers that they couldn't make or market any new passenger cars; instead, the country needed them to use their factories to produce the trucks and the tanks the nation needed to defeat Hitler. Detroit turned on a dime, producing at lightning speed the great arsenal for democracy that saved the world from Fascism.

And less than twenty years after that, President John F. Kennedy boldly announced the Apollo Project, to put an American man on the moon (and bring him safely back) within the decade. The president got virtually every penny he requested for the lofty project on the grounds that it contributed to national security. But the project also had widespread impacts on scientific and technological developments—arguably more important in the long run. And, of course, it made a tremendous impact on our national pride. As JFK noted during a speech several months into the Apollo Project: "[It] has already created a great number of new companies, and tens of thousands of new jobs. Space and related industries are generating new demands in investment and skilled personnel."[6]

My friends at the Apollo Alliance adopted JFK's original Apollo Project as their inspiration (and leitmotif) in their mandate for a clean-energy revolution. As the Apollo Alliance's former executive director Bracken Hendricks writes in his book *Apollo's Fire* (coauthored with Congressman Jay Inslee), JFK's Apollo Project "proved the importance of backing vision with policy and investment. Meeting the challenge meant making a commitment to expanding the capabilities of the nation in both industrial might and intellectual prowess."[7]

In other words, there are precedents—and many more than the three I've noted here—for government support of paradigm shifts and massive world-changing projects. And so, today, the U.S. government must again make a fundamental shift. Right now, the government is spending tens of billions of dollars supporting the problem makers in the U.S. economy—the polluters, despoilers, incarcerators, and warmongers. The time has come for the nation to give greater support to the problem solvers—the clean-energy producers, green builders, eco-entrepreneurs, community educators, green-collar workers, and green consumers.

TOP PRIORITIES FOR THE NEXT PRESIDENT

The Bush administration has been a disastrous failure in the areas of environmental stewardship, climate leadership, economic renewal, and a sane energy policy. At this point, it is tempting to say that we don't need a U.S. president who will fix everything; we just need one who will stop breaking everything. That alone would make a tremendous difference. But to ensure the survival and success of our society, the president must take a number of positive steps.

In fact, at the very beginning of his inaugural address, the new president would be wise to fully embrace the agenda of the climate-solutions group 1Sky. That organization has fashioned an ambitious set of goals based strictly on what the world's scientists say is minimally necessary to avert a global climate catastrophe.

Following 1Sky's lead, the forty-fourth U.S. president should stand before the American people vowing to enact policies that will: (1) create five million green jobs as a part of a plan to conserve 20 percent of our energy by 2015; (2) freeze climate pollution levels now, then cut them to at least 25 percent below 1990 levels by 2020 and 80 percent by 2050; and (3) ban the construction of new coal plants that emit global-warming pollution, promoting renewable energy instead. Better yet, the new president should publicly pledge to meet Al Gore's challenge of making the United States 100 percent free of fossil fuels by 2018. Such bold proposals would immediately signal the end of the status quo, stun the pro-pollution contingent, and begin to rally the nation to meet our crises head-on.

To begin making good on those commitments, the administration would then need to implement multiple policies aggressively, immediately, and at various levels. The task of meeting these challenges would do more than determine the administration's environmental policy. It would also shape America's core economic program, foreign policy agenda, urban and rural policy, and manufacturing agendas as well.

With Bracken Hendricks of the Center for American Progress, I have outlined three policy tracks the new administration must pursue simultaneously to make dramatic, politically sustainable progress on the climate, energy, and jobs policy. The first track involves exerting immediate leadership within the executive branch, taking measures to coordinate U.S. climate and energy policy across all federal agencies and using executive orders, public communications, and other presidential prerogatives to manage carbon, capture energy savings, and promote renewable technologies.

Second, the White House must engage Congress to pass a suite of global-warming and energy legislation, including both a cap-and-trade bill that limits emissions and complementary policies that strengthen standards and drive investment in clean energy. The third track will entail a vigorous diplomatic effort to reclaim U.S. moral leadership abroad through progress on international climate negotiations, clean development, and addressing adaptation and energy poverty.

1. Executive Branch Leadership

The next administration will have many opportunities for executive leadership and agency action in moving the nation onto a sustainable energy path. The next president should take bold and immediate action.

Use climate solutions to frame a positive domestic economic agenda. The president will need to elevate global warming and energy security to the status of a major national commitment. He must place the issue at the center of his agenda for economic opportunity and reconstruction and link it to job creation, rebuilding cities and rural economies, and restoring global competitiveness. This will galvanize new constituencies for action, including labor, business, urban, farm, civil rights, and other stakeholders. By clearly communicating the economic benefits of action for the poor and middle class and for ratepayers and small businesses, the new administration will be able to answer predictable attacks as businesses and markets adjust.

Use the pulpit of the presidency to signal serious commitment. The power of the Oval Office to convene industry and interest groups and drive a national consensus for action should not be underestimated. Efforts should include strong signals in the opening days of the administration, including major national summits and prominent public addresses like the inaugural and state of the union, to underscore the centrality of this issue in defining the leadership and legacy of this administration, aligned with the future not the past.

Build a leadership structure within the White House to sustain this focus. To assure that attention is sustained through the hard political fights and coalition building that will be required, the next administration must establish a key presidential adviser supported by a strong office for building and implementing global-warming strategy and approaches to building a green economy. This leadership and staffing structure should be publicly launched in the early days of the administration and given authority to report directly to the president. It should have strong links to economic and national security advisers and clear pathways of communication with all agencies and White House offices to ensure that a unified strategy is employed across the executive branch.

Enlist all federal agencies in building climate solutions. Agencies across the federal government must play a role in solving the climate crisis. The administration's energy and climate strategy must be systematic and include all line agency budgets and programs.

The Department of Housing and Urban Development can advance community development and housing retrofits. The Department of Labor must ensure that a trained green-collar workforce is available. Agriculture has authority related to biofuels and wind energy. The State Department must play a central role in jump-starting international negotiations, and the U.S. Agency for International Development should shape assistance to impacted countries. The Department of Transportation should guide strategies for expansion of rail and transit, land-use planning, reducing vehicle miles traveled, and air quality and congestion.

The Department of Energy, Environmental Protection Agency, National Oceanic and Atmospheric Administration, Department of the Interior, and others will all play leading roles in the policy and science of climate change, and global warming will increasingly organize their work. Regulatory agencies like the Federal Regulation and Oversight of Energy will shape rules and incentives for smart-grid infrastructure. Meanwhile, Treasury and Commerce will establish mechanisms for carbon trading as well as incentives and financing for public infrastructure, efficiency retrofits, renewables, and transitioning U.S. industrial production.

Utilize the power of executive orders and presidential leadership. Executive orders can play a useful role in immediately implementing policies and using federal powers to make carbon-emission reduction a top priority. The White House could instruct agencies that greenhouse-gas emissions should be analyzed to achieve compliance with the National Environmental Performance Act. It could immediately grant waivers under the Clean Air Act to begin regulating carbon dioxide as a pollutant in automobile tailpipe emissions, a measure that the Bush administration denied in 2007.

Ensure that the federal government leads the way to economic transformation. Federal agencies can do much to accelerate the transition to a clean-energy economy. The president can show immediate leadership by instructing agencies to reduce their carbon footprint through improved purchasing and acquisitions, vehicle fleet management, and facilities management. Such administrative changes would set a tone of urgency and leadership that starts at the top of government.

Launch a signature initiative, the Clean Energy Corps. A national Clean Energy Corps would combine service, training, and employment efforts, with a special focus on cities and neglected rural communities, to combat climate disruption. The work would focus on retrofitting homes, small businesses, schoolhouses, and public buildings; preserving and enlarging green public spaces; applying distributed renewable energy production technology to underserved communities; strengthening community defenses against climate disruption; upgrading infrastructure; and educating children and communities on how they can contribute to ending global warming. These efforts could pay for themselves through energy savings, making the CEC program largely self-financing, while generating enormous demand for new jobs in communities that need them.[8]

A related program, the Civic Justice Corps, could provide the vast numbers of people returning from prison with a path to living-wage green jobs and careers. An excellent training model has been developed by San Francisco State University professor Raquel Pinderhughes. First implemented in Oakland, California, under the leadership of Ian Kim, director of the Green Collar Jobs Campaign at the Ella Baker Center, and also being piloted in Cleveland and Philadelphia, the Pinderhughes Green Job Corps Training combines classroom and on-the-job training, wraparound support, and an internship component. A key innovation of the model is the creation and integration of local Green Business Councils, with the intent of organizing potential employers and providing them with incentives to hire corps members.[9]

2. A Comprehensive Legislative Agenda

Cap, collect, and invest. The highest priority for the new administration is to work with Congress to pass major global-warming legislation that reduces greenhouse-gas emissions.[10] One indispensable component of cap-and-trade policy is the auction of a substantial portion of emissions permits available to greenhouse-gas emitters. The Congressional Budget Office estimates that the monetary value of these permits would range from $50 billion to $300 billion each and every year (in 2007 dollars) by 2020.[11] This money can be invested in the public interest—to equitably transition the country to a low-carbon economy.

Establish the clean-energy smart grid. The second biggest priority for the next U.S. president—besides getting a price put on carbon emissions—must be the construction of a national smart grid for energy. The nation's present energy infrastructure is an outmoded and inefficient patchwork. A wide multitude of renewable sources cannot easily plug into it, and neither the generators nor the purchasers of power ever get enough consistent information to make intelligent decisions. Smart-grid proponents suggest another, better way: the digital automation of the entire energy supply, from the generators to the consumers. Think of the smart grid as an Internet for energy. The grid would be comprised of a network of smart devices, all communicating with each other, to do real-time balancing of energy need and production. As waste is greatly reduced, carbon reduction and cost savings would follow. In the meantime, the project would create tens of thousands of jobs for everyone from electricians to computer programmers.

Whereas our present grid is built around the needs of big, polluting, centralized power plants, a smart grid can be designed to easily accommodate multiple power producers. That means thousands of home producers of energy, perhaps deploying wind and solar, could plug into the power grid to sell or share their energy with others. Once technology for hyperconductive power lines is perfected, a national grid could even move clean energy from windy and sunny places to those regions that lack abundant supplies of renewable energy. Overhauling, linking, and digitizing the U.S. power grid is the biggest and most important piece of work in helping to move the country into a rational, clean-energy future.

There is an added bonus to this idea. A national network of more independent sources of power—home-based fuel cells, stand-alone solar systems, regional wind farms—would make the energy infrastructure as a whole a less inviting terrorist target and much more resilient in the face of natural or human-made disasters. To the best of our knowledge, no terrorist cell has ever blown up a wind turbine.[12]

Support green jobs and worker training. Improving energy efficiency and deploying renewable technology at scale will produce massive demand for skilled labor. Investing in worker training, supportive employment services, manufacturing extension, and community development will be essential to ensure we meet our goals. Legislation like the Green Jobs Act and the Energy Efficiency and Conservation Block Grant program offers an opportunity to use public investment to prime new industries as well as to lift people out of poverty. This legislation not only connects to people's immediate self-interest, but also calls them to the larger moral purpose of cocreating solutions. It is grounded in neighborhood-level actions—restoring communities with green space and green buildings, restoring bodies with parks and clean air, restoring families with purpose and paychecks.

Improve efficiency in energy generation, transmission, and consumption. To achieve immediate efficiency gains, the next administration should implement a National Energy Efficiency Resource Standard to require utilities to cut energy use 10 percent by 2020. Current building stock is wasteful and inefficient—each nonweatherized building is an open spigot for pollution and wasted energy dollars. The next administration should work with Congress to pass a range of efficiency policies, including commercial and residential building codes, retrofitting public buildings to higher standards; establishing incentives for distributed energy; extending energy-efficient home mortgages; and assisting low-income and public housing stock to improve energy efficiency through stronger incentives, better accounting tools, and loan guarantees. Jobs weatherizing U.S. buildings *cannot* be outsourced.

Increase production of renewable electricity. America needs to fully deploy its abundant renewable energy resources, including wind, solar, biomass, sustainable hydroelectric, geothermal, and wave/tidal. At a minimum, the next administration should require that 25 percent of our electricity comes from renewable energy by 2025. As the market for renewables grows (with technological improvements and economies of scale), the objective should be to drive the price cheaper than traditional fossil-based energy in the market, allowing a sunset on any financial incentives. Diversifying electricity and fuel supplies hedges against disruptive spikes in energy costs. Renewable electricity creates *more than twice as many jobs* per unit of energy and per dollar invested than traditional fossil fuel–based electricity. And electricity and heat account for more than 30 percent of all U.S. carbon emissions, a figure that can be drastically reduced by turning to low-carbon, renewable energy.

Invest in low-carbon mass transportation and rail infrastructure. In an era of escalating oil prices, traffic gridlock, hazardous air quality, and the threat of a global-warming tipping point, the next president must reinvest in local mass-transit systems, regional and interstate high-speed rail, and other low-carbon means of transportation of both passengers and freight. Expanding mass transit and rail infrastructure promises to create thousands of good construction jobs, while expanding Americans' transportation choices and strengthening communities.

Increase vehicle fuel economy. In the early years of cap-and-trade, the price for carbon will probably be too low to change driving behavior. A price of $15 per ton of carbon dioxide translates roughly to an increase of 13 cents per gallon in the price of gasoline, not enough to dramatically reduce gasoline consumption. An additional increase in the Corporate Average Fuel Economy (CAFE) standard (to at least 40 miles per gallon) will be needed to spur vehicle efficiency. Increased CAFE standards, combined with incentives for auto manufacturers to retool factories and for consumers to purchase more efficient and alternative fuel vehicles, will support a resurgence of American automotive manufacturing and help move us off both carbon and oil. A new line of ultraefficient vehicles, such as plug-in hybrids that get 100 miles per gallon of gas, will support manufacturing jobs of components—from new battery systems to advanced drive trains—and help consumers.

Change the systems for fueling our bodies. Federal policies and programs can move our farm and food system in a more sustainable direction. Current policies subsidize farm consolidation at the expense of family farms, reduce opportunities for new folks interested in pursuing farming, and encourage industrial, pesticide-based farming practices that hurt the health of the land and consumers. Instead, federal grants and funding could support:

- Fair labor, fair trade, and environmental standards

- A national organic-transition support program that facilitates the adoption of organic standards by conventional farms

- Community-based health-food and nutrition initiatives

- Micro-credit programs to encourage new entrepreneurs in farming and food production

- A matched savings fund for new farmers

- Crop insurance that rewards crop diversification and does not discriminate against organic farmers

- Amendment of the Packers and Stockyards Act to eliminate price preferences that discriminate against small and mid-size livestock operations

- Sustainability criteria to guide the development of agriculturally based renewable energy

- The Outreach and Assistance for Socially Disadvantaged Farmers and Ranchers Competitive Grants Program

We can't use tons of fossil fuels in our fertilizers and massive Robo-tractors just to make a handful of carrots. We need to start preparing now to transition our entire food system to one that relies less on petroleum and pesticides and more on smart people and wise farming techniques.

Block new coal plants that can't safely capture and store emissions. Next-generation coal-fired electricity faces economics similar to those of cars. The cost of carbon dioxide emissions would have to reach roughly $30 per ton before it would be economically rational to deploy advanced technology that captures emissions (carbon capture and sequestration). It may be several years, or even decades, before carbon prices reach such a price threshold—and we don't have that much time. To freeze its emissions and begin serious reductions within the next few years, the coal-fired electricity sector will require a tough performance standard. For the sake of the planet and all future generations, no new coal plants should be permitted unless and until they can safely capture 100 percent of carbon dioxide emissions.

In the meantime, the United States should not build new power plants based on old, dangerous, carbon-spewing technologies. If coal is to play a productive role in our energy mix, the government and private sectors must collaborate on a massive Manhattan Project to achieve dramatic breakthroughs in carbon-capture technology. Even then, the president should move to ban the devastating practice of "mountaintop removal." No coal company should be allowed to blow up mountains—destroying America's beauty, poisoning its rivers, and destroying rural communities—just to scrape out the coal deep inside them. It is time to break our addiction to dirty coal before our addiction breaks Appalachia.

Provide sustainable, low-carbon fuels. The next administration should pursue multiple options to reduce dependence on fossil-based transportation fuels. At the very least it should commit to producing 25 percent of our liquid transportation fuels from renewable sources by 2025. The majority of renewable fuels should come from next-generation biofuels made from nonfood biomass like switchgrass, wood chips, and agricultural waste. To ensure the environmental integrity of biofuels, the administration should implement a low-carbon fuel standard to reduce life-cycle emissions 10 percent by 2020. It should also initiate a certification program with transparent sustainability labeling.

Also, a suite of policies are available—including zero-emissions mandates and consumer tax incentives—to accelerate deployment of plug-in hybrid and all-electric vehicles. To build the infrastructure to supply this energy, a "pump or plug" mandate should require that 15 percent of gas stations retrofit their facilities to deliver either E-85 ethanol, biodiesel, or dedicated electricity charging stations for plug-in vehicles in all counties where 15 percent of registered vehicles can run on alternative fuels. Further, local ownership can provide strong economic benefits to rural communities by producing sustainable bioenergy.[13]

Eliminate federal tax breaks and subsidies for oil and gas. The federal government currently allocates billions of dollars annually in tax breaks and subsidies to the oil and gas industry. With high prices, companies are making record profits and don't need government assistance. It is time to shift investment away from high-carbon energy to the clean energy necessary to power a low-carbon economy. Redirecting investment to help commercialize emerging low-carbon energy sources will help transform our economy and capture the economic and environmental benefits of clean energy.

Trade in "hoopties" for hybrids. "Hoopty" is street slang for an old, unreliable car—often a gas-guzzler. The term is popular in disadvantaged communities because such cars—ugly, noisy, and often belching fumes—can be found everywhere.

Such cars are the least fuel-efficient, least safe, and the most polluting cars on the road. As a result, low-income drivers can end up spending much more money for gas than wealthier people, who can afford to buy newer, more fuel-efficient cars—or even hybrids. Their pain eventually becomes everyone's pain because, in the aggregate, these cars drive up the price of gas for everyone. Maintaining a massive fleet of gas-guzzlers keeps the demand for fuel high—and thus adds to the upward pressure on fuel prices.

To address these problems, the government should adopt—urgently—a policy that helps low-income drivers scrap their inefficient vehicles and replace them with efficient cars. Such a policy would help people of modest means save money on gas; therefore, it would be a great instance of eco-populism in action—showing how green solutions can help ordinary people. It would also decrease the nation's oil and gas consumption, improve air quality, help beat global warming, and hasten the retirement of a whole generation of gas-guzzlers. An added benefit would be that the hard work of deconstructing and recycling the materials in all those old hoopties could be a source of good, green-collar jobs.

There is precedent for a program like this; a few states have already implemented scrappage programs designed to get the most polluting cars off the roads. They are working well. Also, the government already helps low-income households meet their home energy needs through the Low Income Home Energy Assistance Program. This program would help them meet their transportation fuel costs as well.

The question is how to do this in the most affordable manner possible. Eco-visionary Amory Lovins has two solutions. In the first option, the federal government buys a large volume of efficient cars and leases them to low-income people who qualify. According to the Center for American Progress: "The cost of insurance, gasoline, and regular maintenance could be incorporated into the leasing price in much the same way subscription car-sharing programs, like Zipcar and Flexcar, do now. Volume purchasing of insurance and gasoline would lower these transportation costs."

The second option involves helping people who currently do not qualify for new car loans obtain credit to buy efficient vehicles. The Center for American Progress reports: "The risk for this customer segment is similar to that for student loans with the additional benefit of the car serving as collateral. If the federal government guarantees reimbursement to current auto lenders for incremental defaults made to participants in the low-income scrappage program, the existing market mechanisms and financial institutions could be used for this program with little cost to the government."

In other words, just as with student loans, the government would not directly spend much money. Instead, it would use its financial clout to open the doors so that millions of people can get the bank loans they need to improve their own lives. Such a role for government is especially important in the wake of the home-mortgage meltdown. If there is anything we can do to prevent it, those millions of Americans who lost out in the housing meltdown should not be further impoverished every week at the gas pump.

In combination with a reduction of the speed limit back to 55 mph, a national "scrap and replace" program for polluting cars would save low-income drivers money, slash greenhouse gas emissions and lower gas prices for everyone. And of course the side benefit: it would result in serious cool points for the next president. The youth of America would get a huge kick out of hearing the president of the United States say the word "hoopty" on national television. A cooler president could give us a much cooler planet.

3. Leadership in International Negotiations

One great tragedy of the Bush administration has been the abdication of international diplomatic and moral leadership—especially in the arenas of greenhouse-gas emissions and global-warming treaties. The new administration must reengage with the world and simultaneously rebuild American standing abroad. The following steps must be taken rapidly.

Rebuild international credibility through strong domestic action. The most important message we can send is through our own strong action to reduce domestic U.S. carbon emissions. The policies mentioned above will help to restore American credibility in international negotiations.

Reengage international negotiations. In addition, the United States must rapidly reengage international climate negotiations at several levels. This will start immediately in the next administration, with the next UN Climate Change Conference in 2009 in Copenhagen. These talks will set the framework for a successor treaty to the Kyoto Protocol.

Author and climate activist Ross Gelbspan has an ambitious plan to replace the Kyoto agreement, which is widely criticized for its inadequate emissions reduction targets and loopholes that allow for emissions trading and give credits for the use of carbon "sinks" and the provision of emission-reduction technologies, neither of which are adequately regulated. He proposes that the industrialized countries strip away the $250 billion a year that they collectively spend to subsidize fossil fuels—and use that money to support clean energy. Second, he proposes that government tax the $1.5 trillion worth of daily international currency transactions by a quarter-penny on a dollar and use the $300 billion a year generated by the tax to fund wind farms in India, fuel-cell factories in South Africa, solar assemblies in El Salvador, and vast, solar-powered hydrogen farms in the Middle East.

Last, he proposes that every country simply agree to Progressive Fossil Fuel Efficiency Standards. Every country would start at its current baseline and increase its fossil-fuel energy efficiency by 5 percent every year until the global 70 percent reduction is attained. That means a country would produce the same amount of goods as the previous year with 5 percent less carbon fuel. Alternatively, it would produce 5 percent more goods using the same amount of carbon fuel as the previous year.[14]

Connect global warming and trade policy. Climate provisions should be given significant weight in international trade policy. Industry and labor have expressed concern over adverse economic impacts from trading relationships with countries that lack controls on carbon. These concerns should not be an excuse for weak standards, but rather should drive policies that ensure a level playing field for U.S. workers in a world where carbon has a price. As domestic legislation moves forward in Congress, trade implications are likely to receive increasing political attention, and the next president must have answers to calls for a border adjustment tariff, a program for trade adjustment assistance for displaced workers, and a strategy to include climate provisions and broader environmental and labor protections in future trade deals.

Promote adaptation and confront energy poverty. The secretary general of NATO has identified climate disruption as a top security challenge, resulting from water and agricultural shortages and migration of refugees.[15] These global security threats as well as moral imperatives require rapid and forceful attention to two major areas of development assistance. First, increasing the ability of poor countries to access food and water and to ensure public health and public safety must become a top priority for the next administration. Second, we must be ready to help poor countries leapfrog pollution and rapidly deploy clean-energy technology. The goal of international development assistance should be to alleviate the crippling energy poverty that denies much of the world's population basic energy services, without increasing carbon emissions.

Among global activists, a critical mass is beginning to rally around the Greenhouse Development Rights (GDR) framework. It was developed by Paul Baer and Tom Athanasiou, of EcoEquity, and Sivan Kartha, of the Stockholm Environment Institute. The GDR recognizes that the desperately poor around the world have a right to develop themselves economically, even if they add slightly to carbon emissions. In other words, they have a right to bring themselves up to a dignified level of consumption. Meanwhile, it is the rich who must now bring their emissions and consumption down to a dignified level.[16]

The First One Hundred Days

Whatever the next president does, he must act quickly. Diplomatic, scientific, and economic timetables are all running out. The next president must hit the ground running. On energy and climate policy, it is critical that significant efforts be undertaken in the early days of the administration. A hundred-day strategy is key to making real domestic commitments and advancing stalled international climate talks that will result in meaningful global reductions.

The full power of the presidency, both its political leadership and moral authority, is needed to build deep public support to sustain smart climate policies over a generation. Climate solutions must be at the center of the agenda for the entire administration. This effort will also require broader constituencies in support of action and new strategies for public education. Solving global warming should become a centerpiece and organizing principle for the next administration's program for economic revival.

WHAT LOCAL POLICIES CAN DO

Ultimately, the federal government must play the leading and defining role, but local and state governments have important parts to play. And many already are passing laws and creating policies that are moving our society into a brighter, healthier future.

The involvement of city governments is a very good thing, because for the first time in human history, more people on Earth live in cities than outside of them. Urban settlements cover only about 2 percent of the Earth's surface, but they consume more than 75 percent of the Earth's resources and produce 75 percent of the Earth's waste (including air and water pollution).[17] Therefore, what we choose to do in our cities, here and around the world, will either sink the planet—or save it. If we want a planet that can sustain human life, we must create human cities that can sustain the planet.

A Look at Chicago

One American city is quite clearly at the forefront, leading the way toward sustainability, but it's probably not the place you'd guess. "With its strong industrial base, Chicago is perceived to be a meat and potatoes kind of town," says Chicago's chief environmental officer Sadhu Johnston, "so for it to set a green example is different than a city like San Francisco or Boulder doing so." It's true. For such groundbreaking environmental leadership to come out of "The

City of Big Shoulders" rather than the land of tofu and hot tubs is remarkable. And the example that city is setting is a powerful one for industrial centers across the nation and the world.

Okay, perhaps you aren't completely surprised. After all, in the previous chapter, you already met LaDonna Redmond, the Chicago mother who started an organic food revolution in Chicago's black community. But it turns out that she is seriously not alone in trying to green the Windy City.

Mayor Richard M. Daley got to be well known for his commitment to bringing ecological solutions to his city—even before climate change became a front-page story. Johnston says the mayor's initial impetus was economic and social: to improve the quality of life in Chicago and make the city a more competitive place to live, work, and locate a business. Then a team of top climatologists hired by the City predicted a climate like Houston's by 2095 if current emissions weren't halted. That's when Daley added environmental considerations to a list of reasons to build a clean, green economy. (In response, the City set a goal of reducing emissions 80 percent by 2050.)

Johnston stresses that the success of the Chicago model has been building the economy from multiple angles, stimulating both supply and demand. "We're using our purchasing power as a city to attract the kinds of manufacturers we want in the city. For example, we attracted a solar-panel manufacturer by promising to buy $5 million worth of its panels. Now its factory is employing 99 percent local Chicagoans, with a number of ex-offenders among them, to manufacture these panels. Meanwhile, the copper piping and the glass panes and the other parts that go in the panels are being sourced from other Chicago companies."

Chicago also funds incentives for a number of green processes and products, for example, giving away solar-thermal panels made in Chicago to homes and businesses; making green-roof grants, which award $5,000 to anyone installing one; and running geothermal and reflective-roofing grant programs. A Green Bungalow program provides matching grants to homeowners for weatherization and/or renewable energy installation. The Green Permit Program expedites building permits and pays $25,000 toward the cost of building permits for those who are building green. The City is learning it can create financial incentives—and the incentive of speedier processes—to effectively help homeowners and business owners go green.

Last year the City developed an official Green Business Strategy to help conventional companies get greener and expand their green jobs. One of the recommendations resulted in the Waste to Profit Network. It currently has about eighty participants, including utilities, breweries, coal power companies, a huge steel manufacturer, and Abbott Labs, one of the largest pharmaceutical companies. Says Johnston:

> We do a waste audit for every participating business, and an input analysis for every participating business. And then we start to make connections around materials. We've saved them hundreds of thousands of dollars and saved thousands of tons of materials from going into landfills.
>
> For example, Abbott Labs makes IV bags, which need the edges trimmed off. The plastic that gets trimmed is not recyclable, so it has to go into a landfill, and that costs them money. But we've connected them with a tiny start-up company called Curb Appeal that's also in the network, and they have a technique for making parking lot bumpers—what your wheel butts up against in a parking lot—with that discarded plastic. Curb Appeal just needed a client ready to purchase them. So the City committed to buy several hundred of these bumpers for a parking lot we're building. The network is sort of a virtual eco-industrial park, and definitely a win-win-win scenario.

In early 2008, Mayor Daley hosted a union summit that brought together leaders from twenty-four trade unions and their apprenticeship programs to talk about expansion into alternative energy, energy efficiency, and green technology. "It built off existing partnerships we have, for example with our Local 399, the operating engineers, with whom we've been partnering to train their members about green building and how to green existing buildings, and our partnership with the electrical workers union, which has had an apprenticeship program with the City in solar-panel installation," Johnston reports.[18]

Another of the mayor's central concerns has been the reentry into society of formerly incarcerated people. About twenty thousand people are released from prison every year in Chicago. The mayor asks every program in the City to give ex-offenders meaningful ways to contribute. The Department of the Environment provides a particularly beautiful solution: the Greencorps. Since 1994, Greencorps Chicago has been at the vanguard of reentry programs geared toward green opportunities, providing nine months of job training, paid internship, and job placement in an ever increasing variety of green industries.

A complex array of partnerships between government, the private sector, and nonprofit agencies is behind the highly successful model, "so the City doesn't waste any time reinventing any wheels." For example, partner organization Fuller Park Neighborhood Development Corporation manages the home weatherization component. Meanwhile, Computers for Schools trains Greencorps members to fix or disassemble and properly dispose of old computers that are dropped off at the City's Household Chemical and Computer Recycling Facility. These computers are then distributed to low-income households, community centers, or schools, thereby helping to close the digital divide.

A workforce development agency called OAI, Inc. (formerly the Office of Applied Innovations), handles recruitment by partnering with community-based agencies. It also provides certifications in many areas: cleaning up polluted brownfields; getting rid of lead, asbestos, and mold; handling hazardous material safely; responding to emergencies; and complying with the Occupational Safety and Health Act (OSHA). OAI also helps Greencorps students with job readiness (for example, how to deal with sexual harassment), interviewing, and other support services. These are skills that serve graduates well wherever they go.

Another agency called Employ America grounds students in basic financial literacy. Employ America also serves as the employer of record for program participants, providing basic medical benefits and a matched savings program. As the employer of record, Employ America gains tax benefits by employing people from "empowerment zones" (government lingo for distressed and impoverished communities). It then turns those savings around and offers Greencorps trainees a dollar-for-dollar match for the money they save.

And this is only a sample of the more than forty groups that help make the training experience a success. Even more organizations and companies are involved on the placement side, hiring Greencorps program graduates for jobs earning anywhere from $9 to $38 per hour, with most in the $11–$14 range.[19]

With the City's adoption of a Climate Action Plan and a Climate Change Job Strategy Initiative, the program will expand even further. Johnston says the City is analyzing what kind of preparation will be necessary for a workforce that can retrofit thousands of homes, replace thousands of appliances, and install thousands of solar panels, among other activities. "Our initial estimates show this will result in thousands of new jobs per year. Those are contracting, auditing, engineering, labor, insulation—on the retrofit side. And many more jobs in expanding public transit and other initiatives."

Chicago's efforts are already impacting real people's lives at the grassroots level. Take, for example, Chicagoan Jumaani Bates, who has turned his life around and is now a part of the city's green wave.

Bates is a Greencorps graduate. He spent fifteen years in a revolving-door relationship with Chicago's Department of Corrections. Now the people he knew on the streets during his drug-slinging days in Westside constantly ask him for advice, because they see him successfully maintaining a different kind of life. He says:

> I tell them to clean up and then go to Greencorps or Growing Home. With all these new green technologies and jobs in green building and green business, we need to get the word out. African Americans were last on the list in terms of the information age, and are still trying to catch up with that. I keep telling people you need to know about this green economy, whether you believe in global warming or not, because that's where the opportunities are.[20]

Today, Bates works at Wilbur Wright College, one of the City Colleges of Chicago, in the Building Environmental Technologies program. That program trains construction-industry professionals in green building and energy conservation. He's also a member of the local chapter of the U.S. Green Building Council and of a network in Chicago called Blacks in Green. Soon he plans to pursue a degree in horticulture and natural resources at the University of Illinois at Urbana-Champaign. He has a bright future—and so does his city.

LOCAL POLICY IDEAS

Mayor Daley's Chicago illustrates perfectly the powerful combination of setting standards, investing, providing incentives, and fostering innovation. Already many other U.S. mayors and governors are implementing policies that address our environmental problems as well as our social and economic crises.

Below, I highlight some of the most interesting and exciting ideas that local and state governments can embrace. There are dozens of opportunities at the local level to support the greening of America and the creation of new jobs.

1. Green Existing Buildings

Every city should commit to retrofitting its existing buildings and permitting only the construction of efficient, high-performance structures that meet top Leadership in Energy and Environmental Design (LEED) standards. A city's commitment to a comprehensive retrofit of its own buildings demonstrates forward-thinking green leadership, results in savings in energy bills and health-care costs, and creates a ton of work. As a city works hard to make its own buildings more efficient, its leaders can in good conscience require the same of all residential, commercial, and industrial buildings in that municipality.

One big barrier to greening buildings, however, is figuring out how to pay for the work. In theory, the retrofits should pay for themselves in dollars saved on energy costs. But in practice, few building owners have the cash on hand to pay up front for all the necessary audits and repairs. So buildings keep leaking energy, property owners keep leaking cash, and greenhouse gases from overtaxed power plants keep building up in the atmosphere. The key is to create mechanisms that let the cost-saving, retrofit work be done right away, with immediate gains to property owners or renters—but then be paid off easily, over time.

As suggested elsewhere, I think we should be spending much more public money on efficiency efforts. We can do that as direct grants or as low- or noninterest loans in a revolving loan fund. It's a sensible social investment. But what about right now, when the public money for comprehensive building retrofits isn't available, and city leaders must go to banks and private investors to finance their plans?

The COWS-Milwaukee model—Milwaukee Energy Efficiency, or Me2—is a good way of doing this. The Center on Wisconsin Strategy (COWS), led by Joel Rogers, invented the model while trying to figure out how workers in the gutted industrial heartland can move to the center of the clean-energy economy. The idea is to retrofit practically every building in the city to save money and put lots of people to work.

Me2 is an innovative model that allows small-property owners and even renters to use a process similar to performance contracting in order to achieve energy savings. Property owners or renters (with landlords' cooperation) receive an audit listing all conservation measures that can be paid for out of energy savings in a given period. They repay the cost of the measures via their utility bill.

Thus far, COWS has gotten buy-in from labor, business, and community civic and political figures in Milwaukee as well as on the state level. Importantly, it also acquired assurance of private financing from JPMorgan Chase once the meter-based billing scheme is implemented. Public financing has also been promised.

COWS and the University of Florida estimate that for every $1 million invested, about 13 job-years in installation/construction activities and 4 job-years in upstream manufacturing will be created. For single-family residential projects, the distribution of jobs will be 0.5 supervisor job-years, 2.5 skilled labor job-years, 4.7 semiskilled labor job-years, and 5.0 unskilled labor job-years.[21] This is an estimate that should hold true for any city. This is great news for lower-skilled people with barriers to employment, like criminal convictions.

And the really exciting thing about the Milwaukee experiment is that it will in fact be scaled—applied to every building, made a focus of citywide efforts—from the bully pulpit of the mayor to "social marketing" of the concept by community organizations, many of whose members will be getting the new work. This is the sort of beautiful, scalable solution that could be made in any American city or town.

2. Create Green Assessment Districts

Another great idea is using the well-established notion of "assessment districts," which have been proven to work very well for other purposes, for green projects. For instance, a neighborhood decides to put its utility lines underground. Residents opt in to an "assessment district," committing to pay an extra amount, maybe $10 per month, in property taxes. The utility company does the work of undergrounding the lines and is paid back from the city out of the assessment fees. Cities have the opportunity to enact this same model of financing—which is not a tax, but a voluntary, opt-in tax assessment—for efficiency retrofits as well as renewable energy projects, in both commercial and residential sectors.

Suppose residents in an area wanted to get their homes weatherized and outfitted with solar panels. Many would hesitate. For one thing, the interest rate on any individual's home-improvement loan could be discouragingly high. Second, certain homeowners might sell their houses in just a few years and move out—before they had time to make their money back on the investment through savings on energy bills. Therefore, the renewable energy and conservation services might never get purchased—and those homes would go right on using dirty energy in a wasteful manner, despite the owners' contrary desires.

But there is a way out of this dilemma. Neighbors could work with city officials to create a green assessment district. To pay for green retrofits within that district, residents who chose to participate would agree to pay a small assessment added to their local property tax bill. When a large enough number of people signed up to participate, the City could bundle up all of those promises and take them to a bank. There, it could get a big loan to cover these home improvements en masse at a much lower interest rate. Even better, the obligation to repay the loan would not attach to the temporary owner, but to the house itself, like a green lien. Every year, whoever happened to own the house at that time would simply pay back part of the loan as a part of the property taxes. As a result, the cost of the green improvement would be spread out over multiple owners. And for any particular owner, the savings on the energy bill should cancel out the yearly property assessment cost. In fact, the City of Berkeley, California, presently is experimenting with this very model.

Such an approach would create demand for clean, green technology (like solar panels) and the labor to make it happen (like the installation of said solar panels). In fact, an agreement to hire local labor could be specified up front, so the benefits stay within the community at every stage. And those neighborhoods that have the means to opt in and adopt the costs early on end up creating the opportunities for other poorer neighborhoods to green themselves at a lower cost in the future.

Nobody in the district would be forced to participate. Only those who signed up would pay the assessment—or get the benefits. But everyone who did sign up to take part would enjoy the best of all possible worlds—immediate energy savings and home improvements without incurring heavy personal debt.

3. Establish a Carbon Budget

Cities need to assign a carbon impact—a monetary value—to all of their activities and expenditures during their regular budgeting process. This would lead to true cost accounting and show the environmental impact of a municipality's activities. Using this method, a city can assess the real costs of tearing down a building and building a new one compared to the costs of refurbishing the original structure. A carbon budget is an indispensable tool for guiding a city's budget and procurement, ensuring that a city's use of taxpayer dollars supports the clean, green economy.

As in the case of retrofitting their own buildings first, cities have the opportunity to lead by example and prove their commitment to limiting emissions. Cities should quantify and assign a value to all the carbon emissions of the municipality (or county or region)— including all industrial, commercial, and residential outputs. That process is a critical first step in ratcheting down emissions overall.

4. Set Targets for Local Food, Zero Waste, and Renewable Energy

Municipal and state governments can also lead the way in promoting local food, supporting zero waste, and boosting renewable energy usage. Even a light meal might represent a ton of carbon, depending on how far each piece of food traveled to get to one's plate. The closer to the dinner table that a meal is grown, the less distance that carbon-spewing trucks must travel to ship the food to diners. Therefore, increasing the amount of locally grown food that people in a city eat is a smart way to cut global-warming pollution—and simultaneously increase the number of regional agricultural jobs. A campaign to support local food might specify that half of the food for an urban area come from within two hundred miles. This goal could revitalize farming in rural areas, otherwise threatened by economic despair and suburban sprawl. And this goal would also bring into play opportunities for rooftop gardens, urban agriculture, and the conversion of unused urban land to urban gardens and farms. All the better if the food is not just local, but organic, and doesn't rely on hormones and pesticides (poisons).

When a city makes a zero-waste commitment, it is essentially declaring that nothing bought or used within its boundaries can be thrown away. Everything must be reclaimed or used for another purpose. A city can set interim targets, such as a plan to reduce municipal solid waste by 70 percent by 2020. The higher the targets, the greater the entrepreneurial and work opportunities for local residents in the local reuse and recycling industries. A zero-waste economy reduces waste and increases work. The reason for this is simple. Imagine two factories side by side, one putting things together and the other taking things apart, so the parts can be recombined to make other products. In this model, the city would have twice as many jobs as it would if all of the material the second factory deals with was going into a landfill or an incinerator.

Another positive step for city governments to take is setting targets for the use of an increased percentage of renewable energy. Cities set these targets by creating what are called Renewable Portfolio Standards. By setting big targets for the purchasing of clean energy, cities can stimulate investment in solar, wind, and other renewable power and enjoy the growth in jobs that follows.

Additionally, a commitment to replacing the concrete of city streets and other paved areas with permeable surfaces would address the water-management problems that many cities face. Chicago is ahead of the curve in exploring permeable coatings with its Alleyway program. Innovative gray-water systems could be installed to cycle water from streets, medians, or plantings into city irrigation or fire-hydrant systems. In an increasingly water-stressed world, rainwater should be seen as a resource, not a pollutant. When cities set high targets for renewable energy, local food, waste reduction, and even rainwater management, they help the planet and spur the green economy.

5. Use Urban Planning to Create Urban Villages

Utilizing general plans and zoning laws, we need to reconfigure how urban communities are designed and how they function. In 2030, two-thirds of the world's population will be living in urban centers—up from 50 percent today.[22]

In the past there have been powerful incentives for development to sprawl outward from city centers. But sprawl's effects are horrendous. It breaks up the social fabric of society by necessitating cars for everyone, contributes to global warming and climate disaster, and destroys farmland and green space.

The solution is "transit-oriented development," which means the intentional creation of walkable, self-sustaining, mixed-use urban villages. In urban villages, people have access to housing, shops, recreational spaces, and work—or the public transit to get them to work. Cities must commit to infill development (clustering housing and businesses within city limits, not in the suburbs). Leaders in zoning and urban planning should also make a commitment to superhigh density (expanding upward, not outward).

It is strange but true, the gray and unassuming members of the planning commission of every city hold the fate of the world in their hands.

PAYING FOR IT

We need innovators, and innovators need investment. Fortunately, ideas to put muscle behind this slate of policies and programs are in abundance.

1. Create a Federal Revolving Loan Fund for Energy Efficiency

We know that retrofitting buildings produces a return on investment of between 10 and 20 percent. However, in many cases the lack of up-front capital or financing options makes it difficult or impossible to make these investments. The federal government should set up a revolving loan fund for energy-efficiency projects in residential, commercial, and industrial buildings. The fund could issue low-interest or long-term loans to businesses, hospitals, schools, local governments, and others to green their buildings and lower their energy costs.

These loans could complement other energy-efficiency financing mechanisms and help to lower transaction costs or overcome inertia in cash-strapped cities or institutions. For example, any mayor could save lots of money by retrofitting all the city-owned buildings. And a lot of energy service companies would be willing to front the money for the work and get paid back (plus a profit) with the savings from better energy performance. This practice—called an energy savings performance contract—is becoming more widely used for many large projects. But mayors of struggling urban cities or rural towns probably don't even have the resources to research options and broker a good contract. The revolving loan fund could provide them with that capacity.

A successful revolving loan fund could even generate revenue that could be invested in worker training and national service programs, like the Clean Energy Corps. If it were large enough, it could conceivably fund grants to cash-strapped cities for greening projects.

2. Boost Investment by Backing Loans and Matching State Funds

A powerful way the government can support clean and green innovation is by guaranteeing loans. Loan guarantees make capital cheaper for businesses that are experimenting and trying to scale up new methods of water conservation, energy efficiency, and renewable-energy production as well as new products like energy-saving vehicles. When the federal government guarantees the loans, banks can loan money to these businesses at lower interest rates. This also helps drive private-sector funding to the innovators. And the flourishing new businesses create lots of new jobs.

The federal government has long guaranteed loans for industries ranging from maritime interests to nuclear power. In fact, the Department of Energy recently developed a "clean energy" loan guarantee program. But the majority of the $38.5 billion program being launched in 2008 is targeted at nuclear and fossil-fuel industries. The program needs to be redesigned to support only truly renewable energy.

Here's another inventive idea. States can—and many already do—generate money through a small charge on energy use (e.g., one-tenth of a cent per kilowatt-hour, which amounts to an extra one dollar added to an average residential monthly utility bill). They then pool this money in a public-benefits fund. A number of states use some of their public-benefits fund to finance the costs of retrofitting. Energy savings then can be reinvested in the economy, creating increased growth and tax revenue as well as environmental benefits.

The federal government could provide a dollar-for-dollar match to the money that states spend on energy efficiency. Such a program would vastly speed up the retrofitting process. And that would ultimately mean massive savings on energy bills, lessened reliance on fossil fuels and thus reduced carbon emissions, better public health, and lots of green hard hats all over the country.

3. Catalyze Green Businesses with Green Strings

The key isn't always finding new dollars; it's also reallocating existing funding. State and local governments already provide billions
of dollars in economic-development incentives and subsidies every
year. Greg LeRoy, of Good Jobs First, has proposed that government
should attach, where appropriate and reasonable, "green strings"
to all of these programs.[23] If even a small portion of the recipients
of these subsidies had to meet certain green standards to qualify,
it would have a profound and immediate effect on the overall
"greenness" of local economies. Governments can also attach job
standards to the receipt of subsidies or incentives—similar to the
growing number of community benefit agreements negotiated between community groups and project developers—thereby ensuring that people who most need jobs are able to get them.

FROM A LEADER IN POLLUTION TO
THE LEADER IN SOLUTIONS

Our nation has always prospered when we invested in innovative
leadership in technology: from rural electrification, to new transportation networks like the transcontinental railroad and interstate
highway systems, to public investment in semiconductors and the
telecommunications and Internet revolutions. Bold public leadership providing incentives for scientific inquiry, new technology
deployment, and infrastructure have repeatedly enabled the private
sector to flourish while building a growing middle class. Today,
the "clean-tech" revolution and the transformation of our aging
energy infrastructure are poised to become *the* next great engines
for American innovation, productivity and job growth, and social-
equity gains.

With smart federal and local policies, climate solutions can be a progressive force economically. Building a clean energy economy can generate literally hundreds of billions of dollars of productive new investments on a scale equal to that of the greatest periods of past American economic expansion. And globally, the best contribution that we in the United States can make as world citizens is to roll up our sleeves and get our government on the right side of the carbon-cutting, green revolution.

SEVEN

Buoyancy and Hope

I have nothing to offer but blood, toil, tears, and sweat. We have before us an ordeal of the most grievous kind. . . . You ask, what is our aim? I can answer in one word. It is victory. . . . Victory, however long and hard the road may be, for without victory there is no survival.

> —Winston Churchill,
> Prime Minister of the United Kingdom,
> 1940–45, 1951–55

I PRAY THAT this book will give hope, encouragement, and inspiration to those who are working to move our society along the path toward a green future. I believe we can get there. But I do not want to create any false sense of comfort or security about the outcome. The fact that our survival is a vibrant possibility does not mean that it is inevitable. Far from it.

Even the most hopeful ideas discussed here are based on a fundamentally pessimistic premise: that the children of all species, including our own, are gravely imperiled—unless we completely overhaul our outmoded political and economic systems. Such a transformation would constitute one of the single biggest feats in the history of world politics. As Niccolò Machiavelli put it: "There is nothing more difficult to take in hand, more perilous to conduct, or more uncertain in its success, than to take the lead in the introduction of a new order of things."[1] Even if we had skilled leaders in both major parties who were 100 percent committed to the undertaking, it still would be tough for them to produce change of the necessary scope and scale. And so, in this venture, failure is an option. We could lose this crusade, and in losing—lose everything.

No matter what happens, we will need to brace ourselves for a rough ride. Even if our efforts at ecological salvation are blessed with unprecedented success, things will get worse before they get better—probably much worse. In other words, someday we will probably look back on these tough and turbulent times and see them as the "good old days." We may someday sorely miss the kind of relative ecological, economic, and social stability that we are presently enjoying.[2]

But even if our movement fails to avert disaster, the work of building a national Green Growth Alliance to birth a Green New Deal won't be in vain. The effort to reinvent the system will build up important knowledge and establish invaluable relationships. Even in the most dire, "hard-landing" scenario, we can redeploy that wisdom and those networks to make the best of even the worst situations.

And as for me, I do not believe or accept that the fight for the future has already been lost. We should not let the possibility of eco-apocalypse paralyze us; we should let it motivate and propel us. Whatever our fate, we know one thing: hiding out or holding back won't save us.

Many of the best people in the country and the world have not been heard from yet. Many of the best ideas have not yet surfaced or been taken to scale. As the green wave encompasses more people, it will produce more innovation, inventiveness, and passion than we can possible appreciate or imagine. Just as there are unimaginable bad things on the horizon, there are also unimaginable good things. And I am betting on them.

And let's not forget that most people walking around in a mall or on a college campus are carrying on them better technology than the entire U.S. government had when it put a man on the moon. Each one of us is a walking technological superpower. We can access information and communicate instantly with people around the world. Given the capacities available to us, our wildest dreams and biggest hopes are probably too small.

In the coming crises, the only viable response will be collective action, supported by effective government. That approach will demand a different concept of leadership, even among people who are already focused on saving the world.

My friend Paul Hawken, an eco-entrepreneur, poet, and visionary, writes in his book *Blessed Unrest:* "Healing the wounds of the earth and its people does not require saintliness or a political party, only gumption and persistence. It is not a liberal or conservative activity; it is a sacred act." We need leaders with a comprehensive vision and positive agenda, who pursue the most cutting-edge approaches to education reform, health care, violence prevention, job creation, and eco-friendly economics.

Now is not the time to shrink from the challenge of saving our only home in the universe. Now is not the time to pull into ourselves, retreating into either a survivalist or an escapist mode. To the contrary, this is the time for titans, not turtles. Now is the time to open our arms, expand our horizons, and dream big. Big problems require big solutions. World-historic problems require world-class leadership. To prevail, we will need tens of thousands of heroes at every level of human society.

No one great leader can fix this nest of problems. Al Gore has been the planetary Paul Revere on this issue; he could have sat on his hands after 2000, growing increasingly bitter. Instead, he has used his fame to awaken the world to the threat of a climate catastrophe. If we survive, the entire human family will owe a great deal to him. But no one person can do it alone. We need thousands of Al Gores, thousands of Susan B. Anthonys, Rosa Parkses, Martin Luther Kings, César Chávezes, Franklin Roosevelts, and Eleanor Roosevelts. As always, those stalwart heroes will emerge from the ranks of ordinary people just like me and you. So each and every one of us should stop playing small and license ourselves to become one of the giants of the new century. We will need champions by the truckload.

If we stand for change, we can spark a popular movement with power, influence, magic, and genius. We won't just have the movement we have always wanted. We will have the country we have always wanted—and the world for which our hearts have longed.

Now is the time for us to raise our sights. Now is the time for America to dream again. Even in the midst of new dangers, now is the time for us to unshackle our imaginations. Let us envision meeting our economic and ecological challenges with our heads held high—not buried in our hands.

We can put "solution centers" in every town and neighborhood to train young workers in new technologies and ancient wisdom. We can envision our rural and urban youth creating zero-pollution products to sell. We can imagine formerly incarcerated people moving from jail cells to solar cells—helping to harvest the sun, heal the land, and repair their own souls. We can help local communities join hands—across lines of class and color—to honor the Earth, create new jobs, and reduce community violence.

We can create clear skies over our major port cities. Where idling ships once fouled the air, we can build solar-powered energy stations that let docking sea vessels power up cleanly. And we can send trucks using hybrid engines or cleaner biodiesel blends to take fair-trade goods off those ships without polluting the neighborhood.

We can build eco-industrial parks on land once blighted by prisons. We can pass laws that help transform our dying blue-collar towns, struggling rural regions, and poor neighborhoods into dignified, green-collar meccas. We can help our Rust Belt cities blossom as Silicon Valleys of green capital.

And we need not limit the innovation and industry of America to communities within our own borders. We can cooperate globally to give Africa, Latin America, and other developing regions the means to grow economically, while preserving their natural environments. U.S. entrepreneurs can help vast areas of China and India power up with clean energy. And we can learn from the world.

The best answer to our ecological crisis also responds to our socioeconomic crisis. The surest path to safe streets and peaceful communities is not more police and prisons, but ecologically sound economic development. And that same path can lead us to a new, green economy—one with the power to lift people out of poverty while respecting and repairing the environment.

We can lift the sword of war from over the heads of our sisters and brothers across the globe. We will set this country on the path of partnership with, not domination over, the world community. We can retrieve the Bill of Rights from the garbage bin. We can use our powers to heal the Earth, not pave it. We can deepen our nation's commitment to human rights for people of all races, religions, genders, and birthplaces.

These are our sacred duties. And we will meet them. When we do, the United States will, once again, be the leader of the whole world. But this time, not in war. Not in pollution. Not in incarceration rates.

Instead, we will lead the world in human rights and in social justice. In world-saving technologies and sustainable job creation. We will lead by showing the world how a strong, multiracial nation can unite itself to solve its toughest problems. That's where our new movement has the potential to take us all.

Some will call this unrealistic. They will advise America to keep her dreams small. But that cynicism is the problem, not the solution. A national commitment to green-collar jobs will renew this nation. We can take the unfinished business of America on questions of inclusion and equal opportunity and combine it with the new business of building a green economy—and thereby heal the country on two fronts and redeem the soul of the nation. The odds against achieving this kind of miraculous turnaround may seem daunting, but our forebears faced long odds—and overcome them. We can, too.

So I will close with the words and the example of the British prime minister Winston Churchill. As Adolf Hitler's monstrous shadow fell over the capitals of Europe, the prospects for democracy and human civilization had never looked bleaker. The United States was still refusing to fight. All other allies had fallen. And so Britain stood alone against the terror. Most observers doubted the British could last one week against Hitler's murderous onslaught.

But Churchill dared to position his lonely and isolated island nation as freedom's last barricade. On his first day in office, Churchill assigned himself the mission of blocking the advance of the fearsome Nazi death machine.[3] He announced to the Parliament and the world: "I take up my task in buoyancy and hope. I feel sure that our cause will not be suffered to fail among men. I feel entitled at this juncture, at this time, to claim the aid of all and to say, 'Come then, let us go forward together with our united strength.'"[4] His defiance and determination helped turn the tide of world affairs. And so it was that, against all odds and after great and horrendous suffering, the champions of democracy prevailed.

That generation—the so-called greatest generation—looked out and saw two futures: one with a blood-soaked Hitler ruling the world and another with the fascist threat forever eliminated. They decided to go out and do whatever it took to win that better future for the coming generations.

The following generation—the generation of the civil rights struggle and the women's liberation movement—looked out and saw two futures: one with Jim Crow and misogyny forever dividing our society and another with segregation torn from the pages of our law books and bigotry erased from the hearts of our children. They decided to go out and do whatever it took to win that better future for the coming generations.

Today, we are living in the world won for us by the sacrifices of those generations. It is far from perfect, but it is infinitely better than what might have been.

As a result of their heroism, we live in freer societies, with the liberty to act—or not to act. And now we stand at our own cross-roads, looking out upon two futures: one with rising temperatures, rising oceans, and rising violence on a hot and strip-mined planet and another with expanding organic harvests, growing solar arrays, and deepening global partnerships on a green and thriving Earth. Given those same choices, we know in our hearts what our parents' generation—and our grandparents' generation—would have done for us. Come, then, let us go forward together with our united strength—and win that better future for the generations to come.

Winning Already–
For Better or Worse

W HEN I FIRST proposed this book to Harper One in late summer of 2007, very few people had heard the term "green-collar job." What a difference a year makes.

As we go to press in late summer 2008, the idea already has become a mainstay in U.S. politics. Rarely has an idea exploded into political consciousness so rapidly.

The Democratic Party's top three candidates for the presidential nomination—Senators Hillary Clinton, John Edwards, and Barack Obama—all explicitly called for green-collar jobs and specific programs to create them. Community college boards across the land began offering green-collar job training programs. U.S. mayors from coast to coast began proclaiming their commitment to green-collar job opportunities. Media attention to the concept (and Google hits for the term) mushroomed throughout the year. Today, both Democratic Party nominee Barack Obama and Republican Party nominee John McCain routinely celebrate the jobs that can be created in the clean energy field.

McCain is not alone in hoisting a green flag over the Grand Old Party. Conservative Texas oilman T. Boone Pickens has planted his own green stake in the ground—hundreds of them, in fact. He is installing acres of wind turbines and promoting clean energy as the best path to U.S. energy independence. Christian evangelicals— especially the younger ones—have embraced the idea of "creation care"; they see it as a faith-friendly on-ramp to environmental stewardship and activism. Archconservative Newt Gingrich has written a book called *A Contract with the Earth*.

With universal approval and no visible opposition, perhaps the movement for green-collar jobs and a clean energy future has already prevailed? Perhaps we have already won the fight for the future?

Far from it: the battle has just begun.

The positive development is that the twin issues of jobs and energy prices have emerged as two of the central issues of the 2008 presidential election. This development represents a tremendous change from 2004. At the time, the newly-formed Apollo Alliance was promoting clean energy jobs, but the topic was mostly a side issue. Democratic Party nominee John Kerry rarely mentioned it.

By this election cycle, several factors have changed the equation: Hurricane Katrina, Al Gore's advocacy, the pain of the economic recession and—most decisively —rising energy prices. Together, these circumstances have moved the interrelated challenges of energy, environment, and the economy to ground zero in U.S. politics.

But that same convergence has created opportunities, as well, for the enemies of positive change. In the summer of 2008, they advanced three powerful new slogans, under which they launched a brilliant offensive to divert and derail the green movement. These three slogans are "All of the Above;" "Drill Here, Drill Now, Pay Less;" and "Stop the War on the Poor."

The first is perhaps the most pernicious. The main defenders of the planet-cooking status quo have largely given up spreading confusion about whether global warming is a real problem. They lost that fight. So their new tactic is to spread confusion about the real solutions by deliberately blurring distinctions between themselves and the champions of genuine answers to the problem of climate change.

In fact, under the tempting slogan "All of the Above," they have affirmatively adopted the call for clean energy technology. And yet they have not abandoned any of their dirty energy technologies. Instead, they now argue that America should do whatever it takes to lower energy prices—deploying the safest, cleanest energy solutions and the dirtiest, most dangerous energy solutions, all at the same time. This seemingly innocent slogan lets polluters stuff proposals for oil shale development, tar sand exploitation and nuclear power into energy plans that feature solar panels and wind turbines.

In other words: rather than fight the green wave, the proponents of eco-apocalypse have chosen to join it. They cannot succeed by flying their pirate flag of death. They refuse to show the white flag of surrender. So they have chosen simply to grab a green banner and hoist it alongside their true colors.

In some ways, politicians are taking a page from "green-washing" corporations—the ones that change their ads but neglect to change their wasteful processes or toxic products. Today we are seeing "green-washing" politicians, who put solar panels in their speeches and wind turbines in their commercials, but keep their pro-polluter agendas. They say the right words, but their environmental commitment is no deeper than the green sheen on an oil slick. Call it the rise of the "dirty greens."

At least the second slogan is upfront and direct. GOP strategic mastermind Newt Gingrich has led the charge to open America's coastlines to offshore drilling with this mantra: "Drill Here, Drill Now, Pay Less." He has skillfully used rising fuel prices to stoke public support for climate-destroying measures. Despite the reality that offshore drilling would take a decade to produce even a two-cent drop in gas prices, polls show that his slogan has been very effective.

The third slogan is perhaps the most tragic: "Stop the War on the Poor." Using this motto, a black-led, polluter-supported "coalition" is accusing environmentalists of being "punishers of the poor" for not allowing the drilling that the group alleges would reduce gas prices. The group's debut rally featured African-Americans holding signs saying: "Environmental Groups Don't Feed My Family" and "Food or Fuel? Don't Make Me Choose." The backlash alliance of which I warned in these pages is no longer theory. It has arrived—full force.

So the polluters have proven savvy enough to nod in a green direction, while actually accelerating their climate-destroying agenda. Ironically, those who seek a green future have already won the argument for change. But we have not yet won enough public support, at this stage, to implement the kind of changes we need.

Fortunately, we still have time. The next rounds will be fought over the three P's: price, people, and the planet. The debate will be: What's the best strategy to reduce energy prices? What's the best strategy economically to help people? And (in dead last place, but still more important than ever before) what's right ecologically for the planet, especially for the Earth's climate?

The clean greens must convince the public that a true clean-tech revolution gives the best answer for all three. To succeed, we must shift dramatically in the direction of social uplift environmentalism and eco-populism.

Cash-strapped, economically fearful families are emerging as the swing constituency on climate policy. The only way to draw them into the coalition for real solutions is by delivering fully on the promise of a green economy that provides increased work, wealth, and health for them and their children.

Delivering on that promise is the great work of the new century. The real work is just beginning.

Action Items

APPLY PRESSURE HERE

Check greenforall.org for up-to-date information on currently pending legislation that needs your support. Your e-mails and phone calls to Congress help tremendously in the ongoing battles to acquire full funding for green-collar job programs.

HAS YOUR MAYOR SIGNED THE LOCAL GOVERNMENT GREEN JOBS PLEDGE?

The following pledge was created by Green For All in partnership with the Apollo Alliance, Center for American Progress, and ICLEI–Local Governments for Sustainability.

On June 24, 2008, at the U.S. Conference of Mayors (USCM) annual meeting in Miami, 1,139 mayors from around the country passed a resolution to support this pledge.

AS LOCAL GOVERNMENT LEADERS, WE COMMIT TO:
Focus on green-collar jobs as a central strategy for advancing environmental, economic, and climate protection goals.

Green-collar jobs:

- Provide pathways to prosperity for all workers;
- Offer competitive salaries and lead to a lasting career track, thereby strengthening the U.S. middle class;
- Emphasize community-based investments that cannot be outsourced; and
- Contribute directly to preserving or enhancing environmental quality.

Grow an inclusive sustainable economy that creates green-collar jobs that:

- Strengthen and make further progress on our stated commitment to improving the environment in ways that grow both the green economy and green-collar jobs locally;
- Build on climate and environmental commitments to create market demand for green products, services, and skilled workers and create more prosperous local economies;
- Catalyze green-collar job creation and training by supporting policies that drive public and private investment in an inclusive local green economy; and
- Develop education and job-training programs that improve social equity and provide pathways out of poverty for our residents while strengthening our middle class by equipping workers for high-demand jobs in the green economy.

Execute tangible actions that place a priority on building an inclusive green economy that will:

- Involve our communities in developing and enacting green-collar jobs initiatives;
- Drive accountability and resolve to continuously improve and strengthen our efforts to invest in climate solutions that create economic opportunity and build sustainable communities;
- Provide accessible leadership that is responsive to our communities as we evolve the green economy;
- Use the purchasing power of our local governments to create markets for renewable energy, energy efficiency, and other green industries; and
- Invest new local government resources in programs and initiatives that build an inclusive green economy, while leveraging and aligning existing public resources, and private sources of capital and finance, toward these same goals.

We commit to join together as a movement of local governments across the United States to seize the economic, environmental, and social opportunities offered by building an inclusive green economy of high-quality jobs and a thriving green-collar workforce.

The pledge form can be downloaded at:
www.greenforall.org/files/Green%20Jobs%20Pledge%20Packet
.pdf.

Resource List

NATIONAL GROUPS ADVOCATING FOR GREEN-COLLAR JOBS

1Sky
Community dedicated to aggregating a massive nationwide movement by communicating a positive vision and a coherent set of national policies that rise to the scale of the climate challenge.
www.1sky.org

American Council on Renewable Energy (ACORE)
Council working to bring all forms of renewable energy into the mainstream of America's economy and lifestyle.
www.acore.org

Apollo Alliance
Coalition of business, labor, environmental, and community leaders working to catalyze a clean-energy revolution in America to reduce our nation's dependence on foreign oil, cut the carbon emissions that are destabilizing our climate, and expand opportunities for American businesses and workers.
www.apolloalliance.org

Applied Research Center
Center advancing racial justice through research, advocacy, and journalism.
www.arc.org

Blue Green Alliance
Partnership between the United Steelworkers and Sierra Club to spur dialogue between environmentalists and labor on topics of global warming, clean energy, toxics, and fair trade.
www.bluegreenalliance.org

Center for American Progress
Progressive think tank dedicated to improving the lives of Americans through ideas and action.
www.americanprogress.org

Center for State Innovation
Center that helps governors and other state executives advance and implement innovative, progressive policies that better the lives of the people they serve.
www.stateinnovation.org

Center on Wisconsin Strategy (COWS)
National policy center and field laboratory for high-road economic development—a competitive market economy of shared prosperity, environmental sustainability, and capable democratic government.
www.cows.org

Color of Change
Organization that exists to strengthen black America's political voice. Its goal is to empower members—black Americans and their allies—to make government more responsive to the concerns of black Americans and to bring about positive political and social change for everyone.
www.colorofchange.org

Community Food Security Coalition
Coalition dedicated to building strong, sustainable local and regional food systems that ensure access to affordable, nutritious, and culturally appropriate food by all. It seeks to develop self-reliance among all communities

in obtaining their food and to create a system of growing, manufacturing, processing, making available, and selling food that is regionally based and grounded in the principles of justice, democracy, and sustainability.
www.foodsecurity.org

Energy Action Coalition

Coalition of more than forty organizations from across the United States and Canada, founded and led by youth, to support and strengthen the student and youth clean-energy movement in North America. Its Campus Climate Challenge leverages the power of young people to organize on college campuses and high schools to win 100 percent clean-energy policies at their schools.
www.energyactioncoalition.org

The Engage Network

Network that trains leaders to create self-replicating small groups that both take care of people and change the world at the same time. It is creating small circles, including discussion groups and curricula based upon this book in partnership with Green For All.
www.engagenet.org

Green For All

National advocacy organization working to build an inclusive green economy strong enough to lift people out of poverty. It shapes debate and shares best practices, spurs action in the federal government and the private sector to ensure that the United States has an abundant supply of well-trained "green-collar" workers and entrepreneurs, focusing on those from disadvantaged backgrounds.
www.greenforall.org

Intertribal Council on Utility Policy (Intertribal COUP)

Council involved in policy issues and outreach education to Tribal governments, Tribal Colleges, and indigenous environmental organizations on telecommunications, climate change, energy planning, energy efficiency, and renewable energy development. The policy work includes specific proposals to support renewable energy development and energy efficiency.
www.intertribalcoup.org

Lifestyles of Health and Sustainability (LOHAS)

Group of companies practicing "responsible capitalism" by providing goods and services using economic and environmentally sustainable business practices. An annual conference covers industry trends and how to run a successful LOHAS business.

www.lohas.com/

Local Governments for Sustainability

Association of local governments that provides tools and technical assistance to local governments to set and achieve their climate protection and sustainability goals.

www.iclei-usa.org

Reconnecting America and the Center for Transit-Oriented Development

National nonprofit organization that is working to integrate transportation systems and the communities they serve, with the goal of generating lasting and equitable public and private returns, providing people with more housing and mobility choices, improving economic and environmental efficiency, providing concrete, measurable solutions to reducing greenhouse-gas emissions and reducing dependence on foreign oil.

www.reconnectingamerica.org

Transportation Equity Network

National coalition reforming unjust and unwise transportation and land use policies. It works to win funding for transportation and job-training programs.

www.transportationequity.org

U.S. Green Building Council

Nonprofit dedicated to sustainable building design and construction. It established national green building standards, the LEED standards.

www.usgbc.org

The Workforce Alliance

National coalition of community-based organizations, community colleges, unions, business leaders, and local officials advocating for public policies that invest in the skills of America's workers, so they can better

support their families and help American businesses better compete in today's economy.
www.workforcealliance.org

LOCAL, REGIONAL AND NATIONAL GROUPS ORGANIZ-ING GREEN-COLLAR JOBS TRAINING OPPORTUNITIES

African American Environmentalist Association
National nonprofit that works to clean up neighborhoods by implementing toxics education and energy, water, and clean-air programs. It includes an African American point of view in environmental policy decision making and resolves environmental racism and injustice issues through the application of practical environmental solutions.
www.aaenvironment.com

Alameda County Career Center, East Oakland
California county agency providing free job training in the construction trades and other areas to those who qualify.
www.eastbayworks.com/ebw-resources/Oaklandeast.htm

Appalachian Voices
Regional nonprofit that works with communities across Appalachia to restore the region's forests and tackle the dual problems of mountaintop-removal coal mining and the construction of new coal-fired power plants.
www.appvoices.org

Asian Neighborhood Design (AND)
San Francisco nonprofit offering a free preapprenticeship construction training program. Students are automatically indentured in the carpenters union upon completion of the course and provided with a small stipend and tool kit.
www.andnet.org

Bay Area Construction Sector Intervention Collaborative
Regional nonprofit collaborative of service providers and job-training agencies promoting economic self-sufficiency by increasing access to career-path jobs in the construction industry.
www.turner-oak.com/workforce.cfm

B'more Green
Nonprofit providing disadvantaged Baltimore residents with environmental job training and employment development initiatives in the areas of brownfield remediation and hazardous-materials abatement and containment.
www.civicworks.com/bmghome.html

Border Ecology Project
Regional nonprofit that develops solutions to environmental and health problems in the U.S.-Mexico border and other Latin American regions through collaboration with nongovernmental organizations, academic institutions, private consultants, and government agencies. It adds community input to national and international policy discussions and negotiations.
www.borderecoweb.sdsu.edu/bew/drct_pgs/b/bep.html

Boston Connects, Inc.
Boston nonprofit implementing an array of community and economic development initiatives designed to improve communities in Boston that have experienced chronic divestment over the years.
www.cityofboston.gov/bra/bostonez/index.html

Build It Green
California statewide nonprofit that provides a two-day (sixteen-hour) Certified Green Building Professional Training covering all aspects of green building: energy, water, materials, indoor air quality, and implementing green in a company's operations and marketing.
www.builditgreen.org

Building Opportunities for Self-Sufficiency
Alameda County, California, nonprofit offering free job training for the homeless and formerly homeless focusing on building maintenance, computer, and culinary skills.
www.self-sufficiency.org

Business Alliance for Local Living Economies
(BALLE)
National network that creates, strengthens, and connects local business networks dedicated to building strong local living economies.
www.livingeconomies.org

Center for Environmental Policy and Management at the University of Louisville
University center focusing on three project areas: (1) brownfields/smart-growth research, (2) environmental policy and forecasting, and (3) the EPA Region 4 Southeast Regional Environmental Finance Center.
www.cepm.louisville.edu

Center for Integrated Waste Management, Department of Civil, Structural and Environmental Engineering, State University of New York at Buffalo
University center that promotes the development and application of improved technologies and management methods for (1) more effectively remediating past environmental contamination and promoting redevelopment of formerly contaminated properties, and (2) preventing, reducing, reusing, and recycling industrial and municipal waste streams.
www.ciwm.buffalo.edu

Communities for a Better Environment
California statewide nonprofit doing community organizing in working-class communities of color who are bombarded by pollution from freeways, power plants, oil refineries, seaports, airports, and chemical manufacturers.
www.cbecal.org

DC Greenworks
Washington, D.C., business that provides full-service green-roof design, installation, and consulting. All of its contracts serve to train and employ underserved adults in the skills necessary to meet the growing demand for these new environmental services and technologies.
www.dcgreenworks.org

East Bay Conservation Corps
Nonprofit providing free job training for East Bay youth based on environmental stewardship and community service.
www.ebcc-school.org

Ella Baker Center for Human Rights
A nonprofit strategy and action center, based in Oakland, California, working for justice, opportunity, and peace in urban America. It promotes positive alternatives to violence and incarceration through four cutting-edge campaigns.
www.ellabakercenter.org

Federation of Southern Co-ops, Land Assistance Fund
Southern regional nonprofit operating a rural training and research center. It assists in land retention and development.
www.federationsoutherncoop.com

Food from the Hood
Los Angeles nonprofit fostering business, academic, and life skills for challenged young people. It provides tutoring, college entrance-exam training, mentoring, and business-skills development; it is committed to supporting students in business ventures that are socially responsible, environmentally sound, and neighborhood-friendly.
www.foodfromthehood.com

The Garden Project
San Francisco nonprofit that supports former offenders by providing training in horticulture skills. Participants grow organic vegetables that feed seniors and families in San Francisco.
www.gardenproject.org

Greater Philadelphia Urban Affairs Coalition
Philadelphia nonprofit that unites government, business, neighborhoods, and individual initiatives to improve the quality of life in the region, build wealth in urban communities, and solve emerging issues. It offers extensive workforce training.
www.gpuac.org

Green Communities Online
National nonprofit that has a five-year, $555 million commitment by Enterprise to build 8,500 healthy, efficient homes for low-income people and make environmentally sustainable development the mainstream in the affordable housing industry.
www.greencommunitiesonline.org

Green Worker Cooperatives
Bronx, New York, nonprofit that incubates worker-owned and environmentally friendly cooperatives in the South Bronx.
www.greenworker.coop

Greencorps Chicago
City-administered horticultural and green-industries paid job-training program with wraparound and job placement services.
www.cityofchicago.org/Environment

Grid Alternatives
San Francisco Bay Area nonprofit that trains community volunteers in the theory and practice of solar electric installation and provides them with hands-on experience with solar-installation projects.
www.gridalternatives.org

Groundwork Providence
Providence, Rhode Island, nonprofit that provides educational environmental programs such as the Providence Neighborhood Planting Program, Spring and Fall Clean-Ups, Environmental Education Clubs, Brownfields Job Training Program, and Summer Green Teams.
www.groundworkprovidence.org

Groundwork USA
East Coast regional nonprofit network of independent, not-for-profit environmental businesses that work with communities to improve their environment, economy, and quality of life through practical local projects.
www.groundworkusa.net

Growing Home
Chicago nonprofit that provides job training and employment opportunities for homeless and low-income people within the context of an organic agriculture business.
www.growinghomeinc.org

Houston Community College
Texas community college offering associate degrees, certificates, workforce training, and lifelong learning opportunities.
www.hccs.edu

Impact Services Corporation
Philadelphia corporation enabling people in need to attain the hope, motivation, and skills necessary to reach their fullest potential and achieve personal and family self-sufficiency.
www.pacdc.org/cgi-bin/board.cgi?ISC

Isles: Fostering Self-Reliance
Trenton, New Jersey, nonprofit operating activities that recognize the interdependence of physical, economic, health, and social development strategies to address the problems of distressed communities, with the mission of fostering more self-reliant families in healthy, sustainable communities.
www.isles.org

LA City College, CalWORKs program
Community college that partners with the Department of Public Social Services (DPSS) to provide education and successful transition from welfare to work.
www.lacitycollege.edu

Lao Family Community Development, Inc.
California nonprofit that provides free job training in construction trades, health care, building maintenance, and other areas, with a focus on South East Asian refugee and immigrant communities.
www.laofamilynet.org

Los Angeles Conservation Corps
LA nonprofit that provides at-risk young adults with job training, education, and work-skills training with an emphasis on environmental and service projects that benefit the community. It offers a "clean and green" program.
www.lacorps.org

Miami-Dade Community College
Community college providing accessible, affordable, high-quality education, in partnership with the dynamic, multicultural community.
www.mdc.edu

Milwaukee Community Service Corps
Milwaukee nonprofit that provides participants with the opportunity to learn new skills, earn a wage, serve their community, earn a high-school equivalency diploma, and prepare themselves for post-corps college or trade apprenticeships. In the field, corps members renovate vacant homes, plant community gardens, landscape vacant lots, remove graffiti, intern in youth-service agencies, perform lead outreach and reduction activities, distribute food for food pantries, engage in recycling projects, and construct new playgrounds.
www.milwaukeecommunityservicecorps.org

Mo' Better Food
Oakland, California, nonprofit promoting activities that bring generations together and encourage healthy economic development by increasing community leadership, job training, entrepreneurship, community pride, and community ownership.
www.mobetterfood.com

Montana Tech of the University of Montana
University program selected by the EPA for a Brownfields Job Training and Development Demonstration Pilot, in partnership with Crow Nation. The job training pilot will focus on residents of the Crow Indian Reservation (7,900 tribal members).
www.mtech.edu

Mothers on the Move

Bronx, New York, nonprofit that operates community campaigns for decent housing, traffic safety, and environmental justice, including renovated buildings, redeveloped and new parks, and safer streets.
www.mothersonthemove.org

Native Movement

Southwest regional nonprofit that supports projects and campaigns led by youth that are focused on peace, sustainability, youth leadership development, healing, community building, and movement building.
www.nativemovement.org/southwest/

New Jersey Youth Corps

Government agency providing full-time instructional and community service programs for school dropouts, with the completion of a high-school curriculum and employment as the ultimate goals for each student. Students receive academic instruction and perform community service work. A one-month orientation that includes academic and interest/aptitude assessment is followed by placement in community service work crew projects and continuation in basic skills classes.
www.ed.gov/pubs/EPTW/eptw14/eptw14c.html

New York City Environmental Justice Alliance

Nonprofit that supports the work of member groups based in low-income communities throughout New York City. It coordinates advocacy efforts, facilitates networking, and helps to replicate successful projects and activities.
www.nyceja.org

Oakland Private Industry Council

Oakland, California, nonprofit that helps the community maintain no-fee career centers and workforce-development programs. Its goal is to aid the economy by helping job seekers prepare for work, then providing employers with highly trained employees.
www.oaklandpic.org

Office of Applied Innovations

Chicago nonprofit that enhances the capacity of underserved individuals and their communities to contribute significantly to social-environmental

equity, equal access to educational and employment opportunities, and economic self-sufficiency and self-determination.
www.oaiinc.org

Oregon Tradeswomen, Inc.
Regional nonprofit that promotes success for women in the trades through education, leadership, and mentorship.
www.tradeswomen.net

Pacific Energy Center
Center, run by Pacific Gas and Electric Company Corporation, that provides education in energy conservation and green building techniques, systems, and materials.
www.pge.com/pec/

People's Grocery
Oakland, California, nonprofit offering free job training in building a local food system and improving the health and economy of the community.
www.peoplesgrocery.org

Pivotal Point Youth Services
Oakland, California, nonprofit that provides free intensive employment training, vocational skills development, entrepreneurship training, case management, and other comprehensive supportive services for youth ages sixteen to twenty-four.
www.ppys.org

Regional Technical Training Center
San Francisco Bay Area nonprofit providing practical training, resumé and interviewing skills assistance, and job placement.
www.rttc.us

Rising Sun Energy Center
Berkeley, California, nonprofit that provides a demonstration site and education center for renewable energy and conservation techniques.
www.risingsunenergy.org

Riverside New Visions Program
Community college providing eligible welfare recipients the opportunity to attend Riverside Community College in order to receive training in basic skills (computer literacy, English, and math) and enroll in an occupational mini-program. The goal is to help students climb the "career ladder" to higher-paying and more satisfying jobs.
www.rcc.edu

Second Chance
Non-profit working with local and regional architects, builders, and contractors to find old buildings entering the demolition phase and rescue all reusable elements in the Baltimore, Philadelphia, and Washington, D.C., areas. It offers low-income residents training in a wide variety of skill sets ranging from carpentry to craftsmanship.
www.secondchanceinc.org

Solar Richmond
Richmond, California, nonprofit promoting the use of solar power and energy efficiency in order to bring the economic benefits of the green economy to the community. It serves the underemployed by educating a green-collar workforce and opening doors to employment.
www.solarrichmond.org

Southwest Network for Environmental and Economic Justice
Regional nonprofit that strengthens the work of local organizations and empowers communities and workers to affect policy on environmental and economic justice issues as these impact people of color in the southwestern United States and along the border region of Mexico.
www.sneej.org

St. Louis Community College
Community college focusing on residents of economically depressed communities in St. Louis, Missouri, and East St. Louis, Illinois. It furthers brownfields-related redevelopment activities spurred by EPA assessment and revolving loan fund pilots along with recently initiated efforts by the city to address lead and asbestos problems.
www.stlcc.edu

St. Nicholas Neighborhood Preservation Corps.
Brooklyn, New York, nonprofit that spearheads revitalization and sustainability of the multiethnic community.
www.stnicksnpc.org

STRIVE: Boston Employment Service
Boston nonprofit that removes barriers to employment including lack of money, offering programs at no cost to clients. Its core program trains participants within four weeks and gets them into paid employment quickly, with two years of follow-up support.
www.bostonstrive.org

STRIVE: East Harlem Employment Service
Harlem, New York, nonprofit that removes barriers to employment and offers free job-readiness training.
www.strivenewyork.org

Sustainable Economic Enterprises of Los Angeles
Nonprofit that promotes self-sustaining community and economic development activities within the city of Los Angeles, including sustainable food systems, social and cultural programs, and economic revitalization projects.
www.see-la.org

Sustainable South Bronx
Nonprofit that addresses land-use, energy, transportation, water, and waste policy and education in order to advance the environmental and economic rebirth of the South Bronx and to inspire solutions in areas like it across the nation and around the world.
www.ssbx.org

Texas Engineering Extension Service
University service that provides, through contracts and agreements with governments and overseas companies, unique specialized training and technical assistance to workers worldwide, ranging from the smallest volunteer fire departments to some of the largest companies in the world.
www.teex.com

Tradeswomen Inc. (TWI)
National nonprofit that targets outreach, supportive services, mentoring and networking for women interested in the construction trades.
www.tradeswomen.org

Turtle Mountain Community College
An autonomous Indian-controlled community college on the Turtle Mountain Chippewa Reservation focusing on general studies, undergraduate education, vocational education, direct scholarly research, and continuous improvement of student learning.
www.turtle-mountain.cc.nd.us/

Urban Habitat
Alameda County, California, regional nonprofit that builds bridges between environmentalists, social justice advocates, government leaders, and the business community. Its work has helped to broaden and frame the agenda on toxic pollution, transportation, tax and fiscal reform, brownfields, and the nexus between inner-city disinvestments and urban sprawl.
www.urbanhabitat.org

West Virginia University Research Corporation
Nonprofit providing evaluation, development, patenting, management, and marketing services for inventions of the faculty, staff, and students of the university. The corporation also serves as the fiscal agent for sponsored programs on behalf of the university.
www.research.wvu.edu/wvu_research_corporation

The Workplace, Inc.
Southwestern Connecticut regional nonprofit providing a seamless, coordinated system of education, training, and employment that is easily accessible and that meets the needs both of employers and of persons who face barriers to good employment. It collaborates with business, education, government, and community agencies that include economic development, employment and training, and human services.
www.workplace.org

Young Community Developers, Inc.
San Francisco nonprofit that prepares Bayview–Hunters Point and San Francisco residents, particularly those with barriers to employment, for current and future workforce needs.
www.ycdjobs.org

The Youth Employment Partnership, Inc.
Nonprofit providing employment training to Oakland, California, youth.
www.yep.org

RENEWABLE ENERGY TECHNOLOGY, PRODUCTS, AND SERVICES

Austin Energy
Blue Sun Biodiesel
Bonneville Environmental
   Foundation
California Cars Initiative
Cape Wind Associates
Clean Air Now
Clean Edge
Clean Energy Group
Community Energy, Inc.
Community Fuels
Conergy, Inc.
Cooperative Community Energy
   Corporation
Daystar Technologies
East Haven Wind Farm
EcoLogical Solutions
Energy Innovations/Idea Labs
Environ Corporation
Environmental Energy Solutions
Global Resource Options, Inc.
Hawaii PV Coalition
HyGen Industries
McKenzie Bay International
Native Energy, LLC

NativeWind
Northern Power Systems
NRG Systems
Olympia Green Fuels
OurEnergy
Pacific Ethanol
Pioneer Valley Photovoltaics
PPM Energy
Pro Vision Technologies, Inc.
PV Powered
Renewable Energy Access
Sharp Solar
Shepherd Advisors
Solectria Renewables
Sterling Planet, Inc.
Sunlink, LLC
3 Phases Energy Services
United Bio Lube, Inc.
US Renewables Group
Wilson Turbo Power, Inc.

Energy Efficiency

Burlington Electric Department
Conservation Services Group

Engage Networks, Inc.
Johnson Controls
Kinsley Power Systems
Lightly Treading, Energy & Design
McKinstry
Vermont Energy Investment
    Corporation
Virent Energy Systems
Washington Electric Cooperative

Green Buildings, Infrastructure

All American Home Center
Blue Wave Strategies
Center for Smart Energy

CTO, NatureWorks (formerly
    Cargill-Dow)
Duce Construction Corporation
Ervin & Company
High Performance Building Tech-
    nology Team
Mazria Architects
Michigan Manufacturing Technol-
    ogy Center
NYC Transit
Quantec, LLC
Schultz Development Group, LLC
William Maclay Architects &
    Planners
William McDonough Partners

Notes

INTRODUCTION: REALITY CHECK

1. In July 2007, the National Petroleum Council released a report, entitled *Facing the Hard Truths about Energy,* that addressed the future scarcity of fossil fuels: "It's a hard truth that the global supply of oil and natural gas from the conventional sources relied upon historically is unlikely to meet projected 50 to 60 percent growth in demand over the next 25 years."

2. Russell Gold and Ann Davis, "Oil Officials See Limit Looming on Production," *Wall Street Journal,* November 19, 2007, http://online.wsj.com/article/SB119543677899797558.html.

3. *Crude Oil: The Supply Outlook,* an October 2007 report by the Energy Watch Group, conducts a meta-analysis of oil industry papers to arrive at the number of proven remaining reserves. The conclusion: peak oil has arrived. http://www.energywatchgroup.org/fileadmin/global/pdf/EWG_Oilreport_10-2007.pdf.

4. More information about the extraction of bituminous sands, better known as tar or oil sands, can be found on www.treehugger.com at http://www.treehugger.com/files/2006/01/alberta_tar_san.php. Oil-shale drilling in parts of Colorado, Utah, and Wyoming will drain scarce water resources, threaten habitats, and increase air pollution, according to a June 2007 report by the Natural Resources Defense Council (NRDC), *Driving It Home: Choosing the Right Path for Fueling North America's Transportation Future,* http://www.nrdc.org/energy/drivingithome.pdf.

5. Defenders of Wildlife estimates the economic impact of offshore drilling in Alaska's Bristol Bay, based on disruption of the local sustainable commercial fishing industry and related tourism, http://www.defenders.org/newsroom/press_releases_folder/2008/04_08_2008_offshore_drilling_could_destroy_bristol_bay_fisheries.php.

6. Liquid coal results in double the carbon dioxide emissions: first during production, then again from the tailpipe, according to the NRDC report *Driving It Home*, http://www.nrdc.org/energy/drivingithome.pdf.

7. Intergovernmental Panel on Climate Change (IPCC), *Climate Change 2007: Synthesis Report*, November 2007, http://www.ipcc.ch/pdf/assessment-report/ar4/syr/ar4_syr_spm.pdf.

8. Speech by Susan Hockfield, President of MIT, at the American Association for the Advancement of Science (AAAS) annual conference, http://web.mit.edu/hockfield/speeches/2008-aaas.html.

9. American Solar Energy Society, "Renewable Energy and Energy Efficiency: Economic Drivers for the 21st Century," 2007, http://www.ases.org/ASES-Jobs Report-Final.pdf.

10. Daniel B. Wood and Mark Clayton, "California Takes Lead in Global-Warming Fight," *Christian Science Monitor*, September 1, 2006, http://www.csmonitor.com/2006/0901/p01s01-usgn.html.

11. *Biofuels: At What Cost?* an October 2006 report by the Global Subsidies Initiative and the International Institute for Sustainable Development (IISD), reviews the many types of incentives in place to support the ethanol and biodiesel industry. http://www.globalsubsidies.org/files/aseets/pdf/Brochure_-_US_Report.pdf. For example, a $71 million, 20-million-gallon-per-year ethanol plant under construction in Ohio lined up the following sources of public support:
   a $500,000 United States Department of Agriculture grant;
   $600,000 in Appalachian Regional Commission grants;
   $40,000 in training funds from the Ohio Department of Development;
   $400,000 in 629 Roadwork Development funds from ODOD;
   a $7,000,000 Ohio Water Development Authority loan;
   a $600,000 Rural Pioneer loan; and
   $36,261,024 in Ohio Air Quality Development Authority Revenue Bonds.

12. In 2006, over 14 percent of corn grown in the United States went into ethanol production. Jerry Taylor and Peter Van Doren, "Ethanol Makes Gasoline Costlier, Dirtier," *Chicago Sun-Times*, January 27, 2007, http://www.cato.org/pub_display.php?pub_id=7308.

13. Depending on demand, the world's supply of uranium will last only 30–60 more years, making nuclear a nonrenewable energy source, http://timeforchange.org/pros-and-cons-of-nuclear-power-and-sustainability.

14. The idea is to recapture the carbon dioxide produced by burning fossil fuels by photosynthesis: growing algae on the exhaust gas. "The result could then be turned into biodiesel (since many species of algae store their food reserves as oil), or even simply dried and fed back into the power station," according to a July 3, 2007 Economist.com article, "Old Clean Coal," http://www.economist.com/science/tq/displaystory.cfm?story_id=9431233.

15. David Adam, "Plan to Bury CO_2," *Guardian*, Friday, September 5, 2003, http://www.guardian.co.uk/science/2003/sep/05/sciencenews.science.

16. R. Margolis, J. Zuboy, and the National Renewable Energy Laboratory, *Nontechnical Barriers to Solar Energy Use: Review of Recent Literature*, September 2006, http://www.nrel.gov/docs/fy07osti/40116.pdf.

17. David Bielo, "Combating Climate Change: Building Better, Wasting Less," *Scientific American,* May 18, 2007, http://www.sciam.com/article.cfm?id=combating-climate-change-building-better-wasting-less.

18. Thomas L. Friedman, *Hot, Flat, and Crowded: Why We Need a Green Revolution—and How It Can Renew America* (New York: Farrar, Straus and Giroux, 2008).

19. President Jimmy Carter said: "In little more than two decades we've gone from a position of energy independence to one in which almost half the oil we use comes from foreign countries, at prices that are going through the roof. Our excessive dependence on OPEC has already taken a tremendous toll on our economy and our people. This is the direct cause of the long lines, which have made millions of you spend aggravating hours waiting for gasoline. It's a cause of the increased inflation and unemployment that we now face. This intolerable dependence on foreign oil threatens our economic independence and the very security of our nation. . . . To give us energy security, I am asking for the most massive peacetime commitment of funds and resources in our nation's history to develop America's own alternative sources of fuel. . . . These efforts will cost money, a lot of money, and that is why Congress must enact the windfall profits tax without delay. It will be money well spent. Unlike the billions of dollars that we ship to foreign countries to pay for foreign oil, these funds will be paid by Americans, to Americans. These will go to fight, not to increase, inflation and unemployment." From the speech "Energy and the National Goals: A Crisis of Confidence," delivered July 15, 1979, http://www.americanrhetoric.com/speeches/jimmycartercrisisofconfidence.htm.

20. "Congress enacted the Crude Oil Windfall Profit Tax Act in 1980 in response to the excessive windfall profits that oil producers were earning following the deregulation of oil prices. The Act imposed a windfall profit tax on domestically produced crude oil that ranged from 30 to 70 percent of the producer's windfall profit. This act provided a tax credit of $3 per barrel of tar sands oil-equivalent to producers of alternative energy sources. Congress intended to use a substantial portion of the revenues from the windfall profit tax of crude oil to finance the tax credit for alternative fuels. The Omnibus Trade and Competitiveness Act of 1988 repealed the Crude Oil Windfall Profit Tax Act." Robyn Kenney, "Crude Oil Windfall Profit Tax Act of 1980, United States," *Encyclopedia of Earth,* http://www.eoearth.org/article/Crude_Oil_Windfall_Profit_Tax_Act_of_1980,_United_States.

CHAPTER 1: THE DUAL CRISIS

1. Larry Bradshaw and Lorrie Beth Slonsky, "Hurricane Katrina—Our Experiences," September 1, 2005, http://www.emsnetwork.org/cgi-bin/artman/exec/view.cgi?archive=56&num=18427. Although Bradshaw and Slonsky were not New Orleans residents, their story highlighted the compound system failures more comprehensively than any other first-person account I could find.

The fierce Mrs. Phyllis Montana Leblanc, featured in the documentary film *When the Levees Broke* by Spike Lee, composed a poem that better conveys the trauma of a N'awlins family divided by the disaster:

Not just the levees broke—
the spirit broke, my spirit broke
the families broke apart—
I want my momma back,
I want my sister back,
I want my nephew back.
The auction block broke
from so many African American bodies.
The sense of direction was broken
because of the darkness.
There was light from time to time but then?
They broke away and left us.
My being together broke
when I fell apart
The smell broke away from my skin
when I came out of the waters,
the waters that came and stood,
still, with the bodies of my people.
The dogs, shit, piss, rats, snakes, "unheard of" alligators
The broken smiles, the broken minds, broken lives.
And you know something?
Out of all of this brokenness
I have begun to mend
with God, and my deep, deep commitment
to the infinite strength, to never give up.
I am mending
I am coming back
God willing, for a long, long time.
So when you see the waters—
when you see the levees breaking
know what they really broke along with them.

2. Ross Gelbspan, "Hurricane Katrina's Real Name," *International Herald Tribune*, August 31, 2005, http://www.iht.com/articles/2005/08/30/opinion/edgelbspan .php.

3. Emmanuel Saez with Thomas Piketty, "Income Inequality in the United States, 1913–2002," Oxford University Press, 2007, http://www.elsa.berkeley.edu/~saez/piketty-saezOUP04US.pdf.

4. Economic Policy Institute (EPI), *The State of Working America 2006/2007,* Table 5.1, http://www.stateofworkingamerica.org/tabfig/05/SWA06_Tab5.1.jpg.

5. United for a Fair Economy, *Executive Excess 2006,* http://www.faireconomy.org/press/2006/ee06_ceos_pocket_the_spoils_preview.html.

6. Kevin Danaher et al., *Building the Green Economy* (Sausalito, CA: PoliPoint Press, 2007), p. 4.

7. U.S. Census Bureau, *Income, Poverty and Health Insurance Coverage in the United States: 2006,* http://www.census.gov/prod/2007pubs/p60-233.pdf.

8. Economic Policy Institute (EPI), Briefing Paper #171 "Trade Deficits and Manufacturing Job Loss," March 14, 2006, http://www.epi.org/content.cfm/bp171.

9. U.S. Census Bureau, *Health Insurance Estimates from the U.S. Census Bureau: Background for a New Historical Series*, June 2007, http://www.census.gov/hhes/www/hlthins/usernote/revhlth_paper.pdf.

10. Jeanne Sahadi, "President Signs Bankruptcy Bill," www.cnnmoney.com, April 20, 2005, http://money.cnn.com/2005/04/20/pf/bankruptcy_bill.

11. Jonathan Weil, Bloomberg.com, June 18, 2008, http://www.bloomberg.com/apps/news?pid=20601039&refer=columnist_weil&sid=a70JZmfcakF0. In the Bear Stearns bailout, the Federal Reserve is lending $29 billion to a Delaware limited-liability company that will hold a portfolio of illiquid Bear Stearns assets. JPMorgan Chase, which completed its purchase of Bear Stearns this month, will lend the Delaware entity $1 billion and absorb the first $1 billion of any losses. The Fed is on the hook for the rest.

12. U.S. Census Bureau, *Income, Poverty and Health Insurance Coverage in the United States*.

13. U.S. Census Bureau, *Income, Poverty and Health Insurance Coverage in the United States*.

14. Meizhu Lui et al., *The Color of Wealth* (New York: New Press, 2006), p. 34.

15. U.S. Census Bureau, *Educational Attainment in the United States: 2007*, http://www.census.gov/population/www/socdemo/education/cps2007.html.

16. U.S. Census Bureau, *Income, Poverty and Health Insurance Coverage in the United States*.

17. American Civil Liberties Union (ACLU), *Race & Ethnicity in America: Turning a Blind Eye to Injustice*, December 2007, http://www.aclu.org/pdfs/humanrights/cerd_full_report.pdf.

18. Federation for American Immigration Reform, "How Many Illegal Aliens?" http://www.fairus.org/site/PageServer?pagename=iic_immigrationissuecentersb8ca.

19. Applied Research Center and Northwest Federation of Community Organizations, Closing the Gap: Solutions to Race-Based Health Disparities, June 2005, www.thepraxisproject.org/tools/ClosingGap.pdf.

20. Life expectancy statistics from a presentation by Dean Robinson, University of Massachusetts Amherst, at a symposium entitled *Challenges of Black Economic Development: Discrimination and Access Issues*, March 23, 2005, http://www.5clir.org/SlaveryTranscripts/Session%204ABCD.htm.

21. Drug Policy Alliance Network, http://www.drugpolicy.org/communities/race/.

22. Pew Charitable Trust, *One in 100: Behind Bars in America 2008*, http://www.pewcenteronthestates.org/report_detail.aspx?id=35904.

23. A 2008 report by the National Priorities Project based on Defense Department data linked recruiting data to zip codes and median incomes and found that low- and middle-income families are supplying far more Army recruits than families with incomes greater than $60,000 a year. http://www.nationalpriorities.org/militaryrecruiting2007.

24. Intergovernmental Panel on Climate Change (IPCC), *Climate Change 2007: Synthesis Report*, November 2007, http://www.ipcc.ch/pdf/assessment-report/ar4/syr/ar4_syr_spm.pdf.

25. IPCC, *Climate Change 2007.*

26. IPCC, *Climate Change 2007.*

27. Alex Kirby, "Water Scarcity: A Looming Crisis?" BBC News Online, October 19, 2004, http://news.bbc.co.uk/1/hi/sci/tech/3747724.stm.

28. IPCC, *Climate Change 2007.*

29. IPCC, *Climate Change 2007.*

30. IPCC, *Climate Change 2007.*

31. Patricia Reaney, "Climate Change Raises Risk of Hunger," *Reuters,* September 5, 2005.

32. IPCC, *Climate Change 2007.*

33. IPCC, *Climate Change 2007.*

34. International Federation of Red Cross (IFRC), *World Disasters Report 1999* (Geneva: IFRC, 1999).

CHAPTER 2: THE FOURTH QUADRANT

1. M. Kat Anderson, *Tending the World: Native American Knowledge and the Management of California's Native Resources* (Berkeley and Los Angeles: University of California Press, 2005), p. 56.

2. Thom Hartmann, *The Last Hours of Ancient Sunlight* (New York: Three Rivers Press, 2004), p. 158.

3. Anderson, *Tending the World,* p. 64.

4. John Bellamy Foster, *The Vulnerable Planet: A Short Economic History of the Environment* (New York: Monthly Review Press, 1994).

5. William Roscoe Thayer, *Theodore Roosevelt: An Intimate Biography* (Boston: Houghton Mifflin, 1919), p. 20. http://www.bartleby.com/170.

6. Theodore Roosevelt, *An Autobiography* (New York: Macmillan, 1913), p. 17.

7. Roosevelt, *Autobiography,* p. 430.

8. Roosevelt, *Autobiography,* p. 418.

9. Forest History Society, www.foresthistory.org, http://www.foresthistory.org/research/usfscoll/people/Pinchot/Pinchot.html.

10. Gifford Pinchot, *The Fight for Conservation* (New York: Doubleday, Page, 1910), p. 42.

11. Sierra Club, John Muir Exhibit, www.sierraclub.org, http://www.sierraclub.org/john_muir_exhibit.

12. Michael B. Smith, "The Value of a Tree: Public Debates of John Muir and Gifford Pinchot," *The Historian* 60, no. 4, (June 1998).

13. John Muir, *My First Summer in the Sierra* (Boston: Houghton Mifflin, 1911), p. 20.

14. Roosevelt, *Autobiography,* p. 322.

15. Library of Congress Web site, "The Evolution of the Conservation Movement," http://memory.loc.gov/ammem/amrvhtml/conshome.html.

16. Roosevelt, *Autobiography,* p. 447.

17. Kelly Duane, *Monumental* (Loteria Films, 2005).

18. David Brower, *Let the Mountains Talk, Let the Rivers Run* (New York: Harper-Collins, 1995), p. 9.

19. The Wilderness Society, www.wilderness.org, http://www.wilderness.org/Our Issues/Wilderness/act.cfm.

20. Carolyn Merchant, "Shades of Darkness: Race and Environmental History," *Environmental History* 8, no. 3 (July 2003), http://www.historycooperative.org/journals/eh/8.3/merchant.html.

21. Linda Lear, *Rachel Carson: Witness for Nature* (New York: Holt, 1997), pp. 60–72.

22. Rachel Carson, *Silent Spring* (Boston: Houghton Mifflin, 1962), p. 7.

23. Lear, *Rachel Carson*, pp. 414–30.

24. Ohio History Central, www.ohiohistorycentral.org, http://www.ohiohistorycentral.org/entry.php?rec=1642.

25. Jack Lewis, "The Birth of the EPA," *EPA Journal* (November 1985), http://www.epa.gov/history/topics/epa/15c.htm.

26. Population Connection, www.zpg.org, http://www.zpg.org/media/upload/1219thirtyyears.pdf.

27. Environmental Protection Agency, www.epa.gov, http://www.epa.gov/superfund/about.htm.

28. United Church of Christ, www.ucc.org, http://www.ucc.org/about-us/archives/pdfs/toxwrace87.pdf.

29. Federation for American Immigration Reform, www.fairus.org, www.fairus.org/site/PageServer?pagename=about_about4819.

30. *Special Issue on Environmental Equity, National Law Journal*, September 1992.

31. Known as the father of the environmental justice movement, Robert Bullard is a professor of sociology and the author of twelve books, the first of which, *Dumping in Dixie*, came out in 1990, excerpted here: "Unlike their white counterparts, black communities do not have a long history of dealing with environmental problems. Blacks were involved in civil rights activities during the height of the environmental movement, roughly during the late 1960s and early 1970s. Many social justice activists saw the environmental movement as a smoke screen to divert attention and resources away from the important issue of the day—white racism. On the other hand, the key environmental issues of this period (e.g., wildlife and wilderness preservation, energy and resource conservation, and regulation of industrial polluters) were not high priority items on the civil rights agenda.

"Social justice, political empowerment, equal education, fair employment practices, and open housing were major goals of social justice advocates. It was one thing to talk about "saving trees" and a whole different story when one talked about "saving low-income housing" for the poor. As a course of action, black communities usually sided with those who took an active role on the housing issue. Because eviction and displacement are fairly common in black communities (particularly for inner-city residents), decent and affordable housing became a more salient issue than the traditional environmental issues. Similarly, unemployment and poverty were more pressing social problems for African Americans than any of the issues voiced by middleclass environmentalists.

"In their desperate attempt to improve the economic conditions of their constituents, many civil rights advocates, business leaders, and political officials directed their energies toward bringing jobs to their communities by relaxing enforcement of pollution standards and environmental regulations and sometimes looking the other way when violations were discovered. In many instances, the creation of jobs resulted in health risks to workers and residents of the surrounding communities."

32. Peggy Sheppard founded West Harlem Environmental Action, New York's first environmental justice organization; she was the first female chair of the National Environmental Justice Advisory Council (NEJAC) of the U.S. Environmental Protection Agency. New Orleans resident Dr. Beverly Wright works on behalf of communities in Louisiana's "Cancer Alley"; she heads up the Deep South Center for Environmental Justice at Dillard University.

33. Activist and writer Winona LaDuke (Anishinaabe) has twice been the vice-presidential candidate on the Green Party ticket. Tom B. K. Goldtooth (Dine' and Mdewakanton Dakota) is the national director of the Indigenous Environmental Network, at Bemidji, Minnesota; as he says, "Change will occur when the white men realize their testicles are shrinking—then money will flow like water to the environmental movement." Former chief of the Neetsaii Gwich'in, from Arctic Village in northeastern Alaska, Evon Peter has worked in the United Nations and Arctic Council forum representing indigenous and environmental interests.

34. Richard Moore was one of the organizers of the First National People of Color Environmental Justice Summit in 1991. He helped launch the first successful campaign in New Mexico to clean contaminated groundwater. Today he is he executive director of the Southwest Network for Environmental and Economic Justice. A former migrant farmworker and a garment worker, Alicia Marentes has been an advocate for farmworkers for over thirty years, particularly along the U.S.-Mexico border. In 1997 she was awarded the Letelier-Moffitt National Human Rights Award.

35. Peggy Saika and Pamela Chiang cofounded the Asian Pacific Environmental Network (APEN), an environmental justice organization that builds grassroots leadership in immigrant Asian communities. Vivian Chang is the current executive director of APEN.

36. "On the Road from Environmental Racism to Environmental Justice," *Villanova Environmental Law Journal* 5, no. 2 (1994).

37. Julian Agyeman, *Sustainable Communities and the Challenge of Environmental Justice* (New York: New York University Press, 2005), p. 19.

38. Agyeman, *Sustainable Communities*, p. 36.

39. Interview by Amanda Griscom Little of Majora Carter for www.grist.org, September 28, 2006, http://www.grist.org/news/maindish/2006/09/28/m_carter/index .html.

40. LOHAS Journal, www.lohas.com, http://www.lohas.com/journal/article_archives .html.

CHAPTER 3: ECO-EQUITY

1. President Ronald Reagan, Inaugural Address, January 20, 1981, http://www .reaganlibrary.com/reagan/speeches/first.asp.

2. President Bill Clinton, State of the Union Address 1996, http://clinton4.nara.gov/ WH/New/other/sotu.html.

3. Theophilus Eugene "Bull" Connor was the Public Safety Commissioner of Birmingham, Alabama, in the 1960s. A Klansman and staunch advocate of racial segregation, he appeared on national television spewing anti-integration rhetoric and using attack dogs and fire hoses against (anti-segregation) protestors. A brief video clip of his blather can be viewed at http://www.pbs.org/wgbh/amex/eyesontheprize/story/07_c.html.

4. National Energy Information Center (NEIC), www.eia.doe.gov, http://www.eia.doe.gov/oiaf/1605/ggccebro/chapter1.html.

5. Roy Walmsley, "World Prison Population List, 7th edition," International Centre for Prison Studies, School of Law, King's College London, 2007, http://nicic.org/Library/022140.

CHAPTER 4: THE GREEN NEW DEAL

1. Arthur M. Schlesinger, Jr., *The Coming of the New Deal* (Boston: Houghton Mifflin, 2003), pp. 6–8.

2. Member Survey, Women's Business Enterprise National Council, March 20, 2008, www.wbenc.org, http://www.wbenc.org/PressRoom/News/2008_survey_final.aspx?AspxAutoDetectCookieSupport=1.

3. Step It Up, www.stepitup2007.org; Focus the Nation, www.focusthenation.org; Energy Action Coalition, www.energyactioncoalition.org.

4. The League of Young Voters, www.theleague.com; Hip Hop Caucus, www.hiphopcaucus.org; Environmental Justice and Climate Change Initiative, www.ecc.org; Young People For, www.youngpeoplefor.org.

5. Omar Freilla founded Green Worker Cooperatives in the South Bronx, an incubator for cooperatively run green-collar ventures. In 2007 he won the Jane Jacobs Medal for New Ideas and Activism, awarded by the Rockefeller Foundation.

6. David R. Baker, "Economists Weigh Prop. 87 Arguments," *San Francisco Chronicle*, October 15, 2006, http://www.sfgate.com/cgi-bin/article.cgi?f=/c/a/2006/10/15/BUGMKLOCFH1.DTL.

7. Marc Geller, "California's Proposition 87—What Went Wrong?" www.pluginamerica.org, November 1, 2006, http://www.pluginamerica.org/news-and-press/newsletters/2006-archive/2006-11-01-prop-87-missed-opportunity.html.

8. Grover Norquist on National Public Radio, May 25, 2001, http://www.npr.org/templates/story/story.php?storyId=1123439.

9. Bruce Springsteen on the Vote for Change Tour, October 10, 2004.

CHAPTER 5: THE FUTURE IS NOW

1. U.S. Department of Labor Bureau of Statistics, "Employment Situation Summary," May 2008, http://www.bls.gov/news.release/empsit.nr0.htm.

2. Bracken Hendricks and Jay Inslee, *Apollo's Fire* (Washington, DC: Island Press, 2008).

3. Carla Din, "Finding Opportunity in Crisis," *Yes Magazine* (Fall 2004), http://www.yesmagazine.org/article.asp?ID=1030.

4. Interview with Elsa Barboza, February 2008.

5. Elsa Barboza, "Organizing for Green Industries in Los Angeles," *Race, Poverty and the Environment* 13, no. 1 (Summer 2006), http://www.urbanhabitat.org/node/525.

6. In June 2007, the city council of LA established a City Retrofit Jobs Task Force made up of Apollo Alliance representatives, council members, and employees of various City agencies. The task force is identifying the workforce needs, potential job-training providers, and funding sources.

7. Joanna Lee, Angela Bowden, and Jennifer Ito, *Green Cities, Green Jobs*, May 2007, http://www.greenforall.org/resources/green-cities-green-jobs-by-joanna-lee-angela/download.

8. Lee, Bowden, and Ito, *Green Cities, Green Jobs*.

9. Lee, Bowden, and Ito, *Green Cities, Green Jobs*.

10. Center on Wisconsin Strategy (COWS), http://www.cows.org/collab_projects_detail.asp?id=54.

11. Speech by Winona LaDuke at the Dole Institute, University of Kansas, March 31, 2008.

12. Speech by Winona LaDuke at her acceptance of the nomination as Green Party vice-presidential candidate, July 20, 2000.

13. Indigenous Environmental Network, www.ienearth.org.

14. Honor the Earth, www.honortheearth.org.

15. Native Wind, www.nativewind.org.

16. PRNewswire, "U.S. Steel Permanently Closing Most Fairless Facilities," August 14, 2001.

17. Natalie Kostelni, "Progress Being Made at U.S. Steel Bucks Industrial Site," *Philadelphia News Journal*, January 22, 2007, http://www.bizjournals.com/philadelphia/stories/2007/01/22/story6.html.

18. Steven Greenhouse, "Millions of Jobs of a Different Collar," *New York Times*, March 26, 2008.

19. Karen Breslau, "The Growth in 'Green-Collar' Jobs," *Newsweek*, April 8, 2008, http://www.newsweek.com/related.aspx?subject=Technology.

20. "City Crime Rankings," www.morganquitno.com.

21. City of Richmond, http://www.ci.richmond.ca.us/index.asp?nid=1353.

22. All references to Solar Richmond are drawn from interviews with Michele McGeoy, February 2008.

23. Interview with Angela Greene, February 2008.

24. David R. Baker, "Solar Industry Needs Workers," *San Francisco Chronicle*, May 10, 2008, http://www.sfgate.com/cgi-bin/article.cgi?f=/c/a/2008/05/10/BUGD10JVGP.DTL.

25. Interview with Lyndon Rive, June 2008.

26. SolarCity is also planning to bring solar job opportunities to another depressed part of the San Francisco Bay Area: the Bayview–Hunters Point neighborhood. Bayview has been devastated for years by unemployment, crime, and a dirty coal power plant that was finally shut down in 2006. The City of San Francisco has launched an effort to invigorate the area with clean, green companies, and SolarCity is taking the opportunity to open a training academy there. The company

plans to train dozens of new employees every month when the academy opens in late 2008.

27. Lyndon Rive further explains the SolarLease concept: "With SolarLease, the homeowner can pay for the system out of the savings on their electric bill. The lease customer typically provides a low down payment—say $1,000 or $2,000. After that, the monthly lease payment combined with the new electric bill will typically be less than the old electric bill. We're able to capitalize on commercial tax credits and pass the savings on to the homeowner in the form of lower monthly payments. Most people want to do something positive for the environment, but it needs to make financial sense." Interview with Lyndon Rive, June 2008.

28. Lisa Hymas, "We Built This SolarCity," April 11, 2008, http://www.grist.org/feature/2008/04/11/.

29. Daniel Yee, "Obesity Raising Airline Fuel Costs," November 9, 2004, http://www.livescience.com/health/obesity_airlines_041105.html.

30. Anuradha Mittal, speech at the San Francisco Food Professional Society, Commonwealth Club, San Francisco, October 22, 2004, http://www.oaklandinstitute.org/?q=/node/view/100.

31. Diana Deumling et al., "Eating Up the Earth: How Sustainable Food Systems Shrink Our Ecological Footprint," *Agriculture Footprint Brief* (July 2003).

32. United States Department of Agriculture, Economic Research Service, 2006, http://www.ers.usda.gov/Briefing/FoodSecurity/trends.htm.

33. Interview with Brahm Ahmadi, February 2008.

34. The food system also results in a multitude of health problems as our endocrine, immune, and other systems are besieged by pesticides used on crops and the antibiotics and growth hormones with which (usually healthy) livestock is egregiously sprayed. We're seeing a preponderance of allergies, due in part to the lack of diversity of our food crops, as industrial farms grow mostly just one kind of wheat or corn, for example, out of the many strains that exist or used to exist. See Elizabeth Frazao, "High Costs of Poor Eating Patterns in the United States," *Agriculture Information Bulletin* No. 750 (1999).

35. U.S. Department of Labor, *The National Agricultural Workers Survey,* http://www.doleta.gov/agworker/report/ch1.cfm.

36. Christopher D. Cook, *Diet for a Dead Planet* (New York: New Press, 2004), http://www.dietforadeadplanet.com.

37. Interview with LaDonna Redmond, April 2008.

38. Interview with Orrin Williams, February 2008.

39. Growing Home, www.growinghomeinc.org.

40. The Field Museum, *George Washington Carver Educator Guide* (Chicago: The Field Museum, 2008), p. 18.

41. All references to the People's Grocery and the food crisis in West Oakland as well as quotations are drawn from interviews with Brahm Ahmadi, February 2008.

42. Mittal, speech, October 22, 2004. Mittal clarifies the statistics: "There is not a direct correlation between the annual food expenditures and the income to farmers, as not all dollars spent on food go to farmers. These numbers are based on a research paper by Dennis Tootelian for the California Department of Food and Agriculture's Buy California program."

43. Annie Leonard, "The Story of Stuff," http://www.storyofstuff.com.

44. Justin Berton, "Continent-size Toxic Stew of Plastic Trash Fouling Swath of Pacific Ocean," *San Francisco Chronicle*, October 19, 2007, http://www.sfgate.com/cgi-bin/article.cgi?f=/c/a/2007/10/19/SS6JS8RH0.DTL&hw=pacific+patch&sn=001&sc=1000.

45. Leonard, "The Story of Stuff."

46. Meanwhile, the companies primarily responsible for handling waste are making a killing. The monopolization of the industry has the few entities in control extorting higher and higher rates for disposal. The nonprofit Institute for Local Self-Reliance calls it "waste imperialism," which "diminishes democratic local ownership and control of valuable discarded materials . . . hampering recycling and waste reduction progress, promoting the interstate transportation of waste, tightening already slim municipal budgets, and sounding the death knell for recycling-based community development and localism in the solid waste sector." See the Institute for Local Self-Reliance, "Waste Imperialism," http://www.ilsr.org/recycling/wasteimperialism.html.

47. One of the smartest approaches to waste reduction is making the companies who produce the stuff responsible for the damages caused by production processes as well as for the fate of the product and its packaging. This principle is called Extended Producer Responsibility (EPR). See the Institute for Local Self-Reliance, "Extended Producer Responsibility," http://www.ilsr.org/recycling/epr/index.html.

48. Jim Motavalli, "Zero Waste," *emagazine* 12, no. 2 (March/April 2001), http://www.emagazine.com/view/?506.

49. Raquel Pinderhughes, *Green Collar Jobs,* The City of Berkeley Office of Energy and Sustainable Development, 2007, http://www.bss.sfsu.edu/raquelrp/documents/v13FullReport.pdf.

50. Information about Chicago's computer recycling from an interview with Patrick Brown of OAI/Greencorps Chicago, February 2008.

51. Pinderhughes, *Green Collar Jobs.*

52. Environmental Protection Agency, "Characterization of Building-Related Construction and Demolition Debris in the United States," www.epa.gov/epaoswer/hazwaste/sqg/c&d-rpt.pdf.

53. Doug Brown, "Search and Rescue," *Washington Post,* June 19, 2003.

54. All references to Green Worker Cooperatives and ReBuilders Source from interview with Omar Freilla, May 2008.

55. WaterAid, "Statistics," http://www.wateraid.org/international/what_we_do/statistics/default.asp.

56. Storm-water runoff is the result of human intervention in the hydrologic cycle in the course of urban and suburban development. Impervious surfaces, soil compacting, and removal of vegetation alter water's movement through the environment by reducing interception, evapo-transpiration, and infiltration. Storm water is a major source of pollution: in the United States it's the largest pollution source for ocean shorelines, second largest source for estuaries and Great Lakes shorelines, third largest source for lakes, and fourth largest source for rivers. Traditional storm-water management practices focus on the collection and rapid re-

moval of rainwater and snowmelt away from the point of impact through a system of underground pipes and storm sewers. This approach generates vast quantities of polluted runoff, disrupts the natural hydrologic cycle, and adds to the contamination and scouring of streams and rivers. See the Water Environment Research Foundation, http://www.werf.org/livablecommunities/tool_bmp101.htm.

57. Interview with Majora Carter, April 2008.

58. Interview with James Wells, February 2008.

59. Maude Barlow and Tony Clarke, *Blue Gold: The Fight to Stop the Corporate Theft of the World's Water* (London: Earthscan, 2002), p. 233.

60. Barlow and Clarke, *Blue Gold*, p. 235. Another major solution to the global water crisis involves shifting crops to match the availability of local water supplies, which means no longer growing water-intensive crops in arid climates.

61. All references to TreePeople and its LA watershed projects from interviews with Andy Lipkis, May and June 2008.

62. Surface Transportation Policy Project, *Factsheet on Transportation and Climate Change*, http://www.transact.org/library/factsheets/climate.asp.

63. Interview with Sam Zimmerman-Bergman, May 2008.

64. Surface Transportation Policy Project, *Factsheet on Transportation and Social Equity*, http://www.transact.org/library/factsheets/equity.asp.

65. American Public Transportation Association, *Public Transportation Industry Overview*, http://www.apta.com/media/facts.cfm.

66. Surface Transportation Policy Project, *Factsheet on Transportation and Jobs*, http://www.transact.org/library/factsheets/jobs.asp. In fact, according to a study by Cambridge Systematics, although new highway construction does lead to an increase in employment, these jobs are mostly for nonlocal workers: road engineers and other specialists who come in to an area for a specific job and then leave when it has been completed. On the other hand, transit investments create a wealth of employment opportunities in the short and the long run. Transit system construction leads to an impressive level of short-term job creation, and once the systems are finished, a long-term source of high-quality jobs.

67. J. Mijin Cha, "Public Transit Needed in California and Across Nation: California Progress Report," Transportation Equity Network, February 26, 2008, http://transportationequity.org/index.php?option=com_content&task=view&id=62&Itemid=45.

68. Darrell Clarke, "Curitiba's 'Bus Rapid Transit'—How Applicable to Los Angeles and Other U.S. Cities?" *Light Rail Now* (March 28, 2005), http://www.lightrailnow.org/facts/fa_00013.htm.

69. "Solis' Green Jobs Act Signed into Law as Part of Historic Energy Reform Bill," December 19, 2007, http://solis.house.gov/list/press/ca32_solis/wida6/greenjobslaw.shtml.

CHAPTER 6: THE GOVERNMENT QUESTION

1. Civilian Conservation Corps Legacy, http://ccclegacy.org.

2. Stan Cohen, *The Tree Army: A Pictorial History of the Civilian Conservation Corps, 1933–1942* (Missoula, MT: Pictorial Histories, 1960).

3. John C. Paige, "The Civilian Conservation Corps and the National Park Service, 1933–1942: An Administrative History," National Park Service, 1985, http://www.nps.gov/history/history/online_books/ccc/index.htm.

4. Franklin Delano Roosevelt, Greetings to the CCC speech, July 1933, http://www.parks.ca.gov/?page_id=24917.

5. James F. Justin Civilian Conservation Corps Museum Biographies, http://members.aol.com/famjustin/cccbio.html.

6. John F. Kennedy, space-program address at Rice University, September 12, 1962, www.astrosociology.com/Library/PDF/JFK%201962%20Rice%20University%20Speech%20Transcript.pdf.

7. Bracken Hendricks and Jay Inslee, *Apollo's Fire* (Washington, DC: Island Press, 2008), p. xviii. The slogan of the Apollo Alliance is "Three million new jobs. Freedom from foreign oil." More at http://www.apolloalliance.org/.

8. The CEC would mobilize millions of Americans of all ages, particularly the four to six million youth between the ages of sixteen and twenty-four who are neither in school nor able to land meaningful jobs. Working in collaboration with business, labor, schools, and other components of the green economy, the CEC would build on existing service and conservation corps and green-jobs training programs. Regional and community green-jobs training programs need to be vastly expanded to meet the need for skilled workers. An investment of $5 billion a year would support matching grants to states and cities for green workforce development, with a focus on job preparation, matching, and retention efforts for the unemployed or poor. One billion dollars a year would mobilize twice the current number of AmeriCorps members in a dedicated CEC national service corps.

The CEC would have recruiting centers in cities across the country, connecting people to work and service opportunities generated by the implementation of national, state, and local climate-change policies. CEC could retrofit our aging buildings; green America's public elementary, middle, and high schools; expand green space in cities, transforming blacktops into parks or urban farms; assist in food composting and recycling; and build bike trails and organize carpools. Corps members would gain concrete experience, hard and soft skills, and be ready to continue their education, enter preapprenticeship programs, or start their own businesses after leaving the corps.

9. Susan Tucker, director of the After Prison Initiative at the Open Society Institute, is a leading voice on connecting formerly incarcerated people with green-job opportunities. Susan's goal is to scale and institutionalize the CJC as a major federally funded program and to establish a local CJC in every high-incarceration neighborhood.

It may be hard to understand the appeal of such a program, unless you understand the devastating impact on communities of color of the mushrooming incarceration industry. According to the Urban Strategies Initiative, over the past thirty years the United States has become the number-one spender on incarceration in the world, locking up more people and a bigger percentage of its population than Russia or China. Most of the jailed are people of color, the majority for nonviolent offenses—essentially crimes of economic desperation, addiction, and mental illness. Outside of prison there are now 12 million formerly incarcerated people, whose number grows by half a million a year, while more than 40 percent of formerly incarcerated people are returned to prison within three years of release.

A training program with the wraparound services necessary to ensure success for the truly disadvantaged might cost as much as $20,000 per person. But compare that to the $40,000–$100,000 we spend per person in California's prisons—on a system that utterly fails in its "correctional" purpose. According to the Urban Strategies Initiative, more than two-thirds of all adult prison parolees are rearrested within three years of release; an astounding 91 percent of juveniles reoffend. (In both cases, many of those who return to prison are arrested on technical violations or because of legal barriers to their housing, employment, education, and treatment due to their conviction.) The success rate of corps programs that serve comparable populations suggest that a $20,000 investment is a bargain. The mass scale payoffs in reduced costs for prison and social welfare programs plus the gains in peaceful streets and redeemed lives would be simply incalculable.

10. Though variations of the idea are controversial on the left and the right, a cap on carbon is generally thought to be the most effective macro-tool to help society cut greenhouse-gas emissions. A federally instituted cap would set a limit on the total amount of carbon that could be emitted in the United States. Most proposals then call for the government to issue permits that would allow a certain amount of emissions each year. And every year, the number of permits—and therefore the amount of pollution permitted—would decrease. This process would bring down our emissions steadily but gradually, since no one believes a drastic reduction is practical.

And yet those who advocate for carbon trading argue that a "cap-and-trade" system would be a highly efficient and flexible way to cut emissions. In their view, the problem is a simple market malfunction: dumping carbon into the atmosphere has always been free for any individual or firm—and yet dumping all that carbon could ultimately cost us the entire planet. Advocates argue that once businesses are forced to pay the "true cost" of carbon (by buying and trading permits), they will have the necessary financial incentive to seek out low-carbon solutions. Then the magic of the market will kick in and start moving us quickly to safer ground.

As for me, I do not believe that the climate crisis is simply a market failure, nor do I believe that market solutions alone will save us. The climate crisis is a symptom of a much deeper sickness in our souls and our society. I find it distasteful to think of anyone "buying" the right to pollute the planet. And yet I can see few other politically viable, practically workable options. For instance, there is no political will, at this stage, to treat carbon like cyanide and just ban it altogether. And we couldn't do so without plunging ourselves into the Dark Ages anyway.

So in my opinion, as we grasp for a solution, three values are essential. One, we must bring down carbon emissions as fast as possible. Two, the big polluters must start paying for their actions somehow (through carbon taxes, carbon tariffs, buying permits, or even fines). And three, the billions generated by pricing carbon must go toward helping the people and the planet.

Therefore, I propose that we proceed by affirming a new concept: "cap and collect and invest." To ensure equal protection and equal opportunities for everyone, we need the government to *cap* carbon (set a firm limit), *collect* money from big emitters (either by a carbon tax, by selling the limited number of pollution permits), and *invest* the funds (spend them on projects that will further boost the clean, green economy, while protecting people from the worst economic consequences of the changeover).

Neither the carbon-tax ideas nor the permit-trading schemes are perfect. But as long as the United States establishes a firm cap, we could experiment with any number of creative ways to "collect," or make the big polluters pay. But what we don't need, under any circumstances, is for the government to allow polluters to purchase offsets instead of reducing emissions. Offsets are certificates sold by private companies that claim to invest the cost of each certificate in activities that remove carbon from the atmosphere, such as planting trees. Everyone can be encouraged to purchase offsets, but they are no substitute for direct reductions in emissions.

And what we really don't need is for the federal government to institute a "cap and giveaway" policy, in which permits are "grandfathered," that is, given away for free. Although such a policy does still result in a lowering of emissions (providing offsets are not allowed to be substituted for emissions), this proposal rewards longtime polluters, rather than making them take responsibility for their disastrous impacts on public health and the environment. It leaves a big pile of money—in the tens or hundreds of billions of dollars, by various estimates—as windfall profits for major fossil-fuels users.

As we face this global ecological crisis, our largest industries should stop crying and begging for freebie pollution permits—especially our energy companies. We honor their contributions to this nation; they have kept the lights on for us all this time. But in an age of windfall profits for them and worldwide peril for every living species, the time has come for them to let go of their billion-dollar subsidies. The time has come for them to start paying this country back for all the taxpayer support we have given them for decades. They can best begin to do that by paying full price for each and every pollution permit, as an act of patriotic duty.

We should also pass measures to protect U.S. industries, such as a carbon border fee (or carbon tariff), which would impose fees on goods imported from countries where carbon still costs less. And we should also protect vulnerable people as well. The truly needy should get earned income tax credit or direct cash assistance to offset increasing energy and food prices in a carbon-constrained economy.

Of course, everyone will feel the pinch at first. To ease the pain, the government could take part of the money collected from carbon proceeds and send a check to every U.S. citizen. Not only would those checks help everyone defray some of the costs of increased energy prices and prices of basic consumer goods, they also would give every U.S. citizen a financial stake in the transition to a cleaner economy. But I do not believe we should give away *all* of the money. The bulk of the money collected from pricing carbon should go to pay for robust programs to build green infrastructure and create green-collar jobs across the country.

An exhaustive description of cap-and-trade is beyond the scope of this chapter, but can be found in CAP's seminal report, *Capturing the Energy Opportunity*, http://www.americanprogress.org/issues/2007/11/pdf/energy_chapter.pdf.

11. Congressional Budget Office, *Trade-Offs in Allocating Allowances for CO_2 Emissions*, August 2007, http://www.cbo.gov/ftpdocs/80xx/doc8027/04-25-Cap_Trade .pdf.

12. PJM Interconnection, *Bringing the Smart Grid Idea Home*, www.energyfuture coalition.org/pubs/PJMsmartgrid.pdf.

13. John M. Urbanchuk, for the Renewable Fuels Association, *Contribution of the Ethanol Industry to the Economy of the United States*, February 2008, http://www .ethanolrfa.org/objects/documents/1537/2007_ethanol_economic_contribution .pdf

14. Interview with Ross Gelbspan, May 2008. See http://www.heatisonline.org for more information.

15. NATO Secretary General Jaap de Hoop Scheffer, speech at the Security and Defense Agenda, June 3, 2008, http://www.nato.int/docu/speech/2008/s080603a .html.

16. The Greenhouse Development Rights (GDR) framework codifies the right to development as a "development threshold"—a level of welfare below which people are not expected to share the costs of the climate transition. This threshold is emphatically not an "extreme poverty" line, which is typically defined to be so low ($1 or $2 a day) as to be more properly called a "destitution line." Rather, it is set to be higher than the "global poverty line" and to reflect a level of welfare that is beyond basic needs, but well short of today's levels of "affluent" consumption.

People below this threshold are taken as having development as their proper priority. As they struggle for better lives, they are not asked to help keep society as a whole within its now sharply limited global carbon budget. In any event, they have little responsibility for the climate problem and relatively little capacity to work on solving it. People above the threshold, on the other hand, are taken as having realized their right to development and as bearing the responsibility to preserve that right for others. They must gradually assume a greater fraction of the costs of curbing the emissions associated with their own consumption as well as the costs of ensuring that those who rise above the threshold are able to do so along sustainable, low-emission paths. And these obligations, moreover, are taken to belong to all those above the development threshold, whether they happen to live in the North or in the South. See http:// www.ecoequity.org/GDRs/.

17. United Nations, Department of Economic and Social Affairs, Population Division, *World Population Prospect: The 2006 Revision*, http://www.un.org/esa/population/ publications/wpp2006/wpp2006.htm.

18. Interview with Sadhu Johnston, February 2008.

19. Interviews with Patrick Brown, OAI/Greencorps, and Aaron Durnbaugh, Deputy Commissioner, Chicago Department of Environment, February 2008.

20. Interview with Jumaani Bates, March 2008.

21. COWS is working in partnership with the City of Milwaukee, the local area utility, and community leaders to ensure Me2's success. Me2 will mostly use private capital in doing this retrofit work. It has already attracted banks and other private creditors to the effort because it pools expected savings that would otherwise be too dispersed to capture. To minimize risk for the lender, it puts the repayment costs of its capital, and the retrofit work done with it, on the customer utility bills, with standard penalties for nonpayment. It also aggregates individual customers for energy services into a single borrowing pool. To attract wide participation, it selects for efficiency measures that will more than pay for themselves and the cost of capital over a reasonable (say, ten-year) period. That means that, even though customers will be repaying the cost of the retrofits, their utility bills will go down immediately.

Here's how Me2 will work. The utility agrees to administer repayment to Me2 as part of its billing services. A bank agrees to loan or open a credit line for capital at a certain rate. Me2 recruits customers willing to pay for approved work. The bank loans Me2 funds for the expected cost of that work. Me2 sends auditors and contractors to the customer's property, gets agreement from the customer on the scope of work, and has work done and verified. The utility bill drops; customer repayment of Me2 costs begins. The utility forwards that repayment to Me2, which repays the bank.

Me2 guarantees the work for customers, with standards for those who do the work. It assures customers of an immediate drop in their energy costs, even with payment to it, by carefully screening the retrofit measures it will pay for.

Crucially, the payment for Me2 services "follow the meter" or property, not person. That means Milwaukee renters and owners would gain from the program without incurring the obligation to stay in their current property. Whatever they haven't repaid for services simply gets passed (with notice of course) to the next renter or owner. For more details see http://cows.org/collab_projects_detail.asp?id=54.

22. Population Reference Bureau, "World Population Highlights 2007," http://www.prb.org/Articles/2007/623Urbanization.aspx.

23. Greg LeRoy, "Green Strings," www.grist.org, May 1, 2008, http://gristmill.grist.org/story/2008/4/30/113724/493.

CHAPTER 7: BUOYANCY AND HOPE

1. Niccolò Machiavelli, *Il Principe (The Prince)* (Florence: Antonio Blado d'Asola, 1532), p. 12.

2. Lester R. Brown, *Plan B 3.0* (New York: Norton, 2008).

3. Winston S. Churchill, *The Second World War* (London: Cassell, 1948–54).

4. Winston Churchill, addressing the House of Commons, May 13, 1940, http://www.fordham.edu/halsall/mod/churchill-blood.html.

Acknowledgments

First of all, grateful appreciation goes to my parents, Loretta Jean Kirkendoll Jones and the late Willie Anthony Jones, and my grandparents, the late Bishop Chester Arthur Kirkendoll and Alice Elizabeth Singleton Kirkendoll. They gave me the best foundation that any black kid who grew up on the edge of a small Tennessee town could ever hope for.

I honor and acknowledge my life partner, Jana Carter, and our beautiful sons, Cabral and baby Mattai. They have made untold sacrifices so that I could create this book—and do the work that underlies it.

I salute my entire family: the Kirkendolls, the Carters, and the legendary Smith-Jones-Glover clan of Memphis, Tennessee. My twin sister, Angela Thracheryl Jones, and her sons, DeAubrey Jerome and Brandon Demetrious Weekly, are never far from my thoughts.

I also thank Diana Frappier, my steadfast friend, with whom I cofounded the Ella Baker Center for Human Rights in 1996. And I acknowledge my loving godparents, Dorothy Zellner, Constancia "Dinky" Romilly, and Terry Weber.

I thank the many volunteers, supporters, coworkers, cofounders, and board members with whom I have had the pleasure of launching and helping to lead three social change organizations: the Ella Baker Center, Color of Change, and Green For All. We are just getting started.

As a lifelong activist, I have been blessed with scores of friends, allies, and comrades. It would be impossible to name them all here, but any decent list would include Monica Elizabeth Peek, Theda Sevier Hunt, KaCarole Higgins, Karen Streeter, Emilee Whitehurst, Cindy Weisner, Raquel Laviña, Rahdi Taylor, Judy Appel, Craig Harshaw, Lisa Daugaard, Deborah James, Marianne Manilov, Tony Coleman, Priya Haji, Gillian Caldwell, Kolmilata Majumdar, Aya De Leon, Kwame Anku, Michelle Loren Alexander, Bernadette Armand, Alli Chagi Starr, Leda Dederich, Shalini Kantayya, Gita Drury, Billy "Upski" Wimsatt, James Rucker, Tesa Silvestre, Zen DeBruke, Rachel Bagby, Nina Utne, Vivian Chang, Juliet Ellis, Amaha Kassa, Taj James, Gihan Perera, Baye Adolfo-Wilson, Rev. Lennox Yearwood, John Hope Bryant, Bracken Hendricks, Peter Teague, Michelle DePasse, Diane Ives, Kalia Lydgate, Ariane Conrad, Valerie Aubel, Sarah Shanley, ·Monet Zulpo-Dane, Lea Endres, Majora Carter, and Julia Butterfly Hill.

I am the product of a first rate education, thanks in part to Ollye Curry (Alexander Elementary), Helen Mahafy (Jackson Central-Merry High School), E. Jerold Ogg (University of Tennessee, Martin), and Stephen Wizner (Yale Law School). I have also enjoyed the support of world-class mentors and guides. They include: Max Elbaum, Linda Burnham, Bob Wing, Elizabeth "Betita" Martinez, Sharon Martinas, Belvie Rooks, Kathleen Cleaver, Kerry Kennedy, Arianna Huffington, Samsara Becknell, Catherine Sneed, Fred and Ina Pockrass, Jim Sheehan, David Friedman, George Zimmer, Kevin Danaher, Jerome Ringo, Joel Makower, Michael Kieschnick, Jodie Evans, Lynne Twist, John Robbins, Paul Hawken,

George Lakof, Mal Warwick, Josh Mailman, Arnold Perkins, Joel Rogers, and Robert Gass. I especially honor Eva Jefferson Paterson for giving me my first job as a lawyer and supporting all my dreams ever since.

The insights in this book arise as a part of a long-running conversation within a growing community of dedicated thinkers and activists. I cannot claim to be the sole author or lonely originator of all the ideas presented here. For any valuable contribution readers find herein, I must share the credit with my colleagues at organizations like the Apollo Alliance, 1Sky, Bioneers, the Ella Baker Center, the Blue Green Alliance, the Social Venture Network, Center for American Progress, Green Festivals, BALLE/Business Alliance for Local Living Economies, Beatitudes Society, Awakening the Dreamer, the Institute of Noetic Sciences, the Tipping Point Network, Rockwood Leadership, Turning the Tide Coalition, the Alliance for Climate Protection, and all of Green For All's partner organizations. As for the shortcomings in conception or presentation, those are mine alone.

Ariane Conrad has been my tireless copilot in creating this book. She is especially appreciative of Peter Barnes and the Mesa Refuge, the Green For All staff, the San Francisco Writers Grotto, David Levy and Mayacamas Ranch, Cafe Flore, especially Matt—and all her patient Loved Ones. I also thank them.

Plus I deeply appreciate and thank my agent, Patti Breitman, as well as Gideon Weil and his wonderful colleagues at HarperOne.

In closing, I would like to note that my father would have enjoyed reading this book—and grilling me on every point. Unfortunately, he died on March 9, 2008—before the writing was complete. With a grieving heart, I dedicate this book to his memory. Rest in peace. Your spirit and your cause live on.

VAN JONES is the founder and president of Green for All. An internationally acclaimed and award-winning human rights and environmental leader, Jones is a Senior Fellow at the Center for American Progress. He co-founded the Ella Baker Center for Human Rights in 1996, and in 2005 helped found ColorOfChange. org, an online advocacy organization. In addition, Jones is a board member of 1Sky, the Apollo Alliance, and a fellow with the Institute of Noetic Sciences. A Yale Law graduate, Van Jones lives in Oakland with his wife and two sons. Visit the author online at www.vanjones.net and www.greenforall.org.

ARIANE CONRAD is a San Francisco-based writer, editor, and activist. She previously edited a collection of Van's writings entitled *The Future's Getting Restless* (2008). Visit her at www.arianeconrad.com.